UNKNOWN DESIRE

"Francis was a good man."

Luke's eyes darkened. "Francis is gone. And any man who could have been near you without wanting to touch you—and love you . . ."

She could hardly believe the words Luke was saying. Yet she did believe that he truly meant them. "How I wish I could have known you in another life," she murmured.

"Know me in this life," he whispered. His breath was hot against her ear when he spoke again. "I want you to know what it feels like to feel good," he murmured, letting his hands rove down past her waist, over her buttocks, pressing her close. "I want to be here for you, to talk to you, to listen to all your thoughts and hopes and plans." He nibbled at her ear then, taking her lobe between his teeth.

Her knees buckled. "Luke," she whispered—and found that her knees were giving way as Luke pulled her gently to the ground with him.

"Tell me what you want, what you need," he murmured, holding her face in his warm, strong hands. He brushed her hair back from her face, his eyes searching hers with an intensity she found thrilling. "We have to find out what feels good to you. . . ."

LUKE ASHCROFT'S
Woman

ELIZABETH CLARKE

LEISURE BOOKS   NEW YORK CITY

A LEISURE BOOK®

August 2004

Published by

Dorchester Publishing Co., Inc.
200 Madison Avenue
New York, NY 10016

ISBN 0-8439-5391-8

ACKNOWLEDGMENTS

Thanks to Alicia Condon for acquiring a book that will always be special to me because it was my first historical. A special thanks to my agent, Maureen Moran, for her unending encouragement, interest and support. And as always, thanks to my family for knowing that Crabby Mommy eventually gets back to normal when all my deadlines have been met.

LUKE
ASHCROFT'S
Woman

Prologue

Ewington, Illinois, 1834

"Shh," Charlotte whispered to her sister as they hunched down behind the piles of hay in the barn. "I think the fight is moving in here."

Sure enough, a moment later, she heard the sound of her parents' footsteps on the dirt floor of the barn.

"Mind you, I don't think Charlotte's ever going to want to leave the farm," her father said in the raspy, cracked voice that always came with her parents' arguments. "She'll always be as plain as a plain brown sparrow, Helen. No man's ever going to want her. And Lucinda's afraid of her own shadow."

"Those girls have worked themselves to the bone on this place—"

"And so the hell have we, Helen, and I'm sick of your damn backtalk," he growled. "If I want to sell tomorrow, I'll sell tomorrow! If I decide we should stay, then we stay."

Charlotte and Lucinda closed their eyes in anticipation of the sound that would come next: flesh smacking against flesh, followed by soft crying coming from the person they both loved most in the world.

Their pa was a cruel man, no two ways about it.

A second later, their mama ran out of the barn, and they knew their pa would follow—which he did.

Lucinda reached out and touched her sister's face. "Don't you listen to that old meanie, Char. He doesn't know what he's talking about, saying you're plain."

Charlotte shrugged, trying not to care. And in certain ways she didn't, because deep in her heart, she knew she would never want a man. Not if it meant being bossed around, having no say about anything, sometimes even getting hit.

"And anyway," Lucinda went on, playing with her sister's long braid, "Pa doesn't know anything about our plan. We'll marry the two best brothers in the whole world, and we'll show Pa once and for all when we live happily ever after, won't we?"

Charlotte laughed, for a moment feeling like the eleven-year-old girl that she still was. Yet, a few moments later, as she watched her mama through the open doorway of the barn, looking a hundred years older than she should have, the part of her

that had already seen too much swore that even
though she wanted to be with her sister forever,
she would never marry.

"I'm going to see the world," Charlotte heard
herself say. "I can't live like Mama, Luce."

Lucinda's chin quivered. "But you promised!"

Charlotte took her little sister in her arms and
rocked her in her lap. Luce was only eight—a
baby, to Charlotte's way of thinking. "Don't worry
about things like that now," Charlotte chided.
"Worry about whether you fed the horses or
milked the cow or sewed your skirt the right way—
but not about marrying, Luce."

"But we've talked about it near a hundred times!"
Lucinda cried. "And you've always promised."

"Shh," Charlotte whispered, feeling old and
wise. "What's meant to happen will happen, Lucinda. That's the only thing in the world that I
know to be true."

For a moment, she thought about the other
words she knew to be true: that she was clumsy
and plain; her pa didn't lie about things like that.
It was just like when that calf had been born that
couldn't walk, and Pa had said, "I ain't going to
mince words, girls, whether you like it or not.
This calf's going to get her throat cut before sun-
down."

And Charlotte knew she was just the same, someone he wouldn't lie about, no matter whether he
thought it would hurt her feelings or not. Plain as a
plain brown sparrow.

But then she told herself, as she knew she would

for years to come, that it didn't matter, because she didn't intend ever to marry; she would never make the same mistake her mother had made.

Never, not ever ever ever.

One

Mama,

Last night a gentleman told us that Oregon country is the land of milk and honey, a true garden of Eden for those who have the courage to make the journey overland. We are about to leave Independence, and we are all doing fine—me as Francis's new bride (who would have ever thought?), and Lucinda and Marcus excited about the coming baby.

Charlotte reread the words she had written and sighed, wondering if her mother would be able to discern the lies.

"Honey, I think you'd better go tend to your sister," Francis said.

"Not the baby—?" she asked, for it was still too early for her sister's baby to come forth.

Francis smiled and put a hand on her cheek. "Calm yourself," he said softly. "The baby will be fine, and Lucinda will be fine if she can only school herself in."

"What happened?" Charlotte asked.

Her husband shook his head, a lock of dark hair falling across his handsome forehead. "My brother, as usual, could be gentler. Come—seal your letter and go cheer up your sister."

Charlotte sighed, catching a glimpse of herself in what she felt certain would be the last full-length mirror she would see for quite some time. She looked disheveled but excited, her long, dark brown hair done up in an exotic twist she had seen on the cover of *Godey's Lady's Book* back home; and she felt as if even a stranger would have been able to see her excitement about the coming journey.

She looked down at the letter and hastily added a postscript: "Please don't trouble your heart over our journey, Mama. We are all well, and Lucinda shall be a mother herself in a matter of weeks! I love you with all my heart."

"Did you tell her you're enjoying married life?" Francis asked, a smile curving one corner of his mouth.

Charlotte felt a wave of guilt. Francis was funny and kind, certainly kinder than his brother, Marcus. He was gentle, and Charlotte knew with all her heart that he would be gentle with their children, the opposite of her own father. But was there such a thing, she wondered, as being *too* gentle? Since the minister had married them back in Illinois, Francis had yet to touch her beyond giving her a chaste kiss, a brotherly peck on the cheek.

She had told herself that maybe Francis had felt shy or inhibited, since on most of the nights so far, they had camped in strangers' barns or houses. Maybe now, sleeping in their own tent under the stars of the wide, beautiful western sky, he would feel differently.

She looked at him and forced a smile, because he *was* a kind man, and she didn't want to hurt his feelings. "Mama already knows you," she said softly.

He looked at her for a long moment, as if to say he knew she hadn't exactly answered his question. Then he smiled. "Give her my best, Charlotte, and then you'd better tend to your sister before my brother loses his temper again."

Charlotte sealed the letter and walked outside in search of Lucinda. At the far end of the wagon train, past dozens of ox and mule teams, she saw Lucinda in Marcus's arms. She watched as Marcus put his hand up to Luce's cheek—it looked as if he was brushing a tear from her face—and sighed. Lucinda and Marcus always seemed to be fighting or making up. It was the absolute opposite of her and Francis's dull, even-keel marriage, and it made her remember her long-ago vow never to marry.

She looked over at the Dalton family wagon, on which she and Lucinda had yet to perform the artistic miracles they had talked about endlessly, a sign proclaiming that the Dalton family farm would prosper in Oregon country by the following year. As they had started painting the day before, Charlotte had tripped over the paint bucket, and the paint had soaked into the hot, dry ground in the blink of an eye. So the wagon, at that point, just said THE DA, instead of THE DALTON FAMILY FARM, BOUND FOR THE WILLAMETTE VALLEY!

Suddenly, by the wagon immediately in front of hers, Charlotte saw something that made her heart race with fury. Tied to the rear of the wagon bed was a Guernsey cow whose udders were so heavy with milk that Charlotte wanted to scream.

"Whose cow is this?" she called out, not even thinking as she voiced her question, marching to the front of the wagon. Peering inside, Charlotte noticed the distinct lack of domestic possessions common to most travelers' prairie schooners; nearly every married couple of her acquaintance had had bitter arguments about what bureaus, rocking chairs and precious family keepsakes to take along. But this wagon seemed to have been outfitted by someone who owned very little, though the wagon itself was a handsome affair, well built of good oak and a strong, clean, oiled-canvas cover, with pockets sewn along the insides to hold all sorts of implements.

She knew many of the people in the wagon train, primarily those who had traveled from Ewington along with her; but this wagon was new to her. She knelt by the poor cow, which had fastened a pleading, desperate gaze on her.

"All right, I'll get a bucket and come back," Charlotte said, wondering if she would be greeted by fury or thanks when the cow's owner returned.

As she headed quickly back toward her wagon, a low voice called out, "Is there something you need?"

Charlotte turned. The man who had asked the question closed the distance between them in one long stride, and Charlotte looked up to see a handsome, tanned face, pale hazel-green eyes in a broad, strong-jawed, bearded visage that had clearly seen years of outdoor life. The man looked sun-worn and rough, as if he had walked thousands of miles of late, the creases at the corners of his eyes deep beneath dusty, maple-colored brows.

Something in those eyes—too pale, too sharp, too penetrating—made her look away. Her gaze settled on a chest that was broad, muscled, with dark hair curling up at the opening of the stranger's buckskin shirt. Charlotte tried not to imagine what the man looked like beneath the worn leather of his clothes—was he as strong as he appeared?—and she was ashamed of herself for even having such thoughts. She had never even seen her husband unclothed, nor touched any more of his skin than she would have a brother's or cousin's.

"When you're finished," the man said, his voice deep and full of humor.

"I beg your pardon?" Charlotte asked, drawing herself up.

"You've looked me over long enough to measure me for a full set of clothing," he said, giving her a wink with those shocking pale-green eyes. "Will I have the privilege of choosing the fabric—I prefer linsey-woolsey myself—or are you planning to surprise me?"

Charlotte felt the color flood to her cheeks. "Of all the presumption!" she cried out. "I'm trying to find the owner of this poor cow, if you must know."

Those pale-green eyes darkened to an emerald that Charlotte had lately dreamed the Pacific Ocean would become in a rough seastorm. "For what purpose?" he demanded, his voice low and matter-of-fact, all humor gone.

"Is she yours?" Charlotte asked, her heart skipping a beat. She had hoped to have no further conversation with this arrogant man.

"She's mine," he answered in a voice that would brook no arguments. "Or one-half mine, if it's any of your concern."

She took a deep breath. The sooner she could be done with the conversation, the better. "The half that's leaking milk all over the road, sir, is going to be sick indeed if somebody doesn't strip the milk out. Surely you weren't intending to stop milking this fine cow as we begin our long journey—"

He opened his mouth to answer, then closed it, his eyes looking into hers with a questioning intensity that forced her to look away. She didn't know what it was about him that made her at once want to flee and to stay, to speak and be silent. "I hadn't given it much thought either way, miss. She was a small portion of my winnings in a rather profitable poker game last night."

Charlotte narrowed her eyes as she spoke without thinking. "You'll ruin her with your ignorance. I shall buy her from you and you won't have to worry about what you don't know about cows."

A half smile crossed the rugged, sun-worn face, reminding Charlotte of a drawing she had seen on the frontispiece of one of her cherished dime novels—but the portrait, in that case, had been of a swindler, skilled at charming all from whom he later stole. "How much are you offering?" he asked, a silken tease in his voice. "After all, as you just finished pointing out with such passion, she's a fine cow. A *prize* cow."

Offering. In her mind's eye, she saw herself, in the not-too-distant future, being able to buy and sell with ease, trading eggs, meat and milk for everything she couldn't raise on her own. But at that moment, she was the proud owner of nothing except a few personal effects this man wouldn't find the least bit interesting. "Actually," she began, avoiding the man's eyes, "I couldn't pay you anything at the moment, but when I settle myself in the Willamette Valley, I'm sure I'll be able to reciprocate rather well."

At these words, the stranger laughed.

"I can't imagine what you find so humorous," Charlotte snapped. "I expect to do quite well once I'm settled out there."

His gaze fastened on hers. "If you survive," he

warned. "How's a skinny little thing like you going to stay warm in a mountain blizzard? Do you know how many graves line the trail between here and your beloved Oregon Territory?"

"Other women have done it," she snapped.

The man half laughed, scoffing at her optimism. "And hundreds have died. It'll be the start of the rainy season in Oregon country, and you'll be wet twenty-four hours a day when you get there—if you do."

"Which I suppose you have?" she cut in.

His tanned face paled, changing before her eyes from a portrait of health and humor to a ghostly vision of sorrow. "I've made the journey before," he snapped, inviting no further questions. "Now, you still haven't told me what you can offer me for my prize cow." He looked into her eyes, then let his gaze travel down her neck, over her breasts, to her waist. As his eyes moved, Charlotte felt herself—unwillingly—warm under a gaze that felt more like a touch—

And she looked away.

No one had looked at her that way. Ever. Certainly her husband never had.

"That blush is as becoming on you as a wildflower in the middle of a spring prairie," he murmured.

"I have a fever," she answered, feelings and thoughts atumble. Her voice seemed caught in her chest, her heart was pounding, and a delicious, surprising warmth was flowing through her body in a new and utterly unfamiliar way.

The stranger reached out and put his palm to her forehead.

Charlotte felt her knees weaken at the man's touch; and beneath her skirt and starched white apron, a moist wave of desire made her tremble.

"You're healthier than those oxen," he pronounced. "Though you could afford to gain a bit of weight," he added. His gaze steadied on her breasts—always, in her estimation, too small, nothing like the ample bosoms that endowed the women whose portraits graced her cherished book covers and gazettes.

Yet, under this man's gaze, for some reason, Charlotte felt as desirable as any woman on earth, and her nipples tingled under his attentiveness.

What on earth was wrong with her? True, she had broken her childhood vow never to marry, but she had done so with her eyes open. And whatever her own problems were, she certainly couldn't let this man speak to her as if she were a dance-hall girl. "I'll have you know, sir, that I'm a married woman," she declared.

Was she imagining that a look of disappointment flashed in the stranger's eyes? And even if it had, she reminded herself, what of it?

He raised a brow. "What a disappointment," he said softly. "Then I won't be able to strike the sort of trade I had hoped for."

An inner voice warned her against continuing the conversation. Yet, a moment later, she heard her own voice ask, "And what trade was that?"

His handsome, suddenly mischievous eyes twinkled as he hooked his thumbs into his buckskin pants. She tried not to look where the movement had led her eyes, to hands that looked work-worn but gentle at the same time, powerful-looking thighs and long, strong legs. "If you shared my tent with me for one night," he murmured, "I imagine the experience would be worth that cow ten times over."

Her mouth opened and closed, but she could find no words. Indeed, her mind had caught on an image that was created by passion rather than knowledge, for she knew little of how a man and woman actually pleasured each other. But pleasure had swelled into a desire between her legs that was so powerful it was close to pain, yet so deep it was as sweet as anything she had ever felt. What was this feeling, this sense of need that seemed to be flowing through her all of a sudden, most strongly at the spot she had considered secret and private her whole life? And why had she never felt any of these feelings for her husband, a man who was kind and gentle and never teased and taunted her as this man was doing?

She was certain the pounding of her heart must be audible—indeed, she looked down and saw that her nipples were budded tautly against her gingham shirt.

When she looked back into the man's eyes—unwillingly, yet somehow commanded by a wordless connection that was different from anything she had ever felt—he was grinning. "Let me change that. It would be worth a hundred prize cows to me," he said softly.

Charlotte turned and ran.

She ran as if she were running from a knowledge that foretold her doom, ran as if running from a force far more powerful than she would ever be. And she supposed that it was because what she had felt just moments earlier—an exquisite, thoroughly new desire—was a force that would be nigh impossible to reckon with.

She ran past the assembling wagon train toward the eastern sky, knowing she wouldn't ultimately run away from her sister and her husband and the promises she had made, but knowing that she had to be alone, if only for a moment—and that above all, she would have to keep a long, cold distance from this stranger who exerted such a powerful, delicious effect on her.

No. She couldn't even think the word. It was indeed unthinkable, for "delicious" always pertained to something wonderful. And wasn't she anything *but* wonderful for thinking such sinful, forbidden, indeed evil thoughts?

"Charlotte!"

The voice of her husband caught her as she reached the end of the wagon train, and Charlotte hesitated before she finally stopped, feeling like a skittish, flighty colt.

"Are you all right?" he asked, his eyes filled with concern. "Your face is as red as a tomato, and you can scarcely catch your breath."

She shrugged, plagued by a horrible feeling that Francis could read her mind. "I think I have a fever," she blurted out, at the back of her mind thinking that it was as if the stranger *had* made her feverish. Yet now, she merely felt ashamed and extremely disloyal.

Francis was looking at her carefully. "What were you discussing with Luke Ashcroft?" he asked. "You seemed to be arguing with him as if your very life depended on it."

Charlotte felt herself flush again. "Mr. Ashcroft possesses a fine Guernsey that will be good for nothing but beef if he doesn't learn how to milk her," she said.

"Then perhaps you should go back and milk her, Charlotte. I've heard that the animal is owned by Mr. Ashcroft and a Mr. George Penfield, and that her milk is free for any women and children who need it—every day of the journey. And it would be in all our best interests, incidentally, to keep Mr. Ashcroft happy."

Charlotte was filled with questions, but they were ones she dared not ask, fearing she would give her sinful thoughts away. And so, saying not another word, she walked back up the dusty road to where the cow still stood, now with a clean bucket someone had placed on the ground nearby.

"Well, girl," Charlotte said. "I guess I'll be taking care of you at least for a while." She ran her hands back along the cow's spine and down her flanks, waving away whatever flies and mosquitoes she could before kneeling; then she began stripping the milk out of the swollen udders.

"Here," a voice said from behind where Charlotte knelt—a voice she knew all too well.

She didn't want to turn around.

"Mrs. Dalton," Mr. Ashcroft continued. "Put your lovely derriere on this."

Charlotte turned while continuing to milk, determined not to stop or show any emotion.

Mr. Ashcroft had placed a small milking stool behind her and clearly wasn't planning on leaving. "I'll be happy to help you onto it," he said with a grin.

For once, Charlotte wished that her husband—or anyone else, for that matter—was within earshot. But most families were scurrying around, gathering wayward children, hooking plows and other equipment to the sides of the wagons or, in some cases, deciding which beloved pieces of furniture would have to be left behind; no one had the luxury of interesting themselves in Charlotte's torment.

"Certainly not," she snapped, sitting carefully upon the stool. With her luck, she'd fall backwards into Mr. Ashcroft's arms, and then . . .

And then . . .

She couldn't think.

Resuming milking, she tried to ignore Mr. Ashcroft, but he was standing only inches from where she sat, and she couldn't escape a smell that was masculine, earthy, appealing in a deep, mysterious way.

"Tell me, Mrs. Dalton. Why do you run your hands all over the cow before you begin milking her?" Mr. Ashcroft suddenly asked.

"Why, to relax her, of course," she answered, concentrating on staring at the cow's udder. "To get her to trust me a bit, and to know my touch."

Mr. Ashcroft knelt beside her, moving with the grace of an animal. "That makes sense," he said. "That's the way a man should approach a woman, too, I believe: to get her to know him, and then to welcome his touch. Even to need it."

She knew she shouldn't look at him; this she knew with every inch of her being. Yet she was powerless not to.

Her eyes met his, and she felt her lips part. As she looked into that pale green gaze, she felt trapped, yet unwilling to be freed. Without wanting to, she imagined how it would feel if Luke Ashcroft ran his hands along her body, wanting her to want him, forcing her to need him.

"Back home in Indiana," he said softly, never looking away from her, "I once met a man who claimed to read minds." He paused, taking a long, slow, deep breath. "I believe, Mrs. Dalton, that at this moment I can read yours." He reached out and tucked a strand of her hair behind her ear, and Charlotte nearly fell over into the mud.

What on earth was happening to her? This was no trifling joke, she reminded herself. She was no longer an innocent girl who could tease the neighbor's boy and run off laughing; she was a married woman with a duty, and a plan to make an important, productive life for herself and her future family.

And yes, she had always felt uncertain about marrying Francis, wondering whether she was marrying him because she had known him so long and trusted him to be kind, knowing that having children was an important part of farming. But her vague uncertainty was no excuse for shameful thoughts, which she was having despite every good intention.

She knew she couldn't run away again; she was sure that if she tried, her knees would buckle and she'd tip over face-first into the mud. And then she'd have to hear that devil's laugh again, and look into those eyes she knew she could never look at again. So she would have to use words, and words that would work.

She managed to look away from Mr. Ashcroft, to take a deep breath. And then, in a voice as calm as she could muster, she said, "I'm quite certain I don't have any idea what you're talking about, Mr. Ashcroft. But I shall have to ask you again to speak politely to me—or, failing that, to leave me in peace."

He laughed and stood up, smoothing his breeches with his hands as he did so. She couldn't help watching, noticing the strength of his legs and their thick muscles, wondering what sort of occupation Mr. Ashcroft practiced to create such a magnificent, massive body. "And I'm quite certain, Mrs. Dalton, that you're not nearly as good a liar as you are a milkmaid. But I'll forgive you for now, since you're doing such a fine job with Violet."

And with those words, he tipped his black felt hat and strode away.

Charlotte looked back at Violet and thought about the cows she had owned back home, and the dream she and her sister shared: to farm out in the rich, fertile land about which they had heard so much; she would see her sister through the arduous journey, and then together—along with their husbands—they would help settle the new frontier and be a part of history forever.

And if that meant avoiding Mr. Luke Ashcroft at all costs, then so be it.

Two

"Farewell to America!" Charlotte heard a man call out as she walked alongside the wagon train, arm in arm with Lucinda, through the most beautiful meadows she had ever seen. The tall, undulating prairie grasses and wildflowers, fragrant with a wild, sun-warmed sweetness, seemed to be beckoning them onward, promising untold beauty and natural wealth at the end of the long journey.

"Goodbye, America! Hello, prosperity!" another man called, and Charlotte saw it was Mr. Ashcroft's wagon mate, George Penfield. A burly, bearlike man with a beard that reminded Charlotte of drawings of sagebrush she had seen, Mr. Penfield seemed to be a jolly, cheery man intent on enjoying the journey to its fullest. The evening before, she had seen him strolling down Independence's Main Street, singing and probably drunk; the elderly Mrs. Alma Bliss, an acquaintance of Charlotte's from Ewington, had said that he was "Mr. George Penfield, and a finer man you'll never meet, Charlotte, unless you'd consider Mr.

Luke Ashcroft, his traveling partner. I've known each man for a good ten days now, and I can honestly say each one would make a fine, fine husband for any young woman lucky enough to catch their eyes."

At that point, Mrs. Bliss had given Charlotte a long, penetrating look from her ancient, cornflower-blue eyes, and Charlotte had looked away.

Could everyone on earth sense her uncertainty, the questions that filled her heart about love, men and women? She liked Francis a great deal; yet her marriage certainly felt incomplete, and it was as if Mrs. Alma Bliss could sense this as easily as she could sense the beating of her own heart.

Now, as Charlotte walked through the breathtaking meadow, she watched as Francis drove—or tried to drive—their two teams of oxen.

"I thought you were going to be driving the teams," Lucinda said to Charlotte, bending down slowly, holding her belly with one hand as she picked up a dried buffalo chip with the other. She dropped it into one of several canvas bags she and Charlotte had sewn for the purpose of collecting this odd form of fuel for the fires. "Marcus rather liked the idea, since he said you're far better with animals than Francis is."

Charlotte laughed. "That's because he thinks I *am* an animal. Or close to one. What was it he said when he heard Francis and I were going to marry?"

Lucinda smiled, and Charlotte realized it was the first time she had seen Luce smile in days. "Charlotte," she said. "Don't be silly."

"Tell me again," Charlotte said. "It had to do with a mule, I believe."

Now Lucinda giggled. "All right. Marcus said you were a clumsy, stubborn, demanding mule and that Francis would have been better off marrying Beulah Baker, the woman who lost her tongue in that wagon accident up in Castleton."

Charlotte laughed as she stooped over to pick up a buffalo chip. "One thing about Marcus I can always count on is his extreme liking for me."

Lucinda looked at her sister with affection. "Well, at least he knows you're good with animals," she said. "He never tries to pretend otherwise."

Charlotte sighed. "I wish Francis could see my capabilities as well as Marcus can. Francis seems not to want me to lift a finger to do anything. He's afraid the oxen will hurt me, he's afraid walking will hurt me, I believe he's even afraid for me to take a breath on my own; and it's driving me out of my mind."

"Some women would welcome that sort of concern," Lucinda said softly. She had always been the prettier sister, with clear blue eyes, lustrous, nearly black hair and pale, perfect skin. But when something was troubling her—as now—her face pinched into thinness.

"Well, I don't," Charlotte said. "He certainly didn't treat me like a delicate piece of china back home. And I fear we shall have no children if—if things do not change," she murmured. And having had no experience, she had not the least idea how to change the situation. Could a woman reach out and touch her husband, pull him close, kiss him if he hadn't thought of it himself? And what happened after that? She knew what went on with animals, but how different was it with human beings?

Lucinda looked into her eyes. "These things take time," she said quietly. "Francis can be rather peculiar, you know: becoming a lawyer, yet not operating his office in Ewington right away; perhaps it is the same with your marriage."

Charlotte was silent as unwelcome images invaded her thoughts. She couldn't imagine Luke Ashcroft being "peculiar" when it came to the intimacies of marriage; indeed, her breath caught over the mere memory of his earthy and masculine scent.

She watched Mr. Ashcroft up ahead, two wagons to the forefront, a strong, muscular man who walked beside his wagon and drove his teams with an ease that was absent in her husband, whose motions with the whip were fidgety and weak. Mr. Ashcroft moved as if he were yet another animal, strong and sure and powerful.

She wished she weren't looking at him at that moment because every time she looked at him or even thought about him, she couldn't help remembering the curl of dark hair on his broad, muscled chest, or the strength of his long legs, his muscles straining against his pants. Most of all, she couldn't forget those pale green eyes that seemed to look far too deeply into her.

Forcing herself to think of something—anything!—else, Charlotte saw that her and Lucinda's canvas bags were each half full of chips.

She loaded her sister's chips into her own bag and handed Lucinda back the empty sack. "And here you thought you were nearly done, Luce. Let's gather lots of chips so we can have a fine supper tonight—dried beef with beans and bacon, stewed apples, bread if I can figure out how to cook it, and gooseberry jam if I don't burn the bread. I'll go hook this bag on the wagon."

Lucinda nodded, a twinkle at the corners of her eyes. "I know what *you're* doing, so don't think you can fool me, Charlotte Dalton," she said, smiling.

Charlotte saw that Mr. Ashcroft had joined Francis and Marcus and seemed to be giving them a lesson in teamstering. She looked questioningly at her sister, wondering if all her thoughts of the morning had been so simple to read.

"You simply want to see our husbands get taken down a peg or two," Lucinda said. "Obviously, Mr. Ashcroft has a lifetime of experience around animals, and he's trying to teach our husbands not to make such fools of themselves on the trail. So go, and let me know the juicy details when you return."

Charlotte managed a smile, ashamed she was harboring a sinful secret from her own sister.

"Your team would be more responsive if you walked a few inches back from where you're walking," Mr. Ashcroft said to Marcus, who had taken the whip from Francis as Charlotte neared the wagon.

"Yes, yes," Marcus said with irritation. "I've driven these teams for days."

As if he knew Charlotte was watching, Mr. Ashcroft turned in her direction. "And here comes your lovely sister-in-law, who's already taught me something about cows. Pity she won't be farming when you reach Oregon country."

Charlotte stared at Mr. Ashcroft as she caught up to the three men. "I believe I told you before, Mr. Ashcroft, that I'll be farming within a year of our arrival," she said, hoisting the bag of buffalo chips onto its hook on the side of the wagon.

"As you surely did, Mrs. Dalton. But your husband and brother-in-law just finished telling me they would be practicing law, and you—"

"I said if Oregon becomes a United States territory," Marcus cut in, snapping the whip and making all four oxen stumble.

"Marcus, what are you talking about?" Charlotte asked, for a moment forgetting Mr. Ashcroft's presence. She looked at her husband. "Francis? You told me you had finished with the law—'for all time' were your exact words. And now—"

"We don't even know if we'll get there," Marcus snapped.

"Marcus!" Francis cut in. "I'll thank you not to interrupt my wife!"

Marcus gave his brother a black look. "Then speak up for yourself, Francis. We don't know if we'll be able to dominate the Indians," he continued.

"No one has to dominate the Indians," Mr. Ashcroft said. "All my contact with them has been thoroughly peaceful. What worries me are people who expect differently."

"We do expect differently, sir," Francis said. "I've read accounts that make it clear the Indians are dirty beggars who will carry off every woman and child they can get their hands on. If one even looks at my lovely wife the wrong way—"

"You, sir, have been reading garbage," Mr. Ashcroft snapped. "And I caution you: If you truly believe your own words, then stay with your teams or in your wagon when the Indians come to find us—which they will."

"We'll do what we want, when we want," Marcus said, his pale face red with anger—yet even now, quite handsome in a fine-featured sort of way, with gray-blue eyes and lush, nearly black hair.

Mr. Ashcroft looked surprised but certainly not intimidated. "What you believe is of no account to me either way—unless its effects spill onto others in our party. If you act rashly toward an Indian, the rest of the train will be dragged down with you."

"I'm not going to attack anyone," Marcus said disagreeably.

Mr. Ashcroft's eyes darkened. "I'll be watching both of you," he warned, and he walked away, his stride quick and sure.

Charlotte looked into Marcus's eyes—cold and pale, as expressionless as a frog's. "Was that necessary?" she asked.

Marcus rolled his eyes. "Was *his* speech necessary?" he asked, sounding like a petulant child. "All this glorification of the Indians! Does he want the United States to extend its borders or not?"

Charlotte turned to her husband. "Francis, I thought you said we should all try to placate Mr. Ashcroft for some reason."

"He *is* the expert hunter in the group," Francis said. "But I'll make sure to take care of you, Charlotte."

Charlotte felt anger flare deep inside. "I don't need taking care of," she began.

But Marcus interrupted her. "Francis and I can hunt if need be," he cut in. "And the Captain knows the trail."

"Has Captain Tayler crossed before?" Charlotte asked.

Marcus hesitated. "He and Ashcroft have both made the journey. But there's more than one route, and one doesn't have to be an outdoorsman to complete the trip. We're educated men. We can read notes on trail markers as well as the next man."

Charlotte couldn't bear hearing evidence of Marcus's arrogance for another moment. "I have to continue collecting chips with Lucinda," she said. "We're planning a celebratory dinner—"

"Please be careful," Francis cut in. "The two of you, Charlotte, not just Lucinda. I don't want you wandering off by yourself. Do you understand?"

For a moment, she thought of Marcus's assessment of her as a stubborn, crabby, demanding mule, and she wished Francis thought of her, if not as Marcus did, at least as strong and capable.

And yet, back home Francis had known of all the farm work she did. He had always claimed to admire what he called her "animal skills," and she had even once heard him brag that she could split wood "better than any man."

"I shall be fine, Francis," she said, trying not to sound annoyed.

"And you'll remember you're not on your home farm," he warned.

Charlotte turned away, deciding she would try to hold her tongue. If she had married Francis partially because he was congenial, gentle and would be a wonderful father to their future children, did he not deserve her gratitude for being kind and solicitous?

As Charlotte rejoined her sister, she could see that pain was making Lucinda clench her jaw. "Are you all right?" Charlotte asked.

Lucinda sighed. "How I wish the baby would come on the easy part of the trip." Tears began to roll down her face. "Or that we had waited to set forth until after the birth. I can't see what difference another month would have made."

Charlotte said nothing, sharing her sister's thoughts. She knew her mother would have uttered some homily about men, that once their minds were made up, wild horses couldn't turn them back. "It's the way of the world," she would have murmured with a sigh.

My will is as strong as a wild horse's, she said to herself, *and I'd rather be dead than have Francis boss me around the way Marcus orders Lucinda about.* Yet in the end she, too, had agreed to go when the men wanted to, not because Francis and Marcus had been in a hurry but because the grazing would be that much better for the animals.

Charlotte took her sister in her arms. "You'll be fine," she said. "And the baby will be fine," she added, looking into Luce's doubtful eyes. She should have been thinking that they would do their best, with the help of their husbands. Yet there was only one man whose strength filled her imagination, a man she knew she could trust on a cruel, unforgiving journey. And that man was named neither Francis nor Marcus Dalton.

Luke watched as Charlotte prepared dinner. She had driven two forked sticks into the ground and laid a pole across them, Luke assumed for the heavy iron kettle that waited on the ground nearby. But if she didn't get a decent fire going soon, he thought, that kettle was going to stay mighty cool.

He and George, for their part, had been offered more meals by more women in the past few minutes than during both their lifetimes. Nearly every woman was so grateful for Violet's milk—and the buttermilk and butter that had been made in the bucket that Charlotte had tied to his wagon that morning—that all had offered unlimited meals for the duration of the trip. Raspberry jam with bread, dried tomato pie, beans with molasses, fried cakes with cranberries and pumpkin pie were some of the many luxuries that had been promised.

All had made offers except one, the woman he

now watched as she struggled to make a fire, her lovely lower lip jutted out in anger and determination.

She wasn't the prettiest woman in the caravan. But she certainly seemed to be the most determined. And in the fullness of that lip, the curve of her chin, she suddenly reminded him of Parmelia—Parmelia who had begged him not to go, Parmelia who had pleaded with him. . . .

And he looked away.

Don't, he said to himself, guilt already flooding his heart. Wasn't he supposed to be an honest man? Wasn't Parmelia the woman he would love forever?

"Come *on!*" he heard Charlotte cry out.

Luke couldn't help himself. With his callused hands, he gathered some chips that were burning in his own fire, walked over and placed them in the center of the smoking pile Charlotte had created. "Here," he said, kneeling next to her. "These should get your fire burning."

"I don't need your help," she said without looking at him.

"To get your fire burning?" he asked. "I think you do."

For a moment, her eyes met his. And in that moment, he forgot to breathe. He felt as if he were touching her, as if he had known her for a lifetime.

"No, I don't," she murmured.

He laughed. "So you're all heated up then?"

Fury darkened her eyes. He watched her lips part, her breathing quicken, her breasts rise and fall in anger and impatience. "Mr. Ashcroft," she said, settling her dark and hypnotic gaze on him. "I don't need to be teased, and I don't need any help. I'm not some helpless girl from town who's never started a fire before."

"Did I say you were?" he asked, loving the way her cheeks had darkened and a pulse beat rapidly at the base of her neck. "From what I can tell, you're the one who should be driving your teams—not your husband or your brother-in-law. And if you weren't so intent on refusing my help, you'd see that lots of people are sharing their embers." He paused. "Just because your husband feels you're a delicate flower doesn't mean you can't accept some help every now and then from someone who knows you usually don't need it."

Her cheeks darkened more, but instead of seeing the fire he instinctively sought in her eyes, he saw sadness instead. And her silence spoke more than words ever could, making him sorry he had teased her.

"How long have you been Francis Dalton's wife?" he asked quietly.

"Do you think that's a proper topic of conversation between a man and a woman?" she asked, still looking at the fire rather than at him.

"I don't pay too much attention to rules," he murmured. "I never have, and I never will."

Once again, she directed her gaze at him. She narrowed her eyes, the familiar spirit and anger back in full force. "Then perhaps you possess a luxury I simply don't have, Mr. Ashcroft. My mother and sister and I sold our farm to make this journey. My mother, a new widow, gave up everything so that my sister and I could make a new life for ourselves. Unlike you, I have to worry about what my husband would think if he saw you talking to me—again; I have to worry about finding a way to farm when we get there—if we even do—"

"You will," he said quietly.

"You don't know that!" she cried.

"I've been watching you all day," he said. The look in her eyes made his breath stop in his chest; the look as she realized—and appreciated—his attention made his loins tighten. This woman could tell him from morning to night that she didn't want his attention. But some part of her did: the woman who *hadn't* married Francis Dalton, who would never belong to a man as wrong for her as her husband was.

And it was strange, Luke felt, because there were prettier women in the caravan than Charlotte Dalton: her hair, even under her calico sunbonnet, always looked wild and unkempt, and she probably thought her mouth was too big and her breasts were too small. But he had thought she was beautiful from the minute he had seen her.

"You'll be able to handle the weather and your animals," he said. "That much is obvious to everyone." He paused, thinking of her husband. "Or almost everyone. And I'll see that you're never short of buffalo meat and venison and fish. What I fear isn't your competence, Mrs. Dalton. I fear the poor judgment of the men in your life is going to run us all into trouble."

He looked her up and down, and he could imagine what was beneath the layers of her skirt, the soft folds of her femininity ready to be pleasured. He could imagine making her move beneath him and claw at him and cry out his name. "Then again," he went on, his voice husky, "Francis Dalton, inexperienced though he may be out in the wilderness, had the good judgment to marry you, didn't he, Mrs. Dalton?"

All at once, he understood the necessity of her earlier request: He was going to have to leave her alone.

Something had caught at him—something in the way she looked as she watched the horizon; something in the way she would have tried all night to get that fire going rather than admit she couldn't; something in the way she had handled his cow as if she had spent her life being good to animals, which he guessed she had—had caught at him and wouldn't let go.

And in the pleading of her liquid brown eyes, he had finally seen the point: It wasn't fair for him to talk with her as if she were free—to be who she wanted, with whomever she wanted. She was Francis Dalton's wife. She had asked him to leave her alone. And he had no business even thinking about her. Hell—hadn't he always counted himself an honest man, if nothing else?

So if he was going to be honest, then a woman couldn't become part of his life on the trail unless she was going to play a damned minor role, something that wouldn't make him feel terrible at night when he thought of—

Hell. He couldn't even think the words. When he thought of his life back home and those he had left behind, back in Indiana.

Forgive me, Parmelia and John.

But he knew there would be no forgiveness for him—ever.

"All I'll ask of you from now on, Mrs. Dalton, is that you tell me if there's anything you need. Do you understand?"

Her mouth opened, her lush lips parting to reveal pearly white teeth. She looked surprised. "But what about Violet?" she asked. "I'll have to teach you about milking her, or make sure some of the other women get on a schedule—"

He laughed.

"I don't see what's so funny," she said, her cheeks turning the color of sunset. "A cow that's not properly milked will become as ill as a dog—"

"Oh, I know that, Mrs. Dalton. I've raised several dozen myself over the years. But I believe I'll give Violet to the Vestrow family."

Her brown eyes turned black. "Then why on earth did you act as if you needed my—" She stopped. "Oh, I believe I see all too well what you were doing. Trying to make a fool of me in some way—"

He couldn't help himself. "On the contrary," he cut in. "Trying to make the trade of a lifetime," he murmured. And he walked off, swearing he would keep his word to himself—for Charlotte's sake—from then on.

Three

The cold seemed to envelop Charlotte, waking her as it had every night in the two weeks since Independence. It amazed her how the days could be so hot, the sun blistering into the core of her body, and then the nights could be so cold, especially after the afternoon thunderstorms that seemed to come with infuriating regularity, soaking through her bonnet, her clothes, her shoes and her skin, her hopes and her dreams.

She was exhausted, nearly unable to move, desperate for sleep and the peace sleep could bring. But something more powerful than her need for sleep was eating away at her, giving her body an energy she didn't want in the middle of the night.

Every time she closed her eyes, she saw and felt and smelled Luke Ashcroft as if he were lying beside her, on top of her, covering every inch of her and filling her—

She would shake her head, feeling as if she were losing her mind, not understanding how she could be so powerfully in the grip of something she didn't understand.

She didn't know Luke Ashcroft, but she felt as if she already did know him, in important, deep, mysterious ways.

She didn't want to know him, but she felt as if

forces way beyond her control had already thrown her to him, as if fate had meant for her to know him, and to know him well.

She didn't want to think of him, or dream of him, see him with her eyes shut or her eyes open, but at every moment, she felt him; she imagined his touch, she imagined the feel of him, the smell of him, the taste of him, and she felt shame over the sin of her thoughts, and fury that she had been foolish enough to marry Francis—or anyone at all.

It seemed like such a fine idea at the time, she reminded herself, remembering the night she and Francis had been walking through town and Francis had taken her into his arms. "We go together like the moon and the stars, Charlotte. I'd like to go out west with Lucinda and Marcus, and I know you would, too. What if we went there as husband and wife?"

Now, she looked back on the thoughts that had flashed through her mind as crazy. For so long, she had sworn she would never marry. Yet, on that night, she had seen her future in a different light: She had imagined herself under the long, low rays of the western sun, where the soil was fresh and new, the skies high and wide, the land ready and eager for her to farm. And she had seen herself with children, a family. A whole new dream.

Now, as she sat up, adjusting her vision to the darkness, she saw that she was alone in the tent, without Francis, once again.

On so many nights of the journey so far, she had watched other young married couples laughing together, kissing, dancing to after-dinner fiddle and harmonica music, and she had felt an ache in her heart. Was there something wrong with her, some defect or problem that made Francis apparently cringe from her physically? Would Beulah Baker, the unfortunate, tongueless woman from Castleton, have been more to Francis's liking?

Hearing a sound outside the tent, the sloshing of muddy grass beneath someone's feet, Charlotte felt a rush of energy. Tonight would be the night she would try to take the bull by the horns, so to speak, and look her marriage, and her husband, right in the eye. That Francis was kind and gentle didn't mean he could never touch her, did it? Or dance with her and twirl her around under the stars, as she had seen Nora Vestrow's husband do with her?

As Francis came into the tent, Charlotte sat up, noisily shaking her blankets because she suddenly felt too shy to speak. "Is everything all right?" she heard herself ask.

"Absolutely," Francis said, pulling his blanket over himself next to Charlotte. "It promises to be a beautiful day tomorrow."

Charlotte tried to gather her nerve, not wanting to hurt Francis's feelings. "Francis," she finally said, her heart pounding.

"Yes, dear," he said softly.

She swallowed. "Would you like to kiss me?" she asked.

Francis leaned over and kissed her chastely on the cheek. "Good night," he whispered.

Charlotte felt a tear roll down her cheek. She felt as lonesome, suddenly, as she had ever felt in her life, at sea in feelings she couldn't even name. "I meant as a husband," Charlotte said. "To do more than just kiss."

There. She had said it.

But Francis said nothing. She watched in the near-blackness for some sort of movement on his part toward her side of the tent. "We've embarked on a long, arduous journey," he finally said. "Let's save our strength for the trip, Charlotte, and worry about marital duties later."

For a moment, Charlotte closed her eyes, pretending to be somewhere else. It was what she and Lucinda had always done when their parents had fought. They had pretended that they were princesses in faraway lands, with ladies-in-waiting and banquets and all manner of delicacies awaiting them.

Yet she didn't want to be somewhere else. She was thrilled to be part of a wagon train on its way out west. She just wanted to be loved.

Oh, Mama, she said silently. *What a terrible mistake I've made.* She knew that she cared for Francis far more than some other wives cared for their husbands. But the marriage was wrong, she knew—though she knew nothing of how a good marriage worked.

As she lay in the darkness, unable to sleep, she couldn't help wondering whether there was something wrong with her that made Francis feel as he did.

* * *

"I'll trade one of these shirts, sir, for that piece of venison," Charlotte said, trying not to stare at the Indians who had come to the camp to swap. They brought to mind her mother's "Indian book," as they had called it, an old, faded storybook she and Lucinda had once colored in as girls. They had been whipped by their father when their "artistry" had been discovered, but they had always loved looking at the pictures, even afterwards.

Now, looking at her first real-life example of a group that had always fascinated her, Charlotte was filled with questions she was too shy to ask. Why, for example, did they wear ornaments made of silver dollars and Masonic emblems? Why did they all ask for "calico, calico, calico"?

"I swap venison for calico," the Indian said, nodding as he spoke. "Good?"

"Very good," Charlotte said, feeling a thrill as she realized she had completed her first real trade with an Indian. She hadn't made a fool of herself, as far as she knew, and she had ended up with a piece of venison that would make a fine and tasty dinner tonight. And she had to silently thank her mama for helping her to make extra shirts, which the guidebooks had said were highly desired in trades.

All around her, others were trying to make swaps. Mr. and Mrs. Bliss, the elderly couple from her hometown, had traded a flannel shirt for some buffalo meat and were giggling like teenagers as they walked away. Mollie Smithers, the beauty who seemed to be pursuing Mr. Ashcroft with more and more energy each day, was hanging around the edges of the trading circle, looking flushed and gorgeous.

And then, out of the corner of her eye, Charlotte saw Francis heading her way, his face lined with concern and worry. "What did you do?" he called out.

"I traded a shirt for some venison," Charlotte answered.

Francis said nothing, his eyes looking into hers with an intensity Charlotte found unsettling and mysterious.

"What's wrong?" she finally asked, in the face of his silence.

"Those Indians are dirty," he said quietly. "I don't want you near them."

"Are you out of your mind?" she said. "The Indians' help often makes the difference between whether people survive the trail or not, Francis. The Indians actually know what they're doing out here."

"You leave the tracking and the conversations to the others," he said, his voice strange and unfamiliar.

"I don't understand you," she said. "Why on earth—?"

"Did you see the way that savage was looking at you?" he asked. "If he could have undressed you with his eyes, he would have done so."

"Well, at least *somebody* wants to!" she cried out.

As soon as she had said the words, Charlotte could see the pain they had inflicted. Francis's face went white, his lips compressed into a thin line. "I told you, Charlotte. This is going to be a long and arduous journey—"

"And we could give each other comfort," she said. "And pleasure," she added softly, though she had never imagined she could speak so boldly about physical love. "Do you not see that I am a woman, Francis?"

Francis looked into her eyes, opened his mouth, then closed it without a word. Then he stalked off, back toward camp, and Charlotte was left alone in the bright midday sun, the heat shimmering up from the ground.

"Are you all right?" came a voice from behind her.

Charlotte didn't want to turn around. She didn't have to in order to know whose voice had reached her. For almost two weeks now, she had successfully avoided contact with Luke Ashcroft, and he had respected her demand to he stay away.

Yet now, he was back. He came around in front of her and faced her, his shoulders looking even broader, somehow, than before, his hazel-green eyes deeper, a far more attractive man than anyone she wanted to know.

She was half aware that she was out in the middle of the prairie with this man and no one else, that though they could be seen by others, they couldn't be heard.

She was half aware that she should leave, because she had thought far too much about Luke Ashcroft for too many long, tormented nights.

And she was far, far too aware that Luke

Ashcroft was standing close enough to touch her, and that she wanted him to in a way she wouldn't even have been able to imagine before she had met him.

She swallowed and avoided his eyes. "I'm fine," she said quietly.

"Are you? It seems I never see you laugh or smile with your husband."

For a moment, she just looked at him. As the wind shifted, she suddenly heard voices—friends and acquaintances still trading with the Indians, cattle lowing, horses neighing, children laughing and shouting.

Speak! she told herself. "I don't see that my marriage is any of your concern, Mr. Ashcroft. You seem to think about it even more than I do."

"Maybe I do," he said softly.

"But why?" she asked. "You barely know me." She knew she was treading on dangerous ground. Why was it, she wondered, that whenever she talked to this man, she felt as if she were balancing on uneven, dangerous surfaces?

"I know when a woman is unhappy," he said. "Or missing something. And when it's a beautiful woman, it's like watching a beautiful horse tethered twenty-four hours a day to a post. Or watching a neighbor's garden die for lack of care."

A beautiful woman, he had called her. Here this stranger, this man she had been trying to avoid for two long weeks, had called her a beautiful woman.

And her husband—

It was wrong.

"Do you remember when I asked you to keep your distance from me, Mr. Ashcroft?" she asked.

"How could I forget?" he asked softly, his eyes holding hers. "Why do you think I gave the Vestrow family my cow?"

"I—" She felt color rise to her cheeks and down her neck as she remembered that day that now felt like such a long time ago. She had been swept up by wrong thoughts about him back then, even the first time she had ever laid eyes on him, speculating about his broad shoulders and long, muscular legs, imagining what lay beneath his buckskins.

"I don't know," she said softly. "I just assumed because the Vestrows have so many children. . . ." Her voice trailed off as Mr. Ashcroft held her gaze.

"That was one reason," he said. "But I didn't want you milking her, Charlotte. I didn't want us to be near each other every day." He paused. "Isn't that what you asked?" And then he looked into her eyes. "Isn't that what you want?"

Charlotte opened her mouth, but no words came out. What was it she wanted? she asked herself. What she wanted, she knew, was . . . unspeakable. Shameful. A touch from a stranger, words from a stranger, attention that should have come from her husband.

Luke Ashcroft reached out and touched her neck.

"I see you're as irresistible to the mosquitoes as you are to everyone else," Charlotte thought she heard him say.

Thought, but wasn't sure because that touch—just a simple touch—was like fire, warming her neck, spreading heat down her shoulders, over her breasts, sparking across her nipples, his warm, rough hand making her think thoughts she shouldn't have been thinking.

Her breath caught. And her knees trembled. And she couldn't think or move.

"If we weren't out here in the middle of all these people," he said softly, letting his fingers trail down her neck, "I'd brush every one of those mosquitoes off every inch of your body." He took a long, deep breath, looking into her eyes. "And I'd take my damn sweet time at it, too."

She would have laughed if her imagination hadn't been caught by the image. Oh, yes, she could have lived without the thought of all the mosquitoes in her life, but she was thinking more of what it would feel like to have Luke Ashcroft touch every inch of her body.

She had to stop. She had to stop thinking, and she certainly had to stop speaking with this man who always led her down the path of danger, toward thoughts she never should have thought about anyone but her husband.

"But then again, I've made a promise to you, haven't I?" he asked softly.

Suddenly he turned back toward the trading area, and Charlotte followed his gaze. George Penfield, his wagon mate, was running toward them, and for a second, Charlotte had the crazy thought that somehow everyone had heard what she and Mr. Ashcroft had said to each other.

Somehow everyone had read her thoughts and knew how much shame cloaked her heart.

"Luke, there's a men's council meeting in two minutes," Mr. Penfield said, his voice coming heartily out of his big, bearded frame. "And, Mrs. Dalton—I'm sorry," he said, looking into Charlotte's eyes in such a kind, tender way that Charlotte was suddenly terrified something had happened to Lucinda.

"Is it my sister?" she asked. "Is my sister all right?"

"Your sister, as far as I know, is fine," Mr. Penfield answered. "But not five minutes ago, Sam Charlton found your husband in the Charltons' wagon, helping himself to their lifetime savings. The men's council is going to vote on whether your husband will be hanged."

Four

It felt so unreal to Charlotte, and so quick. Captain Tayler was walking back from the group of men that had formed inside the circle of wagons, and judging by how slowly he was moving, Charlotte was certain she knew what the vote had been.

"Mrs. Dalton," he said quietly when he reached her. He took off his hat and made a small, surprising bow. "I'm so sorry."

Charlotte felt her mouth drop open. She had

expected they would vote to hang Francis; yet now that the moment had arrived, Charlotte felt numb.

Captain Tayler looked as if whatever he was about to say was giving him physical pain. "Your husband has already spoken with his brother, but he asked that we let him speak to you before—before the end," he finally said. "Then we'll ask the women to gather the children away. . . ."

"Thank you," Charlotte said. "I'll be there in a moment." She looked into the tent once more at Lucinda, who was sleeping as soundly as a contented cat.

A few moments later, Charlotte felt the eyes of nearly every member of the caravan on her—people who nodded at her and some who simply stared, like the women of the Smithers family, as she walked past their wagon. She had never exchanged words with them, but she knew them as the southerners who spoke to their slaves as if they were dogs.

Now Mrs. Lavinia Smithers gave her a haughty look as she walked past.

"Charlotte!" a voice called out, and Charlotte turned. Alma Bliss, holding on to her bonnet, was running toward her on her spry old-woman's legs, as agile as a woman half her age. "You speak to Francis and then you come with us, do you hear? None of the women except a couple of fools think you had anything to do with Francis's . . . well, his dang-fool stupidity."

Charlotte hugged Alma. "Thank you," she said, and then she took off at a run.

She felt tears well up in her eyes, a sob catch in her throat as she saw Francis, hands tied behind his back. He was talking with Marcus, and though Francis's thievery had made Charlotte realize she hadn't known him as well as she had thought, she still couldn't help thinking that if she had had to wager which brother was more likely to be hanged for his actions, Marcus would have been her choice. If Francis had not been caught red-handed, she never would have believed he could steal. And it made her feel, once again, that a woman could never truly know a man.

As she approached, Marcus patted Francis on the back, then walked toward her. "I hope you're satisfied," he muttered.

"What did you say?" Charlotte asked.

Marcus waved a disgusted hand at her and walked on, and Charlotte hurried up to Francis, not knowing how many minutes she would have left with the man she had married such a short time earlier.

"I *am* sorry," he said softly. "I guess I've botched everything quite badly."

Charlotte said nothing, not knowing where to begin.

"I'm sorry I wasn't a better husband," he said, his eyes full of feeling. "I guess I thought if I got enough money together, you would be happier."

"Money for what?" Charlotte cried out. "We always planned on doing everything ourselves—planting and building, tending the animals—" She stopped because there was no point in making Francis feel worse than he already did.

"Who knows why we do some things?" he asked. "Who knows why I never—" He stopped. "So will you continue on the journey or head back east?"

His question stunned her as much as the news of his thievery had. Had he known so little about her? She would have traveled alone out west to that rich soil and all that free, wide land, even if Lucinda hadn't been going.

But again, there was no reason to go out of her way to hurt him. "Oh, I shall continue," she said. "I wouldn't want to leave Lucinda in her condition."

Out of the corner of her eye, she saw movement, and she turned. Captain Tayler was approaching, followed by thirty or forty men.

Charlotte didn't look at their faces. She turned back to Francis, and in that moment, as she saw the fear in his eyes, she felt pity and guilt and love and regret entwine like ropes tightening around her heart.

"Pray for me," Francis said softly as Captain Tayler turned him around.

"Time will heal you, Charlotte," Nora Vestrow said.

Charlotte turned away, not knowing what to say. What had happened was tragic for Francis—he had been driven to do something rash and crazy, she supposed by her, because he had wanted to make himself look bigger and grander in her eyes.

But she was not a widow grieving for the man she had loved with a wife's passion. She was deeply sad for Francis; but mostly, she felt guilty over the fact that she hadn't been able to figure out how to be a wife. She was exactly the same woman she had been before she had married Francis. She had never been touched by him except for the chastest of kisses, never been given physical pleasure nor given any to him. And she couldn't help wondering if he would still be alive if she had done things—though what, she didn't know—differently.

"Nora is right," Lucinda said, joining her a little apart from the other women. Her eyes suddenly reminded Charlotte so much of their mother's that it nearly broke her heart.

Charlotte shook her head. "I shall be fine," she said softly. "I never should have married Francis in the first place. I will miss him as a friend, but that is all we were, Luce. We were friends."

"Even after all this time?" she asked, her cheeks growing dark.

Charlotte nodded. "It never did happen. And I feel it is one of the many signs that I shall never be the marrying type." She touched Luce's cheek. "Remember what I always vowed, that I would never, ever marry?"

"But if we are to farm together—" Lucinda said.

Charlotte patted Lucinda's belly. "You shall have to have many children, dear sister. Enough for both of us."

Lucinda paled, and Charlotte knew that since even the coming birth terrified her, the idea of enduring several more births was probably unimaginable.

Out of the corner of her eye, Charlotte saw

movement: the men, some forty or so strong, were walking back to camp from the river.

And Charlotte knew what that meant. Francis was gone.

She felt Lucinda put an arm around her, and she prayed for Francis's soul.

Darkness had fallen lightly on camp, the moonlight bright and strong even beneath the trees near the spring.

Charlotte walked lightly, with trepidation. She had heard bits and pieces about Francis's death since it had happened. With the caravan laying over at Alcove Spring—a beautiful spot with cool, clear water the likes of which no one had seen since leaving Independence—there was more gossip and chitchat than on a night when the wagons would be pulling out at the crack of dawn. She had heard Lavinia Smithers say, as the Smithers family walked past Charlotte's campfire, that Francis had left the world "bawling like a baby, according to Jock and Skete."

Now she had to say goodbye one more time, to try to make some sense out of feelings that were as confusing and crossed as a pile of sticks thrown to the ground by a child. She walked under boughs of tall trees that seemed to be protecting her on the way to the spring, past bushes that rustled in the soft, late-night breeze. She would look at Francis, she would say goodbye for the last time, and she would put the past in the past. Deep down, for as long as she could remember, she had always felt different. Now Francis was

gone, partly because . . . what? She had been difficult to please, or mysterious, or . . . something
that hadn't been right.

She walked out into the clearing. At first, she
didn't see Francis's body. She heard a sound, and
she saw movement in the brush. Then she realized she *had* seen Francis out of the corner of her
eye, his body hanging from a tree to her left. And
in the moonlight she saw death, Francis's neck
bent to the side at an unnatural, lifeless angle.

A flood of memories came rushing into her
thoughts: Francis back in Ewington, eating the
overbaked pie she had entered in the church con-
test, claiming it was "excellent, really," even
though Charlotte's own dog later refused to eat
what was left; Francis telling her, beneath the stars
one night outside the barn, that he had loved her
his whole life; Francis—amazingly—going up
against his brother. One Sunday afternoon, Charlotte and Lucinda had been racing Marcus and
Francis to the river, Charlotte having dared the
two to a race. "You two spend all of your time in-
doors," she had taunted—and then had tripped
on a branch and fallen flat on her face. Marcus
had laughed, calling her "the clumsiest girl in all
of Illinois." And Francis had punched him square
in the jaw.

Now Charlotte looked up at his lifeless shape,
and she missed him.

Suddenly she heard an intake of breath off to
her right. A face peered out at her from the
bushes, and Charlotte saw it was one of the
Smithers's two slaves, a young woman who was

probably about Charlotte's age. Charlotte had
heard Mollie Smithers yelling "Biddy *Lee*" at her
more than once, so she supposed that was her
name, though whether that was the name she
wanted to be called, Charlotte had no idea. There
was much about slavery she didn't know, still less
she understood.

Biddy Lee crouched down quickly in the bushes
again, and the leaves were as still as if no one had
ever been there.

It gave Charlotte a chill, a fear she hadn't felt
just looking at Francis. She called out into the
darkness, "Biddy Lee?"

Silence.

"Is your name Biddy Lee?" Charlotte called out.

Silence and stillness. A cloud passed over the
moon, and in that moment of darkness, Charlotte
felt as if she were surrounded by spirits, unknown
forces whose intentions she didn't know. Where
was Francis, exactly? Would he follow her now, his
spirit or essence or soul? Would he no longer love
her, but hate her for whatever she had done
wrong?

"Please," Charlotte said. "If you are Biddy Lee,
will you come and stand near me?"

Silence.

"Whoever you are," Charlotte called out, "if you
come and give me comfort, I shall be forever
grateful."

Silence. Then rustling, and Charlotte saw the
dark-skinned, dark-eyed woman stand, barely visible in the moonlight that had brightened the
clearing once more.

"Are you Biddy Lee?" Charlotte asked.

"Why are you calling me?" Biddy Lee asked, her voice echoing off the spring. "How do you know my name?"

"I've heard you called that by those Smithers women," Charlotte said. "I guess I just want to talk to a living soul, Biddy Lee. My name is Charlotte, and—"

"I know who you are," Biddy Lee said, coming forward. "You're the one my mistress says should be booted off the trail."

"Why is that?" Charlotte asked.

Biddy Lee shook her head. "I wouldn't want to say," she said quietly. "No, those words aren't for my lips to say." Biddy Lee was looking at her sidelong. "She says you and your kind don't believe in slavery."

"That's right," Charlotte said, feeling strange talking as Francis hung not twenty feet from where they stood. "Biddy Lee, do you mind if I ask what you're doing out here? It must be close to midnight. Maybe even later."

Biddy Lee said nothing, just shook her head quickly.

Charlotte sighed. "I had a fright a few minutes ago, Biddy Lee. Did you have one too?"

"You looked into your man's eyes?" Biddy Lee asked.

"I—I think so," Charlotte said, realizing that she had indeed seen his face—bug-eyed, a look of horror frozen forever on it.

Biddy Lee shook her head. "Make peace with your husband, say a prayer right here and now for

him, and then be on your way, Miss Dalton. I
came because—" She hesitated. "I came out because I never saw a dead white man, a white man
who got hanged. Curiosity was what led me out
here. But I didn't look into his eyes. And if you
know what's good for you, you'll make peace with
him. Now I have to go," she said, already walking
quickly.

"Wait!" Charlotte called out.

But Biddy Lee was hurrying off into the darkness beneath the trees, and Charlotte was left
alone.

She headed quickly back toward camp, still
afraid. And then she stopped. *Say a prayer,* Biddy
Lee had said. *Make peace with the man.*

Charlotte took a deep breath, but her mind was
blank. What, she still wondered, had led Francis
to do something as crazy as stealing? Was there
any way it hadn't been her fault? *Please, God,* she
said silently, *take care of Francis's soul as I wasn't able
to in his lifetime.*

And then she ran. She had always considered
herself strong, which was easy when comparing
herself to Lucinda. But now when she had been
presented with something new and mysterious,
she found she wasn't so strong after all.

As she saw her tent limned by the pale moonlight, she felt a rush of gratitude and comfort. She
would lie down in it, wrap herself in the quilt she
had made with her mama what felt like a lifetime
ago, and sleep would claim her.

Only there was a man, a large, tall man, sitting
outside her tent.

Luke Ashcroft.

She would have been able to recognize him in the faintest light, with her eyes clouded by fatigue or blinded by tears.

"What are you doing here?" she whispered, kneeling beside him.

"I've been waiting for you," he said. "Wondering whether I should be going out looking for you. Where were you?"

Charlotte took a deep breath. Why did it feel so natural, she wondered, to have this man she barely knew wonder where she had been? And why did she feel it proper to answer him truthfully?

"I went to see Francis," she said. "To say goodbye to him one more time. I suppose to make it clear in my head and heart that he truly is gone."

"And you saw him?" Mr. Ashcroft asked, his voice as soft as a breeze.

She nodded. "I felt as if his spirit were going to haunt me, though, or as if something bad will happen. I felt something . . . wrong back there." In the moonlight, she looked into Luke Ashcroft's eyes. "Do you believe in that?" she asked. "In spirits that live on, to haunt those who . . ." Her voice trailed off.

"If you believe, Charlotte, that in some way you are to blame for your husband's death, I can tell you that you're wrong."

"But how do you know?" she asked. "I was not—" She stopped, shaking her head. "I tried to be the best wife I could be, but our marriage . . . It was not—"

He waited, but she said nothing more. "Not—?" he prodded.

"It was not all that it could have been," she finally said. "In certain quite private areas. But it was and shall remain a private matter."

His eyes searched hers. "Are you telling me he didn't love you as a man should love a woman?" he asked.

"You must go," she said. "This is so very wrong, Mr. Ashcroft. If you came looking for me because you didn't know where I was, well, now you know I shall be sleeping in my tent, right where I should be—"

"And I will be right next to you—"

"Not in my tent!" she cried out.

Luke's face grew suddenly and completely serious. "I'll be near you because it's the right thing to do, Charlotte. And before you object: I know that you treasure the idea of this journey, and I know that you can take care of yourself. I know you can build your own fires and drive your teams and trade for what you need. But when you do need me, I'll be here for you."

She could not look at him—not when he was saying words that were so wrong and so right, not when she had revealed something terrible and secret, though true enough. For had she not been evil and shameful to tell Mr. Ashcroft that her marriage to Francis had not been all that it could have been?

"You must go," she said, not looking at Luke. She crept into her tent, found her mama's quilt and wrapped it around herself. "Oh, Mama," she whispered into the darkness. "Please help me be a better person." And please, she added silently, make me someone who doesn't think wrong, evil thoughts.

Five

"What makes a man steal from his fellow man, do you think?" George asked. He and Luke had been repairing one of their spare bridles in that silence Luke had always had the feeling only men could stand. Yet now George had broken the silence. And broached a subject Luke felt was much larger than either one could know at that moment. "What makes a man do something so stupid that it's almost as if he wants to be caught?" he went on.

Luke shook his head. "I cut him down," he said.

"You what?"

"I cut Dalton down and buried him," Luke said, softening a lead line with salve. "If folks have a problem with it, including Sam Charlton, they can take it up with me."

George was looking at him carefully. "But why?" he asked. "Why would you bury a thief?"

"There are women and children on this trail," Luke said. "They'll see enough dead bodies between here and the Territories." He stopped, thinking of what Charlotte had said to him about Francis's spirit. She seemed to be a woman of unusual courage. Yet last night, she had truly been afraid.

And he thought of Parmelia's fears when he had left on this same journey four years earlier. He could remember the tears that had streamed down her face when he had left—her pleas, the fear in her voice and her eyes.

He wanted to protect Charlotte Dalton on this trip, to protect her from fear and from danger. But had he protected Parmelia, his own wife?

Forgive me, he said silently.

"Are you going to tell me what's tearing you up?" George asked, setting down the bridle he had been working on.

Luke looked at him, and for the first time in a friendship as deep as any he had ever known, he didn't know what to say.

"Do you miss Francis?" Lucinda asked as Charlotte rubbed a cool, wet cloth against her forehead. Their dinner—bacon, beans and dried plums—was done, the dishes scrubbed, the coffee collecting mosquitoes that they would not be able to avoid swallowing at breakfast.

Charlotte sighed, thinking what would be the truest answer she could give. She and Lucinda had always spoken the truth to each other—"anything and everything," they had always said, meaning "leave nothing out, or forever regret it." But now Charlotte found that she didn't know what the whole truth was, and she was ashamed to speak, even to her sister, of some parts she did know. Would she ever know whether she had been the cause of Francis's death? Had her immoral thoughts about Luke Ashcroft made her too bold with Francis, asking him, essentially, to make love to her when he wasn't yet ready?

"I miss him as a friend," Charlotte finally said. She rubbed the cloth along Lucinda's forehead, then ran her fingers through her hair, back from her forehead, the way their mama had always done. "You always knew you wanted to be a wife, Luce. I always knew I didn't. I tried to go against my true nature, and in the end . . ." Her voice trailed off. "Tell me again how you knew you were in love with Marcus, honey," she said, wanting to hear something true and familiar.

Lucinda smiled. "I've told you a hundred times. Maybe two hundred."

"Then tell me for the two hundred first time," Charlotte said. "Anything and everything, Luce."

Lucinda smiled and leaned her head back as Charlotte ran her fingers through her hair. "I was in town buying that yellow fabric, and Marcus said the blue would suit me better, that it was the same color as the dress I had worn at that dance when Billy James threw up in my lap and Mrs. McGillion's dog tried to lick it up." Charlotte laughed as Luce continued. "It was just one of those moments I knew meant he was the one for me. He had noticed me, and he had a sense of humor, and it just felt right," she said, cradling her belly with one hand. "And it is strange, Charlotte, because just the other night, Marcus was saying again how Francis would have been better off marrying Beulah Baker, and Francis said no, everything was good and that he expected you would be with child any day now."

Charlotte shook her head. "We should never have married," she said softly. In the distance, she heard the sounds that meant a chivaree was beginning—a tentative fiddle, a confident-sounding harmonica, a joyful melodeon—to celebrate the marriage of a man and a girl who had met on the caravan.

"Marcus is livid they're proceeding with the chivaree," Lucinda said, sitting up; "but I suppose life does go on, as Captain Tayler said." She began to stretch her arms over her head but grasped her belly before she had finished.

"Are you all right?" Charlotte asked.

Lucinda nodded. "I'd like to go get some of that water from the spring."

"I can go for you," Charlotte said, feeling she had to go again to see if what she had heard was true, that Mr. Ashcroft had cut Francis down and buried him.

"I believe it is true what they say, that there are almost no bugs in the spring," Lucinda said. "Last night, the coffee seemed positively thin, did it not?"

Charlotte laughed. "I know. I keep thinking that any morning, I'm going to sprout wings and a beak, I've eaten so many bugs."

A few minutes later, Charlotte reentered the beautiful grove and spring that was famous even back in Illinois.

"What's the matter?" came a rough, Southern-accented voice from the bushes. "You saving yourself for that slave boy Ben Lucius, Biddy Lee?"

"Leave me be!" came Biddy Lee's voice.

"Do you know I could have you flogged and flayed for such an unkind remark? I could have your flesh ripped from your bones for such unkind, unfair, positively ungenerous insolence? Now, lie back down—"

Charlotte called out before she had time to even think. "Over here!" she said loudly. "Luke, I think this is the spot." She heard a muffled sound, then whispering.

A moment later, she saw Skete Smithers, the strapping, twentyish son of Jock and Lavinia Smithers, crash out of the bushes. He was blond, with a red, puffy face that looked almost purple at that moment. He glanced at Charlotte, looking daggers at her and then fled.

Charlotte listened, hoping Skete wouldn't change his mind and come back. Then she cleared her throat. "Hello?" she called out. "Biddy Lee? Are you all right?"

Sitting up and then standing, Biddy Lee looked out at Charlotte from the bushes. "That was you?" she asked quietly.

Charlotte nodded.

Biddy Lee narrowed her eyes. "There's no Mr. Luke Ashcroft here, so why?"

Charlotte looked at her and remembered the night before, when Biddy Lee had been the only other living soul out here by the spring.

"I don't like to hear that kind of talk," Charlotte said, "the words Skete Smithers was saying to you. And you helped me last night."

Biddy Lee narrowed her eyes even more. "Helped you how? I came out to see a sight for myself."

Charlotte smiled. "Honestly, Biddy Lee, I don't think I could have moved from where I was standing if you hadn't come over to talk to me."

"You said a prayer last night?" Biddy Lee asked.

Charlotte nodded.

"You feel his spirit now?"

Charlotte thought about it. "Actually, no. No, I don't."

"Then you helped me, and I helped you. And now, we'd best leave each other be, if you don't want to bring a heap of trouble down on your head."

"What will you do about Skete Smithers?" Charlotte asked.

"What I've done all this long time. Fight him off and hope he stays as scared of his wife as a young puppy is of the meanest bull on the farm."

Charlotte thought about Skete's wife, Carlene. Young, blond and pretty, she looked almost like Mollie Smithers's twin. Did she know her new husband was tormenting Biddy Lee this way? And if she did, did she care?

Biddy Lee peered around, then pulled something out from the bushes. As she carried it to the spring, Charlotte saw that it was a doll, with a fine-looking porcelain head and a long, faded dress. "That Skete," Biddy Lee muttered, carefully pulling the doll's dress over her head. "I hid Elizabeth Grace under my apron, but Lord knows if he saw her . . . She's all I own in this world, Mrs. Dalton."

"Charlotte," Charlotte said as she watched Biddy Lee wash the tiny dress.

"You'd best be going, Miss Charlotte," Biddy Lee said. "I don't want that heap of trouble on your head or mine," she said without looking up.

Charlotte was filled with questions—about what Biddy Lee would do about Skete, about spirits, about what Biddy Lee thought of the feelings they'd had last night in the presence of Francis's body. But Biddy Lee had already turned her back to her, and she had been as clear as day: Talking to Charlotte would bring a heap of trouble on her head.

And Charlotte felt she had brought enough trouble onto the trail already, even if she hadn't been the one who had stolen the money from Sam Charlton. She had been tormented by sinful thoughts, dreams of physical passion that had no place in a proper woman's life. Her husband had suffered, and now he was gone.

She dipped her pitcher into the spring, filled it with water and walked back toward camp.

"Hey!" a voice suddenly called out, interrupting her thoughts.

She was only ten feet or so from the circle of wagons and the chivaree inside it, and she thought of running: That voice was the one that made her skin crawl, the one that had threatened Biddy Lee down by the spring.

But something made her turn and hold her

ground. "Yes?" she said coldly, as if Skete didn't scare her, which he did. His puffy face looked like a burned-up side of hog.

"I didn't know you was looking for love," he said, his thick Southern accent almost impossible for Charlotte to understand.

But unfortunately, she had. "Excuse me?"

"You heard me," he said softly, looking her up and down. "I'd service you any hour of the day or night, Miz Dalton."

"Go to hell," she muttered, starting to move past him.

He caught her by the arm. "You dumb slut. You think Luke Ashcroft's going to look at a skinny little thing like you when he can have my sister? Go look at the chivaree and see how much time he's spending thinking about you."

"I don't even—" she began.

"What I'm saying, Miz Dalton, is that Luke Ashcroft wasn't even with you back there by the spring. Which means I know what you did." His eyes were burning with anger. "You cooked up a pretense to try to aid and abet a slave girl. But Biddy Lee Waters is my property. You understand that?"

"No one can—"

He caught her by the jaw. "Repeat after me," he warned. " 'Biddy Lee is your property, Mr. Smithers—' "

"I won't—"

His grip on her jaw tightened. "Biddy Lee is your property," she said softly.

" 'Mr. Smithers,' " he said.

"Mr. Smithers," she murmured, hating herself.

His eyes glittered. "I take her where I want, when I want. You try something like that again, Miz Dalton, and you won't live to see the next day."

Charlotte turned and ran, spilling half the water as she raced along the edge of the chivaree. How was it that a big, stupid man like Skete Smithers had figured her innermost thoughts, thoughts she hadn't revealed even to herself? All because she had chosen Luke Ashcroft as Biddy Lee's imaginary protector?

By the fire, she saw Luke Ashcroft dancing with Mollie Smithers. They were both laughing, and Mollie looked like an artist's model, her long, curly blond hair flowing past her shoulders as she danced in a dress that was obviously brand new.

Charlotte told herself to look away, but she couldn't. In her mind's eye, she remembered that afternoon which now seemed like so long ago, when she had foolishly thought Mr. Ashcroft had described her as "irresistible." She had obviously imagined the word, because in some small part of her heart, she had been yearning to hear it, never having heard anything like it from the man she had married. Or else he had meant she was irresistible to mosquitoes, but to no one else! Of course Mr. Ashcroft would be dancing with a beautiful girl like Mollie Smithers while Charlotte stood off in the darkness—a plain brown sparrow, as clumsy as an ox. Of course!

Finally, Charlotte forced herself to look away. What was important was Lucinda and keeping her well; what was important was surviving the trail, making sure Lucinda gave birth comfortably, and that the baby was well taken care of. Whether Luke Ashcroft liked her, even whether he ever looked at her again, if he indeed ever had—these were questions that belonged in her shameful, foolish past.

Six

"You'll never come back for me," Parmelia said. "I can feel it in my bones, Luke. I'm begging you not to go."

Luke awakened in a sweat, drenched from head to toe. He pulled himself from his dream just as the wake-up rifle discharged, and he leapt up and into his clothes. The sooner he immersed himself in real life instead of the dream, the better.

But that was easier said than done. As he stoked up the fire, setting the kettle with last night's coffee onto the heat, he could hear John as he had cried on that last morning, as if he had known that Luke was leaving, that he would never see his daddy again. As he laid out slabs of bacon in the cast-iron fry pan he had brought from home, he remembered, without wanting to, the day Parmelia had brought the pan home, her face shining like a silver dollar. "My first piece of kitchen equipment that's storebought with my egg money," she had said, as excited as a girl.

"Good morning, handsome."

Luke looked up from the bacon that had just begun to sizzle in the pan. Mollie Smithers was standing there, looking like a blond doll, all done up somehow in clean clothes again, her full breasts obvious and unmissable.

And Luke knew that dancing with her last night had been a mistake. It had seemed like nothing at the time: George had asked Emma Gray, a woman traveling with her father from Council Bluffs, to dance, and Mollie, sitting next to Emma, had stood up and danced into Luke's arms. One dance had led to another, and she had made him laugh and forget his troubles for a few minutes.

But Mollie needed more than a one-night dance partner; he had seen it in her eyes as he had told her it was time for him to turn in. And now, by the light of dawn, he could see there was more energy in those blue eyes than should have been directed at him. "Morning," he said, turning the bacon in the pan with a fork.

"I had hoped to invite you to breakfast," Mollie said softly. "Mother is making flapjacks, my sister-in-law, Carlene, is frying up potatoes, and I said I would cook the bacon if I could bring company."

"Not this morning, Mollie," Luke said as George emerged from his tent. "So the bear has finally come out of his cave?" Luke called out to his friend.

George laughed. "My old bones can't take dancing like that anymore. I'm surprised you lasted even one dance with this little filly here."

Mollie moved to Luke's side and took hold of

his arm. "I would have danced slow dances with Luke all night long if that was what he wanted."

"Look," Luke said. "Thanks for the offer, Mollie, but I won't be joining you for breakfast."

"Tomorrow?" she asked.

He shook his head. He had been a fool to dance with her.

"I don't understand," Mollie said softly. "Last night—"

"Last night I danced with you. Too much, if it gave you ideas."

Her eyes were filling with tears.

"You should be looking for a boy your own age, an unmarried young man who can build a future with you," he said.

Mollie Smithers blinked. "Aren't you unmarried?" she asked.

He could see Parmelia and John as clearly as if they were two feet in front of him, Parmelia holding John in her arms, John's sharp, blue eyes shining into his. His boy, who was the spitting image of Daddy. Far, far too many miles away.

"I've said what I have to say," Luke said quietly. He turned and then walked away, feeling as if his heart were on fire.

Marcus's words were still burning in Charlotte's ears, but she tried to concentrate on what she was doing, helping to heal Mr. and Mrs. Bliss's ox Jake, who had a wound on his shoulder from a rough spot in the yoke. As she spread on the salve, murmuring to Jake as she let her hands do the work, she tried not to think about Marcus. But she

couldn't forget the moment. As she had walked
outside to get the fire going for breakfast, Marcus
was waiting for her, looking wide awake and with
an expression she had learned meant he was
ready for trouble.

"Good morning," she had said, though already
she could sense that maybe it wasn't going to be
such a good morning after all.

"Do you know that you looked like a complete
fool at the chivaree last night?" Marcus began.
"Gaping at the edges, your mouth open like a
frog? How many flies did you catch for your evening meal, Charlotte? Did you think that would
make Mr. Ashcroft dance with you, or even look at
you?"

Charlotte stared at him. She knew that Marcus
had never liked her, that at some level he blamed
her for Francis's death. So perhaps now was the
time to put everything out into the open.

"Do you know, Marcus, that nothing of what I
do is any of your concern? You may feel you can
be rude to my sister, but you have no say over what
I do."

Marcus had spat a wad of tobacco on the
ground and walked off.

Charlotte had gone on to boil the coffee, fry up
some bacon, warm last night's beans and bake a
breadlike something-or-other—and she was soon
joined by Lucinda and Marcus. But Marcus had
not spoken another word directly to her.

Now, as she ran her hands along the soft, sun-
warmed flank of the Blisses' ox, she told herself
once again that none of what Marcus had said,

and nothing he would ever say in the future, mattered. When she arrived in Oregon Territory, she would file a widow's claim and finally own the land of her dreams. She would farm and take care of Lucinda and the baby, and be sure never to marry again.

Yet Marcus's words still hurt, in a part of her heart that for some reason she couldn't protect— and as she looked at Mrs. Bliss, she was glad for the distraction. The old woman looked fretful and obviously worried about her poor ox.

"I think it should heal up all right as long as you keep putting the salve on it and maybe wrap some cloth around the yoke," Charlotte said.

Mrs. Bliss's rheumy old eyes filled with tears, and she extended a bony hand to Charlotte's cheek. "Bless you, child, and ignore these teary old eyes."

Charlotte smiled. "Not at all, Mrs. Bliss. I'm just as fond of my oxen. They're nice, gentle animals who are going to get me clear across this continent. I'd be embarrassed if I *didn't* feel emotional about them."

Mrs. Bliss laughed. "That's very nice, dear, but my eyes are tearing from the wind," she said, wiping at her face with a dust-browned handkerchief.

Charlotte felt a blush heat her cheeks in the hot morning sun. "I guess I'm crazy," she said, looking ahead toward Big Blue, the river they would have to cross. When they had crossed the Kansas River in the first days of the journey, the entire caravan had floated their wagons across after tarring and patching the bottoms. Francis, Marcus

and Charlotte had even managed to team together to pull the wagon along the rope that had
been stretched across the river. But this time, they
would be fording it, which would involve more
skill than strength, Charlotte felt.

At the edge of the river, Charlotte walked up to
Marcus, who looked nervous as he watched the
other teams. "I'll drive the teams across if you'd
like," she said.

He spun around to face her, rage in his eyes. "Is
that so?" he bellowed. "And you've made this offer because you feel I'm incompetent, as you so
obviously felt Francis was?"

"The oxen know me better—"

"Fine," he snapped, throwing the whip at her.
"You're the great animal expert." He stalked off
into the crowd, and Charlotte sighed.

She could feel people looking at her, and the
one whose attention she felt the most was Alma
Bliss. Charlotte felt as if her own mama was
watching her all the way from Ewington, Illinois.
Charlotte Dalton, the woman who could heal animals but couldn't get along with half the human
race.

She peeked into the wagon just as Lucinda was
moving to come out of it.

"I'm sorry about Marcus," Lucinda said.

Charlotte shook her head. "Go get yourself a
good, secure spot inside the wagon, and let's get
across this river while the crossing is good."

Lucinda looked surprised, but she climbed
back in, and Charlotte hopped up onto her seat.
"Come on, boys," she called, hoping her oxen

would be able to hear her over the hooting and hollering of the men driving the other teams.

"Come on, Sam and Pete," she whispered. "Come on, Duke and Tom."

She watched her teams hesitate at the water's edge, snuffling, smelling the water, shocked by the cold.

"Get up, boys, up!"

Finally, they must have appreciated the feel of the cool, rushing water against their bodies as they lumbered in all the way, snuffling some more. Charlotte heard Lucinda cheer from inside the wagon, and she silently promised her boys good grazing in the days ahead.

It took only minutes to cross. When they got to the other side and Charlotte stepped down from the wagon seat, she saw Marcus approach. "Very nice," he said quietly, his face tight-looking and pale as he began lowering the wagon off its blocks, not looking at Charlotte at all. "But do you know, you're a good teamster and a good little farmer, yet you'll always be useless as a woman, Charlotte." He finished lowering the wagon, took the whip from Charlotte's hands, cracked it across the lead oxen's backs and drove the teams forward without a backward glance.

Charlotte turned away and nearly ran into Alma Bliss, who must have been standing only inches away. "Don't take it to heart, his cruel words," Mrs. Bliss said softly. "Any man who feels he has to belittle a woman isn't a man himself."

Charlotte said nothing, a lump welling up in

her throat. She had wanted to shout at Marcus, to scream angry words that had been building inside since Francis had been hanged. But she had stayed quiet, unable to speak, her voice silenced because in a small, unprotected part of her heart, it was as if Marcus was in fact telling her something true.

Charlotte and Mrs. Bliss were both quiet for a few moments as they walked along in the sunshine to the sounds of the oxen's hooves plodding against the hard, dry earth. It was a strange landscape, Charlotte felt—beautiful, wide, undulating, looking truly like God's country, but practically treeless, almost the way Charlotte imagined Africa might look.

"I only know your ma a bit, Charlotte," Mrs. Bliss said. "But I feel if she can't be here with you on this journey, well—I can." She winked. "So I'm going to do a little bit of meddling, and a little bit of advice-giving, because I know your ma would want that. So here it is now, child, my first bit: You're a different sort of young woman. You're not afraid to speak your mind to a man, you're not afraid to show your knowledge of animals. You've made certain people uncomfortable, and now they're going and making you feel uncomfortable. But don't you listen to them, my child. You be yourself or you'll have Alma Bliss to answer to, and being yourself is a damn sight easier than answering to me, Charlotte Dalton." Her eyes looked into Charlotte's. "So don't you dare let your brother-in-law push you around."

Charlotte looked into Alma Bliss's beautiful blue eyes and was grateful beyond words that she was on this journey with her.

She looked up ahead at Marcus, who was savagely whipping the oxen—the same teams that had faithfully carried them across the river.

"Excuse me for a minute, would you, Mrs. Bliss?" she said as Marcus cracked his whip hard against Duke's back.

She found that her body was trembling as she walked toward Marcus. She was so angry that her heart seemed to be fighting its way out of her chest. "Marcus!" she called out, breaking into a run as he raised the whip again.

He glanced back at her but registered nothing in his eyes—no surprise or sense of remorse or change of heart. He cracked the whip down again with a force that made the ox groan.

"I demand that you stop whipping that poor beast this instant!" Charlotte cried out, reaching out to grab the whip.

"You must be insane if you think you can order me about!" he thundered. With another crack of the whip, he lashed out at Duke with a force that made the beast stumble, then kick back roughly and suddenly with his left hind hoof.

With a flash of pain that felt like a burn, Charlotte buckled to the ground. She tried to stand up, but the pain burned in her ankle.

Get up and get your leg washed off, she said to herself, looking at the growing bruise and oozing blood. She knew she would be all right, ultimately, if she could put some salve on. And she would ignore the pain if—

She felt arms beneath her, scooping her up and collecting her, and she knew whose they were; she knew the smell of those arms, their sure strength and breadth and hardness, without having to look.

"Hold on tight and I'll have you fixed up good as new," the voice said quietly, as she laced her arms around Luke Ashcroft's neck.

Oh, no.

For so many weeks, she had patted herself on the back as she had turned in the other direction whenever Mr. Ashcroft was near; she had given herself a little mental check mark every time she had walked past his and Mr. Penfield's campfire at night with a mere "good evening" exchanged. Even the other day, when he had touched her neck, murmuring whatever it was about the mosquitoes, though she had felt too much, and though she hadn't actually been able to walk away from the man, at least she had known that she ought to.

Yet now, she was in his arms. He was carrying her off to goodness knew where, back toward the rear of the caravan.

"Where are you taking me?" Charlotte asked as they passed Mr. Penfield driving the teams.

"Right in here," Mr. Ashcroft murmured, stepping up and maneuvering her into a wagon—his wagon.

A bachelors' wagon, the one she had peered into

on that first day of the journey, when he had been a stranger and she had somehow known—even back then—that she should stay away from him.

Luke Ashcroft laid her on top of two folded patchwork quilts as gently as if she were a fragile piece of glass. "Now let's see that leg," he said, kneeling beside her.

"I beg your pardon?" Charlotte croaked, her voice nearly gone. She cleared her throat and sat up, pulling her skirt back down around her ankles and looking up at Mr. Ashcroft. "I shall be fine as soon as I can put some salve on my wound," she said, her voice still hardly there.

He raised a finger to his lips. "No talking," he whispered.

"Mr. Ashcroft—"

His finger moved to her lips.

She breathed in the scent of his skin without wanting to.

"No talking," he whispered again.

She had never felt a man's finger against her mouth like that. She felt her breathing stop, trapped, as she looked into eyes that were filled with fire. She closed her eyes because the feeling of looking at him, knowing he was so close, feeling the warmth of his skin, smelling his scent, was all too intense for her to take in.

No one had ever looked at her the way Luke Ashcroft just had. No one, not ever. Certainly her husband never had. Luke Ashcroft was pulling at her heart, tugging at her where no man had ever wanted to touch.

When she opened her eyes, she looked at Luke

Ashcroft—she had to call him by two names, or even her thoughts would feel far too intimate— and this time, she saw his breath catch. Then he inhaled slowly, his eyes never leaving hers, and he parted her lips with his finger.

She had never felt anything like it in her life. How was it, she wondered, that he could touch only her lips, yet desire had flooded her from head to toe? She needed him in a place she had barely ever thought about before she met him, and she seemed to need him more each time he looked at her.

She was supposed to have shared all these things with Francis. She should have stolen his breath away; he should have made her heart race. Together, they should have made each other's thoughts go haywire.

But it was another man doing those things to her.

With his thumb, Luke Ashcroft traced her lips—the top one, then the bottom one, slowly, his eyes never leaving hers. His finger felt warm, insistent, intimate. Charlotte thought her heart would jump out of her chest, and she wanted to tell Luke—no, Luke *Ashcroft*—to stop. She wasn't a bad person, and she wasn't supposed to be doing this.

But she couldn't speak.

Suddenly, Mr. Ashcroft took his hand away. He took a kerchief from his pocket, then got a brown glass jar from a wooden box on the floor. He dipped the cloth into the jar and salved her wound, gently but firmly, as the wagon lurched forward.

"I think your leg is going to be all right," Luke said softly, setting aside the kerchief. "What I want to know about is your heart, Charlotte."

Charlotte tried to ignore how even hearing Mr. Ashcroft say "Charlotte" made her feel. She was shaken, and not just by her feelings for this near-stranger. What was wrong with her? Where were the morals her mama had so carefully taught her?

Charlotte looked away, shame washing across her heart.

"When are you going to realize it wasn't your fault?" he asked.

She shook her head, her thoughts atumble, her body still warm and confused by Mr. Ashcroft's touch.

"Did you steal money from Sam Charlton?" Mr. Ashcroft asked softly.

Charlotte shook her head again.

"Did you vote for the hanging? Were you one of the men who agreed as a group, except for Marcus, that hanging was the just and true course of events?"

"Of course not," Charlotte said quietly.

"Were you untrue to your husband?"

She should have been shocked by Mr. Ashcroft's words. She should have raised a fuss, acted properly indignant over such a question. But in a place deep in her heart, she knew that all these questions were important.

"Charlotte," he said, his voice like a caress. "Talk to me."

She took a deep breath, but she couldn't look

at this man she had thought about too much since the moment she had first met him.

"Were you ever untrue to your husband?" he asked again.

She was about to say something—though she didn't know what—when he put a hand on her lower leg—just below her knee, a spot no man had ever touched before.

If it had been any other man touching her like that, she was quite sure she would have screamed.

But this was Luke Ashcroft.

And what she thought, as she looked down at his strong, tanned hand, was that she shouldn't feel the warmth spreading up her leg from his touch, that she should say something; anything would be better than silence.

And that she should move away.

But this was Luke Ashcroft.

She swallowed, her heart knocking in her chest.

"I've been watching you for weeks," he said after a long silence. "I've watched you, and I watched your husband when he was alive. And never once did I see Francis Dalton look at you the way a husband looks at a wife he loves. Or touch you the way a husband touches his wife."

She swallowed again, tears stinging her eyes, though she would be damned if she'd let Luke Ashcroft know his words were reaching her at all. "I didn't know I was such a fascinating scientific experiment," she said softly. Her voice sounded hollow, ragged, weak, and she wanted him to take his hand away from her leg because she couldn't think.

"You're fascinating to me, Charlotte, as a woman. Not as a scientific experiment or anything else."

"I loved Francis," she said softly. "I did love him," she went on, covering her face with her hands.

"And he's gone, and it's not your fault, and you did nothing wrong," Mr. Ashcroft said, pulling her hands from her face. He held her hands in his and looked into her eyes. "You did nothing wrong," he said again.

"Oh, but I did," she said, the words coming out before Charlotte was able to think: For some reason, she always felt compelled to tell the truth to Luke Ashcroft, to blurt out words she didn't want to speak even in the privacy of her own heart.

"Tell me," he said.

She shook her head. "I can't," she whispered.

He took her face in his hands. "Look at me," he murmured. "Talk to me."

She supposed it was his eyes that did it, eyes that promised she would be safe if she spoke the truth.

"Now tell me," he whispered, his hands warm against her cheeks.

"I was untrue in my heart," Charlotte heard herself say, "because I had thoughts about you."

The look in Mr. Ashcroft's eyes was something she had never seen before—surprise, pleasure, deep desire. She couldn't have said whether Mr.

Ashcroft looked into her eyes then for three seconds or three minutes.

And then, still holding her cheeks in his hands, he lowered his mouth to hers.

Charlotte moaned, a sound she had never heard coming from her own body; but then again, everything was strange and unfamiliar. Just the smell of Luke Ashcroft, the warmth of that mouth against hers, the hot desire that seemed to power every inch of his body—it was all so wonderful and terrible and new. She felt as if she were melting as his lips parted hers and his tongue found its way into her mouth.

Luke Ashcroft groaned, and Charlotte melted again. She had never imagined this kind of need, this kind of desire, this kind of pleasure mixed with almost-pain. How could it come so naturally, with few words—

And then she caught herself.

What had she done?

And what had *he* done?

She pulled back, unwrapping her arms from his neck as she moved away, unable to look at him.

"Charlotte," he whispered.

She shook her head. What kind of person was she that she could kiss a man as she had never kissed her husband, and so soon after her husband's passing? Was she so shallow that she thought of Francis not at all?

From deep inside, a voice told her that Francis had not acted as a proper and true husband should. Though thoroughly inexperienced, she had needed love that he hadn't, for whatever reason, been able to give.

Yet she certainly couldn't look to Luke Ashcroft for love. She barely knew the man, and what she had learned after being married to Francis was that she was meant for no man; she was meant to be alone.

"I must go," she said.

He shook his head, his eyes never leaving hers. "You must think," he said. "Of yourself and your feelings, Charlotte. Not what people might think or what the world says is right."

She slid away from him, her body still awake and tingling in a way she had never experienced. "I must go," she said softly, moving past Mr. Ashcroft.

As she passed him, she caught a whiff of his scent, and it made her feel dizzy with need and desire.

She steadied herself and then stepped out of the wagon, for a moment unable even to remember how she had gotten there in the first place. Mr. Ashcroft had been gallant and had carried her in, and she knew that this was the true Luke Ashcroft: He was a man who would always be there for the women of the caravan.

But that didn't mean she had to let him lead her down a path she knew was wrong, absolutely wrong.

And then she suddenly remembered an unwelcome sight from the night before: Mr. Ashcroft dancing with Mollie Smithers, laughing and enjoying Mollie's considerable beauty. He was obviously a rake, a ladies' man, all too happy to help a woman as long as he would be rewarded physically in the end.

She had foolishly confessed her feelings to Mr. Ashcroft, thoughts she had been too ashamed even to share with Lucinda. And she had taken steps down a path whose memory made her cheeks hot with embarrassment. How could she have felt such delicious, amazing feelings in a situation of which she was so ashamed? Well, it didn't matter, and it wouldn't matter, Charlotte told herself. She would put Mr. Ashcroft completely out of her mind, as he had probably, by this time, put her all too easily out of his.

Dearest Mama, Charlotte wrote later on in her tent by the light of the lantern. *I don't know when I shall be able to get this letter to you, but I will pretend we are talking as I write, and so ease my heart.*

I have some sad news, and the only way to tell you is to be direct, I'm afraid. So please sit down and try to shield your heart from shock: Francis is no more. He was caught stealing from another man's wagon and sentenced to be hanged. Mama, I did love Francis, and I am plagued by a sense I did very wrong by him. She stopped writing and wiped at a tear. She was feeling sorry for herself and for a husband she had loved only in a certain way. What was wrong with her, she wondered, that she had never felt on fire with Francis as she had with Mr. Ashcroft, barely even knowing the man?

Luce is feeling well and then unwell, but the event will come soon, I think, and I feel in my heart that she will be fine, and the baby too. Who would have thought Lucinda would be able to walk from dawn to dusk, but that is what she is doing, as marching on foot is less bumpy than riding. We drench in the rains and then bake in the sun, but it is exciting to see such beautiful land with wide-open skies and amazing cliffs in the distance, and know we are among the first to travel this way. Antelopes and grizzlies and buffalo roam all over the place, except, it seems, when the men venture off in a hunting party.

Alma Bliss sends her regards and says to tell you she is keeping a "keen, mean eye" on me. I miss being able to tell you things, Mama. But perhaps when we are settled, raising our chickens and cows and fine vegetables and fruits, we will convince you to join us, and Luce and I and the baby can sit at your knees while you tell us all of our favorite stories. I miss those times, Mama, more than I can say.

Charlotte set down the pen, then thought, for a moment, about writing to her mama about Mr. Ashcroft. But what on earth could she write, and for what purpose? Mr. Luke Ashcroft would mean nothing in her life, nor she in his.

And so she sealed the letter, trying to ignore the cloak of disappointment that these thoughts had pulled around her heart. If she was ashamed to write to her mother about this man, and to tell Lucinda her thoughts, that meant something. It meant everything, she knew.

But as she blew out her lantern and closed her eyes, listening to the night sounds of the crickets and cattle and dogs barking in the distance, she knew that thoughts of Mr. Ashcroft were going to torment her for a long, long time.

Seven

It was before dawn, before the sentinel's rifle wake-up shot, and as Charlotte left her tent, limping slightly from her sore leg, she was surprised to see Lucinda sitting by the breakfast campfire.

"You're up early," Charlotte said.

Lucinda looked away from her, laying three pieces of bacon in the skillet. "I couldn't stop thinking about the unkind things Marcus said to you yesterday at the river. Sometimes I just don't understand why men always feel they have to be cruel."

"Not all men do," Charlotte said, thinking of Mr. Ashcroft. She doubted if he had ever spoken unkind words to a woman in his life. "Never once was Francis unkind to me," she said, deciding to keep her thoughts of Mr. Ashcroft private.

Lucinda's eyes were downcast. "Do you know that looked very romantic when Mr. Ashcroft swept you up in his arms and carried you into his wagon?" She turned a piece of bacon and then looked into Charlotte's eyes. "*Was* it romantic, Char? Was it as romantic as it looked? I do believe

Mr. Ashcroft is one of the handsomest men I've ever laid my eyes on."

Charlotte felt color rush to her cheeks. This was Luce, the sister she loved more than life itself. Yet when she thought of what she had done with Mr. Ashcroft in his wagon, how her insides had sparked and burned with desire, how she knew she would never forget the feel of his lips or the scent of his skin for as long as she lived, shame and desire washed through her all over again. She needed this man in a way that was thoroughly unfamiliar and defied all reason.

"And you wouldn't be blushing, sister dear, if you didn't agree with me. Even Alma Bliss, who says she's old enough to be Mr. Ashcroft's much older sister, says he is as handsome as the day is long."

Charlotte knew she couldn't keep the secret from her sister any longer. "I did a terrible thing, Luce."

Lucinda's eyes widened. "Anything and everything, Char."

"I let him kiss me," Charlotte said. Lucinda's hand flew to her mouth. "He was as romantic as in a dream," Charlotte went on. "And honestly, Luce, I've never felt like that in my life."

"Like what?" Lucinda asked.

Charlotte looked into her sister's eyes. "As if I was meant for him—I mean in a physical way. You must know what I'm talking about, since you . . ." Charlotte's voice trailed off. "Since you are with child."

Lucinda looked down into the pan and turned

the bacon, then busied herself getting a tin plate and forking the bacon out onto it. She decided the bacon was not yet done and put it back into the pan.

And right then, Charlotte knew that Lucinda hadn't felt, with Marcus, the way she had felt with Mr. Ashcroft.

"Do you feel this bacon is done enough for Marcus?" Lucinda asked.

"He gets what he gets," Charlotte said, feeling Luce was so much more than Marcus deserved.

Lucinda seemed rattled. "Maybe in marriage, a wife's wishes come second," she said. "That's the way it was with Pa and Mama."

A rush of anger filled Charlotte's heart. "Mama never should have let that happen," she said. "And *you* shouldn't, either."

As she finished speaking, she looked up and saw Marcus emerging from the tent, slowly buckling his pants as if he wanted all the world to see what a man he was. He glanced at Charlotte and looked away, as if merely looking at her was distasteful.

"Good morning," she said, wanting to irritate him.

He looked at her and said nothing.

"You know, Marcus, this is going to be quite a long journey. I would think you could at least be civil."

"And I would think you could have made an effort to save your husband's life," he snapped. "Did you make an appeal to Captain Tayler? Or to the men of this wagon train?"

"The men of this wagon train, for the most part,

seem to feel that the women are here merely to
serve and feed them, not to give their opinions."

"Did you try?" he cried out, a vein at his temple
bulging.

"You know as well as I do that I couldn't have
changed the course of things. *I* didn't steal from
Sam Charlton; Francis did. He knew it was wrong,
he knew what the consequences would be if he
was caught, yet he did it anyway."

She stopped, and it was as if her words, words
whose truth Luke Ashcroft had tried to make her
see, suddenly made sense for the first time. Francis had stolen, and he had paid the price. It wasn't
her fault, and it never had been.

"That's convenient for you to believe," Marcus
said, grabbing the plate with Lucinda's bacon on it.

"No, it's the truth. And that's your wife's bacon," Charlotte called out. "Yours is the burned
piece!" But Marcus had already stalked off.

"He will change his mind about you before the
journey's end," Lucinda said, forking the blackened bacon out onto a plate.

"No, he won't," Charlotte said, mixing flour
with water she had taken from the spring the
night before. "But I shan't worry about it, either.
When we get out to the Valley, I'll file my widow's
claim and build a cabin—"

"By yourself?" Lucinda interrupted. "What if
Marcus won't help you?"

Charlotte shrugged. "How many times did we
watch Pa and the neighbors put up cabins and
lean-tos? I know how to do it, and so do you. And

if I need help, I'm sure I shall be able to find someone other than Marcus."

"Perhaps Mr. Ashcroft," Lucinda said, giving Charlotte a sly, sidelong glance as Charlotte poured the fried-cake batter into the pan.

"Anyone but," Charlotte said, surprised that she was smiling, that merely the sound of his name awakened feelings in her.

"But why not?" Lucinda asked.

"Just . . . because," Charlotte said. "Because he makes me feel things I've never felt in my life, and because he seems too caring and interested to be true."

"And?"

"And I shall never be with another man, in any way," Charlotte said, turning a thin, burnt-looking pancake in the pan.

Later, as she carried the breakfast dishes toward the spring to scrub, she saw Biddy Lee Waters talking with a tall, handsome young slave who also was part of the Smithers caravan. "Now, you think on what I told you, Ben Lucius," Biddy Lee said.

Charlotte watched the man walk off, slapping what looked like a new hat on top of his head, and then she walked to where Biddy Lee sat by the water.

"Men," Biddy Lee said. "Always with one thing on their minds, even when the world offers millions of other pastimes every minute of the day."

Charlotte had never heard anyone talk like this. Even at home, as close as she and Luce had been to their mama, certain things just had not been spoken of.

"Is he a nice man?" she asked, not knowing where to begin.

Biddy Lee smiled. "Ben Lucius is as nice as can be and as bad as can be. And as handsome as the day is long, don't you think, Miz Dalton?"

"Charlotte, please."

Biddy Lee went back to scrubbing a pot. "Handsome as can be, but I have enough trouble in my life with that Skete Smithers. That Ben—he wants to father a child with me in the worst way. And I can't begin to go understanding an idea like that. Having a baby so it can be a slave?" She shook her head. "No thank you, much as I'd love to lay my head down next to Ben Lucius every night. But let me be free first, and him be free, one way or another." She sighed. "And that Skete. He spends half his day wondering whether Ben Lucius is romancing me. It's crazy."

"Has Skete given you any more trouble?"

"There's trouble in a place as soon as any of those Smitherses walk into it, Miz Dalton, you'll learn that soon enough. But I appreciate what you did for me, scaring Skete off like you did. I don't know if that's why, but that man hasn't tried anything on me since."

"I'm amazed," Charlotte said, thinking of Skete's disgusting words.

"Well, it's a funny thing about some of these slave owners, Miz Dalton. They think they own you, and they believe they own you, they believe they can do whatever they please with you. But they're afraid of their wives, and they're afraid of too much talk."

"Good," Charlotte said. "Then let's hope Skete Smithers thinks I'm the most talkative person in the caravan."

Biddy Lee laughed. "I'm making a bonnet for you. I want you to know that. That's what I do, how I intend to make my money and buy my freedom when I get out west. That hat Ben Lucius was wearing was too small for the Smithers men. The women, they'll be wanting theirs too, but I'll be working on yours in secret. I just wanted you to know." She looked over her shoulder and then went back to scrubbing her plate. "We have company now, so I'll be hurrying up."

Charlotte looked in the direction Biddy Lee had looked, and she saw Mollie Smithers, Skete's sister, approaching. Charlotte had never seen her this close before, and she had to admit that Mollie was a beautiful girl, with flawless skin, a dewy-looking, full mouth and amazingly shiny, long blond hair.

"Biddy Lee, what on earth are you doing?" Mollie cried out.

"Washing the dishes, miss," Biddy Lee answered calmly. "I'm just about finished with the lot of them."

"But Mama didn't have enough bacon," Mollie said. "This is a layover and we'd like to use the time the way we wish, Biddy Lee. Now get back to the campfire and cook up some more breakfast before Mama and Carlene have a fit, you hear?"

"Yes, miss," Biddy Lee said, gathering up the dishes she had just scrubbed shiny clean.

Charlotte watched as Biddy Lee walked off behind Mollie, and she wondered how a whole group of people, state upon state of them, could feel they owned other people. A few minutes later, she began walking back toward the caravan.

"Charlotte!"

Charlotte turned, dropping a tin plate as she did so.

"Don't go dirtying up your plates all over again," Mr. Ashcroft said, bending down to pick up her plate and handing it to her.

They were standing at the edge of the grove of trees that surrounded the spring, and in the distance, Charlotte could hear the familiar after-breakfast sounds of a layover—cattle lowing, roosters crowing, metal against metal as men worked to repair wheels, yokes, horseshoes. *Think of them and not of him,* she told herself.

"I must go," she said, concentrating on not looking at Mr. Ashcroft. She forced her gaze away from his hazel-green eyes, dark and searching at that moment, and away from the dusty light-brown hair that fell against his tanned forehead. She couldn't look at his chest, his muscles clearly defined beneath his threadbare shirt and leather vest. She had seen those muscles, that skin, that flesh at night when she had closed her eyes, in dreams when she hadn't been able to fight against them. And during the day, she had tried to think of anything but the smell of this man, the touch of his fingers, the taste of his lips on her own.

His mouth was curved up in a knowing half smile, and Charlotte felt in that moment that she hated this man she barely knew—for he seemed to know her feelings better than she did.

"And why is that?" he asked. His eyes were dark and dusky, smoky as they took in every detail of her body. She felt her nipples tingle at the very moment she heard Mr. Ashcroft's breath catch; as his gaze moved over her hips, she felt herself ache for him.

"I came out here for one simple reason," he said, his voice intimate.

She dared not look at him. "And that is?" she asked, feeling a thrill as she imagined him saying forbidden words: *I came out to find you so I could sweep you into my arms again. I came out to find you so I could kiss you. I came out to find you so I could hear you sigh against my neck because I know that means you desire me in a way you've never desired anyone in your life.*

"I'm leading a hunting party today," he said. "I want to know what you'd like, what you'd most like to preserve for the trip. Venison for jerky, or buffalo?"

At this, Charlotte had to laugh. "I see you're not lacking in confidence, Mr. Ashcroft. Most men are content to come back to camp with any meat at all."

"Most men aren't bringing back supplies for Charlotte Dalton."

She had to look into his eyes. She had to tell him the truth, because she owed him that, even though it wasn't exactly the whole truth. "I won't ever keep company with a man, Mr. Ashcroft. It was wrong the first time, and I shall never make the same mistake."

His eyes darkened. "Your only mistake was in marrying the wrong man, Charlotte—"

"Francis was a kind man," she cut in.

"I never said he wasn't. He might have been the perfect husband for someone else, but he wasn't the perfect husband for you."

He took her chin in his hand then, and she caught a whiff of his scent: sun, smoke, musky sweat. With his thumb, he traced the outline of her lips, then parted them gently, and slowly. "You deserve to be made happy as a woman, Charlotte."

She felt damned and desired and consumed by a heat that seemed to affect every part of her body. She couldn't speak, nor could she breathe without an effort that felt as if she were gasping for air. She was aware that her heart was pounding—knocking against her chest—and she wondered if Mr. Ashcroft could hear it.

"And you intend to make me happy?" she asked, her voice coming out as a breathy squeak. She knew she should move back from this man; yet something held her close. Mr. Ashcroft knew how, with the slightest touch, to make her body throb as if he were pressing naked against her, skin against skin. He knew what words would give heat and life to her imagination. He knew how to make her want him, how to make her lose her breath, her voice, her reason.

And she knew she couldn't let this happen; it was wrong. She looked past Mr. Ashcroft at the lushly swaying prairie grasses, lit fiery orange in the morning light, burning with life, mystery, promise. Her destiny was the West, an adventure she held deep in her heart and her dreams. She belonged to no one except Lucinda, and the baby when it came. She belonged to family and to no one else.

"What did you think about when you thought about me?" he asked, putting his arms around her. "The thoughts you weren't supposed to have."

She felt his hard length against her, and it took her breath away. She looked up at Mr. Ashcroft.

"Knowing" was the only word she could think of when she saw his eyes. She had already learned that he seemed to know her thoughts; but now, she found that he seemed to know her body as well. He knew that in her most secret, intimate place, she felt wet and hot and swollen, that the feel of his body was doing things to her that she had never even dreamed of only days earlier. He knew what the touch of his hands on her back did; he knew that as she looked into his eyes, she could no more think clearly than if she were in the middle of a deeply pleasurable, confusing dream.

"I've had thoughts of you too, Charlotte. Wrong thoughts, since the day I first saw you," he said, his voice husky, his body strong and hard against hers. "Maybe I always knew you were meant to be Luke Ashcroft's woman."

"You don't even know me," she said.

His eyes were stormy and filled with passion as they looked into hers. "I know your spirit, Charlotte. I know you're as determined as a wild horse to get out west, that your love for your family is as deep as the ocean we're traveling toward." He reached up and put a warm, strong hand at the back of her head. "And I know you need loving, that you're meant to be touched and tasted and kissed and treasured," he murmured, as his lips closed over hers.

She felt warmth, pleasure, desire in her most secret place; she felt weak in the knees, needing more. Mr. Ashcroft parted her lips and gently slid his tongue into her mouth.

Charlotte moaned, desire burning inside her. Mr. Ashcroft did know her, it seemed. The thought of being touched and tasted, kissed and treasured by this man made her heart soar and her body melt. Mr. Ashcroft was holding her tightly against his long length, one hand around her waist, the other around her shoulders. He moved his lower hand down, over her buttocks, and Charlotte felt a surge of need so hot she thought she might faint. Her tongue danced with his, and she moaned again, surprised and pleased and frightened by the new and strange needs that had overtaken her body.

And then, in the distance, she heard sounds of the caravan, a gunshot, a dog barking, one cow and then another beginning to moo.

And Charlotte tore herself from the hold of this man she was beginning to need in ways she understood not at all. "Mr. Ashcroft," she said.

He was smiling, his tanned face as handsome as any she had ever seen. "Don't you think it's about time you called me Luke, Charlotte?"

She shook her head. "I shall continue calling you Mr. Ashcroft," she said.

He looked perplexed, though he was still smiling. "And why is that?"

"Because I want to keep my distance from you," she said, struggling to regain her voice, her strength, her thoughts. Her heart was still racing, her mind a jumble of need and desire and somewhere, fortunately, resistance. "Because I've told you I shall never keep company with another man again," she went on, gathering strength. "And though you do seem to know much about me, there's one thing you apparently don't know—and that is that I'm as stubborn as a mule."

He laughed. "We'll see who's more stubborn, Charlotte." He bent down and picked up a tin cup. "I believe this is yours," he said with a wink.

Charlotte felt her mouth open, but no words came out. She hadn't even heard the cup drop! Chiding herself, she broke away from Mr. Ashcroft and began heading back toward camp. "I'll win this battle, Mr. Ashcroft. I know myself quite well. Now, good day," she called out, and broke into a run.

Luke laughed again as he watched Charlotte run, a strong, pretty woman who did seem to know what she wanted. Yet he had seen her lose her breath as he had touched her; he had heard her shyness turn into lust as she had moaned against his neck.

Don't break the heart of another one, an inner voice said. He and George had made firm plans over the course of many months. They would log out west, alone, with no women to complicate their lives.

But now, he couldn't stop thinking about Charlotte. Hell—he hadn't stopped thinking about her since the day she had been so angry about that cow of his.

Don't break the heart of another one, he said again to himself, as he watched the woman he couldn't get out of his mind walk quickly back to the caravan through the tall prairie grass, the sun shimmering all around her.

Eight

"So how did the lovely Charlotte Dalton like the venison?" George asked, forking a mouthful of venison, beans and bacon into his mouth after he spoke.

"I don't know," Luke answered. "She was down at the spring when I brought it to their campfire. But her sister, Lucinda, was quite pleased."

George was giving him an odd look. "Charlotte wasn't there and you just left the meat off? What's gotten into you?" he asked.

"I'm using my head, dammit," Luke snapped. "Easy for you to joke around about a woman like Charlotte, but she isn't some dance-hall girl."

George was looking at him in amazement. "I never said she was. She's a hell of an animal healer, she's pretty and she's a stubborn, energetic spitfire. I'm saying, what more could you want in a woman?"

"And I'm saying how many more hearts do I have to break?" Luke asked. "How many women do I have to leave in the dust?"

"We're *here,* Luke. On the Oregon Trail. Not back in Indiana—"

"Mr. Ashcroft! Mr. Ashcroft!"

Luke looked up and saw Zeke Bliss running toward him, waving his skinny old arms and half-hobbling, half-running on his skinny old legs. "Tip went down five or ten minutes ago, and he's blown up like a blowfish. Big as the Smitherses' showoff wagon, I reckon."

Luke said nothing as he and Zeke ran ahead and poor old Tip came into view. He was lying on his side, his legs unnaturally straight, his eyes bugged out. Running up from the other direction were Alma Bliss and Charlotte, who had come armed with the "animal medic" bag he had heard people talk about.

"You could say hello," he murmured as she walked past.

She ignored him, kneeling by Tip and pulling a long wooden rod out of her bag. "Help me tie this across his tongue," she said to Alma. "Grab that twine out of my bag, would you?"

"Quick as I can," Alma said, moving so fast she looked half her age.

"I'd put him out of his misery," Luke said to Zeke.

"You'll do no such thing," Charlotte said sharply.

Old Zeke raised a brow as Charlotte tied the rod into place across the ox's tongue. "Quite the little spitfire," he murmured. "I know if I were a single man and ten or twenty years younger, I wouldn't let *her* get away." He looked Luke up and down. "So what about it, my friend?"

"You know I'm not in the market," Luke snapped as he and Zeke walked away. He was surprised Zeke had forgotten his situation. Had George forgotten too? Did no one but him care about the past?

"Sorry," Zeke said quietly. "But tell me: Does she remind you of your wife?"

Luke felt as if a cloud were passing over him, as if a force had reached into his chest and taken hold of his heart. He shook his head, for a moment not even knowing where he was. "I wouldn't say that," he said. "No, I can honestly say that from what I know of Charlotte Dalton, she's not like anyone I've ever met."

"You're acting as if you're the first woman who has ever carried a child," Marcus snapped, his voice reaching far beyond their tent into the evening air.

"I never said that, and I never thought that," Lucinda said. "All I said, Marcus, was that I fear the birth."

"And all *I* said was that you should learn to school yourself in. Lucretia Clayton has borne eight children, with a ninth on the way, due any day now. Do you think she's huddled in her tent crying to her husband?"

Charlotte had to walk away, her heart pounding with fury. True, she hadn't married the right man; but at least Francis had been kind, even sweet, where Marcus seemed on his way to being as cruel as her pa had been.

Charlotte walked on, nearly blind with fury, toward the Blisses' stock so she could check on Tip. Even from a distance, she could see that he was feeling better. He had stood up, and he was trying to shake the rod out. "All right, Tip," she said. "It can come out now."

The flap on Alma and Zeke's tent flew open. "Is it time?" Alma asked.

Charlotte smiled. In the darkness, she could see that Alma was already in her sleeping garb. She and Zeke were usually first in bed of all the people Charlotte knew in the caravan. "Go back into that cozy-looking tent and cuddle up with your husband, Alma," she called. "I can take care of Tip."

She unlashed the rope on one side, let the rod drop halfway out of Tip's mouth, then steadied him. "Easy, boy. One more side," she murmured.

She was in the middle of untying the other side when hands came and held the rod, steadying it so it wouldn't drop to the ground.

She didn't have to look to know whose hands they were. They were the tanned, strong, rough hands she had dreamed of, needed too much. She had thought of them touching her neck, her arms, her breasts, and she had tingled and warmed, unable to tear her mind from needs too great to ignore. She had imagined those hands touching her more intimately, and she had moaned with desire at even the thought, her body on fire with need.

"You shouldn't sneak up on people like that," she said, not looking at Mr. Ashcroft.

"Sometimes it's necessary," he said, pulling the rod away from Tip's mouth. "It's a skill I learned from some Indian friends on my last journey out here."

Tip waved his head and then walked away, without a look back.

Charlotte smiled and stole a glance at Mr. Ashcroft. "I guess that means 'thank you,'" she said. "He does look better, does he not?"

Mr. Ashcroft laughed. "Much better than if I had treated him."

Charlotte was dying to ask Mr. Ashcroft what the West was like, if it was all she had dreamed, all that people promised. If it was, why had he come back east, she wondered?

But he spoke first, walking with Charlotte as she followed Tip out into the night. "You're out too late in the evening," he said. "You should be getting your sleep instead of worrying about an ox."

"Then I could say the same of you," she said, "though I doubt you were worrying about poor old Tip."

Mr. Ashcroft half smiled. "I promised Zeke I would keep an eye on him."

Charlotte sighed. Somehow when she was with Mr. Ashcroft, she always was compelled to speak all her feelings. "I had to get away from the mad ravings of my brother-in-law," she said, "before I spoke words I would regret, or that would hurt my sister."

Mr. Ashcroft frowned. "About what?" he asked.

"Oh, Lucinda fears the birth of their baby in a way that you would understand only if you know her as I do, Mr. Ashcroft."

"Luke," he said.

She took a deep breath. "Luke," she said, feeling as if she were stepping into deep waters. "Lucinda has always been afraid, partly because our father was a very rough, very cruel man. And Marcus is just so uncomforting. It reminds me of when Mama gave birth to my littlest sister, Adrietta. She was a dark-haired little angel, but too tiny, and she died when she was two days old. Mama was out of her head with grief, and Pa had to pry that little baby girl from my mama's arms to bury her. And not once did he give her a word of comfort. Not once."

It was as if a dark cloud had passed across Mr. Ashcroft's—Luke's—heart; Charlotte could see it as clearly as if a shadow had passed in front of the moon. "Perhaps he was grieving for your little sister in his own way," Luke said quietly.

Charlotte shrugged. "Perhaps he was. But for my mama, and even for me, I think we needed him to act more upset than if a chicken had keeled over in the yard. Or even as upset. And that's one reason I never will marry again."

"Why?" he asked, walking in a westward direction through the moonlight. "Because Lucinda married a fool and your pa was a cruel man? Do you truly believe all men are like that?"

"I remember Mama telling me that Pa was so charming when she first met him, Mr. Ash—Luke. And Marcus—I saw with my own eyes how wonderful he was to my sister—laughing with her, complimenting her at every turn. Now, Francis truly *was* kind, but . . ." Her voice trailed off, halted by guilt and desire.

"There was something wrong there," Luke said. "And that was Francis's problem, Charlotte. Not yours. But to judge all men—" He reached up and brushed her hair back from her face. "That would be like me thinking you're the same as Mollie Smithers just because you're both pretty."

"Mollie is beautiful," she said.

"Mollie is boring-looking," he said as he ducked under an overhanging branch. The dappled moonlight gently illuminated Luke's handsome features, and Charlotte wished she couldn't see him as well as she could.

"You didn't look too bored the other night when you were dancing with her," she blurted. This always seemed to happen when she was with him.

Luke Ashcroft shrugged. "Live and learn," he said. "I'm looking at real beauty right now—a woman who knows what she wants out of life, who's headed for the adventure of a lifetime, who isn't afraid of anything."

Charlotte had to laugh. "Do I truly strike you as someone who knows what she wants?"

His eyes were penetrating. "You want to farm in the Territories, where the soil is as rich as rich can get. You want to take care of your animals and crops, and have a mess of children—"

"You don't know me as well as you think," she said.

He raised a brow. "Is that so? Which part didn't I get right?"

"The part about a family," she said, trying to fight against the memory of that long, deep kiss. "I plan on being alone—well, with my sister and her family—for the rest of my life."

"Then what a waste of a beautiful woman," he said as he stopped near a grove of saplings. He took her into his strong, warm arms. "You said there were things in your marriage that weren't right. Are you telling me you've never been loved? I mean loved as a man loves a woman?"

Guilt stabbed at Charlotte's heart as desire sparked inside. "Francis was a good man."

Luke's eyes darkened. "Francis is gone. And any man who could have been near you without wanting to touch you—and love you . . ."

She could hardly believe the words Luke was saying. Yet she did believe that he truly meant them. "How I wish I could have known you in another life," she murmured.

"Know me in this life," he whispered. His breath was hot against her ear when he spoke again. "I want you to know what it is like to feel good," he murmured, letting his hands rove down past her waist, over her buttocks, pressing her close. "I want to be here for you, to talk to you, to listen to all your thoughts and hopes and plans."

He nibbled at her ear then, taking her lobe between his teeth.

Her knees nearly buckled. "Luke," she whispered—and found that her knees were giving way as Luke pulled her gently to the ground with him.

"Tell me what you want, what you need," he murmured, holding her face in his warm, strong hands. He brushed her hair back from her face, his eyes searching hers with an intensity she found thrilling. "We have to find out what feels good to you," he whispered as his lips gently brushed against hers.

Charlotte opened her lips as surely and naturally as if she had been making love to this man for a lifetime. She moaned as his tongue found hers. And that same new, shocking need suddenly flooded her, warming and liquefying her from her belly down between her legs.

Luke drew his head back, and in the moonlight, she could see that his eyes looked wild, filled with desire and also some kind of torment. "You deserve to be pleasured," he whispered, his voice hoarse with need. He ran the palm of his hand along the side of her face, then along her neck, searing, teasing a path down her chest until his hand cupped a breast. Slowly, gently, so tenderly Charlotte thought she might faint, he teased her through the fabric of her blouse, circling her taut, tingling nipple with his fingers, then circling her breast with his palm.

And then he moved his hand inside her blouse. Charlotte was shocked at how it felt—how wonderful and surprising and new—to feel a man's hand on her skin, on her breast. He took her nipple between his fingers, then pulled her blouse open. He lowered his lips to the top of her breast, and then ran his tongue downward until it caught her nipple and circled it. She grabbed at his hair as heat gripped her body, making her throb as his tongue flicked at her breast.

"How does that make you feel?" he whispered as his hand trailed down her stomach.

She felt as if she was burning in the spot she could only half believe he was headed toward, and she knew she should tell him to stop.

Gently, he reached under her skirt and began a slow, tormenting path up her leg with his hand as his fingers made light, teasing circles up her calf, over the inside of her knee, up to her thigh.

She wanted to tell him to stop, but she didn't want him to, not in the least, except in a part of her head that had apparently been shut down.

"How does that feel?" Luke asked softly.

"Too good," she answered honestly, scared but also happy. Too good felt wonderful, and she wrapped her arms around Luke's neck and kissed the rough, wet skin beneath his ear. She loved the scent of musky sweat that was more intimate than anything she had ever smelled, and she felt more connected to Luke than she had ever felt to anyone.

"What about this?" he asked as his palm moved over the mound of her femininity.

She was shocked, but it was as if somehow, in

some deep place, she already knew what was meant to happen, and she instinctively rose to meet him, moving her hips as the heel of his hand circled and pleasured her, as her insides throbbed with desire for this man she hardly knew. She felt liquid with need, an ache made of pleasure and sweet, hot torment.

"Luke," she whispered. "I've never felt—" Her voice broke off. What on earth was happening to her? She felt pleasure so strong. . . .

"Enjoy it," he murmured. "We have all the time in the world, Charlotte."

She couldn't speak. She had never felt such exquisite desire and pleasure mixed together. "Luke," she whispered.

"You're going to be my woman," he said as his hand moved surely, expertly.

And then Charlotte cried out, exploding with a rush of pleasure so intense she forgot, for a few moments, where or even who she was. She wrapped her body around Luke, climbed on top of him, pressed her lips against his neck . . . feeling too much.

She felt as if her life had changed in some way, so profound had been the pleasure Luke had given her. She lay there, breathing in his scent and her own, listening to his heart pound in his chest, closing her eyes as he ran his fingers through her hair.

And then she told herself to wake up and face the truth. What on earth was she doing? What on earth had she done? She was a new widow, someone who had no business frivolously heading down a path of . . . what?

"What's wrong?" Luke asked softly.

"Nothing," Charlotte half-lied, not knowing how she felt.

"I just felt you tense right up," he said, running a warm hand along her back. "Everything's going to be all right, Charlotte. I'm going to keep my tent near yours at night, and I'm going to watch over you, and we're going to learn everything about each other that there is to know. All right?"

Charlotte said nothing. This was the way she was supposed to have felt as a married woman. But she wasn't married to Luke.

"Listen to the sounds of the night," Luke whispered. "And listen to my heart. And let yourself enjoy the moment." Charlotte listened to the pounding of Luke's heart, to the soft wind rustling the branches around them, and she wished she could just lie there and enjoy the moment, as Luke had said.

But she felt a dark sense of foreboding, a sure, deep knowledge telling her that what she had done was wrong. *Charlotte's a plain brown sparrow,* she could hear her father saying. *No man's ever going to want her.*

That, she realized, was the deep voice resonating in her heart as the voice of truth. And as she listened to the beating of Luke's heart against her ear, she told herself not to fall in love. Because if she did, she knew absolutely that her heart would get broken in the end.

Nine

It had been a long, hot day, and twice Charlotte had thought Lucinda was going to go into labor. But each time had been a false alarm.

Charlotte had yearned all day to tell Luce what had happened with Luke. But something stronger than her desire to share anything and everything with her sister had stopped her. *It was wrong,* she told herself. *I can't fall in love with this man. And if I tell Lucinda, the telling will make it all the more real.*

Now, at near-darkness by the spring, as Charlotte scrubbed a pot beside Biddy Lee, she watched as Alma and Zeke walked up from the spring back toward camp, hand in hand, their heads tilted toward each other as they talked.

"There's a couple who's in love," Charlotte said.

"Made for each other, I say," Biddy Lee answered. She set her last pot up on the bank and began to wash her doll, carefully dipping her head in the water and gently wiping her face.

"Do you wash Elizabeth Grace every day?" Charlotte asked.

Biddy Lee blushed, her brown skin darkening red. "When I have the chance," she said softly. "Some days I still can't believe my mama even gave her to me since I drove her near crazy with my whining. But then one day, she was mine, and the tears ran like a river down my mama's cheeks. It was after that that she died."

"I'm so sorry," Charlotte said. "Was it something sudden?"

Biddy Lee's face darkened. "Female trouble, I think, from Mr. Jock Smithers. I think another baby was coming due." She stroked Elizabeth Grace's hair and looked into Charlotte's eyes. "Did you have a doll growing up?"

Charlotte thought of the rag doll her mama had made for her. Liddy, Charlotte had called her, and she had a linsey-woolsey dress, a white apron and a crisp white bonnet. "I had one for a bit," Charlotte said. "Pa threw her into the fire when I back-talked him one night."

Biddy Lee stared. "Your pa?"

"My pa was as cruel a man as I ever met, Biddy Lee. That's why I always swore I'd never marry, not after I heard the stories Mama would tell about how Pa had courted her, how he was so romantic. And handsome, of course," she said.

Biddy Lee looked down for a moment. "I never met my father," she said quietly. "He was the owner of the plantation where Mama worked, and then he sold her to the Smithers family."

Charlotte didn't know what to say.

Biddy Lee quickly filled the silence. "So your pa was handsome, then? As handsome as Mr. Luke Ashcroft?"

Charlotte shrugged. "Probably I would have to say yes, Biddy Lee. I saw a picture of him when he was courting Mama, and you would have said he was as handsome as the day is long. Like Mr. Ben Lucius. And yes, like Mr. Luke Ashcroft. Which is why I don't intend to let Mr. Luke Ashcroft make me—" She couldn't utter the words Luke had said to her about making her his woman.

"Make you turn as red as a ripe tomato?" Biddy Lee asked.

"What?"

Biddy Lee laughed. "You're as red as a tomato. Redder, I think."

Charlotte was about to say that proved Mr. Ashcroft was bad for her, but she heard voices all of a sudden. And Charlotte could see that Biddy Lee heard them as well: Mollie Smithers and someone else.

Charlotte saw Biddy Lee set Elizabeth Grace down and begin gathering her pots and pans. Mollie and Carlene were walking quickly toward the spring, and Charlotte wanted to pick up Elizabeth Grace and tuck her under her arm. No need to court trouble.

But as Charlotte headed for the doll, she saw Mollie spy her as well. And quickly, moving like an animal, Mollie bent down and picked the doll up.

"That's Biddy Lee's doll," Charlotte snapped.

Mollie laughed and looked at her sister-in-law. "These Yankees," she sighed. "So ignorant of the ways of the real world. Imagine thinking a slave girl can own property or own anything at all in the course of her whole miserable, pitiful little life."

"That doll belonged to my mama," Biddy Lee called out.

"Another slave. Another woman who preyed on her owner's husband—"

Charlotte felt as if her blood were boiling as she looked at Mollie holding Elizabeth Grace. "If you don't hand that doll over to me or to Biddy Lee, I'll knock you to the ground and roll your face in the dirt, Mollie Smithers."

Mollie opened her mouth and stared. "You wouldn't dare," she said.

"Hand me over the doll," Charlotte said, holding out her hand.

Mollie stared at her, and Carlene stared, both somehow looking as clean and pretty as they had back in Independence. Mollie raised her chin and tossed her hair back. "You don't have the nerve," she said, starting to move past Charlotte.

Charlotte grabbed her around the waist with one arm and grabbed the doll with the other hand, tossing it into the air. "Get her!" she called out to Biddy Lee, who ran forward and caught Elizabeth Grace in one hand.

Mollie lunged forward, but Charlotte didn't let go, and she landed on top of her on the ground.

"Let me up!" Mollie said. "Let me up, for goodness' sake. I'm as dirty as a pig in slop!" she cried.

Charlotte moved off of her. "Then next time, Mollie, don't even think about stealing something that's the real and true property of a slave—in God's eyes, where it matters."

Mollie stood up and tried to rub the mud off her skirt. "I will agree only to keep this incident from the public's ears."

Charlotte laughed. "I imagine you would agree to that, Mollie, so people don't mock you for trying to steal something that so obviously belongs to another." She took Biddy Lee by the arm. "Come, Biddy Lee. Together we shall decide who will know what happened tonight and who will not." She had been smiling, but when she saw Biddy Lee's face, her smile faded.

"You think this is a joke, Charlotte?" Biddy Lee asked as she walked quickly back toward the caravan.

"No, I didn't think it was a joke," Charlotte said. "But I do find it satisfying that someone like Mollie can be afraid of us."

"There's nothing funny in it," Biddy Lee said. "Miss Carlene thinking I'm looking to be with her husband and Mollie thinking I want to cause trouble. I don't need stories now—"

"I understand," Charlotte said. "I hadn't realized, but now I do, Biddy Lee. So we will keep it quiet, and just be happy we got Elizabeth Grace back."

Biddy Lee was silent as she walked along.

"What's wrong?" Charlotte asked.

"I don't know where it ends, Charlotte," Biddy Lee said. "This morning Miss Carlene was looking daggers at me, and Mollie told me to keep my distance from Skete. I would *love* to keep my distance from that man," she said with a sigh. "But he's back to his old ways. Following me . . ."

"Do you think—" Charlotte hesitated. She knew so little about slavery and how it worked. "Do you

think you'll be able to buy your freedom when
you get out west?"

Biddy Lee shook her head. "My mama told me
a long time ago to take one day at a time, Charlotte. Make my plans, hold on to my dreams, and
take one day at a time." She nodded her head in
the direction of the caravan. "Looks like you have
some company of your own looking to find you,"
Biddy Lee said.

Charlotte turned and saw Luke walking toward
her. A moment later, Carlene Smithers and a
mud-covered Mollie, both holding up their skirts,
came running from the spring. Charlotte could
see that Mollie was surprised and upset to see
Luke. She smiled shyly at him and then, as if remembering she was covered in mud, covered her
face and raced past him.

Luke looked at Charlotte and Biddy Lee. "Am I
right in thinking the two of you know a good deal
about why Mollie is as muddy as a spring sow?"

Charlotte laughed. "I wouldn't begin to know,
Biddy Lee. Would you?"

"Mr. Ashcroft is a trustworthy one, Miss Charlotte. You can go and tell him all you want about
whatever you want, and he'll keep the facts close
to his own heart. But I'd best be getting back.
Good night to you both."

Charlotte watched Biddy Lee hurry off toward
the caravan, holding Elizabeth Grace close
against her chest. As she watched, Charlotte could
feel Luke's eyes on her. And she wished, in certain
ways, that last night had never happened, because

it had changed her heart and her body forever. Until she had met Luke, she had never known desire that could rob her of sleep, of breath, of thought. And until Luke had touched her, in her deepest, most private spot, she had never known pleasure so intense it had made thoughts and reason shimmer into nothing but bliss.

But now . . .

Now, as she looked up at him, as she fought the memory of his touch, of a need that was already building inside her, she saw that he knew. He knew how he had changed her, altered her forever.

And he was pleased. Maybe even smug about it.

"Is your sister all right?" he asked.

"I don't know," Charlotte said, alarmed. "Is she? Did you hear anything?"

He was shaking his head, his gaze never leaving hers as he closed the distance between them. "Nothing," he answered softly. "Everything was quiet when I passed their tent. I was just making sure . . ." His voice trailed off. "Do you know, Charlotte, that I can't get you out of my mind?"

She had to fight this, she knew. She had to fight her feelings, her needs, her desires and Luke.

She knew what she should say. She knew she should tell Luke that she was made for no man, that whatever they had had was over, that he should stay away from her.

But he had taken her in his arms, his long length firm against hers.

And she could feel his thoughts.

And his desire.

And her own.

So instead of saying the words she knew she should say, she spoke the truth. "I can't get you out of my mind, either."

With a hoarse cry, Luke covered her mouth with his. His tongue danced with hers, dared hers, teased her.

"Come," Luke whispered, taking Charlotte's hand.

She knew she should say no—as she had known the night before.

But she followed—because she was falling in love, because she knew how much she needed Luke, because she knew the pleasure that lay ahead.

And so she followed him to a small grove of shrubby, scrubby-looking trees that was dark on this nearly moonless night.

Luke pulled her into his arms with hunger. He tore off his shirt and laid her gently on its softness, and then he kissed her on her lips.

His fingers worked quickly, pulling off her blouse, opening her chemise.

His breathing came hard as he lowered his lips to her neck, and Charlotte found that her body was aching for him in a new way. She knew what the touch of his lips could do, knew that the warm sensations that were making her moist and hot and full of need would only grow stronger and sweeter now that Luke was here. Even in the darkness, Charlotte could see the hunger in Luke's eyes as he lowered his head and took one of her nipples in his mouth. With the tip of his tongue, he circled it wetly, and Charlotte moaned, needing more.

She moved against him, kissing his neck and loving the smell of him.

With a warm, strong hand, Luke trailed along her thigh beneath her skirt, teasing her with taunting, knowing fingers, making her remember a pleasure deeper than any she had ever known. And though Charlotte still felt shy and confused, her body grew brazen—remembering, needing as her hips danced in a primitive rhythm, wanting Luke's touch.

"I need you, Charlotte Dalton," he whispered, his lips hot and wet against her ear.

She wanted to tell him she didn't need him. She wanted to tell him she neither wanted him nor needed him. But as always, with Luke, the truth tumbled out as velvety fire smoldered inside of her.

"I need you too," she whispered.

With a moan, he pulled her skirt down over her legs. In seconds, she was naked before his eyes, and even in the near-total darkness, she could see him looking at her—with pleasure, with appreciation, with need.

She felt desired and . . . pretty, even beautiful, for the first time.

"Yes, you're beautiful, Charlotte Dalton," Luke whispered, lowering his lips to her mouth. She began to drink in his kiss, but he trailed his lips away on a liquid path of pleasure, his tongue teasing lightly down her neck, over one breast, then the other.

"I want to touch you," Charlotte breathed, her

voice hardly there. "I want to make you feel good, Luke."

"Not yet," Luke whispered.

Brazenly, Charlotte reached down. She trailed her hand down along his flat belly, and Luke moaned as she found his masculinity, hard and straining beneath his breeches.

"That's how much I want you," Luke whispered. "But not yet, Charlotte. I want to teach you . . ."

His sure, commanding fingers began teasing her, circling her mound of curls in an intoxicating, possessive pattern as Luke moved away from her touch.

Charlotte's breath grew choppy, shallow as the flames of need grew hotter. She felt a shimmering, wet path along her stomach, and she grabbed for Luke's hair as his tongue suddenly probed the curls of her pleasure. Luke teased her, circling expertly and then flicking at the core of her need.

Charlotte clawed at Luke and her hips writhed as Luke's tongue skillfully, ruthlessly possessed her.

"Luke," she cried out, hot with molten pleasure. "Oh, Luke!"

With velvet-soft strength, Luke reached his fingers into her silky recesses as his tongue flicked at her, and Charlotte's heart, body, soul and mind dissolved in a blaze of pleasure so fierce she barely knew what had happened.

"I'll take you when you're ready," Luke whispered, stroking her hair as she closed her eyes, loving the feel of his chest, the steady thump of his heart. He smiled down at her. "When you're more than ready, Charlotte, and not a minute before. Remember, we have all the time in the world, sweetheart."

"Charlotte," Luke whispered.

Charlotte jerked awake, for a moment not knowing where she was, even who she was.

And then she remembered what she had just done, what Luke had done with her only minutes before. Or was it hours? She could hardly believe she had dropped off into a sound, deep sleep in his arms.

"How long have I been asleep?" she asked, sitting up and rubbing her eyes.

He was smiling as he reached out to tuck a lock of her hair behind her ear. "Long enough for me to know you'll want to be getting back to your tent. But before you do . . . What happened between you and Mollie?"

Charlotte shrugged. "She had the nerve to take Biddy Lee's doll—I would imagine the only possession that woman has." She shrugged again. "I got it back."

"They're a rough crowd, that Smithers family," he said as he pulled Charlotte up. "So you be careful," he said. "Promise?"

She nodded, still feeling dazed from as full a sleep as she had ever experienced.

"Now that I've found you, I'm not about to lose you," Luke said.

She looked into his eyes. "Luke—" she began.

He put his thumb across her lips. "I'm not about to lose you," he said again.

And Charlotte wished he meant his words in the way she wanted, because she knew she was already losing her heart to him.

Ten

"Help me! Oh Lord, Mama!"

Charlotte dropped her bag of buffalo chips and raced to the wagon. As she clambered in, she saw at a glance that the time had come. "I'll call Mrs. Gunderson," she said, squeezing Lucinda's hand. "All right, honey? I'll be back in a minute."

Lucinda shook her head. "No. Wait," she whispered. "We must talk."

Charlotte brushed her sister's hair back from her dampened forehead. "It's going to be all right," she whispered, feeling as if she and her sister were still little girls, hiding from their father's rage.

And now, just as then, Lucinda worried. "But if it's not," she said. "If it's not, I want you to promise you'll take care of the baby if something happens to me."

"Nothing's going to happen to you," Charlotte murmured, willing her words to be true. Yes, Lucinda had been the weaker sister all her life, but couldn't she be strong this one time, now that she was going to be given such a precious gift? "Try to imagine the best instead of the worst, Luce."

"Promise me," Lucinda whispered, clutching at Charlotte's hand.

"I promise," Charlotte said.

Lucinda nodded. "And that means fighting Marcus if you have to. I want *you* to have the baby, Char."

Charlotte said nothing, thinking about how marriages indeed seemed never to turn out as people intended. Why marry, she had to wonder, if in the end you didn't even wish for your own husband to care for your baby?

"Better call Mrs. Gunderson," Lucinda whispered, and immediately after, her face twisted into a vision of fear and pain.

Memories of four years earlier clouded Luke's heart as he set off to see some of the Kanzas who had come to trade before dinner. The Kanza chief, White Fox, had been generous and great company four years earlier, and Luke hoped he was still around. He could still hear White Fox's voice as if he were speaking at that very moment. "When you go back to your woman and child, they will be happy you find such a generous land. Your heart will no longer be heavy, my friend."

Luke closed his eyes as he remembered Parmelia's tears. "We won't see each other again, Luke. I can feel it. I'm begging you not to go!"

Suddenly he heard a sound coming from his and George's wagon, the sound of something being moved—which was strange, because George was outside, trading with some of the Kanzas. He leapt up into the wagon and saw Mollie Smithers standing there—holding his picture, the last photograph ever taken of Parmelia.

"What the hell are you doing?" he asked, his voice rough with rage.

Mollie's mouth dropped open. "I—I needed to see you," she stammered.

"And go through my things? You couldn't see me outside, where I've been all morning?"

"I just—I need to talk to you," she said, moving toward him and setting the picture down on a pile of blankets as if it were just some random household object. "I don't think you know how I feel about you."

"Stop right there and get out," he said.

"What?"

"I have an idea how you feel about me, Mollie. I think a dead man would know how you feel. I'm not interested. I thought I made that clear."

"But you don't know me," she murmured. She reached up and undid her skirt, letting it drop to the floor.

She stood there naked from the waist down, her long legs creamy white, her triangle of hair pale and curly, her face expectant as she waited for him to do or say something.

But he felt nothing but anger. "You can get dressed and you can go, Mollie, or I can pull you out of this wagon now, for everyone to see."

Her eyes flashed. "You wouldn't do that."

"Why not?"

"What about your precious Charlotte Dalton?

What would *she* think? And what about whoever *this* is?" she asked, picking up Parmelia's photograph again.

"Put that down and get dressed. Right now."

Something in his tone must have scared her, he figured, because she did both, more quickly than he could have imagined.

"Who is she, Luke?" Mollie asked. "Aren't you and Mr. Penfield bachelors? Is that your mother when she was younger?"

He took a deep breath and moved her toward the wagon entrance. "That's my wife, Mollie," he said quietly. "Now get out."

God forgive me, he said in his heart.

The birth went better than Charlotte had imagined it would, and it went worse than she had imagined. She had thought Lucinda would be torn right up the middle, what with her screaming, crying, not listening at all to what Mrs. Gunderson was telling her. Luce should have known she had to push, from having seen so many animals on the farm being born, Charlotte felt. But Charlotte knew, too, that a part of Lucinda's mind just wasn't working.

Finally, Lucinda began pushing. Her face grew red, then purple.

"Is she all right?" Charlotte whispered.

Mrs. Gunderson didn't answer. "Push harder," she commanded. "I see the head now, Lucinda."

And Lucinda pushed.

"Give her more of the powder," Mrs. Gunderson whispered, as Charlotte put a pinch of dried-up sow bugs on Lucinda's lips. But Lucinda shook the powder off, sobbing, her face red, tear-stained, exhausted.

"Dear, you'll have to push when I say push, and you'll have to take the powder when your sister gives it to you," Mrs. Gunderson shouted, as if Lucinda couldn't hear through the pain. "I wish we had put the ax under her blankets to cut her pain. Now push, dear. Right now, Lucinda. Just push as if your very life depends on it."

And Lucinda pushed.

The baby came out all at once, as if it hadn't been any trouble at all for him, and Charlotte fell in love that very moment.

"Now, I'll make three knots in the cord," Mrs. Gunderson said, "for health, wealth and happiness, Lucinda, and your sister might better bury the afterbirth as soon as we get you cleaned out, just for that extra measure of good luck."

Charlotte handed Mrs. Gunderson the one clean cloth they had left, a little quilt their mama had made for just that moment.

"You've got a fine little baby," Mrs. Gunderson said, briskly rubbing the blood off him with a rag and then wrapping him in the quilt. Her brows knit as she looked down at all the blood still oozing from between Lucinda's legs.

"You might better find some ergot from these Indians, Charlotte. Sooner than soon, do you understand?"

Charlotte did, knowing that on the farm, you never wanted animals to bleed like that after giving birth.

"Here, just a minute," Mrs. Gunderson said as she bundled the baby into Lucinda's arms. "Now don't be shy after all we've just seen together, Lucinda. Let me see about this afterbirth, this bleeding down here."

A few minutes later, her whole attitude had changed. She had "freed up" the afterbirth, with firm instructions to Charlotte to bury it. And Lucinda's bleeding had stopped.

"She'll be fine is my feeling," Mrs. Gunderson said. "But to be safer, Charlotte, find some ergot from one of the squaws before we pull out of the area. Just in case she picks up bleeding again."

She reached down and laid a hand on Lucinda's brow. "Dear, you'll be just fine, and you have a fine boy with three fine knots in his cord. Now let him drink, dear, like this," she said, putting his tiny, dark head to Lucinda's breast. "And let me get my own self cleaned up, and your sister will take care of that afterbirth and the ergot."

Charlotte hesitated before leaving. She just couldn't believe there was a whole new person in the world. "I'll go now, then," she finally said, taking one last look at little Jacob and wondering, just for one brief moment, what it would be like to have a baby of her own.

But now that she was an aunt, she could hold Jacob as much as she wanted, and she would be able to watch him and his brothers and sisters grow up.

Maybe her worries about Lucinda's strength had been wrong, too, she thought hopefully. Maybe Luce *would* survive the journey after all.

"One piece of advice before you go," Mrs. Gunderson suddenly called out, gathering up the birthing supplies she had brought with her. "You stay away from the Smitherses' slave girl, and any other slaves for that matter. Do you understand?"

Charlotte was shocked. Mrs. Gunderson was from Illinois, and as far as Charlotte knew, not a supporter of slavery.

"I beg your pardon?" Charlotte asked. "Don't tell me you condone the idea that the Smithers family *owns* Biddy Lee and Ben Lucius in some way."

" 'Tis not for me to condone or condemn, and the same truth goes for you. There's been talk, Charlotte, more than a little talk, that you're scheming with that girl. You'll be more than a mite sorry if you get painted with that brush, my dear."

Charlotte could feel Lucinda's fear even without looking at her, the same dread that had always been able to take hold of her heart since she had been a little girl.

"I won't listen to nonsense," Charlotte said.

"But Charlotte," Lucinda pleaded. "If Mrs. Gunderson says—"

"I don't care what Mrs. Gunderson says," Charlotte snapped. She looked into Mrs. Gunderson's eyes. "I can't have Jock Smithers, Skete Smithers or anyone else telling me who I can and can't speak to, Mrs. Gunderson—"

"You don't know these people," Mrs. Gunderson said.

"Then maybe I'll find out more about them that I ever wanted to, but I'll be damned if I let them tell me whom I can talk to."

She knew Lucinda wanted to talk more about the issue, even in her pain. But Charlotte didn't want to hear the fear in her voice, and she didn't want to say something she'd later regret. And so she left, with the afterbirth in a bucket and in search of the ergot.

"The ergot should help if you begin having a problem," Charlotte said, not wanting to discuss feminine details in front of Marcus. "The squaw said it should heal you right up."

Marcus made a sound from across the campfire, a dismissive snort, but Charlotte ignored him.

"How do you feel?" Charlotte asked, surveying her sister's pale face.

"Fine," Lucinda said. "Weak, but isn't that to be expected? I feel better than I would have thought."

Charlotte nodded. "Good. I'll get more of it. I heard willow-tree bark tea might be good to have on hand, too. I think I'll try to get some more this evening, since so many of the Kanzas are still around."

Another dismissive snort came from Marcus.

Charlotte couldn't tolerate any more. "Do you have some sort of breathing problem, Marcus, that you need a remedy for? Or do you have a problem with the Indians you'd like to share with us?"

Marcus set down his plate. "I'll tell you what the problem is. The problem is that all of you people treat these savages with kid gloves, as if they can heal you and supply you with everything you need. Don't you see they're filthy beggars?"

"They're sharing meals!" Charlotte cried out. "It's called hospitality—on the part of Mr. Ashcroft and Mr. Penfield, the Blisses, Captain Tayler and the other right-thinking members of this caravan. The Kanzas are no more begging than you and I are when we go to trade with them."

"Oh, no? How much food do you think they've eaten at all these little gatherings tonight?"

"And what of it? How do you know that in a week's time, we won't be stuck somewhere, or need something that only the Indians have? Besides which, some members of this caravan know them personally."

"And so we return to the illustrious Luke Ashcroft once again," Marcus muttered.

"Everyone benefits from knowing them!" Charlotte cried out.

"They're dirty, scheming thieves," he said, crossing his arms. "Nothing will ever convince me otherwise."

Charlotte felt like screaming. There was no use trying to change Marcus's mind, of course; she could see that. But what about Lucinda and baby Jacob, who was lying in his mother's arms, his little lips forming a perfect pink rosebud?

"Are you going to raise your son with those beliefs?" Charlotte asked, looking at Lucinda.

"Charlotte," Lucinda said softly. "He's sleeping. Please."

"I'm not asking him, I'm asking you!" she said.

Lucinda's pained look made her angrier than any of Marcus's words ever could have, and she grabbed one of the shirts their mother had made and stormed off—past families who were sharing their meals with the visiting Indians, past horses and oxen nibbling at the sparse, overgrazed prairie grass, past thin, trail-worn dogs wandering the hard ground, looking for scraps of anything edible. Outside the wagon circle, she saw the squaw from whom she had gotten the ergot trading with the Vestrows. She thought about the words Marcus had used to describe the Indians—filthy beggars—and she was tempted to go back to the campfire and pummel him.

But she held her tongue and her fury and asked the squaw for some more herbs in trade for the calico shirt. "I not have more ergot, but I know who does, for that swap. You wait," she said. "They are for you?"

Charlotte shook her head, thinking she would probably never need any ergot if it was only for women who had given birth. "No, for my sister," she said.

"You wait here," the Indian woman said gently, and took off at a run.

Half an hour later, the darkness had quickly blanketed itself around Charlotte. The campfires glowed in blackness, evening sounds had turned into those of night, and Charlotte waited, wondering what had happened.

She knew that it probably would make sense to approach one of the Kanzas tomorrow morning before the caravan decamped, and make the trade then. But what if the Indians had moved out of the area for the day, in search of another caravan?

Charlotte felt torn, her mind snagged on the earnestness of the woman's manner and how definite she had been: "You wait here," she had said.

Yet her uneasiness was growing. She was outside the circle of wagons, beyond the protection of the night guards, and she couldn't help thinking about the Smithers family and Mrs. Gunderson's words of warning.

She knew in her heart that she had done nothing wrong, but people like the Smithers family didn't share her views about anything. She would head back for the caravan and find the Kanza squaw in the morning.

"Are you trying to look for trouble, Charlotte, or just not thinking?"

She turned. She certainly would have recognized Luke's voice without seeing him. But seeing him, his large, handsome shape, a man she had grown too used to meeting in the moonlight, made her heart stop for just a moment.

In seconds, he had closed the distance between them and enveloped her in his arms. "I hear your sister had a healthy baby boy," he murmured.

She nodded, breathing in the scent she loved.

"And I hear there's talk against you—lots of talk."

"I'm not listening to any of you," she said. "I'm so disgusted with all these people thinking we should tiptoe around everyone else's opinions. Do you know that Marcus doesn't even want us dealing with the Indians? And now my sister won't even argue with him?"

"Your brother-in-law is a fool, Charlotte. I knew that the first day I met him. But what do his opinions have to do with you?"

"He's affecting Lucinda's judgment!" Charlotte exclaimed.

"Charlotte," Luke said, putting his hands on her shoulders. "Listen to me. And think about what I'm saying. You're going to have to let Marcus and Lucinda and their boy live their lives. If he's a terrible husband, that's their business. Let Luce make her own decisions and be the kind of wife she wants to be. You live *your* life." With his thumb, he parted her lips, making her remember that first time, when she had been shocked by how just the touch of a finger could make her feel.

And now . . .

"You have a lot of new things going on in your life," Luke said softly. "I think you should concentrate on those."

She was falling in too deeply.

She was a woman who had vowed never to want or need a man, yet she was in the arms of a man she was falling in love with.

"Tell me what you're thinking," Luke said softly, brushing her hair back from her face.

Anything and everything, she said to herself. She had never dreamed she would meet a man with whom she shared all her thoughts—albeit unwillingly.

"This is going too fast," she finally said. "I feel that when I'm with you, I always end up telling you everything I'm feeling."

"And what's wrong with that?" Luke asked, his lips nuzzling her neck.

"It's not something I want," she murmured, fighting to concentrate.

"What *do* you want?" Luke whispered, his hands splaying over her hips.

For a moment, she couldn't speak. She was caught in the memory of an explosion of pleasure.

"Tell me," Luke said.

"I don't want to need you," Charlotte said.

Luke smiled. "Then that makes two of us," he said. "*I* don't want to need *you*. I had it all planned out, Charlotte—logging out west, no women, no ties. And then I meet Charlotte Dalton, and I can't get her out of my mind. And then I kiss her," he whispered, brushing his lips against hers, "and I'm done for."

Charlotte shook her head, loving Luke's words but not believing them—because she knew that any man could change from day to night, from Mr. Wonderful to a man who could strike his wife and children and throw his daughter's doll into the fire.

"I don't want this to go anywhere," she said.

He shrugged. "Then it won't," he said. Simply, as if she had asked him the simplest arithmetic problem in the world. "I told you: George and I are logging out west. Women aren't part of the plan."

"But I don't want to be your mistress," she said.

"You're my woman," he whispered, his lips nuzzling her ear. "That means the woman I love to kiss. And to touch. And to taste."

Their bodies knew what to do, though Charlotte wouldn't have dreamed she could act with such wanton disregard for everything but her needs. She undressed as he helped her, and she longed for his touch. As his lips teased her nipples, as his tongue trailed a delicious wet path along the skin of her stomach, she moaned for him, knowing the pleasure he could give her.

She longed to see more of him, to touch his skin, to feel the wiry curls she had once glimpsed on his chest. She longed to run her hands over the strong muscles of his chest, to touch his firm, flat stomach, to make him groan as she touched his hardness.

"I want to see you," she whispered. "I want to see you and feel you."

"Not yet," he whispered, his hands moving up her thighs.

Luke's touch was sure and hot and skillful. He slid her pantaloons down and off, then slid his hands slowly back up her thighs.

But she wanted more. She covered his mouth with hers, bit at his lip, edged his earlobe with her teeth. She pulled his shirt open and reached inside, loving the feel of the coarse hair and hard muscle she had thought about too much. She caught his nipples in her fingers and Luke moaned, his male need hard against her.

And she burned inside, wanting him.

"Charlotte," Luke whispered, moving his fingers to the center of her need, working her as he caught her buttocks in one hand and plundered the silky recesses of her desire with the other.

Her breath came in gasps as she bit at his neck, clawed his hair, raked his back.

"Come for me," he commanded in a whisper, and Charlotte gave herself over to him.

She had no thoughts at all as she whimpered, bucked, arched in a blaze of pleasure that was like nothing she had ever felt in her life.

Spent, she sank her lips into his hot neck, and she felt waves of love, and sadness, because she knew it was all an illusion.

Luke stroked Charlotte's hair, and as he spoke into the night, she felt that his voice sounded as kind and tender as any she had ever heard in her life. "The time has to be right, Charlotte. You have to be ready in every way."

She said nothing, and Luke closed his eyes, telling himself he was doing the right thing.

Don't break the heart of another, his inner voice said.

He cared a lot about Charlotte, and it had taken all his strength not to respond to her touch. He didn't think he had ever wanted a woman as much.

Don't break the heart of another, he said to himself again.

And he knew this was the path he had to take.

Eleven

They had traveled six miles since morning in the dry, dusty heat, the midday break a too-quick rest for everyone. Charlotte felt as if she had just packed away the lunch dishes and gotten back on the trail when she heard a sound she had hoped not to hear until Oregon—the snap of a wheel spoke as the wagon lurched over a rock.

"Whoa. Steady," she said to her teams, holding up her whip as a signal for them to stop.

Marcus, Lucinda and the baby had been riding inside the wagon, Lucinda feeling too poorly to walk. Now, Marcus stuck his head out the front of the wagon and glared at Charlotte. "What the devil was that?" he cried.

"Come and see for yourself," she answered.

Marcus jumped out, his face nearly purple with rage. "If you drove the teams like a normal person—"

"Then what?" Charlotte said. "Everyone's spokes snap, Marcus. I'm the one who *hasn't* been pushing the teams."

Marcus said nothing, and Charlotte began the work of putting blocks under the wagon so the wheel could be taken off.

She had just taken off the wheel and laid it down on the ground when she heard teams coming toward her. She looked up just as the Smitherses' oxen stumbled over her wheel, then crushed it with the wagon. On the other side of the teams, she could see Skete walking, whipping the oxen as they followed the course he had directed.

A second wagon, with Jock driving it, passed over the same spot, over the iron and splintered wood that had once been her wheel.

"Jock Smithers—" she called out, about to say that she was going to ask Captain Tayler to call a men's council meeting about him.

But then she saw the back of the Smitherses' wagon. Biddy Lee was lying in the rear, looking out, her eyes full of fear. Charlotte couldn't imagine what had happened, but she thought Biddy Lee might be hurt or ill if she was riding. And she didn't want to cause trouble for her friend.

"What the hell happened here?" Marcus asked, eyes blazing, when he returned and saw the wheel, split into a dozen pieces.

"Ask your friends the Smitherses, the ones I'm not supposed to cross."

Marcus's eyes narrowed. "You're telling me they broke the wheel?"

Charlotte nodded. "I don't even think they'd deny it if you asked."

Marcus shook his head. "I have *you* to thank for that, of course," he muttered, lying on his back to get one of the spares he and Francis had fastened to the undercarriage, what now seemed like a lifetime ago.

"Would you like some help?" she finally asked.

"No!" Marcus yelled. "I don't need any!"

Shrugging, she went into the wagon to check on Lucinda and the baby. Lucinda looked positively blissful nursing Jacob, and Charlotte decided she wouldn't say anything bad—about the wheel, about Marcus, about the Smithers family.

"His bark is worse than his bite," Lucinda said softly. "And he's *my* husband, not yours, Char."

Luke's words of the night before echoed in Charlotte's ears. What was it he had said? That Charlotte should let Lucinda live her life, make her own decisions, be the kind of wife she wanted to be. Charlotte flushed as she thought of all that had followed, Luke's too-appealing words and skilled, persuasive touch.

She looked into her sister's eyes and wanted to tell her what had happened, but she was ashamed. "Luke said the same thing last night," she said, feeling as if she were dipping her toes into a pond of cool water. She would see if Lucinda was shocked, interested, or something else.

"Last night?" Lucinda asked, a corner of her mouth curved in a half smile.

"He warned me not to be out alone because of the Smithers family."

Lucinda looked skeptical. "And then he told you Marcus is my husband and not yours?"

Charlotte laughed. "Not exactly. When I'm with Luke, we talk about anything and everything. For some reason, I say what I'm thinking; it's as if I have no choice. And he wants to know everything. My hopes, my dreams—"

"He's a good man, Charlotte," Lucinda said.

"Too good to be true, you mean," Charlotte said.

"But why?" Luce asked. "Why *can't* it be true? Why can't Luke Ashcroft truly be what he seems to be?"

"Because look at Pa," Charlotte said. "And Marcus. You have to admit he isn't what he was when you married him, Luce. *I* even liked him back then."

Lucinda's cheeks darkened, but she said nothing. Then she nodded toward the open end of the wagon, and Charlotte followed her gaze.

Luke Ashcroft, carrying tools, was walking toward them.

Charlotte felt butterflies in her stomach, a shallow, not-there feeling that had never before come over her.

"Looks like you could use some help," he said as Charlotte left the wagon.

Marcus's face darkened. "Not from you. And I'll thank you not to pitch your tent an inch or two away from ours tonight."

Luke's eyes flashed. "I didn't realize you had staked a claim to this land. So you're not finishing the trail?"

"You know what I mean," Marcus growled.

"And I know what I have to do," Luke shot back. "Make sure these women get where they want to go, if you're not going to."

"If you want to impress my sister-in-law by fixing a wheel any idiot could fix with his eyes closed, then be my guest," he sputtered. And then he stormed off.

Luke laughed. "I guess I'll do my best to impress you," he said. But then his eyes grew serious. "Now do you see what I mean about the Smithers family?" he asked. "We could bring them up before the men's council for what they did, but I don't want it to backfire on Biddy Lee. But do you see what I was talking about?"

Charlotte nodded as Luke began gathering the broken spokes. "So you watch your back, Charlotte. Because I can't always be here to watch it for you." He looked her up and down. "Pleasurable though that would be," he murmured.

* * *

"That's some fine filly you were helping out back there," George said, cooking up a pan of beans and venison. "She seems just about perfect for a man like you. Just about perfect." He stroked the big, bushy beard Luke had teased him about since the day they had first met more than ten years earlier.

"Oh, go back to untangling that matted old beard and leave me be," Luke said. "You're the one looking for a wife, George."

"Oh, no, friend. A tiger never sheds his stripes. You're the one who needs a wife. And if I live to be a hundred ten years old, I'll never again see a woman block up a wagon and repair it as quick as that little thing did today."

Luke laughed. "That *was* pretty good, the way she helped me," he chuckled.

"Helped you? Hell, boy, you would have been lost without that woman!"

George was laughing, but Luke's smile faded. The wounds of the past were too deep, too recent, his guilt way too strong. He shook his head and said nothing, knowing George already knew his thoughts.

"It wasn't your fault," George said. "When are you going to realize that?"

"Why would I, when it's not true?" Luke asked, his voice rough with grief and raw regret.

"You have to move on," George said. "Parmelia and John are gone and buried. And here's a woman who's smart and strong, your match in spirit—"

"I married once," Luke growled, the pain in his heart nearly physical. "Forever. Now, are you going to eat or lecture for the rest of the night? Because if you're going to lecture, I can find a different place to eat."

George shook his head sadly, and Luke forked some buffalo meat into his mouth, sorry that White Fox, still traveling nearby, hadn't taken him up on his offer of dinner. He could have used that kind of company—or none at all. What he didn't need was George questioning him like a woman.

Then what have you been doing with Charlotte these last few nights, an inner voice asked, *making her cry out in the darkness?*

He didn't want to think about it. He needed her as a man needed a woman; he had needed to pleasure her, to show her what it felt like. He had needed, for some reason he'd probably never understand, to show her what it felt like to have someone be good to her. It was as simple as that. Nothing more.

But he didn't need her or want her in his life. He didn't.

He looked up and saw Charlotte and Lucinda heading his way, Lucinda carrying her newborn baby, Charlotte carrying something that looked like a pie.

"We wanted to thank you for fixing our wagon," Charlotte said as they drew near. "So far I've had two left hands when it comes to cooking on this trail, so this may end up tasting just awful." She seemed not to want to meet his gaze. "It's *supposed* to be a dried cranberry and hickory nut pie, but it smells suspiciously . . . odd," she finally finished. "But you two can be the judges of that."

George stood up and walked over to the women. "I think *I'll* be the judge," he said, laughing and taking the pie. "It smells delicious."

Luke was purposely not looking at the boy. Jacob, he had heard his name was.

He could remember John at exactly that age, the way he smelled, the way he had felt in his arms, strong but so breakable, and his round, warm weight as he had slept on his chest, a weight Luke had expected to grow and grow and grow. Luke had always thought John would grow even taller than himself.

Forgive me, he said for the ten thousandth time. But what forgiveness could there be for him? It was too late; he bore too much guilt.

And then he looked. He looked at Lucinda, holding the baby tentatively—anyone could see she was a nervous person, frightened and insecure—and then at the boy, who was beginning to squirm.

Lucinda smiled and held the baby out to Luke. "Would you like to hold him?" she asked.

Luke opened his mouth but said nothing. In his mind's eye, he could see Parmelia holding John out to the banker on one sunny March day, saying the very same words. "Babies and I don't mix," he muttered. "George is the family man."

George laughed and handed the pie to Luke, taking the baby in his big arms. "That's a fine little boy you have there, ma'am."

Luke noticed that both Lucinda and Charlotte kept looking over their shoulders, back in the direction of their tents. "What's wrong?" he asked.

Charlotte's eyes finally met his. And when they did, he was pulled in as if by long threads of silk. "Marcus," she murmured.

Luke's heart raced. "If Marcus has a problem with me, he should take it up with me, not you two. I'll watch over you as many hours of the day as I think you need to be watched."

Lucinda held her hands out for Jacob. "I think I should be going," she said softly as George handed the baby back to her.

"I'll go with you," Charlotte said.

Luke felt Charlotte was unwilling to meet his eyes again. And he wanted to tell her they had done nothing wrong. He had shown her—a bit— what it felt like to be physically loved by a man. She had a right to know, a need to know.

Yet, he knew—he could feel—that she was shamed by what they had done, maybe because she already sensed that he would never love again.

"If that Luke Ashcroft pitches his tent half on top of ours tonight, I'm going to bring it up in front of the council," Marcus muttered.

Lucinda put the quilt she was mending down in her lap. "Do you think that's wise?" she asked.

Marcus looked furious. "Obviously I do, yes, or I wouldn't have said it."

"But Charlotte—" She stopped, her voice gone. He narrowed his eyes. "Charlotte what? Charlotte has no respect for the dead, and you wish everyone in the caravan to think about this fact?"

Lucinda's mouth opened, but no words came out.

"Charlotte is behaving like a fool and a slut, and you wish everyone in the caravan to know *that* fact, as well?"

"That will be enough, Marcus," Charlotte said as he stood up. "If you have a problem with my behavior, then tell me, please, and leave Luce out of it."

"*If* I do?" he cried out. "Francis must be rolling in his grave every night as you run off with that man and make fools of us all."

"And he wouldn't have even *had* a grave if it hadn't been for Luke," she snapped. "I didn't see *you* lift a finger to bury him, and he was your own brother!"

Marcus's face darkened. He opened his mouth, closed it, then stalked off into the half-light of the dusk.

"This will end," Charlotte said as she watched Lucinda bundle Jacob up into her arms. "At least with me, Luce. I won't let him talk that way to you." She remembered, suddenly and once again, Luke's telling her to let Lucinda live her own life. But how? And why?

"The trail changes people," Lucinda said quietly. "You yourself saw how it changed Francis. And yes, it has changed Marcus too. I just think Francis's death hit him awfully hard, and then you . . ." Her voice trailed off, and her cheeks darkened. "You with Mr. Ashcroft." She stopped as Mollie Smithers came toward them.

"I want to apologize for what my family did to your wheel," Mollie called out.

Charlotte could hardly believe she had heard correctly. "Excuse me?"

"As long as my heart beats in my body, Charlotte, I'll never apologize about that doll, because everyone knows a slave can't own property. But what my brother and pa did back there today, I do feel that was wrong."

Charlotte glanced at Lucinda, who was feeding Jacob beneath a shawl hanging from her shoulder with the nonchalance of a woman who had borne half a dozen children. Maybe, Charlotte thought, bearing a child changed things in a woman, just as she herself felt so changed simply because of Luke Ashcroft's attentions.

And now, as she looked at Mollie Smithers, she wondered what had changed Mollie in a way that had compelled her to apologize for her own family's actions. "I'm surprised that a woman who feels a slave can't even keep a doll would feel it's wrong for her family to run over someone's wagon wheel, Mollie."

"They're entirely different things, Charlotte, entirely different." She looked into Charlotte's eyes then. "But I did want to tell you something else, because I know that you and Luke Ashcroft have been spending time together."

Charlotte felt as if her whole body were suddenly on alert. "I don't feel that that's anybody's business but my own and Mr. Ashcroft's," she said.

Mollie shrugged. "Woman to woman, I want to

tell you something. Because I was sweet on Luke
myself for a couple of days."

Charlotte still felt on guard. "That's *your* business," she said.

Mollie looked into her eyes, her own shining
clear and blue and triumphant. "Did you know
that Luke is married?" she blurted.

Out of the corner of her eye, Charlotte saw Lucinda look up quickly. But she thought about that
for only the time it took to see it. No, what she
thought about after that was far more painful: the
image of herself shuddering beneath Luke's fingers, crying out his name, holding him.

And loving him, falling in love though she had
sworn she never would. Loving all those words he
had used as he asked about her hopes and dreams
and desires.

As if he liked her, or even loved her.

"I can see you're surprised," Mollie said. "I was,
too, Charlotte. That was why I thought I'd mention it to you." She sighed, looking into Charlotte's eyes. "I know there are probably quite a few
things we disagree about—slavery and so on—"

"You mean thinking you can own a person
when there can be no such thing, Mollie? Thinking things that are an abomination against God
and nature?"

"That's your opinion," Mollie said quietly.

"It's a fact," Charlotte said. "And you'll find
that out, Mollie, sooner or later, when you're punished for what you've done."

Mollie narrowed her eyes. "In your opinion,"
she said. "Maybe *you'll* be punished for being with

a man who's married, who has a beautiful wife back east. I saw her picture, Charlotte. Ask Luke to see it." She shrugged. "Anyway, I thought I'd let you know, as a friend. You have a beautiful baby, Lucinda," she called out as she turned and walked back toward her wagon.

Charlotte could hardly bear to look at Lucinda. She felt as if shame had stained her skin a different color, as if dishonesty had shrunk her whole body.

"He's an amazing man, Char," Lucinda said. "Strong and courageous and as handsome as the heavens are high. I'm sure lots of women have had thoughts of him." She paused. "You didn't know," she said gently.

Married, Charlotte thought. Luke was married.

And a liar. Or a dissembler, at best, for even though she had never asked him if he was married, certainly he had never given any hints that he was.

She thought of what she had done with him only the night before—crying out his name, quivering beneath his touch, throbbing with pleasure beyond any she had ever imagined. And for what? Luke's amusement? She thought of all he had said to her, convincing her that she deserved to know what it felt like to be cared about, what it felt like to be given pleasure.

All lies.

But just punishment, she told herself, for having had thoughts, from the moment she had met him, about a man who wasn't her husband. Evil thoughts.

"Did you hear what I said?" Lucinda was asking her. "No harm has been done, Charlotte."

Charlotte squeezed her eyes shut tight.

No harm had been done.

Then why did her heart ache so much for something she knew she shouldn't ever have wanted?

Twelve

When Charlotte awakened, she tried to shake off the bad dream she'd had: Luke was married, and . . . and it hadn't been a dream.

She sat up and wiped the sleep from her eyes, wondering how she could have been crazy enough to fall in love when she had always known, even as a child, that she wasn't meant to love anyone but her family and her animals. She had known when she had listened to her father yell at her mother day after day and night after night. She had known at age eight, when her baby sister Adrietta had died and her pa hadn't shed a tear. She had known when her father had said she was plain and that no man would ever want her. Only now . . .

She thought of all the words Luke had said, and hated herself for having believed him.

And trusted him.

And loved him.

"Char," Lucinda said as she peeked into Charlotte's tent. "Nora Vestrow says there's a lovely grove of serviceberries a bit north of here. Do you want to come pick with me? Nora says she made three pies with them."

"That sounds fine," Charlotte said, her voice wooden and without feeling. What difference would it make whether she picked serviceberries or not? She felt as if a hole had been cut deep in her heart, and she was furious that she had ever let herself feel anything for Luke. She had been wrong, and now she was being punished for the sin of having wanted him from the very first.

At breakfast, Charlotte wished she had the courage to dump the pan of johnnycakes over Marcus's head. He seemed to be glowing every time he looked over at baby Jacob, and she felt it would be well worth the loss of the morning's breakfast to see his mood blacken to at least a fraction of what hers was.

But later, as she and Lucinda set off with baskets and the baby, Charlotte told herself that her mood was her own fault. She had opened her heart, and look what had happened.

It didn't matter that she had fallen in love with Luke Ashcroft. It didn't matter that he had told her things no other man—in fact, no other person—had ever told her. It didn't matter that he would now occupy her thoughts night and day, and there would be a place in her heart that would ache for him forever.

He was married, and she had sinned. She was selfish and flighty, passionate when she should have been stoic and cool-headed. She should have been deaf to Luke's words, to all of his sup-

posed interest in her life; she should have been
blind to his strong, handsome features, those sea-
green, storm-filled eyes and his strong, beautiful
jaw. She should never have let herself taste him,
or feel him.

And she should never have let him touch her.

She walked on, wondering what she could do to
change things. It was almost funny that for most
people, the overland journey was a question of
physical survival; yet, it was her heart that had
been wounded on this journey, and all because of
a man.

Because of a man who wasn't her husband.

Up ahead, Charlotte saw Biddy Lee walking,
the prairie grasses shimmering beneath the sun's
heat all around her. And Charlotte felt a rush of
shame. She had spent the night and morning feeling sorry for herself, yet she knew that compared
to Biddy Lee's, her life was a picnic.

"Let's catch up with Biddy Lee," she said to
Lucinda.

Lucinda laughed. "*You* run to her, Char. We'll
catch up. I've got a nice, quiet little baby here, and
I'd like to keep him that way for a few minutes."

A moment later, Charlotte caught up to Biddy
Lee. "Is everything all right?" Charlotte asked,
walking beside her. "I saw you riding in the back
of the Smitherses' wagon. I didn't know what that
meant."

"It meant I hurt my ankle, and Skete told me to
ride in the wagon, and then Miss Carlene
screamed bloody murder and I jumped out and
walked."

"Are you all right?"

"I've been better and I've been worse," Biddy Lee said. "Now are you going to tell me what's making you look sadder than a girl who lost her best friend and doll and mama all in the same day, or do I have to try to guess?"

Charlotte smiled. "Do I look that bad?"

"Maybe worse," Biddy Lee said as they reached a grove of berries.

Charlotte shook her head, not wanting to speak—because she knew that if she told Biddy Lee about Luke, she'd start to feel even sorrier for herself; and her heart felt as broken as she could imagine right at that moment.

Biddy Lee sighed. "You tell me when you're ready, girl. And concentrate on this special sight right here and now: To see fresh fruit is an amazing thing, isn't it?"

Charlotte picked a berry and ate it, letting the juice tingle on her tongue. It was sweet and sour, bitter and fruity, and Charlotte truly felt she hadn't tasted anything that wonderful in her life. "Berries," she said, taking another one. "I think I'd like to just stuff myself right here and now and forget about jam and pie."

Biddy Lee laughed. "Me too. I'll tell Carlene and Mollie and Mrs. Smithers they were all gone," she said, shoving a handful into her mouth.

Lucinda caught up with them, and Charlotte told her to close her eyes and open her mouth, then dropped a handful of berries in.

"Mmm," Lucinda said. "I haven't tasted anything this good in years." She moved Jacob more to the side, against her chest. "I need a quicker way to eat these," she said, laughing and wiping the juice from her chin.

Charlotte laughed, and for a moment, she felt like a girl again, happily picking berries down by the creek at home with Luce, some for themselves and some for pies their mama would make— never fewer than four pies, Mama always said, because you never knew who might stop by.

And then she remembered the knowledge that had blackened her morning like a thundercloud moving across the sky: Luke. And his wife. And her own foolish heart, emotions that had been stronger than her will.

But she knew she could be strong. She had been happy a moment earlier, sharing berries in the sun with her sister and her friend. She hadn't needed Luke in that moment, and she would force herself not to need him ever again.

"Your eyes are troubled," White Fox said, looking carefully at Luke as he passed him his pipe.

Luke laughed as he drew on the smoke he hadn't tasted in years. "I think my whole body is troubled," he said. "I'm getting old, White Fox."

The Indian—himself an old man, his long hair streaked with gray—didn't smile. "Man who teaches boy to shoot bow and arrow not old," he muttered.

Luke was lost in the memory for a moment, a memory that seemed to come from another life, though it had happened only four years earlier. It was at this same time of year that he had gotten to

NAME: _____

ADDRESS: _____
_____
_____

TELEPHONE: _____

E-MAIL: _____

_____ I want to pay by credit card.

__ Visa   __ MasterCard   __ Discover

Account Number: _____

Expiration date: _____

SIGNATURE: _____

*Send this form, along with $2.00 shipping
and handling for your FREE books, to:*

Historical Romance Book Club
20 Academy Street
Norwalk, CT 06850-4032

*Or fax (must include credit card
information!) to:* 610.995.9274.
*You can also sign up on the Web
at* <u>www.dorchesterpub.com</u>.

Offer open to residents of the U.S. and
Canada only. Canadian residents, please
call 1.800.481.9191 for pricing information.

If under 18, a parent or guardian must sign. Terms, prices and conditions
subject to change. Subscription subject to acceptance. Dorchester
Publishing reserves the right to reject any order or cancel any subscription.

know the Kanzas a bit during a layover. White Fox's grandson, a boy of five or six, had been crying because his brothers were teasing him about not being able to hit anything with his bow and arrow.

Looking angry, the boy shook off help from his father and White Fox and walked off into the desert, dragging his bow and a few worn-out arrows with him.

Luke had figured it was worth a try, offering to teach the boy. Either Quick Feather would accept his help or not. Luke had walked up to him and motioned to aim at a bush, then showed him to hold steady before letting go, covering the boy's hand with his and exaggerating what Quick Feather had been doing wrong. "That's your only mistake, son."

Quick Feather had practiced with Luke, the look of pride shining strongly in his eyes. They had walked back to camp together, and then Quick Feather had showed his taunters his new skills.

And White Fox had beamed as he and Luke had watched. "You will make a fine, fine father," he had said.

"You were a happy man when you helped my grandson," White Fox said. "Yet now you are dying of sadness."

It would have to stop, Luke told himself, this feeling of sharp, raw pain and guilt. But he knew it never would. When did the grieving for the two loves of one's life end? Or did it go on forever?

He could still remember—now more than ever,

since he was with White Fox again—the joy he had felt when Quick Feather had looked up at him after making his first good shot. He had imagined teaching young John all the skills he had learned on the trail, and he thought of how amazing it was that they would have a whole lifetime together in which to teach each other.

He had felt the pride of fatherhood in that moment of triumph, thinking of his little boy back home—when young John had already passed away, because Luke had been following a selfish dream.

"Tell me the trouble," the chief said.

Luke shook his head, remembering how Parmelia had always said John had been sent to them by an angel, that no harm could ever come to him because he had been wanted so much.

"What's done is done," he muttered. He had never been one to talk an issue to death, and he wasn't about to start now. A man's feelings were his weaknesses.

"But it isn't done," the chief said softly. "It dulls your mind and your heart. It causes you pain all day and all night. You will make mistakes because of it."

Luke just looked at him.

"Your wife and son?" the chief asked.

Luke stared, feeling as if his stomach had been punched, but also feeling the edges of a strange relief. "How did you know?"

"It is the kind of grief that destroys a man. You are being destroyed in that way."

Luke felt himself closing off again. "Maybe so, but there's nothing to be done about it."

"It will eat you alive, your grief, unless you let it go."

"No offense, White Fox, but you don't know what you're talking about."

White Fox raised an eyebrow. "I know exactly what I'm talking about, my friend. I lived my life. I went on. I started another family."

Luke's curiosity almost drew him in. What exactly had happened to the chief's family? But then he backed off. "That's you," he said. "I'm different."

White Fox looked long and hard at Luke. Luke felt as if time had shifted somehow, as if he were unable to move as White Fox looked him up and down; it was almost as if he were putting him under a spell, Luke felt.

"Now listen," White Fox said.

"To what?"

"Just listen," White Fox said. "And tell me what you hear."

In the distance, Luke could hear children—he thought the Vestrows' little ones, who were almost always singing. "Uh, someone's singing," he said. "And there are the usual stock sounds—oxen, horses—"

White Fox narrowed his eyes. "And?"

"And . . ." Luke laughed. "And an old, nosy chief asking me a bunch of never-ending questions."

He saw the corners of White Fox's mouth curve up. But then the old chief's face grew serious. "If you listen hard," he said slowly, "you will hear your wife and your boy."

Luke didn't want to hear the words. He could still remember what John's voice sounded like—sometimes. But there were days he couldn't, days when he awakened and tried to remember young John's voice and he couldn't, days when his boy's face faded to a blur, when he couldn't even remember the feel of that soft, soft skin, or exactly the way his nose had looked, or his mouth, or his chin, or how perfectly, exactly, the boy's little hand fit into his.

"My boy is dead," he said. "And my wife is dead."

"And their spirits have much to say," White Fox said, still looking deeply into Luke's eyes. "If it had been the other way around, and you had died, and your wife and boy had lived, would you want them to live like the walking dead?"

Luke didn't say anything. He was caught in a half-memory, John's face only partially clear.

"Are you able," White Fox asked, "are you able, Luke, always to remember their faces? Are you able always to remember what they smelled like? Are you able always to remember the sounds of their laughter?"

Luke said nothing.

"If you are not, my friend, I will tell you why," White Fox said. "If you want to know why," he added, drawing on his pipe.

Luke said nothing.

"I will tell you what I know," White Fox said, passing Luke the pipe. "There are times you want to see the face of your boy, but you cannot. There are times you want to see the face of your wife, but you cannot. The more you try to picture her face, the less you see. And the reason is because you are not living. You are between life and death. When you live again, my good friend, your people will live again in your mind."

Luke drew on the pipe and passed it back to White Fox. "You're an old friend," Luke said. "And I trust you. But you don't know the guilt I bear—"

"Make me a promise you will live your life," White Fox said.

"I won't—"

"Make me a promise," White Fox said again.

Luke sighed. "I promise," he said.

"And mean it with your heart," White Fox said.

Luke nodded, but he knew there was too much that White Fox didn't know and would never understand.

"Help!" came a voice, suddenly, in the distance. "Oh, God. Somebody!"

Luke took off at a run.

The voice, a female one, had come from near camp. One lone steer was running wildly, as if it had been wounded, and it was dragging something in the dust, ten or fifteen feet behind.

"Darius!" Nora Vestrow was screaming. "Darius, let go!"

Luke saw that a few of the men had realized what was happening: The steer was dragging Darius Vestrow, Pete and Nora's six-year-old. Two men were now running after the steer, knives brandished, probably planning to cut the line the boy was tangled in.

But Luke didn't think they'd make it. The steer was wild, running like a mad animal, and Pete Vestrow and George weren't running nearly as fast.

But George had a lasso.

"The lasso!" Luke called out to George as he neared.

George was a beast, a bear, about as quick on his feet as a slow-moving tortoise, so Luke went for it.

He grabbed the lasso and ran.

Pete Vestrow ran behind the steer, heading him at a diagonal so he wouldn't be spooked by Luke.

Luke tossed the lasso. The rope sailed through the air, landed perfectly . . . and then slid.

The lasso had the steer by one horn. Which wouldn't last, wouldn't work, wouldn't mean much unless Luke raced as if his life depended on it.

And Darius Vestrow's life did, if he wasn't already dead.

Luke's feet pounded the ground. Gasping for air as he reached the steer, he took his horns, twisted his neck and threw him to the ground. And was gored in the shoulder, a pain that was sharp and hard and stinging.

But Pete and George had reached Darius. George cut the lines—Luke saw they were horse lead lines, so Darius had probably been playing—and a shot rang out.

The steer bucked and went limp, and Nora Vestrow came running, her face covered with tears as she scooped Darius into her arms. "Darius!" she yelled.

Luke heard a moan come from the boy as Nora held Darius's limp but breathing body in her arms. A second later, Pete joined them.

And Luke thought about what they must feel, joy that their son was alive, uncertainty whether he would continue to live; and he wondered, if he had been home, if he would have had that chance with young John.

Darius was scraped badly, blood oozing from too many parts of his body, and Luke tore off his shirt and began ripping it into strips.

"We'll want to stop the bleeding where we can," he called out to Pete, who took off his own shirt as well.

"Might better keep him warm sooner than any-thing," George said, taking his own shirt off. He smiled down at Nora, who was still crying. "Use mine as a blanket, Mrs. Vestrow, and you'll want to save your tears. Your boy will be fine."

"But how do you know?"

"Trust me," George said, wrapping his shirt around Darius.

Luke certainly hoped George knew what he was talking about.

"You two take whatever meat you want off this devil," Pete called out. "I want no part of— Good lord, Luke. You're bleeding half to death!"

"I'll be fine," Luke said. "And you won't feel that way later about the meat when you have no more than a length of lead line and a dried-up piece of timothy to eat, Pete. We'll butcher him, but the meat is yours. He was your devil."

White Fox suddenly appeared, seemingly out of nowhere. "Get him warm," he said, moving to pick Darius up. "Put him by a fire."

The four men carried Darius while Nora ran along, covering her mouth with her hands. As they got closer to camp, they were joined by others—Alma and Zeke Bliss, Lucinda Dalton with her baby, then Charlotte.

Luke's eyes met hers for a moment, but it was only a moment. She looked away with an expression he couldn't read. And when Luke next looked up, it was into the eyes of White Fox. "Live your life," were the words he mouthed.

Thirteen

The next day, the caravan was finally going to move on again, and many felt it was only right to celebrate Darius's quick recovery with a chivaree, complete with a buffalo roast, a bonfire, and dancing to fiddle music. Some of the women had baked serviceberry and currant pies, and Zeke Bliss had said he'd share his jerked buffalo hump with anyone brave enough to eat it.

Charlotte didn't plan on going. She knew she had to speak to Luke, because even if Luke *was* a liar, she owed him the question: Was he really, truly married? Because at the back of her mind, a voice kept telling her that Luke was honest and Mollie was not.

Yet she almost couldn't bear to ask because she wouldn't be able to bear the truth if Mollie had in fact been right: *Yes, I am married. Yes, I lied. Yes, you let yourself feel things you haven't ever felt with anyone else because you are a fool.*

She had watched as Luke had helped save Darius Vestrow, and she had known that she loved him. He had acted, and would always act, without a thought for himself because that was the kind of man he was, the kind of man he always would be. He was the brave, appealing man she had always—

She shook her head, stopping her thoughts as if they were words she was speaking aloud—because she *hadn't* been looking her whole life for a man like Luke.

She didn't believe in men like Luke.

She was sitting by the campfire—Lucinda and her family had already gone into their tent—when Alma Bliss came along.

"You're sitting there like a lump on a log for what reason?" Alma demanded, hands on her bony hips.

Charlotte couldn't help smiling. "I'm really not in the mood—" she began.

But Alma was already pulling her up by the elbow. "That makes no difference to me, young lady. Now get into your tent, put on something pretty and meet me out by the bonfire."

"I really—"

"I told you, missy. I really don't care what you think. Now, go!"

Charlotte shook her head and went into the tent, knowing it would do no good to argue with Alma. But just because she was going to the party didn't mean she would have to dance.

She put on the cleanest skirt she could find, and her embroidered blouse, and she pulled her hair back with a ribbon. In the small, now-cracked mirror Lucinda had kept, Charlotte could see there was a mark where her sunbonnet had dug into her forehead day after day; and her skin was blotched with enough mosquito bites to make it look as if she had measles. And her dark brown hair looked more like old string than hair. But she figured no one would get close enough to see it or care.

She walked quickly in the direction of the music and the crackling flames of the party, laughingly thinking she couldn't handle being dragged by that bony but surprisingly strong hand of Alma's.

"Wait a minute!" Luke called out as he came toward her, a cocky smile making his handsome face even handsomer.

"Yes?" she asked, her voice brittle. She hated how easily this man could affect her. Just looking into his deep green eyes made her nervous and giddy and furious all at once.

"I don't think you want to go to the party like that."

"Is that so?" she snapped. "And why would that be?"

He burst out laughing. "Look behind you," he said.

Oh, wonderful. She had tucked her skirt into her pantaloons; all the world could see her droopy off-white underthings! "Well, fine," she said, flustered but determined not to show it. She pulled her hem down as quickly as she could.

"Don't be in such a hurry," he said, still laughing. "I've already seen everything there is to see."

She felt color flood her face as she continued pulling at her skirt. It was unnecessary to go on fussing with it, but she needed something to do with her hands, a distraction that would prevent Luke from seeing how embarrassed she was.

Luke reached out for her then, catching her by the waist, pulling her close, encircling her with his arms. "We need to talk," he said.

This was going to take all her strength. She pushed at Luke, putting her hands on his chest and pressing. But he didn't budge.

She put her hands on his wrists at her waist and tried to pull them off. But he didn't budge. "I want you to let me go," she said.

"Tell me why," he murmured, his lips close to hers. "Tell me what's bothering you."

"I should think you would know," she answered. Her heart was pounding.

Luke reached up and tucked a strand of her hair behind her ears, his eyes searching hers. "Tell me," he said softly.

Well, the time had come. He wanted to know what was bothering her. She hated the idea of saying the words, but she knew she had to. "When were you going to tell me you were married?" she asked.

He looked surprised, and then angry. "What did you say?" he asked. "Why would you think I—" He stopped. "Ah—I can guess why, I think. Mollie?"

Charlotte nodded, and she could feel the edges of happiness beginning to lighten her heart.

But Luke's face had grown so serious—indeed, so heartbroken—that right away, she knew the truth was probably not as simple as she had hoped.

"I'm not married," Luke said. "But I was. And I should have told you." His face crumpled as he spoke his next words. "My wife and boy—he was three months old—passed on when I made this journey four years ago."

"I'm so sorry," Charlotte said, knowing her words were completely inadequate.

"Regret is a weakness," Luke suddenly said, his face ravaged by the pain of memory. "You can't change mistakes you made in the past." He looked into her eyes for such a long time that she began to wonder if he was under some sort of spell. Then, suddenly, he took her in his arms. "Do you know what? I hear music, and I have a beautiful woman in my arms, and tonight, I'm going to live in the present. Or maybe not just for tonight," he murmured.

She knew she had to fight against everything that was happening. She felt too raw, too inexperienced when it came to love. One minute, she felt she was falling in love with Luke; then she had to tell herself, with the clear-thinking part of her mind, that she knew it was crazy to trust any man. And with Luke, one minute he was obviously in so much pain over what had happened to his wife and child. Yet in the next, he was claiming that the past was in the past.

He lowered his lips to her neck and brushed them against her skin, pulling her tighter against him. "Tell me what you're thinking," he whispered.

She almost had to laugh. Luke made it sound so easy. What was she thinking? She felt raw and confused and naive, happy that Luke wasn't married, sad for his sorrow and the loss of his family. She felt half in love with Luke, completely in love when she simply let herself be, when she watched him save a boy, drive a team, laugh with his friends. She felt completely in love when he looked into her eyes, when he drew her into his arms, when he touched her.

Yet she trusted none of her feelings. Nor did she trust his.

"I can't," she murmured, shaking her head.

He put a hand at the back of her head and drew back. "Don't say that, Charlotte."

"But there's too much," she said. "All your feelings about the past, all my feelings for you. They're too strong, and I don't want to need you the way I do—"

"We need each other," he whispered, gently swaying as he held her, his hips urging hers to move with his rhythm. "Dance with me here and now, Charlotte. When we get too far away from the music, we'll make our own."

"I can't," she said.

He looked at her with eyes that swirled dark with passion. "Never say you can't. Not to me,

Charlotte. Haven't you already felt more than you've ever imagined here on this trail?"

She thought about how he had made her feel the other night, and the memory made pleasure and desire throb unmercifully between her legs. There was so much she didn't know.

But wasn't that the point? She didn't possess much experience, either with her heart or her body, and that was the way she wanted to keep it. She was an independent woman who was absolutely thrilled at the idea of farming on her own out west. She didn't need a man for anything.

"The only way a man and woman can get along is to talk," he whispered, his hard length urging her softness to melt against him. She felt liquid and weak and completely confused. "To talk and then talk some more."

"I don't want to need you," she finally said. "Luke—"

He lowered his lips to hers, and her mouth opened, needing the taste of this man who knew how to reach her as no other person in the world did.

She felt as if she were drowning, as if the liquid, molten desire that burned in her most secret place was growing deeper, filling every part of her body until she would no longer be able to breathe.

He drew back, his eyes dreamy with desire. "I told you I wouldn't make love to you until you were ready," he murmured, his body hard against hers, crying out for her. "I'd never rush you."

She couldn't tell him the truth. Oh, she loved

what he had said about talking to each other. She loved everything he had said. But she couldn't tell him that she was already ready, that her body was on fire, willing her to do what she knew was wrong.

Suddenly she felt wetness beneath her right hand as she gripped Luke's shoulders. Blood oozed from his wound.

"Luke!"

He shook his head. "It's fine. I'm fine," he said.

"But have you put gunpowder on it? Have you bandaged it?"

"I'm not thinking about my shoulder right now, Charlotte," he said softly.

"Well, I am!" she said.

He tried to pull her to him again. "I want to make you feel good again, Charlotte. Tonight."

The dark red of his blood was spreading down the front of his shirt, and Charlotte looked into Luke's eyes. What she saw were eyes she could never say no to—not if she stayed with him for even one more minute. What she saw were lips she loved too much—whose taste she knew and dreamed about, whose soft touch she needed even in her sleep. She saw the strong jaw of the first man who had ever wanted to talk to her about anything and everything, and she knew she had to get away. Luke was the first island she had ever been able to find in an otherwise stormy sea, and though she wanted him with every part of her heart, she didn't understand him, and she didn't know him—because no woman could ever know any man; it was the one fact about men of which she was absolutely sure.

"Please take care of your wound," she said, not looking at him. "I must go this very moment." She broke away and ran back to her tent.

Inside, she felt like a caged animal. She plopped herself down on the cold ground, her body still feeling as if Luke were near. Her nipples tingled as if his fingers were touching them, and the heat between her legs pulsed with every beat of her heart, every wave of need growing stronger, as if that amazing thing Luke had done might happen again.

She thought of the words he had said tonight, how he knew she had already felt things she had never before imagined, and she squirmed with desire, wishing Luke were with her, or that she could think of something else!

She thought of what he had said as she had tried to push him away: "I want to make you feel good again, Charlotte. Tonight," and how much her body wished she had said yes.

She thought of the other things he had said to her as well, how he had promised he would never lie to her; and how he had said the only way a man and woman could ever get along was to talk; and she knew that those words were as stimulating to her as his touch, that those words of promise and affection made her simmer and burn as much as his fingers and lips.

She didn't understand why; she had never wanted a man. She had never wanted to want one, or to need one. And if anyone had asked her even a week ago whether she would believe a man if he said those words to her, she would have laughed out loud.

Yet for some reason, a part of her believed Luke.

No! an inner voice cried. Luke Ashcroft was only doing what thousands of other men around the world did every day: trick a woman.

And she wouldn't be tricked.

"Oh, please!" she suddenly heard Lucinda cry out. "For pity's sake, Marcus, can we have one evening in which you're not picking at me?"

Marcus growled an answer Charlotte couldn't hear, and Charlotte left her tent, not wanting to hear any more, all desire gone from every part of her body.

The chivaree was going at a full roar, and Charlotte watched from the sidelines, marveling at how easily the single men and women of the caravan paired off. Did none of the other women share her doubts about men? Did none of them care?

"I didn't see you dance even one dance, Charlotte," Alma said, coming up alongside her. "Here Zeke and I have been dancing like a couple of kids, and you've been a sorry stick in the mud from start to finish." She shook her head. "It's a crying shame, young lady, and you being a widow now and all."

"Alma, Francis has only been gone for a short time," Charlotte chided.

Alma narrowed her eyes. "Don't you be pretending with *me*, young lady. Francis was a kind and gentle man, but he never lit a fire in your heart the way another man on this trail has. Don't forget that I'm doing a bit of watching over you, missy, and that means I'll tolerate no lies whatsoever." She sighed. "And poor Luke, with no one to tend his wound, bleeding again like a poker-stuck pig."

"Still?" Charlotte asked.

" 'Tis flowing like a river," Alma said. "I offered to bandage it again, but he said a good night's sleep was probably all he needed."

Charlotte knew what she had to do. She had been around enough injuries in her life to know that you didn't ignore wounds, breaks or any kind of injury unless you wanted trouble. *You're looking for trouble of another kind,* an inner voice said, but she shook her head as she got her medical bag and her lantern and walked toward Luke's tent.

She cared about Luke in a different way than she had ever cared for anyone in her life. She was definitely falling in love with him, and her feelings were new and strange, like nothing she had ever experienced.

But that didn't mean she had other motives when she told herself she was going to check on his wound, did it? If Luke was awake, she would be completely businesslike and professional. And if he was asleep—

Well, if he was asleep, she would figure out what to do when she got there.

"Luke?" she called out softly at the entrance to his tent. With the music from the chivaree playing loudly off in the distance, she felt fairly comfortable. Probably no one would even notice she was here.

As she opened the tent flap, she was immediately relieved: Luke was fast asleep, his breathing even and deep.

She set the lantern on the ground, knelt beside Luke and looked down at him, this man she had felt was too handsome, too smart from the first day she had met him. Somehow, her heart had known even then to stay away from him.

She could see the blood caked against the shoulder of his shirt, and she wondered how much more it had bled since she had seen him.

She wanted to make sure he was truly asleep. "Luke?" she whispered.

His breathing was as deep and regular as before, and she began unbuttoning his shirt.

Her breath caught as she saw the broad, muscled expanse she had dreamed of and loved touching. It was covered with curls of brown hair at its center, and Charlotte parted the shirt more, remembering how Luke had moaned as she had touched his nipples.

She parted the fabric as far as she could, and she brushed her fingers lightly through the hair that grew at the center of his chest. His chest was hard, firm, warm. His flat, muscled belly was bare except for a thin line of hair, and she had an urge to run her hand down that dark line—

But she knew better. Or at least knew that she *should* have known better.

She began pulling the left side of Luke's shirt over his shoulder to expose the wound and caught her breath again as she saw that although the wound wasn't deep, it was dirty, with fresh blood only at its center, as if Luke hadn't cleaned it or taken care of it.

Well, Charlotte reasoned, salve was the ticket for tonight. If she hadn't awakened him yet, salve would help without robbing Luke of precious sleep. She could treat him and be out of his tent before three minutes were up.

She pulled his shirt a bit more off his shoulder—

And felt a hand on her buttocks.

She jumped, and the first thing she saw was that grin on Luke's face as he pulled her to him.

"What are you doing?" she cried.

"What I've wanted to do since you walked off," he said huskily, pulling her on top of him.

Oh, no.

She had never been on top of Luke, never even thought about being on top of him. Her breasts were pressed against the chest she had been admiring, her hips were against Luke's, her body already warming against his hard length.

"What are you doing here?" he asked, his hands running lightly over her buttocks, tracing hot circles through the fabric of her skirt.

"I came to treat your wound," Charlotte whispered, barely able to find her voice.

Luke raised a knowing brow. "Is that right?" he murmured, his hands knowing otherwise as they moved persuasively up and down her body. "Now, why couldn't you have done that outside, honey, with all of the caravan looking on?"

Charlotte opened her mouth. "I—I didn't know it was bothering you. Alma said—"

He laughed. "Alma said. Do you know what I say, Charlotte?"

She didn't want to know. But she heard herself ask, softly, "What?"

"You're an intelligent, pretty woman. It's time you started knowing yourself, inside and out. Knowing your thoughts, knowing your body."

She looked into his eyes and said nothing, amazed that this man always seemed to say things no one else had ever said to her. Sometimes he said things she had never even dared to think.

"Now tell me," he went on. "Why did you come?" He reached under her skirt, hiking it up and running a hand over one hip and then the other. His touch was light, but warm and powerful. Charlotte could hardly breathe when his hand reached her upper thigh.

"I can't do this," she whispered. "Maybe I don't want to know myself that well, Luke."

His eyes were dreamy and full of affection and feeling. "Do you remember I told you I'd never make love to you before you're ready, honey? I'll never break that promise." He was hard beneath her, sending a message she didn't know how to fight. "I want to make you feel good again," he whispered. "I want to see you tremble. I want to feel you let go of everything but how good I'm making you feel. I want to do that ten times a night."

She had to laugh. "We'd kill each other off before we reached the Territories."

His face was stormy with passion. "Then what a way to go," he whispered, his hand brushing her hair back from her face. "I told you the first time I met you that it would be worth a hundred prize cows to spend one night with you." She took a deep breath as a hand moved over the skin of her buttocks. "Now I know it would be worth anything." He moved her onto his blanket and looked down at her with eyes filled with fire.

She knew she should move away, do something, say something, as his fingers opened her blouse and she heard Luke's breath catch. She knew she should move away, do something, say something, as his fingers encircled her nipples. He lowered his mouth to a nipple and took it into his mouth, edging it with his teeth, as his hands traced circles down her stomach, unfastened her skirt and pulled it off in one long, silky motion.

She knew she could say nothing, that her breath was caught somewhere deep in her chest as desire and need were spreading up and down her body. She yearned for a touch she knew was coming, yet Luke teased her, suckling one nipple, then another, his hands tracing lightly along her thighs, up over her hips, across her stomach, spreading fire.

"Listen to your body," he whispered.

She listened and she knew. She knew she needed Luke, she knew she wanted him, and she listened to his body as well, feeling how much he wanted her in the hardness pressing against her belly, a male need she wanted to slake and satisfy for the man she loved.

"Let me make you feel good," he murmured, as his hand circled the private spot between her legs. She moved her hips, wanting more of his touch, but Luke's hand slid up to her belly, tormenting her as his wet lips roved across her breasts.

"I want you," she heard herself say. "Please, Luke. Make love to me."

With a groan, he covered her mouth with his. His fingers slid down her belly and gently parted her lips, entering her and making her cry out. "I need you to be sure," he whispered, using his thumb to stroke her sensitive core of pleasure. "There's no going back, Charlotte. I'll always be your first man."

"That's what I want," she whispered, letting her hand slide along his belly until she reached the massive shaft straining against his pants.

Within seconds, Luke had torn his pants away, and Charlotte stared at his arousal. "I'll be gentle," he promised, as if reading her mind. "As gentle as I can be."

She wanted him so much that she trusted him—the man she had sworn to avoid, the man she had vowed not to like, the man who had somehow always known her too well. "I trust you," she said as she felt his hot, muscled chest against her breasts.

Bracing himself on his elbows, sweat dripping onto her face, expertly, gently, Luke entered her, only a bit at first. "If it hurts, Charlotte, it will only hurt once, and I'll make it up to you a thousand times over."

He moved with her and she felt as right as she ever had in her life, her need engulfing him inside of her.

She felt a sharp pain then, and he covered her lips and kissed her wetly, tenderly. "That's the last pain you'll feel, honey," he whispered, and she felt as if a fire had moved inside her. And with every rhythmic stroke, as he gently went deeper and deeper, he took possession of her heart and soul.

She throbbed with need that melted with pleasure as her hips rose to meet his. And she knew that this pleasure, having him inside her, knowing she was stoking his fires as much as she hers, was way beyond anything she had ever felt. She moaned as he moaned, raked his back as he urged her on . . . and then, she opened her eyes. Luke was staring at her intently, his eyes dark with pleasure and passion, intense with emotion and desire. "You fit me like a glove," he whispered.

Their bodies moved in a primitive rhythm made up of desire and knowledge and molten need. Luke's thrusts were like velvet fire. And then a wave of pleasure and hot need swept Charlotte under, as she clawed at his back, as she bit into his neck, as she bucked under a white-hot explosion of searing pleasure. "Luke!"

"You're going to come again, honey," he whispered.

Moaning, sweat dripping from his brow as he

looked down at her, Luke moved with a rhythm that was different, faster, his thrusts like a powerful animal's as he held himself up on one elbow and cupped her buttocks with his other hand. What she would have told him if she could speak, if words or even clear thoughts were possible, was that she wanted him to feel as good as he had made her feel. She wanted to give him that kind of pleasure, as deeply as if the need were part of her own body.

But thoughts weren't possible at that moment. All that she felt was pleasure, getting hotter and deeper again, and then Luke cried out, a moan that went right through her as he tugged at her hair and his hips ground against hers.

And she went over a brink, for a moment not even there but in some other place she had never been. She felt as if she were floating, all needs gone from her body and soul. And then Luke fell against her, soaked, spent, and Charlotte kissed his hard, firm shoulder, loving the salty taste, wanting to know every part of the body of this man she loved.

Luke was The One, she absolutely knew it now; she didn't know what being The One meant, what it would mean in her life. But she did know, deeply, that he was the one and only man with whom she had been destined to make love.

And she didn't feel shy; that was the amazing part. Luckily, the chivaree was still in full swing, so she and Luke hadn't been moaning and crying out into the silent night.

Charlotte wondered if this amazing, blissful pleasure was what made good girls "go bad," as her mother would have said, and she guessed that it was, and she knew that she should feel bad. She had lost her husband only days earlier; yet, she had given herself over, body and soul, to this man who now lay by her side, running his fingers through her hair and looking at her with what she was pretty sure was affection.

"Well, thank you a thousand times over, Charlotte Dalton," Luke whispered. "I needed a woman tonight, and I got myself a woman and a wild animal rolled into one."

Charlotte felt as if she had been slapped. Would any woman have done? she wondered. Would Mollie have been just as much of a pleasure to him as she herself had been? Would Emma Gray, or any woman at all?

She felt as if, with those few, all-too-casual words, Luke had erased the entire encounter. Something she had guiltily thought of as pure bliss had now turned into *How I Made a Fool of Myself on the Oregon Trail.*

She felt tears burning behind her eyes and was even more embarrassed. "I must go," she said quietly, sitting up and gathering her things. "Make sure you clean that wound."

She looked at him quickly, and for a second, in his eyes, it looked as if he knew he had hurt her. He opened his mouth, looking troubled.

But then he closed it again, and she turned away, feeling like the world's biggest fool.

Fourteen

Charlotte tossed and turned all night long, her body tormented by a need for more of what Luke had given her, her heart in pain from the memory of Luke's cruel, casual words. She knew that the rest of the caravan was asleep, dead to the world from the exhaustion that to Charlotte usually felt like a black cloak dropping over her head, putting her to sleep within seconds.

But on this night, sleep eluded her, and she walked outside when it was not quite light, in those moments before dawn in which everyone slept, even the women.

Except that one person, Charlotte saw, was awake as well, creeping out from Ethel and Martin Crowley's wagon. Dawn drew one second nearer, and Charlotte saw that the person was a woman, holding her skirt as she climbed into Ella Mae and Stanton Jespersen's wagon. Now this was strange, strange enough that Charlotte forgot about her troubles with Luke as she waited.

The figure emerged from the wagon after only a few moments, and the dawn half-light shed one more shade of darkness. And Charlotte saw that the figure was Mollie Smithers, now running back toward her own wagon, holding up her skirt with one hand and a satchel in the other.

And Charlotte was left wondering thoughts that were pleasantly, juicily ungenerous to Mollie: What had she been doing in the wagons?

Charlotte had heard many stories of thefts and crimes in the last few weeks, stories of men, like Francis, who had been driven out of the wagon train or hanged for their actions. She had heard of a woman, Maisie Claypool, who had been hanged because she had stolen money from her cousin.

And now Mollie . . . what else, Charlotte wondered, could she have been doing except stealing? Unless she had been searching for . . . what, in the darkness, creeping around like a frightened mouse?

Charlotte began preparing breakfast, setting out her pans and flour and water and jam on the flattened grass outside the tent and imagining, as she always did, how her mother would have cringed at all the bugs and dirt and dust.

Suddenly, a scream shattered the morning quiet. Three tents away, Ella Mae Jespersen was running around like an overly plump chicken with her head cut off. "They're gone!" she shrieked, her gray-streaked brown hair flying in all directions. "My life savings, the only thing I had that was worth more than a hill of beans!"

Out of the corner of her eye, Charlotte saw Mollie Smithers peek out of her tent. Then the flap closed shut again.

"Are you right positive, Ella Mae?" Grace Brinton asked, stepping forward into the knot of women who had quickly gathered around Ella

Mae, eager for the intrigue her loss had promised. "I wasn't going to say anything, but my Irish linen table runner went missing just last night. I was looking through my pine chest, wondering how long it'd be afore Jess tells me we'll have to pitch the chest out on to the trail, and—"

"Good lord, Grace, we'll all be dead and buried before you finish telling 'em!" her husband snapped, spitting onto the ground. "You prob'ly forgot where you put the danged thing is all—"

"I most certainly did not—"

"Well, *my* wagon looks like a squirrel burrowed through half my possessions this morning," Ethel Crowley said, wringing her hands.

Out of the corner of her eye, Charlotte saw Mollie Smithers whispering to her father, her beautiful mouth moving quickly, her hands gesturing with great animation as she spoke. Jock Smithers seemed to puff out and grow larger as Mollie spoke, his face getting redder and redder as he listened.

And then he stormed off toward his tents and wagon. "Where in hell is that Biddy Lee?" he called out, his voice booming.

It couldn't be happening. But as if Charlotte had read all of the details in a book, she could guess: Mollie was the one who had committed the thefts; and now, before she could get in any trouble, she was going to blame Biddy Lee.

"Wait a minute!" Charlotte called out toward Mr. Smithers.

She could see all eyes in the crowd on her as Mr. Smithers stopped and turned.

She had always been a little bit afraid of the man, of his tiny blue eyes set deep in that puffy red face. And of how big his body was, a huge, beefy frame with enough muscle and fat to make Charlotte think of the largest steer her family had ever owned.

"I beg your pardon?" he asked as Charlotte reached him. Mr. Smithers narrowed his eyes as he looked Charlotte up and down. "Was it my imagination you called out to me, Miz Dalton, or did you have something to say? Something so important you had to stop me from what I was doing?"

Charlotte's throat was dry, and her heart was thudding in her chest. She looked back toward the Smithers wagons and saw Biddy Lee standing beside it.

"I asked you a question, Miz Dalton," he barked.

"Biddy Lee didn't do it," Charlotte said.

She wouldn't have thought Mr. Smithers's eyes could get any smaller and still stay open, but she was wrong: They narrowed to fury-filled slits that were sparking with hatred. "Just what is it that you're so sure my Biddy Lee didn't do, Miz Dalton?"

Charlotte struggled to find her voice. "I had thought *you* thought Biddy Lee took those things from the Jespersens' and Crowleys' wagons," she said.

"What I think," he said, stepping forward so he was only inches away from Charlotte, "is my business and no one else's. What trouble Biddy Lee may be in is my business, and no one else's. Do you understand that?"

"She's over here!" Carlene Smithers called out, holding on to Biddy Lee's upper arm with both hands. "Jock, that thieving whore is right here!" Hatred and excitement had made her voice shrill.

"I know for a fact that Biddy Lee didn't do it," Charlotte heard herself say, feeling as if it were years earlier and she was arguing bitterly with her father.

"And just how would you know that, less'n you've spent twenty-four hours a day with a slave who's s'posed to be working for *me*, not you?"

"Let's string her up now and get it over and done with!" Lavinia Smithers called out.

"Biddy Lee did nothing!" Charlotte cried out. "I absolutely know that!"

Out of the corner of her eye, she saw a shape move toward her—she thought Luke, by the size and coloring, but she wasn't sure. "I saw your daughter leaving those wagons this morning," she said. "I saw it with my own eyes."

A murmur rippled through the crowd, and Charlotte thanked God there were enough good people in the crowd—the Vestrows, Alma and Zeke, George Penfield and many others—that she and Biddy Lee would be protected . . . she hoped.

"Why, you lying whore," Jock Smithers whispered. "And that would be right after you finished servicing Mr. Luke Ashcroft—"

The punch came from nowhere, a flash of rage and power as Luke's fist connected with Smithers's jaw and knocked the man to the ground. Luke moved on top of him and grabbed him by his shirt, forcing his neck into an odd, painful-looking bend. "You ever speak to Charlotte like that again and you're a dead man."

Charlotte wouldn't have believed she could ever see fear in eyes like Mr. Smithers's, but there it was, fresh and new and real. "Take your hands off me," he breathed. "Get off me, Ashcroft."

"Apologize to Mrs. Dalton and I might consider it," Luke said, pulling the shirt tauter.

"She accused my daughter—"

"Because your daughter probably did it," Luke said. "If Mrs. Dalton says she saw Mollie, then she saw her. Now, apologize or you can start eating your words in the form of dirt."

Smithers closed his eyes, and Charlotte realized, in that moment, that she had never had a grown man apologize to her.

Then again, maybe she never would: Smithers had said nothing.

"Fine. Have it your way," Luke began, reaching for some dirt.

"All right!" Smithers cried out. "I apologize."

"To what?" Luke demanded. "The sun? That ox over there? Who are you apologizing to?"

Smithers sighed. "I apologize to Miz Dalton," he finally said.

Luke glared at him as he let go of his shirt and then stood up. "You stay away from Mrs. Dalton, Smithers. And from Biddy Lee. You understand?"

Jock Smithers dusted himself off as he stood up. "What makes you think I'd have any truck with—"

"One wrong word," Luke whispered. "In fact, let

me help you find your way back to your tent," he said, taking Smithers in a rough grip by the arm.

Suddenly Smithers began yelling over his shoulder. "What the devil is everyone staring at?" he called out.

The crowd—almost all women—began dispersing, shuffling back to their tents and wagons and campfires. All except for Mollie Smithers, who stood quietly next to Charlotte as if she were her best friend.

"You know, no one's going to believe you—no one *did* believe you—and Biddy Lee's just going to suffer horribly because of you—"

"You mean because of you," Charlotte said. "You told your father Biddy Lee had taken those things before anyone could think it might have been someone else—"

"And? So what?" Mollie asked, her eyes glittering smugly. "Biddy Lee is a colored girl," Mollie said with a shrug. "If she had been lucky enough to be born white, she'd be free—"

Charlotte shook her head. "You're going to be sorry for what you've done, Mollie. Someday—"

Mollie laughed in her face. "Do you know, Charlotte? The truth is that *you're* going to be sorry for what you've done. Because of what you've done—not me—everyone in the caravan knows you've been in Luke's tent. Everyone thinks you're a whore, and everyone thinks Biddy Lee is a thief." She took a deep breath, her cheeks flushed with anger. "And do you know, you probably still think you've gotten what you want—

Mr. Luke Ashcroft—but you have no idea he's just having some fun with you on a long, lonely journey."

And with those words, she flounced off, as carefree-looking as if she were at a Saturday night dance at her hometown church.

The words echoed in Charlotte's ears as if Marcus were still yelling them, though hours had since passed: "I can't understand why you would stick your neck out for a slave when you wouldn't even defend your husband!" he had shouted.

"Maybe because Biddy Lee didn't do anything wrong!" Charlotte had shouted back, feeling bad when she saw how upset Lucinda looked.

"Charlotte only did what was right," Lucinda suddenly said. "Biddy Lee happens to be a good friend of ours, Marcus, whether you like it or not." She shot Charlotte a look that said they were sisters of the heart, sisters who stuck together no matter what.

Marcus must have been too stunned, Charlotte figured, by Luce's outburst to say anything more about it.

Now, as Charlotte walked outside in the middle of the night, she could hear the baby crying inside Lucinda and Marcus's tent, and worry settled around her heart like a heavy, wet cloak. Would Marcus take his feelings about her out on Lucinda and the baby? Would he slap the boy across the face as her father had done to both her and Lucinda? Or slap Luce because she had finally spoken her mind?

"Have they woken up?" came a voice from behind Charlotte—low, affectionate, concerned.

In the moonlight, Luke's handsome features
looked darker, rougher, than she remembered.
She tried to stop herself from being happy that he
had come to search her out. The only conclusion
she had been able to come to about the night before was that she felt like a stranger to her own
heart. She knew she loved Luke, yet she knew she
would never trust a man. She knew she needed
him physically, but she knew, too, that this was a
weakness she had to fight.

And most important of all, she knew that Luke
was clear about *her:* He had needed a woman, and
probably any woman would have done.

Charlotte was about to answer Luke when she
heard the sound of Lucinda's voice, and then
Marcus's, talking quietly.

Luke put his arm around her and led her off toward the edge of the caravan. "No need to inter-
fere," he whispered. "As long as we know the
baby's all right."

Charlotte looked up at him, saying nothing.
She hadn't ever heard him say "we" to include
her, and she had never thought he'd have any
feelings about someone else's baby, one way or
another. "I'm not used to hearing a man worry
about someone else's baby," she said quietly.

Luke was silent, leading her through the blanket of thick darkness that lay beyond the edge of
the circle of wagons.

"When you lose one," Luke said, his voice
rough with emotion, "you think your life can't go

on." He stopped and faced Charlotte. "But life does go on. And you start closing yourself off, because there's too much pain. And then you see something, or hear something, a young'un who looks like yours." He took a deep breath. "Your Lucinda's boy is the image of my John," he said softly.

Charlotte didn't know what to say. "That must be very hard," she finally said, wishing she could comfort him. But she didn't even know where to begin.

At first, Luke said nothing. And then, in a voice that was cold and hard, he said, "What's done is done." He began walking again, and Charlotte followed, wanting to hear more. "Which is one reason I'll be logging out west. No commitments, no feelings. Just me, George, and acres of trees."

His words stung. Not that she had wanted to plan a future with Luke, because she didn't; but to hear Luke be so blunt . . .

"You're very quiet tonight," he said softly, stopping to face her in the moonlight, by a hillock of scrubby trees.

She didn't want to talk. She didn't want to have heard the words he had spoken, because she didn't want to be vulnerable.

"Talk to me," he said softly, taking her into his arms. "Remember what we said? A man and woman have to talk. About anything and everything."

"You overheard me and Lucinda saying that," Charlotte said.

"Saying what?" he asked, looking mystified.

"'Anything and everything,'" Charlotte answered. "Those are the words Luce and I have always used—our promise to each other to keep no secrets."

He was shaking his head, his length pressed against hers, his eyes fiery with passion. "I've told you from the beginning, Charlotte. I know you. I want to know everything about you, but I know you in some deep, natural way." He moved against her, hardening into her softness, running his warm, strong hands over her hips. "We need each other," he whispered.

She shook her head. "Last night you said you needed a woman—" she began.

"I needed *you*," he said, his voice husky. "I've hardly begun showing you what it feels like to feel good," he whispered before he covered her lips with his.

Charlotte tried to fight her own body, to tell herself that the heat that flooded between her legs wasn't her own, that it wasn't her heart pounding in her chest, that her nipples didn't feel as if they were on fire.

She pulled back from him and shook her head, forcing herself to speak words she didn't fully mean. "Luke, I don't want to be your mistress," she said.

His eyes were smoky with passion. "Then we'll stop whenever you want," he whispered. With a light but knowing touch, he moved a hand inside her blouse as he unbuttoned it with his other hand. As he pulled off her chemise, it felt like silk against her skin. Every touch was somehow new and different, luxurious and pleasurable. Cupping her breasts, thumbing her nipples, he never took his eyes from her. Daring her, knowing how she was feeling, knowing how her most secret, private spot was flowing with need. "If you want me to," he said, undoing her skirt, letting it drop to the ground, "I'll stop, Charlotte. Always."

He pulled her pantaloons down and scooped her up in his arms, carrying her over the hillock into a small gorge. Carefully holding her, naked in his arms, he managed to tear off his shirt, laying it on the ground. As he laid her on the shirt, she couldn't believe she was lying there for him to see in the moonlight; his eyes were hungry, passionate, as he looked her up and down. "Don't forget what I said," he whispered, his palm gently trailing fire below her navel. The heel of his hand circled her mound, moistening it as it circled slowly, insistently. "I'll stop. Whenever." He lowered his lips to her neck, tracing hot, wet kisses, running the tip of his tongue in teasing circles down her chest, around each nipple, as his hand worked its own secret, velvety liquid magic between her legs.

Charlotte knew she could never, would never tell Luke to stop. He was right in some deep way that had nothing to do with logic or reason. She *was* his woman, in her heart, her body and her soul. Her mind, through words she couldn't even speak, said No, but of what use was that?

Luke trailed his lips down her stomach, and

Charlotte could say nothing except "Luke," over and over between moans of pleasure.

She clutched at his hair as his tongue began stroking her most sensitive spot. "Luke," she whispered, her hips arching.

"Take your time," he murmured as his hands moved along her inner thighs, then held her hips as Charlotte writhed in sweet torment. His tongue flicked and teased her, and Charlotte was caught in pleasure that was white-hot. And then she went over the edge, rippling wave after rippling wave of ecstasy, crying out the name of the man she loved.

Luke moved up, on top of her, parting her legs and entering her, making her insides flame even deeper. "Go with it, Charlotte," he whispered, looking down at her with eyes heavy-lidded with passion. "Let yourself come as many times as you want. For yourself and for me."

She hadn't ever thought she could feel so much pleasure, hadn't ever thought she could feel that way so soon after having it happen once. But she felt it burn as Luke's hips quickened, his thrusts grew deeper, drops of sweat cascaded from his forehead onto her chest.

She raked her hands into his back and moaned into his shoulder, tasting him as she exploded in pleasure. And Luke let go, searing her as he groaned, quickened, and quietly, so quietly she almost wasn't sure she had heard it, said "Charlotte."

Fifteen

It had been a hot, dusty, difficult morning, starting with one of Charlotte's oxen's hooves going
sore to the point that even Charlotte thought
about turning the poor animal, Dan, into meat.
Baby Jacob had cried all morning and Lucinda
had been acting strangely, too, crying nearly con-
stantly. "I just need to be left alone, by both of
you!" she finally said, looking from Marcus to
Charlotte.

Charlotte had walked on ahead, gathering
chips and weeds for the night's fire, trying not to
give in to the flood of feelings about Luke that
threatened to invade her every moment, and
wondering why she hadn't been able to tell Lucinda all that had happened with Luke.

She knew now that she would never be able to
put him out of her mind. She knew it with a deep
certainty that was like an engraving on a grave-
stone. He was The One for her, the one true love
she and Lucinda had always talked about finding,
the one she had sworn she would never want.

Of course, as Luke had said himself, he was a
man who would never marry again, never even
love her as she wanted to be loved.

Oh, she had certainly believed she wanted to
be alone all these years, independent and without

a man. And part of her wouldn't ever trust a man: Men always did change, and always for the worse.

Yet she wanted Luke.

She knew in her heart that she *could* survive on her own, that she knew enough about animals and the sun and the soil to live alone and do fine. She knew, too, that it was better to have no husband at all than to have the wrong husband.

Yet she wanted Luke.

She suddenly realized she hadn't heard a sound from either Lucinda or Jacob in quite some time. She hung up the bag of chips she had been collecting and stepped inside the wagon.

"Marcus!" she called out.

Lucinda lay on the floor of the wagon with her eyes closed, her skin as pale as the moon, a dark pool of blood spreading out beneath her. Baby Jacob lay by her chest, sleeping as well, his little bow-tie mouth open, his thin little cheeks pale.

Marcus poked his head in. "What?" he asked.

Charlotte felt the oxen grind to a halt. "Better go get Mrs. Gunderson," she said quietly.

From his face, Charlotte could tell that he had seen the blood. A moment later, he was gone.

As carefully as she could, Charlotte picked up the baby and laid him down on the soft patchwork quilt her mother had made for the grandchild she would probably never see.

And then Charlotte began gathering what clean cloths she could, knowing she was already acting panicked. Yes, the bleeding had to be stemmed, but Lucinda had to be given more ergot—or something other than clean cloths!

She's not going to survive this, an inner voice said, and Charlotte shook her head, the panic making her hands begin to go numb. *Think!* she said to herself. *Think!* What if Lucinda were a horse or a cow? What medicine would be given?

And then another question sliced through the panic: What if Mrs. Gunderson didn't come? Several people in the caravan had been distant toward her since the incident with Biddy Lee and the Smithers family. What if Mrs. Gunderson had turned on her as well?

But at that moment, Mrs. Gunderson peeked her wrinkled, no-nonsense face into the wagon and stepped in. "So many days after the young'un's birth," she said, shaking her head. " 'Tain't good, Charlotte. You know that."

"I know you can help her," Charlotte said. "You saved Euphemia Brice and Jessamine Grant."

Mrs. Gunderson was still shaking her head as she lifted Lucinda's skirts at the same moment that the wagon jolted back into its slow, uneven rhythm.

So Marcus was driving the team again, Charlotte said to herself. There was little choice, of course, but to go on.

Lucinda's legs looked rail-thin, her veins merely suggestions of color, her ankles nearly as thin as her son's.

Charlotte held her breath as Mrs. Gunderson raised Lucinda's skirt higher. She didn't want to see how much blood had seeped from her body, didn't want to think what it meant that Lucinda wasn't waking up.

"The poor thing," Mrs. Gunderson murmured. "I always say if men had to endure the pain and death of childbirth, we'd find our get-togethers with them to be few and far between."

With guilt and shame, Charlotte thought of her pleasure the night before, of her selfish thoughts about her own needs and desires. And she pushed another thought out of her mind, one that had tried to nag at her since morning: childbirth; a child; a baby born of a passion she hadn't been strong enough to control.

"Put compresses on your sister as often as you can, Charlotte," Mrs. Gunderson said in a queer, frightened voice. "If you have no clean cloths—"

"I'll find them," Charlotte cut in. "There's nothing else—?"

Mrs. Gunderson looked into her eyes. "You must work from the inside, dear, and with your sister in this dreamy state . . ." Her voice drifted off as she wiped her hands on a handkerchief and then reached into her satchel. She pressed a sachet of powder into Charlotte's hand. "You force the poor thing to take one pinch of this every four hours if she wakes up. It's my own trail concoction, ergot with a trace of willow bark and a bit of gunpowder for good measure."

"She has to wake up," Charlotte said, glancing over at Jacob, who, miraculously, was still sleeping. *She has to wake up,* Charlotte told herself. How could anyone with a baby like that not wake up again, if only just to breathe in the smell of the top of his head or to feel those tiny fingers even one more time?

Wake up so we can have a long talk about anything and everything, Charlotte thought. *Wake up so Marcus can tell you I'm a clumsy, demanding shrew, and you can say we're sisters and that is all that matters. Wake up so you can tell me not to be in love.*

Mrs. Gunderson put a hand on Charlotte's cheek. "It'd be a miracle, child, but then if we didn't believe in miracles, not one of us would have made this journey."

A moment later, she was gone. Charlotte applied compress after compress, but to no avail. She had no idea how much time had passed when Jacob woke up with a wail. Charlotte felt certain it was a signal of what the world would be like without her sister.

Jacob's wails turned to screams, his little hands waving in the air, and as Charlotte picked him up and held him against her chest, she hoped against hope that his cries would wake Lucinda.

But she lay motionless, in some place that was too far away for her to return.

"I'll find milk for you," Charlotte whispered. "I promise I will, honey."

She told Marcus she was taking Jacob to look for someone to nurse him, and Marcus nodded absently. "Mrs. Gunderson said there wasn't anything she could do for Lucinda," he said quietly, as if speaking in a dream.

Charlotte walked on, heading for the nearest woman she knew who was nursing. She hadn't ever said more than a few words to Amelia

Wetherwax, one of the older mothers of babies in the caravan. But they had bathed near each other at Alcove Spring, and she was close by, and Charlotte couldn't imagine anyone turning down a newborn baby who might very well lose his mother.

Mrs. Wetherwax was driving her teams of oxen, her children riding in the wagon. As Charlotte approached, Mrs. Wetherwax—gaunt, with light brown, stringy hair and gray, worried-looking eyes—glanced at her and then looked away.

"My sister is quite ill," Charlotte called out. "I was wondering if you'd be able to put her boy by you for a few minutes later on, Mrs. Wetherwax."

Mrs. Wetherwax whipped at one of the oxen as if Charlotte hadn't spoken.

"Mrs. Wetherwax?"

"Up!" she called out, urging her worn-out oxen to pick up their pace.

"The boy's got no mother!" Charlotte heard herself say, wincing at words she hoped weren't true.

"And I'm a churchgoing woman with a church-going husband," Mrs. Wetherwax snapped. "I'd like to keep it that way, Mrs. Dalton."

"And why on earth would I want to change that?" Charlotte cried out. "I just want to get the baby fed!"

"Maybe you should have thought of that before . . ." Her voice trailed off. "Maybe you should have thought of that before all your meddling and . . . and indecent ways." With another crack of the whip, she moved on.

Charlotte turned and walked away, holding Jacob against a chest that felt useless and stark.

Lucinda. She was going to slip away and die, and in Jacob's overheated, hungry little body, Charlotte felt all the life that was probably slipping away from her sister at that very moment.

"Well, well, well," came a female voice from behind Charlotte. "Visiting Amelia Wetherwax all of a sudden?" Mollie asked. "Do you really think she'd have anything to do with the likes of you? Most women in the caravan—"

"You'd think most women in the caravan would have the decency, if they possessed any milk for a baby, to share it."

Mollie shrugged. "I told you before, Charlotte, you've made a big mistake if you think Mr. Luke Ashcroft is ever going to marry you when you've already given him what men hope to get when they marry. My mother says—"

"Get out of here before I knock you to the ground," Charlotte said. "I have more important things to worry about than what you and your mother think—"

"But—"

"I mean it," Charlotte yelled as she walked away, making Jacob wail.

Not five minutes later, Nora Vestrow took Jacob more than willingly. "You saved our mule, Charlotte. I wouldn't say no to you for anything in the world."

"If you can keep him for a few minutes," Charlotte said, "I'll run back and check on Lucinda. Is that all right?"

"You take your time," Nora called out. "Do what you must do."

To Charlotte's ears, it sounded as if everyone expected Lucinda to die. And in her thoughts that were ruled by logic, she knew that these people had to be right. In the miles they had traveled so far, Charlotte had already counted more than a hundred graves. And those were just the ones that had been marked by families who had possessed the strength and time to do more than dig a hole in the ground.

Somewhere in her heart, somehow deep inside, Lucinda had always been sure that she wouldn't be able to complete the full journey.

As she walked, Charlotte was visited by one memory after another, as if her life were passing before her eyes. As if it were yesterday, she could remember pulling Lucinda along in their sled, Lucinda's little face frozen but determined. She could remember making cookies as a surprise for their mother, Lucinda's cheeks and nose covered with molasses and butter. She could remember holding her at night after she had awakened from a nightmare, and holding her as they had listened to their pa rant against their mama.

And suddenly, she was certain that the same memories were reaching Lucinda, touching her for the last time.

"She didn't wake up?" she asked Marcus.

He gave her a stony, desperate look. "What do *you* think?" he asked. "The captain says one more mile and we'll camp for the night," he added, as if this information had some bearing on Lucinda's health.

Charlotte moved past Marcus and stepped up into the wagon.

Lucinda had moved! She had changed position and was now lying on her side, her breathing slow and even.

Charlotte moved closer and knelt down by Lucinda, preparing to pray for what seemed like the hundredth time that day . . .

And Lucinda opened her eyes.

"Luce," Charlotte whispered.

"Shh," Lucinda whispered. She reached out and put a cold, thin hand against Charlotte's cheek. "I'll be all right," she murmured.

"I can give you Mrs. Gunderson's cure now that you're awake!" Charlotte said, starting to stand up.

But Lucinda grabbed her by the wrist and held on, surprisingly tightly. "It's too late," she said softly. "I came back for your promise."

"What?"

"Do you truly promise to watch over Jacob? I want you raising him. Not Marcus and—and whoever."

"I—" Charlotte began, but tears blocked her voice.

"Just swear," Lucinda whispered, squeezing Charlotte's hand.

"I promise," Charlotte finally said, her voice cracking. In a story Charlotte had read often, an old Indian woman had known exactly when she was going to die, and she had simply lain down at the top of her favorite mountain, crossed her arms and passed on.

Now, she looked at her sister as she closed her eyes, and she whispered, "No. Please, Lucinda."

Her sister had read the story, too—their mother had read it to them by the fire even when they were nearly grown up.

Lucinda had taken in the words.

And the spirit.

"Lucinda," Charlotte whispered.

The sweat ran off Marcus's forehead, down his neck, down his thin, weak-looking arms. He chopped at the earth as if it were a massive oak, making as little headway as if he were a small boy with a toy shovel.

"If you'd let me take a turn, Marcus, we could make it deep enough—"

"It's deep enough now," he said, throwing down the mattock.

Charlotte stared. "Are you out of your mind?" she cried out. "You haven't even dug two inches down!"

"It's pointless and you know it," he said, wiping off his hands on his pants.

He had barely dirtied them, and he was calling the job done.

"Do you know what Lucinda's greatest fear about the trail was?" Charlotte asked.

"No, but I'm sure you're going to tell me," Marcus said, beginning to walk away.

"Her greatest fear was that wolves would dig up her body. I want to dig a grave deep enough to make sure that doesn't happen—"

"Then you're a fool!" he snapped. "We're moving on in the morning."

"Then I'll have it done, or I'll catch up with you. I'm not leaving her—"

"She's dead!" he said, spitting on the ground near where Lucinda's body lay wrapped in the quilt Charlotte had made her for her tenth birthday. "Nothing's going to change that," he muttered, and he walked away.

Charlotte knew he was in pain, that Lucinda's death was hurting him, even if he had a strange way of showing it. He had to be worried about raising Jacob without a mother, and probably the truth of Lucinda's death hadn't yet sunk in.

As Charlotte heard him walk away, tears rolled down her cheeks. She'd keep digging, she told herself as she picked up the mattock and swung it into the hard soil, so if there was one thing on earth she was sure of, it would be that Lucinda's bones would never be dug up, and her body would truly rest in peace.

But there was so much to regret, so many last moments she would never be able to recover. She had wanted to tell Lucinda more about Luke; she had wanted to tell her everything. But somehow, she had always found some reason that the time wasn't right. She had been afraid, she now knew, to tell Luce how she had fallen in love with Luke, because that would have made it real and final and true. Deep in her heart, she had believed that if she didn't tell Luce, then she couldn't have been foolish enough to have actually fallen in love.

And now, it was too late to tell her anything, much less anything and everything. She would never again hold those thin shoulders in her arms, never again remember sewing with Mama together, or feeding calves together, or trying to hide a litter of new kittens from their pa, or holding each other after a whipping.

"Oh, Luce," Charlotte said out loud. "I'm going to miss you so much." And poor baby Jacob, who had more of a need for Lucinda than anybody. For how long would he wonder where his mama was, Charlotte wondered, before she finally faded from his memory? When he cried in the night, would she be able to comfort him at all? Would he know to stop expecting to see his true mother?

Suddenly Charlotte saw a shadow pass across the shallow grave. And then someone put an arm around her waist.

"Over here," Luke said, leading Charlotte away from the grave.

"I'm digging my sister's grave!" Charlotte screamed, shaking Luke away.

"Come with me," he said softly, taking her hand. "If you'd like to visit your sister sometime in the future, maybe with Jacob when he's older, you'll want a spot you'll always be able to find."

Luke stopped by some cottonwood saplings, where three huge boulders lay in a group as if a giant had set them down. At first, Charlotte didn't even see a hole. She had been looking at the collection of boulders because it was so perfect.

And then she saw a hole, a grave Luke had already made three feet deep.

She had known that Lucinda was dead; she had been digging her own version of a grave and watching Marcus dig for more than an hour. Yet, somehow, this sight—a gaping, dark hole—suddenly brought the truth of Lucinda's death as sharply into Charlotte's heart as if it were a knife.

And she began to sob against Luke's chest, to cry deeply for the first time since Lucinda had died.

"That's just what you need to do," Luke whispered, wrapping his arms around her and swaying softly. "Cry as hard as you can, Charlotte."

He breathed in her hair and held her close and remembered the night before, when he had heard her cry out his name. He rubbed her back and closed his eyes and imagined they were the only two people in the world.

He would protect her forever, he knew. He could remember feeling this perfect with Parmelia, mornings when they had lain together and he had smelled her hair, stroked her skin, loved her. And wanted it to last a lifetime.

Suddenly he opened his eyes. He had a grave to finish digging.

And a life to lead. The one he had planned down to the last detail. Logging and money. No ties, no family.

"Let's get back to digging," he said softly, "so we'll know nothing can ever get to her, Charlotte. And then we'll mark the stone. Other people will bury their kin here soon enough, thinking the same thoughts we've had."

Even in the darkness, he saw her eyes fill up

with tears all over again. "Oh, Luke," she whispered, and she fell into his arms again.

He wanted to hold her like that forever. He wanted to hold her, breathe in her scent, feel her in his arms. Believe it would last forever.

And then he caught himself. He wasn't going to be drawn in by her. Never, not ever. He would never love again, never feel the way he had felt about Parm and John. There would be no attachments, no ties, no guilt.

"We'd better get to work," he said quietly, letting go of her.

And he told himself that he must keep his distance from Charlotte, no matter how much she tempted him.

Dearest Mama, Charlotte wrote, tears streaming down her face. *I am so sorry to tell you that I have bad news about Lucinda . . .*

Sixteen

Charlotte had thought she wouldn't sleep that night. How much would she be able to sleep, she had wondered, after burying her sister?

Luke had carried Lucinda's body to the grave and laid her in it with the quilt. "Do you have anything else you'd like to put in?" he had asked softly. "Something of Jacob's and something of yours?"

Charlotte had gone and gotten a soft cloth of Jacob's, a kerchief of hers, and a letter their mama had written, years back. And then sobbed as she and Luke had covered Luce's body with moist, cool earth.

And then sleep she had, because her exhausted body had forced her to, mercifully making her forget what the day and night had brought.

Nora Vestrow had nursed baby Jacob until he was, as Nora had put it, "drunk with milk, the poor thing," and thankfully, he had slept in a small, peaceful bundle on top of Charlotte's chest the whole night.

Now, though, as Charlotte awakened to pitch-black darkness, for a moment she thought she was still dreaming. "Don't be scared," a female voice was whispering.

The baby made a small sound, and Charlotte rubbed her lips against the top of his head as she had often seen Luce do. It was soft and silky and warm. Carefully, she laid Jacob in a nest of blankets.

"It's me," the voice said. "Biddy Lee."

"Biddy—? What time is it?"

"Shh," Biddy Lee whispered again. "An hour till dawn. I didn't know you'd have the baby with you."

Charlotte shrugged in the darkness. "I'm amazed I didn't have to fight Marcus about it. But he probably wanted his sleep. What are you doing here?"

"Hiding," Biddy Lee said. "And I swore, Char-lotte, no more trouble on me or you, but that Skete crawled into my tent five minutes ago and started pawing at me, and all that kept me from screaming bloody murder was—you remember how Mr. Luke Ashcroft swung that punch at Jock Smithers and shoved him into the dirt?"

Charlotte couldn't help smiling at the memory. "I could never forget."

"Do you know he couldn't stop himself? Jock Smithers was threatening his woman, and a team of wild horses wouldn't have stopped him defending you. Well, if I had screamed the way I wanted to, Ben Lucius would have come running and punched Skete till he killed him. And then Ben would be a dead man, too."

Jacob stirred for a moment, moving his lips, rosy and full, as if he were kissing someone in his sleep.

Biddy Lee looked down at him and shook her head. "So innocent," she said. "Why they have to change into men, I'll never know."

Charlotte laughed, and Biddy Lee laughed, and Biddy Lee put a hand on Charlotte's shoulder. "It's all right to laugh, you know," she said, reading Charlotte's mind. "There's an ache in your heart for your sister that will never go away. But you have to live, too, Charlotte. Lucinda would have wanted that."

Outside, dawn arrived suddenly, in that rippling, bright way that Charlotte knew meant it was going to be a white-hot, cloudless day.

Jacob opened his eyes, looked at Charlotte, and began to wail.

Charlotte gathered him up into her arms. "I'll take care of you," she murmured, holding him against her chest and wishing she didn't have to depend on another woman to give him milk.

He shifted unhappily, a movement she could recognize even though she had never felt it before: fists dug into her hair, his little body went rigid, and then he began to wail. And Charlotte felt the pain of missing Lucinda more sharply than ever: She had been missing Luce as a girl, thinking of all the times, both good and bad, that they had shared as children. But in Jacob's cry, she heard the loss of all the years of Lucinda's motherhood that would never happen now.

"I'll get some milk from that nice Mrs. Vestrow," Charlotte said, pulling on her clothes. Suddenly she saw that Biddy Lee was holding Elizabeth Grace under her arm.

Now Biddy Lee held the doll out. "Would you keep Elizabeth Grace for me? I keep thinking on them Smitherses throwing her into the fire the way your pa did."

"Of course," Charlotte said.

"Well, I'll be late less'n I go yesterday," she said. "I just pray those girls slept through all that went on."

"Do you think they saw Skete crawl into your tent?"

It was as if a dark cloud had passed across Biddy Lee's face. "Those two already imagine worse than that, Charlotte. Pray for us both that Ben didn't see, most of all." And then she was off.

"Waa!" Jacob screamed, and Charlotte held him tightly against her chest.

"I'll get some milk and then we'll see about becoming a new family, just you and me, and your dad sometimes." She looked into his big blue eyes and wondered if he was questioning why his mama wasn't with him. "Your mama is in a beautiful place right now, Jacob. And she's watching to make sure I feed you enough, and kiss you enough, and love you enough. And I'm not going to disappoint her. All right?"

His eyes looked beautiful and mystified.

"Even if you don't understand, honey. I'll never forget the promise I made to your mama, and she'll never, ever forget you," she said.

As she walked out into the already bright light of the Western sky, she promised herself that she wouldn't let anyone, even Marcus, get in the way of her keeping her promise to Luce.

The sun was hot and bright in the sky, and Charlotte felt the heat shimmering up from the ground made it seem as if Lucinda had been gone far longer than she really had been. It was as if they were entering a different world now, drier and more desolate, almost like what Charlotte imagined another planet would look like. A place Luce had never seen and never would see.

She had taken Jacob over to Nora Vestrow to nurse during breakfast, bringing a jar of jam to thank her, along with some dried plums.

"You can leave him in the wagon with mine," Nora had said as she had handed Jacob back to Charlotte, but the offer had sounded half-hearted, and in any case, Charlotte would have said no. Wagons overturned, accidents happened . . . and she and Jacob had to get to know each other.

Yet now, as she walked with Jacob back to the wagon, she realized there was something she had never thought of as far as Marcus was concerned: another woman.

Penny Clusen, a pretty red-haired girl of eighteen or nineteen who was traveling with her sister and her parents, was at that moment talking with Marcus as he drove the teams, walking quite close and hanging on his every word.

"Oh, there he is!" Penny cried out, holding out her arms as Charlotte approached. "May I hold him?"

Before Charlotte could say anything, Marcus had grabbed the baby.

"He was just falling asleep!" Charlotte yelled at her brother-in-law.

Marcus gave her a warning look. "I daresay he has all day to do that, Charlotte. Penny's never met my boy."

"Oh, he's lovely," Penny cooed. "And he looks *just* like his handsome daddy!"

Marcus's pace grew lively and proud as he walked next to Penny and his son.

And Charlotte had to walk away.

Yes, she knew that Marcus deserved to be proud of his boy. And yes, she knew that he would probably marry again. But she hadn't ever thought of it in terms of Jacob.

She had planned on collecting buffalo chips and checking up on the oxen. But all of a sudden, she wanted nothing but to get away—before she said something she'd regret, before she grabbed

Jacob back from Penny Clusen's arms, before she dissolved into tears.

Marcus seemed to be courting Penny Clusen. Or the other way around. Or both. And Penny seemed to want to take care of Jacob.

"I promised Lucinda," Charlotte said out loud. "It simply cannot be."

She didn't know what she would say, what she would do, but she knew she had to do something. She had promised Luce, and she had promised her little nephew.

She turned and headed back for the caravan and was just passing one of the Smithers' tents when she heard screaming.

It was Carlene's voice, impassioned, high-pitched with fury. "You're nothing but a pig and a liar!" she screamed. "If I stay in my right mind, Skete, I swear on my honor never to let your filthy, slave-loving hands touch me again!"

"You're imagining things," Charlotte heard Skete say. "I swear it's in your head, Carlene."

"Don't you even *look* at me!" Carlene shrieked.

She must have torn out of the tent, for suddenly Charlotte found that she was face to face with Carlene.

Carlene Smithers was trembling, pale with fury, and beautiful, Charlotte felt, like a porcelain doll or a wealthy woman from France or England. Carlene's eyes, pale-blue violet, seemed to be trembling too, their lashes dark against milk-white skin. "Your kind and your filthy friends should be banished from this caravan," she seethed.

"That sounds like a fine idea," Charlotte said. "Give your slaves their freedom, Carlene. I'd love to travel with them."

Carlene pursed her lips, looked long and hard at Charlotte and then spat at the ground. "That's what I think of you and your kind," she said.

Charlotte laughed. "Spitting? I never would have thought you had it in you, Carlene."

"Then just you wait," Carlene said. "By the time this journey is done, you're going to learn all kinds of things about what good, right-thinking people can do."

It was near darkness, and Charlotte was cradling Jacob in her arms. She had eaten dinner alone with the baby, and she had tried not to think about why it was just her and Jacob, that Marcus and Penny were off somewhere together. Luke had been busy helping friends, and each time he had walked past Charlotte, he had been eating something—jerked beef, a potato, a hunk of bread—and smiling. "I think I'm eating more this way than if George and I had sat down to a meal," he had said one time as he was walking past, eating what looked like an actual piece of town-made pie.

Charlotte had smiled, but she had felt doomed. She loved everything about the man. She had loved him even in her grief, as he had dug Lucinda's grave. She had loved him as he had helped Zeke with his ox, even if she hadn't known it at the time. And every time he spoke to her, touched her, made her cry out . . .

Yet she could feel as certainly as she knew her own name that she was meant never to love a man, that she would be destined to fulfill her childhood vow never to marry.

"It's going to be you and me, Jacob," she said out loud, stroking the top of his head as he lay curled in her lap. "And that's going to be just fine." Nora had said he had had "enough milk to feed a family of six, Charlotte. Where does the poor little thing put it all?" And now, Charlotte could see Jacob's eyelids growing heavy, his little mouth relaxing, lips curling like the petals of a flower—and Biddy Lee coming toward her, walking quickly and with obvious purpose.

"I need to know something," she said, whispering when Jacob's eyes closed. "Have you seen anything strange? Heard anything strange with the Smitherses?"

"You mean stranger than the usual?" Charlotte asked. "I know Carlene must have seen Skete going into or leaving your tent, Biddy Lee, because she was screaming bloody murder at him this morning."

"My Ben must have seen," she said, letting the words rush out like water. "My Ben must have seen, and he's a man fit to be tied."

"But what did he say? What did *you* say?" Charlotte asked, rocking Jacob in her lap.

"I told him I ran. But he still went crazy. He says Skete isn't going to leave me alone till I'm nine months with his child. And nohow will he let that happen."

"Where is he now?" Charlotte asked.

Biddy Lee shook her head. "I don't even rightly know, Charlotte. I don't know where Skete is, or Jock. I never thought so many men could disappear, but they're all . . ." Her voice trailed off. "I'm scareder than scared, Charlotte."

As if sensing Biddy Lee's fear, Jacob woke up. He looked up into Charlotte's eyes, then Biddy Lee's, then squeezed his eyes shut tight.

"Your mama's kissing you from heaven, sweet thing," Biddy Lee said, laying a hand on his head. "Go to sleep and let your aunt rest up for tomorrow."

Charlotte looked around at the nearly dark campsite. Some fires were still glowing, some lanterns still shone, but many people had already gone to sleep, obeying Captain Tayler's suggestion. "We've had too many layovers so early in the journey," he had said at a meeting at lunch. "We have to push harder tomorrow. So anyone with a head on their shoulders would do well to lay that head down at dusk. That especially goes for wild partygoers like Alma and Zeke Bliss," he had added with a laugh.

"Maybe Ben's back by now and I don't even know it," Biddy Lee suddenly said. "Maybe all the men are back."

Charlotte cradled Jacob in her arms. "Come back and tell me if there's trouble, Biddy Lee," she said before she took Jacob into the tent.

She had seen Luke and George over at Emma Gray and her father's campfire, and she planned to put Jacob to sleep and then to tell Luke about Biddy Lee's worries. She nestled Jacob with his warm little face against her chest and told herself she would get up soon, as soon as she felt his hot, sweet breath waft out of his mouth against her skin, as even and as regular as the clock ticking on the mantelpiece back home. . . .

It was a cry of pain and terror, and Charlotte jerked awake. Where was she?

When she felt Jacob's hot little body against hers, she remembered where she was: in a tent, with her tiny love. Without Lucinda.

Had she heard something or not?

She remembered that she had fallen asleep before she had been able to speak to Luke . . . and that Biddy Lee had been worried about Ben.

She rubbed her eyes, listening for that awful sound. And she heard nothing.

But she couldn't get the memory of that blood-curdling scream out of her mind. It had reminded her, in sleep, of the sound the pigs had made as her father had cut their throats.

Yet now that she was awake, she knew that the sound she had heard—if she hadn't been dreaming—was one she had never heard in her life.

She looked down at baby Jacob and brushed her lips across his cheek. "I'll be back in a second," she whispered, hoping she would find nothing unusual outside, that she had only dreamed of the scream.

But the moment she stepped outside, she knew she had been wrong to hope. In the distance, she saw a fire crackling behind a grove of saplings.

And that alone was strange. Indians wouldn't have had a big fire going like that, Charlotte was pretty sure, but she also saw people moving—jumping up, walking around, moving in a way that looked strange, infused with too much energy, too much enthusiasm for the middle of the night.

Biddy Lee, she suddenly said to herself. Something strange was going on, and Biddy Lee had had a fear that something wasn't right in the caravan.

Charlotte began running, and she ran the way she and Luce had run as girls when they were running from one of their parents' fights, quick as the wind and as light on the ground as kittens, because if their pa caught them running, it would mean a beating.

Only this time, she was running toward something, and as she drew close, she couldn't believe what her eyes told her, what it looked like—

Charlotte covered her mouth.

Her knees buckled.

She cried out something—"Oh no oh no oh no," and then turned and ran back toward the caravan.

She had to find Luke, she told herself. If she found Luke, somehow that would change things, it would make what she had seen—what she thought she had seen—an illusion, something she had imagined in a horrible nightmare.

She stumbled against the rough ground, but she was almost there. She could see Luke's tent in the moonlight, and she knew that if she could only reach him . . .

"Luke!" she called out, her breath and voice nearly gone. She ran in to the tent and nearly bumped into Luke, who was already coming out of it.

"What is it?" he asked, taking her by the shoulders. "Is Jacob all right?"

She shook her head, her voice gone, stolen away by a sight she'd never forget. "Ben," she finally blurted out. "Those men, those awful men, they killed Ben and hanged him, and—" She shut her eyes, sobbing against Luke's chest, unable to say the rest. What she had seen in the moonlight was even worse than what she had told Luke. "They cut off his private parts and flogged him, and he's . . . it's almost not even a body hanging from that tree."

"I'm getting George and the captain and Pete," he said. "You find Biddy Lee."

Charlotte watched Luke run off and then she went looking for Biddy Lee—hoping Biddy Lee was still in her tent.

"Biddy Lee!" Charlotte called, standing outside her tent. "Biddy Lee!"

Charlotte heard a rustling behind her, and she turned.

Carlene and Mollie Smithers were standing there, wrapped in blankets. Both looked giddy, wide-awake and excited.

"What a night!" Mollie said.

Biddy Lee came out of her tent and looked from Charlotte to the two Smithers women, then back to Charlotte. "What—what's going on?"

"Your man is dead!" Carlene said. "He tried to have his way with the two of us, and our men brought him to justice."

218 Elizabeth Clarke

Biddy Lee's hand flew to her mouth.

"Of course, that's what everyone in this caravan has been told," Mollie said.

"Maybe if this slut slave girl hadn't been drooling over my man day and night," Carlene said, "our people wouldn't have had to go after hers."

With a scream, Biddy Lee lunged for Carlene, but Charlotte caught her. "Not now," Charlotte whispered, holding onto Biddy Lee with all her might.

Suddenly it was obvious Biddy Lee saw the campfire in the distance and knew in an instant that Ben was there. And she began running, shaking Charlotte off.

Charlotte ran too, crying as she ran. She felt a sickness in her stomach thinking about what those men had done to poor Ben; hatred welled up in her throat.

"One at a time!" she heard Captain Tayler scream. "You sound like a bunch of jackals! And what you've done." He shook his head. "It looks as if the man was torn limb from limb by an animal."

"We had no choice, sir," a contrite-looking Skete Smithers said as he walked up to Captain Tayler, hat in hand. "Think if you had come upon a slave trying to violate one of your women. Are you telling me you wouldn't have hanged the man before dawn, even if he was one of your own slaves, even if you would take a loss killing your own man?"

"We have a men's council—" Captain Tayler began.

"And we almost couldn't pull that man off my

wife. It took all the strength we had, Captain. He came at us like a crazy man."

"Says who?" Pete Vestrow called out. "You mutilated the man and then you murdered him! By what right?"

"By the right of God!" Jock Smithers thundered. "I challenge any man to say he wouldn't wreak vengeance after an attack like this. You do what you have to do to save your women—"

"And that means cutting up a man like an animal?" Charlotte called out. "You two are so weak that you couldn't hold Ben Lucius down until a council meeting could be called, if any of what you've said is even true."

"Somebody get those women out of here!" Jock Smithers cried out.

Charlotte saw Luke pushing through the crowd of men. "You two go back to camp," he said in a voice that wouldn't allow argument. "Biddy Lee, Ben surely didn't deserve what those men did. But things will only get worse if you two stay here."

Charlotte swallowed against a throat that ached with sadness. Was this what the journey had come to—her sister lost to illness, a man tortured by hatred and ignorance?

"Go," Luke said. "Now. Before it gets worse. Biddy Lee, I can't promise you anything more than this, but I promise I will bury your Ben Lucius for you."

"Mollie and Carlene and Mrs. Smithers were lying," Biddy Lee said. "They told us as much. And I know as much in my own heart, Luke."

"I believe you," Luke said. "And probably all the

right-thinking people in this caravan would believe you, too. But that doesn't amount to more
than a few words from a friend, Biddy Lee. Now
go. Get back to the baby."

The tears flowed down Biddy Lee's face as she
and Charlotte walked back to camp. Charlotte
held her tightly, feeling her shoulders tremble
with sobs.

And then suddenly, the trembling stopped, and
Biddy Lee wiped away her tears. "I'll tell you a secret," she said. "I was thinking of running. I've
been thinking of it ever since Skete first laid his
fat, sick hands on me."

Charlotte knew it was thoroughly selfish of her,
but she didn't think she'd be able to bear another
person leaving, after Luce. "Are you going to do it
now?" she asked softly.

"Now, Charlotte, now this girl is going to stay,"
Biddy Lee said, narrowing her eyes. "Just from
spite and hate and revenge. That Carlene and
Mollie probably thought I'd be halfway to the Territories and quaking in these worn-out rags they
call shoes, but they don't know Biddy Lee Waters
the way *I* know Biddy Lee Waters."

Charlotte didn't say anything. She couldn't
imagine where it would all end. And she couldn't
bear thinking about the pain Ben must have felt
before he was killed.

When she reached the tent, panic gripped her
as she realized she had left Jacob for so long. Mollie and her family knew no boundaries; Marcus
and Penny weren't to be trusted; how could she
have left little Jacob all by himself for so long?

But as soon as she entered the tent, she heard the even breathing that meant Jacob was sleeping peacefully, his nose just a little bit stuffed. She knelt down and scooped him into her arms, needing to hold him.

"That boy there is your future, honey," Biddy Lee said. "I see it as clear as day. That boy and Mr. Luke Ashcroft."

Jacob stirred and nestled against Charlotte's chest, and Charlotte closed her eyes, taking in the smell of the top of his head, warm and soft and downy.

"You can fight it and you can deny it and you can say you don't believe in it, but that doesn't make the truth about Mr. Luke Ashcroft go away," Biddy Lee said. In the half-light, Charlotte saw that Biddy Lee's eyes were glistening with tears. "I fought that Ben Lucius every day of our lives. He would have done anything for me, and now he's gone," she said quietly, tears running down her cheeks again. She gathered up her skirts and moved toward the tent flap.

"Biddy Lee. Wait. Where are you going?"

"I can't stay," Biddy Lee said. "I won't be sleeping tonight, Charlotte."

"Neither will I," Charlotte said. "Neither will anyone who knows what happened, Biddy Lee. Stay with me and Jacob. We'll talk until morning."

Charlotte heard a rustling outside the tent, and she looked at Biddy Lee. Biddy Lee began to move toward the closure, but Charlotte shook her head and handed Jacob to Biddy Lee. "Let me," she whispered.

She opened the flap and saw Carlene and Mollie Smithers walking away. "Stay away from here! How dare you show your faces around here?" Charlotte shouted. Her voice seemed to dissolve thinly into the darkness, and for a moment, she wondered if she had imagined the two shapes she knew so well.

But then she heard laughter. "Don't frighten us, Charlotte. It's just so cruel."

And then they laughed again.

Charlotte's voice rang out in the dark. "On my sister's grave, I swear you two will suffer for what you've done."

More laughter, like high-pitched bells ringing in the darkness, and then Charlotte heard the rapid footfalls that meant the two women had run off, scampering in the darkness like two carefree young girls.

Seventeen

At some point, Charlotte realized as she opened her eyes, she must have fallen asleep. Baby Jacob was sleeping on her chest, and . . .

And then she remembered the horror of the night before. She bolted up, laid Jacob in a nest of blankets, crawled outside—and bumped into Luke.

She stood up, and he took her in his arms. "We

buried Ben," he said softly. "Biddy Lee is with George. She's going to be all right."

"And the Smithers family?" Charlotte asked. "Has someone hanged them from a branch and cut their private parts off? Has someone flogged and flayed them?"

"It's over," he murmured, holding her tight.

"What do you mean, it's over?" she demanded. "What about justice? Are you telling me the men's council thinks it's just fine to murder a man because you feel like it?" She felt like pounding Luke's chest, like punching him to make his words change.

"Listen to me," he said. "It's over, and Ben is dead, and nothing is going to happen to Jock or Skete or their friends. It's wrong, but it's true. The story they've given is that they had to fight for their lives and pull Ben off Carlene and Mollie—"

"But it's a lie! Ben was probably defending Biddy Lee against Skete! He knew Skete was always going after her."

"And it's their word against the word of a slave. Francis was hanged for stealing. The punishment for what they accused Ben of doing is much worse—and should be."

"And you're saying that was *right?*"

"Of course not," Luke said, as a cry rang out from the tent. "I'm saying it's frontier justice."

Charlotte went into the tent, scooped Jacob into her arms and came out, only to see Luke walking away. Walking away?

She wanted to call out to him, but at that mo-

ment she hated him for understanding what had
happened, even for being able to explain what
had happened.

She laid Jacob on the tiny quilt her mama had
made "just for a baby's bottom," and she wiped at
his little bottom, small enough to fit in her hand.
Jacob screamed, and Charlotte realized she felt
like screaming too, at all that had gone so unex-
pectedly wrong on the journey. Why was Jacob
destined to grow up with no mama to hold him
and watch him grow? Why had Ben had to suffer
such pain?

As she laid a soft cloth between Jacob's thin, little legs, he began to scream more loudly, and
Charlotte put some salve for horse and cattle
sores on the chapped, raw spots. There were some
things that she knew, she told herself: She knew
that a salve of chamomile and beeswax and honey
would help soothe baby Jacob's pain; she knew
how to hold him and love everything about him,
the way he smelled, the softness of his skin and
the sweetness of his breath. But there were so
many things she didn't know because she wasn't
Jacob's real mother; and her body felt useless in
the face of his hunger.

"I'll get you some milk as soon—" she began,
and then she stopped as she saw Luke coming
back, holding something in his arms: It looked
like a pitcher and a cup.

Luke was looking at Jacob, and in his face,
Charlotte could see the passion and pain of losing
his son. "You'd do well to learn how to feed your
boy, Charlotte, so you don't need to go running

to other women every time Jacob wants a drink. Now, give him to me and you pour some of that milk into this cup."

She finished bundling Jacob into his clothes and handed the wriggling, hungry boy to Luke. Jacob had stopped screaming, but Charlotte could see, in his angry, impatient, jabbing movements, that he was on the verge of squalling.

Luke held him, and calmed him, and looked as if his heart were breaking, and Charlotte imagined he was remembering his baby son.

She began pouring the milk into the cup Luke had brought, a little silver one with the initials J. A. on it, and she guessed it must have been Luke's son's cup.

"That should be enough," Luke said. "All you want is a few sips, Charlotte."

Charlotte swallowed, wondering how it was that just hearing Luke say her name could have such an effect on her. Since Luce's death, she had been so unsure of everything—unwilling to love, wanting to feel nothing for anyone, least of all for a man. And Luke, she was certain, had sensed this. But now, just hearing him say her name made her feel as if he was holding her. And as she saw how he was holding Jacob, as comfortably as if he had done it for a lifetime, she knew that her heart was in danger.

"Now, you want to put some on your finger first," Luke said as she handed him the cup and he cradled Jacob against one arm. "Make him think you're his mama." He put his finger to Jacob's lips, and Jacob took the milk, moving his lips tentatively at first, then looking up at Luke with surprise and enthusiasm. "Then you tip the cup up," Luke said, "and make him sip it, but not too much; just touch his lips with the milk. Do you see?"

Jacob was drinking, not really sipping at it, but taking the milk in with his lips from the edge of the cup.

As Charlotte watched, she knew that if she hadn't fallen in love with Luke before, she certainly would have right at that moment. He barely knew Jacob, yet he was treating him as if he were his own.

"You'd better try it while I'm here," Luke said, putting Jacob into her arms.

Luke felt the weight lift from his arms, a hungry life force the likes of which he hadn't felt since he had last held John.

And he felt too much—too much loss, too much tenderness for a baby he didn't even know, too much regret for a wrong decision made years earlier.

He looked at Charlotte and saw in her eyes a look he had seen so many times in Parmelia's eyes: She was in love with him. Clear as day. The woman who claimed not to need a man, the woman who planned to farm all on her own when she reached the Territories, was in love with Luke Ashcroft, a man who sure as hell needed her.

But love? It was something he didn't want to see in a woman's eyes and sure as hell didn't want to feel in his heart. If he was going to feel love in his heart ever again, it was going to be for a piece of land, period. End of story.

Jacob cried and reached out for Luke, his little hands clutching at the air, and a voice inside Luke's heart said, *You already feel love for this baby.*

And it was wrong. When he felt the warmth of Jacob's body, he was forgetting John's. As he got used to the smell of Jacob's skin, he would forget the smell of John's; he could feel it happening already.

He had lived a life of love—a life full of love, for his wife and son. He'd had one chance; and now that chance was over.

"Like this?" Charlotte asked, squirming and starting to giggle as Jacob sucked the milk from her finger.

He couldn't love her; he couldn't let her love him, no matter how strong the attraction between them.

"Now tip the cup up," he said. "Now that he wants more, give him more."

Charlotte's eyebrows were nearly up at her hairline as she waited for Jacob to sip. And when he did, she looked amazed. "It worked!" she said.

"Of course it worked," Luke said. "He has this wonderful, beautiful woman feeding him. Who *wouldn't* drink under those circumstances?"

Charlotte's cheeks flushed, and the corners of her mouth turned up—barely. She let Jacob have another sip, and then another and another. And then he curled against her chest, his fists in balls, his eyelids heavy.

"Looks like someone's halfway into a nap already," Luke said.

Charlotte smiled and then looked at him in a

half-reluctant, sidelong way. "I want to thank you for helping me figure all this out," she said, her voice soft and tentative. "I know I couldn't have done it without you."

She looked too pretty and full of feeling. He had to stop things before he hurt her. "Charlotte," he said. He hated to go on, but he knew he had to.

"Yes?" she asked softly.

"You know I'll always help you, every day of this journey. Night or day."

She said nothing.

"You know that. Right?"

"Yes," she said, her voice almost a whisper.

"And you know—" He stopped. How could he tell her he would always want her? Wasn't he trying to do the right thing, to steer her toward someone else, someone who deserved her, who wouldn't hurt her? "What you need to do, Charlotte, is find yourself a partner who wants to be partnered up. God only knows there are enough men on this trail and you should have your pick of the lot."

She looked crushed, as if he had struck her. And for a long moment that felt like a physical pain, he thought she was going to cry. "How is it— why is it—that you've always, from the day we first met, thought you could read my mind, Luke? What makes you think you could possibly know what I want?"

"Because I've always known you," he said, hearing his own voice crack with emotion. "From the moment we first met. As you say."

"Well, you don't if you think I want to be married again, Luke, because I don't."

"Yes, you do. You want to be married, and you want children, in addition to Jacob. You deserve someone who wants those things too."

Tears finally sprang from her eyes. She opened her mouth, closed it, then wrapped Jacob more tightly in her arms and ran back into her tent.

He had broken her heart, and for a moment, White Fox came into his vision. *You must live in the present,* he had said. *You must live your life.*

But White Fox didn't know him. White Fox didn't know him, George didn't know him, Zeke Bliss didn't know him. He had been given a gift in Parmelia and John, and he had failed them.

Charlotte deserved better.

He looked down at the pitcher of milk she had left, the silver cup with initials that broke his heart.

Go to her.

He took a deep breath and walked toward her tent. Then he stopped, set the pitcher and cup down outside the flap, and walked back toward his wagon. Time was a' wasting, and it was time to hit the road.

Eighteen

Charlotte closed her eyes against the hot, sandy wind as she held Jacob tightly, hoping he could somehow continue sleeping in the miserable swirls of dust. She walked on, clucking to the oxen like an old, worn-out mother hen, and she told herself that her lot in life was walking right beside her: She had healed Dan's sore hoof, something she hadn't thought she'd be able to do. But she had; so that was her talent and her future, she guessed: fixing up animals and being good to them. Which, in a certain part of her heart, was what she had always wanted: to farm, to be part of nature.

She had never thought she was being smart when she had first kissed Luke Ashcroft. Even when she had first *looked* at the man, she had known it wasn't a wise thing to do. And oh, why had she ever let him touch her, even that first time, when he had parted her lips with his finger, or when he had carried her into his wagon and put salve on her wound—and then touched her heart? *Those* parts of her life were never meant to have happened.

Off in the distance, she saw Marcus walking hand-in-hand with Penny Clusen, and she felt a surge of hatred.

After dinner tonight, there was going to be another chivaree, this time for a young couple who had met in Independence and decided just yesterday to tie the knot. Charlotte had already decided she'd spend the evening in the wagon with Jacob. Let Marcus dance or do whatever he wanted. She had no use for parties.

"Charlotte!" Biddy Lee's voice called out as Captain Tayler called for the caravan to encamp.

Charlotte saw that Biddy Lee was holding something small and blue. "I finished your boy's bonnet," Biddy Lee said. "The Captain says chill winds are going to blow tomorrow, and I don't want Jacob going sick."

"You finished it today?" Charlotte asked. How could Biddy Lee even have put one foot in front of the other, she wondered, after what had happened to Ben?

"Those women would love for me to crawl into a hole," Biddy Lee said. "My mama taught me my whole life to take one day at a time, Charlotte. One minute at a time if you have to. If I go and fall apart, then they killed me too, as much as they killed Ben Lucius."

Charlotte felt petty and shallow for all her self-pitying thoughts about Luke. She took the bonnet—a beautiful little thing made of gingham and ribbons. "Your mama would be proud of you, Biddy Lee."

Biddy Lee gave her a pitying look. "She *is* proud of me, Charlotte. Just like your sister is proud of you for taking care of her boy. She watches you two night and day. Now I have to go get dinner ready for that lovely family that claims to own me. Put that bonnet on Jacob when he wakes up, and go and enjoy the chivaree tonight."

As Charlotte watched Biddy Lee walk off, she clucked her teams to a halt, right behind the Vestrows' wagon.

"Luke? George? Can you please help me for a minute?" Emma Gray called out. Her father had taken ill last night, and Charlotte didn't know whether he was all right.

Luke and George took off running like greased

lightning, and Charlotte watched as Emma spoke with them. She was pretty and seemed quite kind, having given Biddy Lee a shawl the other day when Biddy Lee's had fallen apart.

But Charlotte felt as if Emma were a different species, someone interesting to watch but totally foreign. It made Charlotte remember one night when she was nine and she had managed to fix the gate to the pigpen before her father had come home from town. She had been sure that he would be proud of her, but he had been furious. "What makes you think any man is going to want to marry you if you do men's work all the time?" he had snapped, almost blind with anger.

Charlotte had opened her mouth but said nothing, crushed. The only man in her life thought she was clumsy and plain and headstrong, and he always would.

"You take my words to heart and don't you forget them," her pa had seethed.

Now she watched George and Luke help Emma with a spoke on one of her wagon's wheels, and she turned away, thinking about Biddy Lee. Her man had suffered a horrendous, painful death, and she had gone on. Charlotte had always wanted to be on her own, and now she was, with a baby boy and the wide, Western sky looking down on her. She had to look forward, toward the future, as Biddy Lee seemed to be doing.

She hugged Jacob close against her chest, took off the worn little bonnet Lucinda had sewn for him and breathed in the smell of his head. He was dusty and dirty, even beneath the thin cotton fabric of his little hat, but oh, what a sweet smell. She would save the bonnet for Jacob, even though it was weak with wear and washing, so that Jacob would always possess something his mama had made for him.

Charlotte felt him squirm, and he opened his eyes and blinked at her—clear, blue, as if he was surprised to be looking at her, but happy all the same.

"Oh, honey," she said softly, "we'll keep each other company tonight and not think about any-one else at all. Does that sound like a plan?"

Charlotte couldn't say she had been expecting any kind of agreement or even a smile. But she hadn't expected what she ended up getting: a big, milky burp in her face.

"I'll assume that means yes," she said with a laugh as she headed off to the Vestrows' wagon to get some milk from Violet for Jacob's dinner.

Jacob cried and cried, and cried some more.

Luke watched Charlotte struggle—she had fed him, and he had drunk his milk and cried. She had changed his clothes and dried him off, and he had cried. Luke thought the sounds of the chivaree might have soothed the boy—Zeke was playing a mean fiddle, Alma was singing, Captain Tayler was playing the harmonica and George was dancing with Emma Gray, kicking up his heels like a man half his weight and age.

But Jacob was sobbing against Charlotte's chest as she paced back and forth in the darkness.

And Luke knew he had done wrong. He had

hurt Charlotte, he had gone against advice from White Fox that he knew in his heart was right.

With his lantern, he climbed into his wagon and looked for something he had always vowed he would hold on to forever—the sling Parmelia had used to hold young John against her chest, a sling he had made out of buckskin before he had left on this same journey all those years ago. Under a quilt Parm had made when she was pregnant, he found it—a soft, brown object that was smaller than he remembered.

Carrying it out into the dusk, he saw Charlotte walking over by her oxen, Jacob's arms flailing out on either side of her.

"Try this," Luke said when he reached her.

Her eyes were etched with anger. "What is it?" she asked, her voice flat.

"It was John's," he said. "Parmelia always said it calmed him right down when she carried him in it."

Charlotte hesitated, looking torn. "But you've saved it," she said.

"My wagon isn't a museum," he said. "You need it. Here, I'll show you how to use it." He took Jacob from her arms, tucked his little legs and arms in, and then held him against Charlotte's chest as he wrapped the straps, one behind her neck and one behind her waist. "Now if you walk, he'll calm right down."

He waited, but Charlotte didn't move. "So walk," he said, slinging an arm around her shoulder.

She moved away. "I can't do this," she said.

"Do what?" he asked.

"I can't spend time with you, Luke. I can't be

with you and have you do nice things and—" She stopped. "I can't have you be the kind of man I've never known before, and then have you say I have to find someone else."

"Charlotte!" a male voice called out.

Charlotte turned around, and Luke followed her gaze. Marcus and Penny Clusen were coming toward them, Penny all dolled up and looking breathless, Marcus looking like his usual irritable self. "We're taking Jacob to the chivaree," Marcus said.

Charlotte's cheeks flushed. "Are you out of your mind? He's exhausted."

"What on earth is that contraption?" Marcus sputtered.

"It's mine," Charlotte said. "To help him sleep when he needs to, Marcus, instead of being paraded around like some traveling circus exhibit."

"I'm going to take him," Marcus said, holding out his hands.

"You will not!" Charlotte said.

At the sound of her voice, Jacob, who had just fallen asleep, woke up with a start and began screaming.

As Jacob screamed, Luke watched Penny Clusen's face. She was wincing, as if Jacob's screams were giving her physical pain.

"Charlotte," Luke said. "Let them take him."

"Are you out of your mind? He needs to sleep."

"And he *will* sleep, if he needs it that much. Let them take him."

Charlotte's eyes were filled with rage, even more so when Marcus said they wouldn't be needing the sling.

After they walked off, Charlotte demanded, "How could you let them take Jacob when he's exhausted?"

"The boy is Marcus's too," Luke said. "You'll do well to remember that."

Tears sprang from her eyes, and he pulled her against him.

Right away, she fought him, trying to pull away. But he held her. And stroked her hair. And held her some more.

"Be mad at me if you want," he said. "But think about what I'm saying."

"I can't keep listening to you," she said, looking not at him but at the ground. "I don't even want to be near you."

He tipped her chin up so she was looking at him. Her face was streaked with tears, her eyes filled with emotion. "Tell me," he said softly.

"Why should I?" she cried. "Why should I listen to you at all when according to you, I'm supposed to find myself someone who wants to be partnered up?"

"Because I know you," he said, wiping the tears from her face. "I know you want certain things in your life. And I know you're hurting because of Lucinda, and because of Ben."

"And I don't want to hurt because of you!" she cried out.

"Then don't, anymore," he murmured, kissing her tears. "Come," he said softly. "Talk to me in the tent." He took her by the hand, and she hated him for understanding her, for knowing too many of her feelings. She claimed she wanted no man, but she wanted Luke. And as for children . . .

Luke knelt and took her face in his hands. He kissed one eyelid, then the other. "I don't want you to hurt," he said softly. "And I don't want to hurt you. But this is too big to ignore, what's between us."

"What *is* between us?" she asked.

"I need you," Luke whispered as he laid a hand on her thigh and brushed his lips against hers. "And I think you need me," he murmured.

Charlotte's body responded even as her mind commanded against it. Just the feel of Luke's hands on her thigh made her body remember what her heart and brain wanted to try to forget. She grew warm in her most private place, as Luke's hand teased her thigh with soft, gentle caresses.

"Tell me the truth," he whispered, planting kisses on her lips, her neck, her chest. "And tell me to go if you want," he murmured as his fingers parted the front of her chemise. He cupped her breasts in his hands, edging her nipples with his thumbs, and she parted her legs, needing him already.

"I don't know what the future will bring," he said against her neck. "But I know I don't need just anyone, Charlotte. I need you."

Looking into his eyes, she suddenly knew that at some level, he was telling the truth. He didn't need her fully, as a man needs a woman as his wife, but then again, she didn't want a husband.

What she wanted was Luke—Luke the man,

Luke who could give her so much pleasure, who could do what no one else ever had.

She trailed her hand down his stomach, flat and muscled, to his thighs, strong and broad, to his maleness, straining against his pants. She could hear his breathing stop, could see the passion in his eyes, could feel the power her hands had over his body just as his did over hers.

In seconds, they were in each other's arms, flesh against flesh, lips against lips, as she ached for him to enter her. He teased her with his fingers, his mouth, the heel of his hand, making her moan with desire. She found his need and wrapped her fingers around it, and Luke buried his face in her neck, crying out, "Charlotte!"

"Hold on, honey," he whispered, his breath hot against her ear. "Are you as ready as you feel?"

"Yes," she said, her insides swollen with desire.

He lay back and hoisted her on top of him, and when he entered her, she cried out, pleasure blazing inside her. Luke moved beneath her, his hips commanding her rhythm, his eyes never leaving hers.

"I want every time to be better and better for you," he whispered.

It can't get any better than this, she thought, unable to talk, pleasure pushing all reason out of her mind.

"Look at me," he murmured.

She could hardly hold her eyes open, hardly do anything except succumb to the growing wave of hot need mixing more and more with pleasure, getting closer and closer to ecstasy—

"I want you," he said, holding her hips, moving her up and down his shaft. "Just you, Charlotte. No one else."

It took her over the edge. She fell into a pool of pure bliss, crying out "I love you" as she went over the brink.

He picked up his rhythm then, and moaned, finally closing his eyes, giving in. He exploded inside her and pulled her to him, stroking her back, wet and slick, with his warm hands. She felt as if they had both gone swimming—their skin was soaked, her hair, his hair—and then she thought about what she had said. Wondering if she had said it, hoping she hadn't; knowing, in the end, that she had.

He hadn't said it back. She hadn't expected him to; she had cried it out without thinking, calling from her heart in that place that had no boundaries. Making love with Luke was like being in another world, a world without inhibitions or rules or embarrassment.

But it wasn't, in fact, another world.

He had heard her, and said nothing.

Well, what could she have expected, if she had thought about it beforehand? Luke had never lied to her, nor made any promises. On the contrary, he had told her from the beginning that he wouldn't be looking for any future attachments.

Yet, as she lay in his arms, she knew her heart was doomed. As surely as a person could halter-break a horse, she would have to break herself from loving Luke—once and for all, forever.

* * *

Charlotte felt panic seeping from her heart to her fingertips, a fear that was great and huge, yet nameless. She felt a sense of dread that went far beyond her trepidations about Luke, deeper even than her sadness over Lucinda.

Jacob. She shouldn't have left him with Marcus and Penny. She had been selfish, horribly so, giving in to a passion that was wrong for a million reasons. She had known she shouldn't hand him over, and now she could feel his absence as if her heart had been cut from her body.

"I must find Jacob," she said, pulling her blouse on.

"He's probably sleeping," Luke said.

"He's probably not!" Charlotte retorted, panic curdling her voice. "I never should have agreed to let them have him. Never!"

Luke caught her by the shoulders. "Marcus is Jacob's father," he said. "You have to acknowledge that, or Marcus is going to end up raising Jacob all by himself."

"He wouldn't even be able to care for him in his dreams," she snapped.

"That isn't the point," Luke said.

Charlotte looked into his eyes and moved out of his grasp. "The point is that I know something is wrong. I can feel it," she said, pulling on her skirt.

She moved out of the tent before Luke said any more, and she felt a rage over the words he had said, and at his power over her. When Lucinda had been alive, Charlotte had felt ashamed by her powerlessness against her feelings of attraction for Luke. And now, it was as if her need for him was wrecking her ability to think, to plan, to live her life the way she wanted.

The chivaree was still going on, couples and families dancing in the moonlight, drinking wines and brews and a "newfangled trail elixir of youth" Zeke had invented, eating jerky and fried potatoes and roast buffalo meat. Charlotte saw Alma and Zeke dancing cheek to cheek, Zeke's hands firmly around Alma's skinny, girlish waist. She saw George Penfield dancing with Emma Gray. And she saw Marcus dancing with Penny in an intimate, easy rhythm that made her head hurt.

She felt fury rise in her throat like bile, and she could hardly see as she marched toward Marcus and Penny. They were framed in a haze made up of Charlotte's anger, everyone else at the chivaree suddenly invisible.

"Where the devil is Jacob?" she asked, grabbing Marcus's arm with venom. She wished her hands *were* venomous, something that could hurt this man she hated.

"Sleeping in my tent, where he belongs," Marcus said, shaking her off.

"He fell asleep like a little angel in my arms," Penny said. "He doesn't need constant attention, Charlotte. He went to sleep feeling very happy, and he'll probably wake up feeling very happy."

Charlotte turned and stormed off, hating Penny as much as she hated Marcus. As she neared Marcus's tent, she heard screaming, a cry that gripped her body at once and made her heart race. She ran into the tent and found Jacob flailing his arms and legs, sweating, his face and chest as red as a ripe apple. "Oh, honey," she said, gathering him into her arms. "I'm here."

His breath was hot against her neck, and she unbuttoned her blouse and held him against her skin. And he seemed to settle, to gather strength, and his breathing slowed, his crying now all but gone.

"Let's see how wet you are," Charlotte whispered, stroking his hot, damp head. "But let me just hold you for a second more. And love you," she added, because she suddenly felt, for the first time ever, that Jacob truly did know her. And that he might even love her. In the calming of his little body, she had felt his acceptance of her, his need for her, maybe even the beginnings of love coming from his little heart. And she knew it was an important new beginning for both of them.

Nineteen

"Take your time," Charlotte whispered, nuzzling the bonnet Biddy Lee had made that now lay snugly on Jacob's head.

Jacob sipped eagerly at the milk in the little silver cup that said J. A., and Charlotte had to laugh. He reminded her of a little calf she had raised as a girl, a calf who had always drunk so hungrily from her bucket that Charlotte could hear her slurping from the barn as she walked all the way up to the house.

For a moment, Charlotte felt as if she were back home in the barn, with Luce's small, warm hand in hers, the sounds of the animals all around them. Despite their father's cruelty, there had been so many good times. And as Charlotte looked around, she felt the absence of her family like a chill, biting wind.

Yet she had Jacob. And she knew that Jacob loved her.

Over by the campfire, Marcus sat with Penny, scooping the fried cakes Penny had cooked for breakfast off their plates like two hungry bears. Charlotte had gotten up early, started the fire, made herself a bitter, bug-filled cup of coffee and a few fried cakes, and then had tended to Jacob. She would be damned, she had told herself, if she lifted a finger for Penny.

Yet Penny was already eating food made with flour Charlotte had packed with her mother. "You'll need more flour and saleratus than you think," her mama had said as they had filled the barrels together. "And if we pack these eggs in corn meal, they'll be less likely to crack, and then you'll have eggs when you think you're down to nothing." Charlotte tried to think generously, the way her mother would have: "God blessed us with food so we may share it with others," she would have chided.

Still, Charlotte knew she wouldn't be able to abide Penny for long. Not in her wagon, using all the food and dishes and tools she and Mama and Lucinda had so carefully chosen for the journey. "Mama," she said softly, just to hear herself say the name. "Make me a better person," she added, knowing that without her mother's presence, there was no hope.

Suddenly, Penny set down her plate and began walking toward Charlotte.

"I'll take Jacob now," she said, holding out her arms, "so you can get on with your morning chores."

"What did you say?"

"I *said* I'll take Jacob now so you can get on with your morning chores. You might as well get used to me having him, Charlotte."

Charlotte wondered if Lucinda could see or hear any of this. The thought made her eyes burn. "I'm feeding him," Charlotte said. "When he's done, and he's ready, and I'm ready," she added slowly, "then you can hold him."

Penny looked as if she had been slapped. She turned on her heel and stalked back to Marcus. A few words were exchanged, and a moment later, Marcus walked over and wrested Jacob from Charlotte's arms. "I'll take my son now, thank you."

"He hasn't finished eating!" Charlotte cried out.

"We'll see that he eats," Marcus replied. "I believe you have chores to do."

"As do you!" Charlotte said. "As does Penny, with her family. I don't intend to be that girl's handmaiden, Marcus. And she's not Jacob's mother—"

"And if I marry her, you will have no choice but to travel with her, Charlotte, with Penny as Jacob's mother—"

"Over my dead body!" Charlotte called out as Marcus walked away.

Her eyes met Penny's then, and Penny looked relaxed and pleased with herself, smiling as she held open her arms and Marcus gave her the baby.

This can't be, Charlotte said to herself, tears starting to burn in her eyes. *I won't let this happen. I can't let this happen.*

She wanted to wrest Jacob from Penny's arms, to grab him and then knock Penny to the ground. "My sister is watching," she would say, "and she forbids you ever to touch her baby again."

Yet she knew she wouldn't do this, or anything even close to it, partly because of the annoyingly sage words Luke had spoken earlier. "Jacob is Marcus's son," he had said. And Marcus probably did feel a deep, genuine love for the baby.

Charlotte walked over to the campfire and picked up the pan that she and Penny had both used. "I'm washing this because I used it, Penny, but don't think I'm going to be doing your dishes for you. If you cook for Marcus, you use your family's cookware, and you clean up or face leaving your things behind."

Penny opened her mouth, looking surprised. "Why, Charlotte Dalton, I do believe you're the least generous woman I've ever met in my life."

"Good," she said. "Then I've made myself clear."

As she walked toward the river, she found that her heart was still pounding so quickly and loudly that she thought she might faint.

But then she saw Biddy Lee, crouched by the water and scrubbing pots and pans. And immediately, her heart lightened at the sight of her friend.

"Tell me what's wrong, girl," Biddy Lee said. "It can't be that bad."

Charlotte shook her head. "It's Marcus and that Penny Clusen," she said. "Acting married already." She knelt beside Biddy Lee and began scrubbing the pan with a bunch of horsetail she and her mama had made for the journey. "I know Jacob is Marcus's, Biddy Lee, but I can't bear seeing him in Penny's arms."

Biddy Lee raised an eyebrow. "You might just have to go learning to bear it, child. No sense pretending it isn't going to happen. It's like me with that Skete. I sleep with a knife in my hand, and I'll cut that man's throat if he so much as lays a hand on me again."

"But the men's council—"

"If the men's council hangs me, then they hang me, Charlotte. Do you know what he said to me this morning? 'Now it's just the two of us, Biddy Lee. You ain't got no man to protect you.' "

Charlotte shuddered, her body and mind disgusted by the man and his words. "What did you say?"

"I looked right in his eyes and told him the truth. 'My Ben Lucius is here as sure as you are, day and night, Skete Smithers,' I told him. He laughed, but that man's a fool because I'm speaking the truth." She put a hand on Charlotte's cheek. "You keep your eyes on the prize, Charlotte Dalton. You and me both are meant to go west, to reach the Territories and start a new life. Eat your citric acid and your dried berries to stop the scurvy, keep your feet clad in the best shoes you can find, take care of your boy. And head west, child. That's all it's in your power to do."

The wind whistled and howled, swirling, shifting, an ominous, low-pitched moan that sounded almost like a wolf. Charlotte lay alone in her tent, wishing Marcus hadn't taken Jacob for the night, wishing she had simply been able to say no.

None of the livestock liked the storm any better than she did. Outside, she could hear cattle lowing, tack clinking and clanking against wagons, too much activity during a time of night when there should have been none.

Oh, how she missed that sweet, warm body; but Luke was right, she knew. Marcus was Jacob's father, whether she liked it or not. And with thoughts of anger and bitter resentment, Charlotte finally fell asleep, feeling alone and bereft.

In the morning, the wind still howled fiercely, relentlessly, and Charlotte decided to get Jacob; surely they would hand him over for a while. . . .

But the wagon was gone.

Charlotte shook her head, for a moment sure she was dreaming. She had slept not twenty feet away . . . Surely she was confused, turned topsy-turvy because of the unceasing howling of the wind.

But it was gone. Gone! Marcus and Penny had taken Jacob, taken the wagon, taken everything. They had taken the oxen she had trained and loved, they had taken the quilts her mother and Lucinda and she had made, they had taken all her supplies, her childhood diary, letters her mother had written for her and Luce to read on the trip, Biddy Lee's doll . . .

But as Charlotte sank to her knees, holding her head in her hands, she knew she would have traded it all, every bit of it, if only they had left her with the baby.

She didn't know how long she sat in the gusting wind like that, pelted by blinding dust, deafened by a howl she could only imagine was terrifying poor Jacob at that moment. She thought about Penny's careless attitude toward Jacob's feeding, and she prayed that the fact they had taken Jacob meant they truly wanted to care for him. Yet what would they feed him? How would they survive?

She felt arms around her shoulders, felt herself pulled against a chest whose smell she knew and loved. "Get out of this wind before you're blown back to Missouri," Luke shouted, shielding her face from the wind with his massive frame. "Go on in," he said, pointing to his tent, still standing staunchly against the wind. He followed her in and took her in his arms. "This is yours, and anything else you need."

"How do you know what happened?" she asked. "You didn't see them—?"

His eyes darkened. "I didn't. But everyone's

pretty much figured out what must have happened. When the storm picked up, Marcus and Penny must have decided it was a chance they might not get again. Penny had told her sister they were planning to head back east with the boy."

"Can we go after them, do you think? Could you catch them if you rode? Do you really think they headed back east?" Charlotte fought back tears. "They'll never make it," she whispered. "Jacob—"

"I couldn't save my own boy," Luke said. "I wasn't there for him, I didn't even know he was sick." He paused. "It was the biggest mistake of my life, leaving when I did, and I'll never forgive myself. And if you want me to turn back, I will. But in my heart, Charlotte, I think they're heading west, and that we'll find them. So you tell me. I promise I'll do everything I can to find him."

Charlotte said nothing, looking into his eyes and feeling a wave of faith and love that shook her to the core. Luke was the most courageous and gallant man she had ever met. And for some reason, she had a strangely strong faith that Luke would find them. "I can't imagine how they think they'll manage," she said. "Marcus is about as capable with those oxen as a tree."

She thought of those pale blue eyes of Jacob's, his little rosebud mouth and soft cheeks and sweet, warm breath, and her heart ached. She thought of what it took to feed him, to change him, to keep him dry and comfortable and happy, and she felt panic and rage and a fear that was bottomless.

And she thought of her promise to Luce, the most important promise she had ever made. "I promised my sister," she said to Luke, tears suddenly flowing. "I promised I would take care of him."

"I know," Luke said softly, enveloping her in his arms. "But remember, Charlotte, even though you might not like to think about it: Marcus does love his son; that's one of the reasons he took him. He does love him."

At some level, Charlotte knew Luke was right. But she also knew there was a chance she would never see her nephew again. And as she looked out toward the West, into a distance that was unseeable, swirling, ominous, she felt a piece of her heart being cut away to die.

Twenty

Charlotte walked toward the river and told herself that life would go on, that as Biddy Lee always said, you had to put one foot in front of the other, set your eyes on the prize, and keep going.

She had confronted Penny's sister, Olive, demanding to know if she knew anything more about Marcus and Penny's flight. "They wanted to get away from you," Olive had snapped. "You were like a thorn in their sides, Penny told me."

Charlotte had felt the ache of regret, remembering how Luke had warned her to respect Marcus's rights.

Now she felt herself dragging, her vision a bit hazy. As she walked over the soft ground near the river, she saw Skete Smithers out of the corner of her eye, walking quickly to catch up with her. And she walked on.

The only good thing about having Jacob gone, she realized, was that the enormity of her loss made almost everything else unimportant.

"Must be nice," Skete said.

Charlotte didn't answer.

Skete walked by her side then. "You don't care what people are saying?" he asked, his voice cracking. "Them saying you're a whore and worse, that you'll shack up with anyone who talks nice to you? 'Cause if that's the case—"

"Drop dead," Charlotte said, not breaking her stride.

Skete Smithers stopped in his tracks. "You want to say that again?"

"I'll say it as many times as I need to," she said, scooping her pitcher into the water and then turning back toward camp.

She felt aware of dizziness for a moment, felt her knees begin to buckle, and she steadied herself, hoping Skete hadn't seen her. And hoping she wouldn't feel dizzy again. She could remember that Lucinda had felt dizzy at the very beginning of being with child. Well, Charlotte had felt this way before in her life; she was certain of it. And certainly a lot of people felt weak on the trail, people who weren't sick but weren't at their best. If she felt dizzy at times, it certainly didn't mean she was carrying Luke's baby.

"You know, Charlotte," Skete called out from behind her, "I see you talking to Biddy Lee day and night, night and day."

Charlotte kept on walking. "And? What of it? Are you going to string me up and hang me, cut off parts of my body and torture me before you kill me?"

"You don't know what went on that night," he said.

"Anyone who knows anything about bodies, whether they be animal or human, knows exactly what happened," she said, still walking. "And you and your father and whoever helped you will suffer the consequences someday, for the evil you've done."

"By your hand?" Skete asked, his heavy pink face creasing into laughter. "Don't make me laugh."

"And don't make me ill by asking me to speak to you for one more second," Charlotte said.

"What I know," Skete said, catching Charlotte by the arm, "is that Biddy Lee's protector is gone. So you know what that means."

She wrenched her arm back so Skete was swung off of her. "If you ever touch me or Biddy Lee again, I'll kill you," she said, stalking off.

She told herself not to look back, that Skete's reaction to her words didn't matter. He had tortured and killed Ben Lucius; that was all that mattered.

Yet something compelled her to look back—

partly a need to look strong, partly plain old curiosity. And when she did turn and look, she wished she hadn't. Hatred filled his eyes, and evil seemed to hang like a mist around his head.

As she neared camp, she saw that a large group of caravan members had gathered. "What I'm saying is that we don't know if the Platte's going to go down or not," Captain Tayler said. "Two years ago, in this very spot, it was as fast and high as it is today, and it didn't go down for five days. That's five more days than we have to spare." He took off his hat. "That's all I'm going to say about the matter, ladies and gents. Those who want to try to hang back, I wish you well. I won't be looking at the South Fork of this river after this afternoon, so to those who plan on staying, the best of luck, and may God be with you."

Many of the husbands and wives who had gathered to listen to Captain Tayler began talking softly to each other, and Charlotte almost had to laugh at her own situation. With no wagon, no possessions and no children, the question of whether to cross now or later was hardly worthy of debate.

She felt hands on her shoulders, coming from behind, and she jumped.

Luke turned her around to face him, lifting her face with a gentle hand. "Don't tell me the invincible Charlotte Dalton is scared of crossing the puny old Platte River," he said.

She swallowed, not exactly sure what she was feeling. "Of course not."

"Then let's get our oxen ready," he said, beginning to walk away. Charlotte didn't move, and Luke turned and looked back at her. "What's wrong?"

"They're not 'our' oxen," she said. "Everything I had is gone."

He shook his head. "Not anymore. It's our wagon, and our oxen. Practice saying 'our,' Charlotte."

A blinding fury surged through her. "I won't," she said. "Why *would* I? Why would I say it's our wagon when it's not? It wasn't going to be our wagon yesterday. You're only saying it because Marcus and Penny ran off with mine."

He was looking at her with an emotion she was afraid to name. His eyes were filled with affection and feeling, an intensity she had longed to see on so many other days and nights. He seemed—almost—to be looking at her with love.

Yet now, the look only infuriated her.

"I told you a long time ago you were Luke Ashcroft's woman," he said, pulling her into his arms. "If circumstances have thrown us together as far as our possessions go, then so be it."

"Circumstances?" she cried, trying to pull away. "Is that what you call it when people steal a baby and everything you own? As I recall, you told me I should find a partner who wants to be partnered up. Those were your exact words!"

His eyes seemed to be shining with even more of that nameless emotion, and Charlotte wanted to hit him, to wipe the light from his eyes and the half-smile off his face. Suddenly Luke seemed to shimmer and swirl in front of her eyes—and

Charlotte saw blackness beginning to drench the edges of her vision. She fell against Luke, and he caught her. And held her.

"Are you all right?" he asked, his voice soft, his arms warm around her.

"I'll be fine," she said, breathing in the scent of his chest and feeling too much.

"Do you know what I think?" Luke asked, his voice even warmer. "I think you have a little one growing inside of you," he whispered, stroking her hair.

His words were too much.

Charlotte broke away from him and she ran, not knowing where she was headed, feeling hot tears against her cheeks and stifling sobs that racked her chest.

She heard footsteps, and then Luke caught her in his arms and held her. "It's not a bad thing if it's true," he said. "It's a *good* thing."

As tears cascaded down her cheeks, Charlotte felt an anger that nearly took her voice away. She saw little Jacob in her mind's eye, and she felt a pain in her heart that was like the slice of a knife. "What are you saying?" she cried. "Now that Jacob's gone, we'll just have another? We'll just substitute one baby for another?"

"Of course not," Luke said. "You ought to know me better than that. I promise I'm going to do everything I can to find Jacob. But if there *is* a baby, Charlotte, that little one is going to need its daddy," he said, his fingers splaying across her belly.

And Charlotte felt rage flare again. Luke seemed

always to say words she had longed to hear, only to say them too late, and for all the wrong reasons. He hadn't talked about sharing, about a baby needing its daddy, until he had thought those things were necessary.

He didn't love her. He was a man for whom honor was supremely important. If she were indeed carrying his child, he would want to marry her, no matter what.

And it was all so wrong. She missed Jacob as if her own heart were missing. And yes—in a small, secret part of her heart, she could feel a sliver of pleasure and happiness and hope as she thought of the future Luke had painted: She would spend the rest of her life with the man she loved—the man she would always love—and the family they had created together.

But it would be a future based on obligation, a sense of duty. Luke had already been married before; he had already felt that kind of love. And she knew he didn't want it again. What he wanted wasn't to love her; he wanted to be a man of honor.

And she knew that if she were indeed carrying his child, and he found out about it, he would never stop demanding that she marry him.

She swallowed, not knowing what to say, but knowing that she was trapped, and that she had to find the exact right words. If she said the wrong thing, he would never let go of the idea of doing the honorable thing.

She stood up straight, finally looking him in the eye when she was about to act as dishonestly with Luke as she ever had. "I could never marry you," she said. She ignored the look in his eyes—surprise, a deep shock darkened by anger—as she went on. "I married once—to a man I only *thought* I loved. And it was a mistake. I vowed never to repeat that mistake again." Her heart was pounding as she spoke her next words. "What we had, what we shared, is over." She nearly passed out from the untruth of her words, but she went on, ignoring the pain in his eyes. "I'll help you prepare the wagon and continue traveling with you if you want. But if you prefer that I make other arrangements—"

His jaw was clenched, his eyes pained, but he said nothing. Then, "The day is getting late," he suddenly said, starting to take boxes out of the wagon. "You can help unload the wagon and block up the wheels."

She could hardly look at him. She knew that he had taken her words as she had meant him to take them: that she didn't love him, and never would.

For a moment, recent memories flashed before her eyes as if they were still occurring: Luke kissing her for the first time, after he had carried her back to his wagon; Luke digging the grave for Lucinda's body; Luke teaching Jacob how to drink.

Be strong, she told herself, *and say no more.* Because if lying to Luke was the only way to prevent a marriage based on duty and nothing more, then lie she would.

To Charlotte, the water didn't look threatening, possibly because so many of the wagons had already crossed. At that moment, she was holding on to the back of the wagon, where they had piled some things Alma was afraid would fall out of the Blisses' wagon; Luke was driving the teams from the front seat, George at his side; they were just about a quarter of the way across the Platte.

Off to the left, moving perilously close, was the first of the Smithers family wagons. Jock Smithers, driving, stood screaming and cursing, flailing his whip from the wagon seat. Next to him, Mollie Smithers clutched the seat, looking terrified.

For some reason, either because Jock Smithers had no control over his oxen or because he wanted to get closer to the front of the line, his teams had plunged in and were coming up so close that Charlotte could nearly touch them from where she sat at the back of the wagon.

Charlotte heard a scream—"Daddy!" Mollie Smithers cried—and a moment later, a splash as Mollie fell headfirst into the swirling, muddy waters.

She looked terrified, gulping for air as her head sank and then came up again, as she paddled against currents that would have been overwhelming even for the strongest of men.

Suddenly, Mollie's father screamed from his seat, and Charlotte saw Lavinia Smithers peeking out from inside the wagon. She began screaming at the top of her lungs. "My baby! Oh, my baby!"

And Charlotte remembered the night when they had tortured and cut Ben Lucius apart. She remembered the flames, the figures dancing near the fire with unnatural energy, a fever powered by evil.

And then she remembered something from childhood, pulling Lucinda out of the water when she had gone out too deep and panicked. She reached for the rope at the back of the wagon and threw it into the water. *You can't let a person drown,* she said to herself. Yet what had that family done to Ben Lucius?

"Grab the rope!" Lavinia Smithers shrieked. "Baby, grab the rope!"

Charlotte looked down at Mollie, her blond hair dark and muddy, her face slick with dirty water. She was crying, swimming for the rope. And then she caught it.

And Charlotte knew what she had to do.

"You owe me Biddy's freedom!" she yelled down to Mollie.

Mollie looked frightened, and for a second her head sank under the water. But then she pulled herself up, coughing and sputtering. "What? Pull me up!"

"You owe me Biddy Lee's freedom!" Charlotte yelled, feeling someone at her side.

Luke.

"Now swear Biddy Lee can go free!" Charlotte called out.

"Yes, yes!" Mollie called out, sobbing. "Please, Charlotte!"

"What the devil—?" Luke muttered, moving behind Charlotte and pulling the rope along with her. With one huge tug, they pulled Mollie up into the wagon, and she fell, sobbing and soaked, into Luke's arms.

"Thank God for you, Luke, thank God for you.

I would have drowned if you hadn't come along."

"What the devil are you talking about?" he snapped. "Charlotte's the one who saved you." He moved past her quickly, through the crush of boxes and clothes and supplies, to the front of the wagon, where George was now sitting and driving the teams through the churning water.

Ignoring Charlotte, Mollie moved through the wagon to the front, plopped herself down behind Luke on the floor and began to sob.

And a feeling of horrible foreboding settled around Charlotte's heart. She had extracted a promise from Mollie. But now what?

And Luke—she had lied to Luke, lied in order to protect her own heart. And she felt suddenly as alone and vulnerable as she ever had in her life.

Twenty-one

"It was like a nightmare," Mollie was sobbing, hugging her father and talking to a group of her parents' friends at the campsite. "Charlotte made me promise ten or fifteen things, each crazier and more horrid than the last."

"You mean she would have dropped you into the Platte if you hadn't said yes to everything?" a young girl named Juliette asked.

"I couldn't take the risk of finding out," Mollie cried. "Could I have, Daddy? I couldn't have said no."

"Of course not, Butternut. You did the right thing."

Charlotte walked away, unable to listen anymore.

She was being painted as evil, and from what Charlotte could tell, Mollie hadn't even mentioned the one promise she had actually been asked to make.

She walked up to Luke, who was already unloading the Blisses' possessions. "I could have done that," she said.

"I know you could have," he said. "But I didn't ask you to, did I?"

She felt as if he had slapped her. "I need your help," she said, trying to ignore the way he refused to look at her.

"You said you needed my help," he said, his voice expressionless. "Are you going to tell me what you need my help with, or am I supposed to guess?"

Charlotte sighed. So this was the way it was going to be. Well, she supposed she couldn't blame Luke. He had asked her to marry him, and she had made it clear that she would never say yes.

"Were you watching Mollie and her little theatrics over there?" she asked.

"I have better things to do with my time," Luke said.

"Mollie's acting as if she never promised to let Biddy free."

Luke set down Alma and Zeke's carved wooden hope chest, stood up and looked into Charlotte's eyes. "Tell me something, Charlotte," he said. "Would you have let Mollie go if she had said she wouldn't free Biddy Lee?"

Charlotte shrugged, pondering a question she had thought about many times in the minutes since it had happened. "I really don't know," she answered. "It all happened so fast, and I didn't think about it in advance. But I honestly don't think that anything can compare with what that family has done to Biddy Lee—and Ben Lucius." She shook her head. "And I'm afraid that if I say anything more, they're just going to take it out on Biddy Lee."

"They have to be stopped," Luke said quietly.

He walked past her then, without another word, and Charlotte took a deep breath and closed her eyes, trying not to love him. Another man might not have been able to see past the troubles he was having with her; another man might have said, "You want to be by yourself, so solve your problems by yourself too."

But not Luke. She watched as he walked quickly and purposefully toward the Smithers family. And she tried not to love him. But with every step he took, she loved him more.

As Luke walked toward the Smithers family, he saw Jock Smithers smile and then laugh. Luke felt like punching the man's face to bits. Did he think it was all a joke, that no one would consider all the hatred their family had stirred up when the time came—as now—to judge one of them?

Smithers was laughing with another man Luke didn't like, a merchant who had no idea how to treat his livestock.

"Smithers!" Luke called out.

Jock Smithers narrowed his eyes, staring at Luke but saying nothing.

Luke felt the hairs at the back of his neck stand up as if he were an old hound dog. "We can talk here or in private. The choice is yours."

Smithers glanced at Hank Calloway and then at Luke. "I'll be back in a few minutes," he said. He began following Luke toward the river, then stopped. "If I'm not back in ten minutes, Hank," he called out, "you'd better come looking for me."

Luke laughed. "You have a reason to think you won't come back?"

Smithers said nothing, and they walked on in silence, Luke enjoying what he knew was Jock Smithers's growing sense of fear. The ground beneath their feet, rutted with the marks of thousands of hooves, showed the enormous struggle their fellow travelers had made to cross before them, and Luke thought of how wrong it was that a man of Smithers's poor moral character was going to be one of the first pioneers in the new western lands.

"I'm surprised you didn't make Biddy Lee swim across the Platte with your oxen," he said as he stopped at the edge of the river.

"There's a lot you don't understand about slavery, Mr. Ashcroft."

"Well, that's the first and last thing we'll ever agree on, I imagine," Luke said. "You think you can own that girl or anyone else, that's just crazy to me. That girl has a momma and daddy just like yours does—"

"And they's slaves too," Smithers cut in. "It's the way of the world."

"Not *my* world," Luke said. "And your daughter made a promise. I believe you already know that."

"To that little—" Smithers stopped. "What kind of a person would make a drowning young girl bargain for her life?"

"What kind of family would do what yours did to Ben Lucius?" Luke cut in. "It's time to set Biddy Lee free, Smithers."

Fury made Smithers' eyes spark. "Like hell," he growled.

Luke grabbed him by the throat and threw him to the ground. He climbed on top of him and crushed his chest with the weight of his body. "Now, this is the way it's going to be," he breathed. "You sell Biddy Lee to me. My payment—what I give you—is that I let you live."

"You're insane," Smithers gasped.

"I think it's the other way around," Luke said. "Now do we have a deal or not? And don't think you can go back there and pretend this didn't happen the way your daughter did, Smithers, because you'll pay right then and there, in front of your family and friends. Understand?"

"Why are you doing this? She's a slave girl. She's nothing. Unless you're wanting some of that brown sugar for yourself—"

Luke punched him square in the jaw, his fist connecting with a solid mass of flesh and bone. Smithers groaned in agony, his face twisted in pain.

"Do we have a deal?"

Smithers tried to reach up to touch his swelling jaw, but Luke's thighs blocked him. "All right," Smithers finally gasped. "We have a deal."

"I don't imagine I should have to tell you this again," Luke went on as he swung himself off Smithers, "but you stay away from Biddy Lee, and you stay away from Charlotte. That goes for your family too. Understood?"

Smithers said nothing.

Luke lurched forward and grabbed him by his shirt.

"All right, all right," Smithers finally conceded, holding up his hands.

Charlotte watched as Luke and Jock Smithers came back from the river, a knot of Smithers's friends still gathered near his wagons.

"Go get Biddy Lee," Smithers growled at his son.

Skete Smithers's mouth dropped open, and he stood there, slack-jawed.

"What are you waiting for?" Jock Smithers barked, looking as if the veins in his neck would pop at any second. "You heard me: Go get her!"

"But Daddy—"

"But nothing! Mr. Ashcroft has bought her and he wants her. Now!"

"Bought her!" Skete cried. "You told me when we got to the Territories, she'd be mine and nobody else's—"

"You even *look* at her wrong," Luke said, "and you answer to me."

Skete's mouth dropped open again and hung there, and Charlotte loved the moment, wishing one of the photographers who occasionally traveled the trail was there to capture the look of stunned stupidity on that cruel, ignorant oaf's face.

He loped off then like a wounded animal toward the Smithers's wagons.

"Wait!" Luke called out. He caught up with him in a few long, graceful strides. "Biddy's mine now, so she's mine to go get," Charlotte heard him say.

It was strange to hear Luke talk like that, to pretend he now "owned" Biddy Lee. But she knew Luke; he thought the idea of slavery was as horrible and crazy as she did. And as she watched him walk away for the second time that afternoon, she tried again not to love him.

A moment later, Biddy Lee was walking slowly toward Charlotte, her eyes looking into hers and avoiding everybody else's.

Charlotte wanted to run to her friend, to hug her and dance her around the way she used to dance her sister around when they were kids.

But Biddy Lee's expression was impossible to read. "Mr. Ashcroft said we would be sharing a tent," she said quietly.

Charlotte couldn't hold herself back. She took Biddy Lee's hands in hers. "You're free, Biddy Lee."

Biddy Lee shook her head. "It can't be this easy. There's too much you don't understand."

"I understand that the Smitherses will be doing 'slave work,' Biddy Lee. They'll be washing and cooking and scrubbing, and burning their arms with soap, scrubbing their fingers raw, and let's see. What else?"

At first, Biddy Lee just looked at her.

"It's the truth," Charlotte said.

After another long silence, Biddy Lee suddenly spoke, the glimmer of a smile curving her lips. "They'll be digging trenches to make their fires," she said softly. "And hitching up the teams and washing and scrubbing some more," she went on, her eyes almost twinkling.

"Not too terrible, is it?" Charlotte asked quietly. "You can think of worse things happening, can't you? Because I can."

Biddy Lee frowned, looking doubtful. "It was too easy, the way I was freed," she said quietly, all merriment gone from her face.

Charlotte looked from Biddy Lee over to Skete Smithers. His eyes were pale with fury in his dust-caked face, his lips set in a line of rage. And she knew that for her and Biddy, if they were smart, they could never truly rest or relax for as long as the journey continued.

"I want to thank you for what you did for Biddy Lee," Charlotte said, kneeling next to Luke in front of what remained of the night's campfire as Luke worked on a tear in a lead line. "Biddy says she can't believe how different the simplest things feel—'Washing dishes isn't half bad now that no one's forcing me to do it,'" Charlotte went on in a poor imitation of Biddy Lee's voice.

She was beginning to feel uncomfortable, em- barrassed at the way she was rambling on, but unable to stop herself. "So I just wanted to say—"

"Thank you," he cut in, finally looking at her. He gave a brief nod of his head. "Biddy Lee has thanked me enough, Charlotte, and in any case you were the one who arranged for her freedom."

"Well," Charlotte said, feeling panicked and engulfed in confusion, "since we haven't had a chance to talk all day . . ." Her voice trailed off, and in the grim set of Luke's jawline, she could tell she had said the wrong thing. But what on earth was the right thing to say?

He stood up, lifted his head, and smoothed his hair back from his forehead. "Things are going to be different from now on," he said. "I didn't think I would have to tell you we won't be spending a lot of time together anymore." He shook his head, looking deeply into her eyes. "You and Biddy Lee may share any of my belongings, keep the tent, share my meals. Don't stop any of that. But we won't be spending time alone together anymore, so don't go looking for that, for any reason."

Charlotte's mouth dropped open.

Luke walked away with his fixed-up lead line, and Charlotte watched, waiting for some kind of misstep, for Luke to turn around, change his mind, tell her he hadn't meant any of it. But he kept on walking.

"You look like a lost soul, girl. What's the matter?" Biddy Lee asked as she emerged from the tent.

Charlotte began stacking dishes, worn-out tin clanking against worn-out tin. "Luke doesn't want to have anything to do with me anymore."

Biddy Lee laughed in her face. "Isn't this the man who asked you to marry him?" she asked. "Weren't you the one told him no?"

"He only asked because he thinks I'm carrying his child," Charlotte said quietly. "I told you that, Biddy."

"And my mama told me I was the prettiest girl in the whole state of Missouri, but that didn't make it true, did it? That was what she thought; it wasn't the truth. That man is in love with you, Charlotte."

Charlotte shook her head, suddenly missing her sister and mama so much that her heart ached. "That's what you see because that's what you'd like to see."

"And what if you're carrying his child like he thinks?"

"Then I'll act like the widow I am when I get out to the Territories."

Biddy Lee narrowed her eyes. "And keep the child from its daddy?"

"It's been done," Charlotte said flatly. "Now, tell me, Biddy Lee. Do you feel different? Do you think about your freedom every minute, or are you already used to it?"

Biddy Lee laughed. "Now, tell me, Charlotte, are you always this clumsy at trying to change the subject?"

Charlotte smiled. "Always," she said softly, remembering that her mama had teased her about the very same thing.

But she couldn't talk about Luke anymore—not if Biddy Lee was going to persist in refusing to see the truth.

Charlotte knew what the truth was. She had promised herself she would never fall in love, but she had fallen. Hard. And Luke—Luke was a man who would always take the heroic, honorable course of action. But even Luke, a man of so much honor, even he had shown that the only reason he had asked her to marry him was because he had thought she was carrying his child.

And so she was destined to love without being loved back. She had created her own fate, by mistake, by falling in love when she had sworn she wouldn't. And now, she would pay the price, by having loved—too much—and then lost.

And poor little Jacob. She had fallen hard for him, opened her heart to him, but she had failed him, and failed her sister, breaking the most important promise she had ever made in her life.

Twenty-two

It wasn't the biggest piece of news in the world, but right then, Luke felt as if it was. That afternoon, he had met a man who was traveling in the "wrong" direction, which meant he might—just might—have seen Marcus, Penny and Jacob, if they had continued heading west, as Luke suspected.

He had invited Ezra Pine to share his and George's meal of buffalo and bean stew, with George's sure-to-kill-innocent-bystanders coffee, and it had worked out better than Luke could have imagined.

True, he still didn't know how he felt about Charlotte: Her words had cut deep. But he had promised he would aim to find baby Jacob.

Now, Luke howled outside Charlotte's tent—a low wolf howl, a trick he had perfected as a boy after months of practice and which now seemed just about right for getting Charlotte's attention.

She stuck her head out of the tent flap, looking as alarmed as if a real wolf had come knocking at her tent on its hind legs.

And for a second, Luke felt as if the world had stopped. This wasn't going to be easy, ignoring Charlotte when he—

Well, when he felt so much.

He thought about how if it had been a few days earlier, he would have been able to joke with her about how he had fooled her into thinking he was a wolf. And he would have taken her into his arms and kissed away the surprise.

No more, never again.

"Oh, it's you," she said. "What's wrong?"

Suddenly he didn't know what to say. Looking at her up close, having her look into his eyes, he felt as tongue-tied as a teenager at a barn dance.

Well, hell. That hadn't been the plan at all.

"Not here," he said. "Come walk with me."

He could see her stealing glances at him as they walked along, away from the caravan, and he couldn't guess how she felt.

He had to ask himself, as he walked with her

past the ring of wagons, what he was trying to do. Well, hell, part of him said. He was trying to give her some news.

Liar.

They walked in silence as the sun hung low and red in the broad, endless sky. They walked on along granite ledges, with the foothills of the Rockies ahead of them in the distance, until the sun had sunk below the horizon and the moon had appeared low and bright.

"Unless we're planning on walking all the way to the Territories, Luke, don't you think it'd be a good time to stop?" Charlotte asked.

He laughed. "I guess this is far enough."

"Far enough for what?" she asked, her voice wary.

"To tell you something we've both wanted to hear since Jacob was taken," he said softly. "The man who ate with us tonight saw Marcus and Penny and the baby at Courthouse Rock."

"Oh my God," Charlotte whispered. "Is he sure? How could they have made such good time? Why would he even have noticed them?"

Luke fought against taking her into his arms, holding her, covering her with kisses. "He noticed them because they were traveling alone. They had joined up with another caravan, he said, but then had broken off."

"Oh, Luke, how will they survive on their own?" she asked.

For the first time in days, she was looking into his eyes without guarding herself, and he felt as if he was looking into her soul. "They'll join another group," he said softly. "Have faith, Charlotte. I promised I'd help you find them. You trust me to do that, don't you?"

She tried to turn away, but he caught her. "Answer me," he said.

She shook her head. "I can't, Luke. I don't know the answer. I don't know you, I feel as if I don't know myself anymore. What I said to you was a lie—"

"What lie?" he cut in.

"I can't have this conversation," she said. "What I said about not wanting you—"

It was all he needed to hear. "We're meant to be together," he murmured. "You know it, and I know it." In his heart, he knew he wasn't saying the right words. Her body was responding, he could feel her soft shape melting against him, he could feel a need she couldn't deny—but he knew her heart needed more.

"This has got to end," she whispered. "I can't be your mistress, Luke."

"It will be the beginning if you'll agree to be my wife," he said, putting a hand on her belly. "We'll be a family of three or four or five, whatever you want."

As she pulled away, he thought he saw tears in her eyes. "I can't, Luke. Ever," she said, and she ran off into the night.

He felt an ache in his heart—she shouldn't have run off; she should have been wrapped in his arms at that moment, and he should have been making love to her.

But then he stopped himself. Who was he kidding? He had sounded like a stranger when he had asked her to marry him.

And with damn good reason, he suddenly realized.

He would never be the marrying kind again; never. Asking her had been a reflex—doing right, doing the right thing. But he would be breaking a promise to himself, breaking the past and throwing it into pieces.

He looked out into the night and breathed in the fresh air, the prairie earth and smoke and grass, and he told himself it was good that Charlotte had run off. She had known his proposal had come from the wrong place—an empty place, no heart there at all. And so she had run. And the world was the way it should be.

Let her go, he said to himself, and wondered why that felt so wrong.

By the breakfast campfire, Charlotte began mixing flour and water for fried cakes, buoyed by the knowledge that Marcus, Penny and Jacob were still headed west.

For some reason, she believed that she and Luke would find her little nephew. She couldn't imagine how; if too much time passed, how would they even recognize the boy? But somehow, deep in her heart, she did believe.

Then why, she wondered, couldn't she trust in a future with Luke?

For one thing, she answered herself, because he had never said he loved her. And she knew he was a man who didn't lie. He would never tell her he loved her if he didn't. And so, he hadn't.

She looked at him as he walked toward her, searching for the expression she sometimes saw in his eyes: an affection she could fool herself into believing, if only for a few seconds, was love.

Only now, she saw worry and fear. "You and Biddy Lee are going to have to go on ahead," he said. "Just leave us two of the horses and we'll catch up with you."

"What's wrong?" Charlotte asked. "What happened?"

Luke shook his head, sadness darkening his eyes. "George has been hit with dysentery. Worse than he realizes, I think," he said quietly.

Charlotte thought of the young man in their caravan who had died the night before, a twenty-year-old farmer who had been the picture of health only days earlier. And Emma Gray's father had passed on the day before, a victim of the bloody flux.

"You don't think he'll make it?" Charlotte asked.

"I'll do whatever I can to make George comfortable," Luke said. "And I'm not going to think beyond that, except to tell you to be more careful than you've ever been in your life, Charlotte. Watch your back, and don't go off alone—"

"You mean because of the Smitherses—"

"I mean because of everything. Because I won't be there to watch over you—" He stopped, for a second not having any idea what to say. "I'm only leaving you because I'm trusting you not to do anything crazy—"

It was too much like his last goodbye to Parmelia,

he felt—only worse because he knew what it felt like to say goodbye, thinking you would see the other person again when in truth you never would.

He could remember kissing Parmelia for minutes, her soft lips opening for his, her hair that unforgettable combination of perfume and wood-smoke and sun. He could remember kissing her, loving her, holding her, never thinking it would be the last time, never guessing he would know his son for only three months of his pathetically brief little life.

He looked into Charlotte's eyes, soft and brown and shining, and a voice said, *Don't do this.*

A voice said, *Go with her.*

A voice said, *Do what's right.*

"What's the matter?" Charlotte asked. "You look as if you've seen a ghost."

He thought about George as he had looked only yesterday, fat and happy and never thinking he wouldn't reach the Territories. "I'll see you before you know it," Luke said, taking Charlotte into his arms. He closed his eyes and was swept up by too much emotion, feelings he didn't want to feel or to name. He breathed in her scent, felt the heat beneath his fingers, felt the strength emanating from every part of her body.

God protect her, he whispered in his heart. *And don't let me make the same mistake twice in one lifetime.*

Twenty-three

Dearest Mama, Charlotte wrote.

It has been raining for three days and three nights in torrents. Biddy Lee and I have saved enough buffalo chips to make small fires under a tent flap, but keeping the flap up is rather a trick, so we are eating cold, jerked meats, cold beans, cold, old bread and washing our dishes in cold, muddy water. She stopped, knowing that someday she would have to tell her mama about Jacob.

But not yet—because if she wrote the words, the truth that he had disappeared, she believed that those words would seal his fate. And so she went on, the lie like a stone in her heart. *Yet there are people who are faring far worse . . .*

"Mrs. Dalton," someone called, and Charlotte saw that it was Charlie Mews, an odd but friendly fellow, riding his bedraggled-looking mule. "Mr. Ashcroft is hurt. I found him when I saw a campfire all by itself up north a ways. The Vestrows are coming with Mrs. Gunderson's stretcher, but I'd best take you now, maybe with your friend there to help, and the others can follow later on."

Charlotte dropped her letter, not wanting to think or hope or feel anything at all. She found Biddy Lee and told her what had happened, and a moment later she and Biddy Lee were riding

Pontiac, Luke's best horse, and following Mews out of camp.

Charlotte didn't know how far away Luke was, but Charlie Mews's mule looked as if it wouldn't be able to walk even half a mile. "Will your mule make it?" she asked as Mews kicked it sharply.

Charlie Mews smiled, his surprisingly healthy-looking teeth shining out from a dirt-covered face. "She's lasted this long!" he said. "I expect she's got some life left to her yet. And we don't have time to be dawdling, Miz Dalton. Just follow me."

"What sort of wound does Luke have?" Charlotte called out. "Or is he sick? And did George— is George still alive?"

"I think you'd best wait until you see Mr. Ashcroft for answers," Mews said.

"Then he's alone?"

After a moment's thought, Mews nodded. "He's alone."

Charlotte sighed. So George had passed on. She had feared he would, but somehow, hearing it made it seem sadder.

George was no more. She would never hear that funny laugh again, never see his eyes crinkle up until they had almost disappeared in those ruddy, puffy cheeks.

And he had seemed so healthy—as had Luke.

Charlotte estimated they had traveled a mile across the prairie when Mews's mule began stumbling worse than before.

"Mr. Mews!" she called out as her horse pulled up next to his mule. "You'd better rest your mule, don't you think?"

Mews looked back. "I don't see the others," he said quietly.

"Well, how much farther is it?" Charlotte asked, looking out at the long rays of red stretching away from them across the ground. It seemed the sun had come out that afternoon only to tease them, after so much rain. All the swaying prairie grasses had been flattened, the landscape was a gently rolling, graceful sea of muddy green-brown stretching as far as Charlotte could see. "We've been traveling due north, which is easy enough for us to keep doing if you can't make it. You're going to kill your mule if you don't let her rest."

"Mr. Ashcroft needs you now, Miz Dalton. He's lost a lot of blood."

"Then we'll go to him if you tell us how," Charlotte said.

Mews swallowed, looking nervous and unsure of himself. "All right," he finally said. "Keep going due north, in line with the trees over there in them groves. Maybe ten minutes more riding if you keep right on. Ashcroft is laid up in a hollow, and I built a good fire by him so you should be able to see the smoke. The others will probably catch up soon enough."

"All right," Charlotte called out. "Take care of your mule, Mr. Mews, and wish us luck, because we surely need it."

He nodded and tipped his hat, and Charlotte clucked Luke's horse on ahead as Biddy Lee held on tight behind her.

"Strange, wasn't that?" Biddy Lee said.

"What?" Charlotte asked.

"Didn't he look a little funny?" Biddy Lee asked. "So nervouslike."

"I imagine this desolate terrain does make him nervous." She looked up at the sky, darkening now with its long rays of western sun, clouds rolling in—again! And she hoped Luke wasn't too much farther away. Hadn't Mr. Mews said it would be another ten minutes or so of riding?

She looked back and saw nothing of the Vestrows, and she wondered if she had veered off too far in the wrong direction.

"Look!" Biddy Lee cried, pointing ahead.

Charlotte's heart skipped: A plume of smoke was curling up ahead, in the distance, in a grove of trees. Luke!

When they got to the campfire, they both dismounted quickly, and Charlotte studied the fire closely; it looked as if it had just been tended, its coals glowing brightly beneath new sticks not even yet burned. So Luke had to be nearby.

"I'll see if he crawled into that brush," Biddy Lee said.

"I'll check over here!" Charlotte called out, hitching Pontiac to a water willow and starting to search nearby. "Luke!" she called out. "Luke!"

It was an eerie silence, a sort Charlotte realized she hadn't heard since before the rains had come. For days now, the constant drumming of the rain on the wagon, the tent, the waterlogged ground and oxen and paths, had been the backdrop for every conversation. Yet now, Charlotte heard . . . nothing.

No wind, no livestock, no animals of any sort,

no tools being worked, problems being resolved or worsened, babies being fed or scolded or sung to.

And then she felt a hand around her mouth, an arm around her waist, violence in a grip she knew wasn't Luke's.

"You dumb little bitches just walked yourselves into a trap," a voice whispered in her ear. "My dad's got Biddy Lee over there, and you done drawed yourself the lucky card and got me. Till we switch," he added with a laugh.

Charlotte felt her eyes close for a second as a wave of nausea gripped her. This was not the time to feel weak or dizzy. She had to protect herself and her baby.

"Now just come on over here, little lady," Skete Smithers said, "and start acquainting your pretty little self with me and my body parts."

Charlotte went limp, forcing Skete to drag her through the brush, and she tried to imagine grabbing the rifle off Pontiac's saddle. But how would she even get to it?

"So this is how you're going to play?" Skete asked, his grip tightening on her upper arms. "You might find yourself sorry, Miz Charlotte, if you don't show me some of that famous passion. Why, if I'm not mistaken, I think I heard your lovely voice the other night, making some mighty, mighty fine sounds." He looked into her eyes. "That moaning must have had some heaving and huffing and grinding behind it, and my pa and I done decided we'd have to get a taste of that before this trip comes to an end." He smiled. "Of course, *your* trip, yours and Biddy Lee's, is going to come to an end right here and now, after Pa and I get our fill of you."

"You'll be caught," Charlotte heard herself say.

Skete laughed. "Who did you have in mind, little lady? A prairie dog? A coyote? I don't think your so-called gift with animals includes talking them into rescuing you from two horny sons of bitches aiming to make the most of some time alone with you two whores."

In the distance, Charlotte could hear Biddy Lee's voice. Was she arguing with Jock, berating him? Cursing him?

"Now don't go telling me you think Mr. Luke Ashcroft is going to come to your rescue, because that would just be plain pathetic."

"You *will* be caught," Charlotte said again. "I can promise you that."

Skete laughed. "And I can promise a hell of a good time, Charlotte, for you and for me. I'm going to make you scream for more. And then I'll have Biddy Lee screaming for more while my pa takes you—"

From out of nowhere, it seemed, a shot rang out.

Skete looked around, letting go of Charlotte, and Charlotte ran toward Pontiac. She had just gotten hold of her rifle when Skete yelled out.

"You can drop it right now, Miz Dalton," he cried out hoarsely.

Charlotte thought about it. She didn't move, she didn't blink, she didn't breathe. But some inner voice told her she couldn't let go of the gun.

"No, sir, Skete," came another husky voice. "You drop your gun. Now."

Biddy Lee was standing there, a rifle aimed at Skete Smithers's back.

His mouth dropped open, he spun around, and he took dead aim at Biddy Lee.

Charlotte pulled her trigger. Even as she did it, she realized she hadn't had time to think about whether Biddy Lee would be hurt if she shot.

She heard a cry from Skete Smithers and saw blood as he fell to the ground, blood pouring from a hole in his chest, a hole she had made.

Biddy Lee stepped forward and looked down at the man Charlotte had killed. "Good riddance," she said, and she looked into Charlotte's eyes. "You shot him in the heart, Charlotte, same as I shot Jock. Isn't that strange?"

"I can't believe it," Charlotte murmured. "I didn't even think—"

"Well, *I* thought plenty," Biddy Lee cut in. "That Jock Smithers was so intent on getting what he wanted that he forgot I have a brain." She suddenly looked panicked, like a spooked, flighty horse in a storm. "I'd best be on my way right now, then, girl."

"No!" Charlotte cried out. "They were going to kill us, Biddy Lee."

Biddy Lee narrowed her eyes. "And you think that's going to matter to half the wagon train?"

Charlotte didn't answer. But she knew that if Biddy Lee ran now, she would be hunted down for sure. At least if they went back . . .

Twenty-four

As if it was a physical need, a hunger or thirst, Luke wanted to catch the caravan that had occupied his every thought for the past four days, and he tested his horse to her limits as they galloped west.

George had died, finally, a death he hadn't deserved—slow, painful, with the knowledge that the end was near and there was nothing either man could do about it.

Close to the end, as the two men had lain by the last campfire they'd ever share, George had spoken out into the near darkness long after Luke had thought he had fallen asleep. "So now you'll catch her and marry her, my friend. Do we have our last deal? Are you going to make me the last promise I'll ever force you to make?"

Luke had chuckled into the cool night air. "You never made me do anything in your whole life, George, and you know it."

There had been a silence then, as they both remembered the truth: George was the one who had convinced Luke to make the trip west one more time, something that had felt impossible to Luke after Parmelia and John had died.

Now George wanted him to do something else that would change his life. "I said I'd never marry again," Luke said quietly, sitting up and rolling himself a cheroot.

"You never thought you'd fall in love again."

Luke laughed too loudly, a sound that rang false and jarring in the dark night. "Coming from a dyed-in-the-wool bachelor, George, I'd say your words don't carry a hell of a lot of weight. Ask me something that makes some sense."

George leaned up on one elbow, the largest movement he could make in his condition. "It isn't a joke, Luke. The trail has changed everyone. And if I were going to make it to the Territories, the first thing I'd do is marry Emma."

"You're asking the wrong man," Luke said, not wanting to hear George say he wouldn't make it. "Now leave me alone and get some sleep."

As it had turned out, it was the last conversation they would ever have—one with sharp words and unspoken thoughts, another conversation to regret for a lifetime.

As Luke had slept, George had passed on.

Now as Luke rode along, George's last words echoed in his ears as no others ever had. And the promise . . . well, somehow the fact that Luke hadn't agreed made George's wish all the more compelling.

But dammit, it was George's wish—not his own, he told himself over and over as he sped along the prairie trying to catch up to his woman. Oh, he wanted her. Body and soul, heart and mind, he wanted her.

But he was the only person who knew the truth:

George didn't, Charlotte didn't, White Fox didn't really know him; none of them did.

He didn't have the heart they thought he possessed; he didn't have the soul.

He was a man who had cut off his best friend's words with sharpness in the last conversation they would ever have. He was a man who had walked away from a newborn son and from a wife who had begged him to stay.

He was a shell, like stone, not the lover Charlotte or any good woman deserved.

But he still had to see her, had to know she was all right.

Don't lose her, an inner voice said as his horse galloped toward the setting sun, blazing from a West he hadn't ever expected to see again.

He didn't love Charlotte. He would never love again. But he did need to see her.

Suddenly, in the half darkness, across a distance that let him barely make out the details of the wagons, he caught sight of the Blisses' wagon, and he felt he was breathing for the first time in days.

When he saw his own wagon, with the tools he and George had lashed onto the outside together, he felt more emotions than he would have thought possible. He missed George sharply, with a pain that felt physical. But he also felt he was home, with the woman he—

Well, the woman he needed to see.

Though everyone else was settling down for the night, some even already asleep in their tents, he saw no sign of Charlotte, or Biddy Lee.

The wagon was in place and the livestock looked good . . . but there was no campfire from supper, he saw. None of his dishware, nothing set up in that homey fashion Charlotte had developed, the way she set the fold-up wooden table he had made as if they were a pioneer family already living in a cozy cabin, always with bread or cakes, beans and meat. . . .

When Luke asked Zeke about the women, Zeke said only that he had seen the two ride off in the afternoon, going north and following someone— a man—whose identity he couldn't make out.

Luke tried to control his flash of anger at Zeke—hadn't he wondered whom Charlotte and Biddy Lee were following? But Zeke knew nothing more, and Luke reminded himself that Zeke was an old man, and a friend.

A man going north, he repeated to himself.

They couldn't have been crazy enough to go anywhere with the Smitherses.

He asked the Vestrows, but they hadn't seen anything, and then Mrs. Gunderson, who had: Charlotte and Biddy Lee had followed Charlie Mews.

That piece of news wasn't good, Luke felt. Charlie Mews was the kind of man Luke never would have expected to see on the trail: someone who would have been a drifter otherwise, maybe the town drunk back home.

Luke found Charlie in his tent, supposedly already asleep, his breathing rasping and steady. "Mews," Luke said as he crouched at the tent's entrance, holding his lantern near Mews's legs.

No change in the breathing, but Luke had the feeling he was only pretending to be asleep.

He took hold of Mews's ankle and squeezed it. "Mews."

Charlie Mews jumped as if he had been singed with a brand. "Holy smoke!" he cried out. "What are you trying to do, Ashcroft? Scare a man into an early grave?"

"What were you doing taking Mrs. Dalton and Miss Waters off the trail?"

Mews laughed. " 'Miss Waters'? That's a new one."

Luke grabbed him by his shirt. "Miss Waters is a free woman, and in a year's time will probably own more than you'll ever acquire in your miserable life."

Mews narrowed his eyes. "Maybe so, maybe not. That remains to be seen. I wouldn't know anything about it."

Luke let go of him and looked into his eyes. "And what do you know about where the two women are? People saw you riding north with them."

Mews swallowed, looking nervous. "I spied a campfire and told Mrs. Dalton about it," Mews answered, swallowing. "She begged me to take her to it, and I did. She thought it was you, maybe wounded or some such thing. But when we got there, no one was there."

Luke looked at him carefully. "And then— what? You just left them there? They left you? What I want to know is why they're missing and you're in your tent, sleeping like a baby."

Charlie Mews looked up, down, everywhere but at Luke.

"Cough up the truth, Mews."

Mews said nothing, but Luke could smell the sweat spurting from his pores. "My mule went lame," he finally said. "I never even reached the campfire. I came back, and they didn't. I don't know what happened."

Luke narrowed his eyes, a bad feeling gnawing at the edges of his heart. "And Skete and Jock? Where were they?"

"Where were they when?" Mews asked. "I don't know anything about that."

"So if I went to their tents, they'd be sleeping like babies too?"

"Am I married to them?" Mews cried. "I don't know where they are. They're probably asleep. But I don't know anything about that."

Luke stood up. "There's a hell of a lot you don't seem to know about. Now, tell me what direction you sent the women in, and face the consequences when I get back if you lied to me, Mews."

"It was north," Mews said quickly. "Due north, Mr. Ashcroft. I swear."

Luke took a deep breath. "If anything happened to Mrs. Dalton or Miss Waters, Mews, you'll be the one to pay," he muttered, and walked out.

As he tightened the girth on Canton's saddle, he thought about George and how much he had loved the horse. *Don't let another person who's important to you just vanish from your life.* He shook his head, not wanting to listen. And then, in the distance, he saw something: two women coming back into camp, riding one spent-looking horse.

Charlotte and Biddy Lee were back.

A few moments later, he was holding Charlotte in his arms and she was kissing him, and she put her arms around him as if she never wanted to let go. . . .

And he felt himself falling. . . .

No!

Just hold her, he told himself. *Don't think about anything but holding her and keeping her safe.*

"Tell me everything," he whispered.

She shook her head. "Tell me about George. Is he—is he gone?"

Luke nodded, the memory as sharp and painful as if he were still looking at his friend. "He hung on as long as he could," he said quietly. *And he wanted me to promise him something,* he added silently.

Biddy Lee came up and whispered something in Charlotte's ear and then looked up at Luke. "I'm glad you're home safe," she said. "Now your woman needs taking care of, Luke, and I'll leave that to you. I'll water Pontiac and Canton."

"What are you doing?" Charlotte asked as Luke pulled her along toward the tent.

"Biddy Lee gave me my orders, Charlotte. I'm supposed to take care of my woman. Now go. Into the tent."

Inside, he pulled her into his arms and kissed her mouth, her nose, her eyes; he kissed her neck, smelled her hair, breathed in her scent, looked into her eyes.

What he felt for her, what he had felt when he had thought he had lost her . . .

Tell her.

Instead he kissed her, long and hard. Their bodies melded, melted, subsided, and then were swept up all over again. They cried out for each other, moaned, drenched each other in sweat. And held each other some more, spent and exhausted.

Afterward, as Charlotte lay with her head against Luke's chest, his arms wrapped around her, she craned her neck to look up at him. "Luke," she whispered.

And then a moment later, she was asleep.

Twenty-five

"Charlotte Dalton and Biddy Lee Waters! Charlotte Dalton and Biddy Lee Waters!" Charlotte thought she was dreaming the deep-pitched voice. "You're summoned to report to Captain Tayler at once!"

Her eyes flew open. It was still dark, yet she was certain she had heard those strange, terrible words.

Luke had stood up and was heading for the tent's entrance.

"Is Mrs. Dalton in here?" Charlotte heard a male voice ask.

"What the hell business is it of yours?" Luke demanded.

Elbridge Chant, a gaunt, old-looking man in his mid-thirties, looked past Luke. Charlotte was holding a cover over her chest, but she felt naked—and frightened as the events of the previous afternoon filtered back like a bad dream. How could she have slept for so long? And how could she not have told Luke any of it? "Mrs. Dalton, the captain needs to speak to you. Immediately."

"Get the hell out of here before I cork you!" Luke cried, shoving at Chant as he followed the man outside.

Charlotte dressed quickly, pulling on her blouse and skirt and apron, still feeling as if she were in a dream. And wishing she were in a dream, one from which she could wake up.

She didn't know who had said what to whom, but she knew, as surely as she knew her own name, that she should have said something to Luke last night.

She already heard raised voices: Luke's, Lavinia Smithers's, Captain Tayler's.

"Biddy Lee?" she called as she walked out into the near-dawn.

Biddy Lee looked petrified, her eyes like moons in her dark, smooth-skinned face. "This is it," Biddy Lee whispered. "I think we'd best tell the truth, Charlotte."

Charlotte felt a chill as Mollie Smithers's eyes met hers. "You can't say you did anything, Biddy Lee. Just follow my lead," Charlotte whispered as they headed for the growing crowd. "I can only beg you, Biddy Lee, but it is for your own good."

Captain Tayler looked grim, his face drawn and

pale beneath the thin, grizzled gray beard that covered his chin and jaws.

Charlotte could hardly look at Luke. But when she glanced at him, she could just imagine what he was wondering, and she could only wonder those same things herself: Why hadn't she been able to tell him the night before?

"What we're here to find out," Captain Tayler boomed in his frightening, low voice, "is what has happened to Jock and Skete Smithers."

Charlotte's heart was already racing. She could hardly find her voice, yet she knew that she wanted to be the one to speak for both of them— before Biddy Lee spoke the truth. "We were lied to," she said. "And I'd like to know where Charlie Mews is because he set the wheels in motion."

Her voice died in her throat as Lavinia Smithers's eyes met hers. Charlotte didn't think she had ever seen so much hatred in her entire life.

"Those whores are what started the trouble," Mrs. Smithers hissed. "Charlie Mews didn't have nothing to do with it except being a victim was all. They fooled everybody."

Captain Tayler held up a hand. "I'll have no more accusations until we can start looking at the truth. Now, someone go fetch Mews—"

"Charlie's gone missing!" a voice called from the back of the crowd. "His horse is gone and his tent and his own self!" the voice piped up.

A skinny, pale-haired young man Charlotte knew only as Clem came forward. "I looked for Charlie this morning, and he's gone!"

Captain Tayler's face darkened, and he looked at Charlotte as if she and he were the only two people in the caravan. "Begin at the beginning, Mrs. Dalton, and let every word of yours be the truth."

Charlotte looked at Biddy Lee, but she couldn't read her friend's eyes. Oh, how she wished her mama were here, at least to stand by her side!

Charlotte took a deep breath. "Charlie Mews came to tell me he had found Luke, that Luke was wounded. He said the Vestrows would be following, but that he'd lead us out there while the others were readying themselves." Charlotte looked into Captain Tayler's eyes. "I had no reason to doubt Mr. Mews, Captain Tayler."

"She's a *liar!*" Carlene Smithers cried, her blue eyes bulging.

Captain Tayler held up a hand. "You'll have your turn in due course," he pronounced. "For now, it's Mrs. Dalton's turn to present her version of what happened." He frowned. "So Mews led you where?"

"Well, about two thirds of the way toward a campfire. His mule seemed awfully lame and weak, so we—I—told him he should head back. We were heading due north and felt fairly sure we could find Mr. Ashcroft on our own—"

"Two women!" Lavinia Smithers cried out. "Finding a man alone out on the prairie? Who would believe a story like that?"

"It's the truth," Charlotte insisted. "I would have crossed hell or high water to get to Mr. Ashcroft, and so would Biddy Lee. As it was, it wasn't hard to find the campfire. Except that Luke wasn't there. Jock and Skete Smithers were."

"You're a liar!" Mollie screamed.

"You hold your tongue, young lady," Captain Tayler warned. "Go on, please, Mrs. Dalton."

Charlotte shivered. "They said all sorts of hateful things to us. And they made it clear that after they had had their way with each of us, they were going to kill us—"

"They're lying!" Lavinia Smithers screamed. "Those whores led my men out to the woods like lambs to the slaughter, and now they want to be given a medal for what they did!"

Amelia Wetherwax grabbed hold of Lavinia, and Mollie put her arms around her mother, and the screams turned to sobs as Captain Tayler spoke. "No one has said Mrs. Dalton and Biddy Lee will receive a medal," he said calmly. "We still don't even know what Mrs. Dalton claims happened."

Charlotte didn't particularly like the way the captain had said the word "claims," but she went on, telling herself it didn't matter that the next part was a lie. It was for Biddy Lee's sake, and for Biddy Lee, a lie was worth telling. "Jock and Skete seemed intent on hurting Biddy Lee." She shook her head. "It was horrible to hear what they planned to do to her, and to think that they had planned everything. And that we were no closer to knowing where Luke was than we had ever been."

She looked down as she told her biggest untruth of all. "I had one chance to defend us—and that was when Jock and Skete were both holding

Biddy Lee down. I reached for my rifle, and I warned them to stop, to let Biddy Lee go. They didn't, even though I had the rifle pointed at them."

"And so you *shot* them?" Captain Tayler asked, his voice incredulous.

Charlotte wondered where she had gone wrong. True, she had made up the details, but they were based on the truth; yet Captain Tayler was acting as if she hadn't had cause to do what she and Biddy Lee had done. "If I hadn't shot Skete Smithers, I wouldn't be here right now—"

"And my brother would be!" Mollie cried out.

Charlotte set her gaze on her longtime rival. "Maybe," Charlotte said. "But I had my own life to defend. And my friend's. And I don't know of any laws out here that say those men had a right to do what they did—"

"But your whole story is a lie!" Mollie called out. "It's your word against the words of three men who can't tell their story!"

"Now you're saying I killed Charlie Mews as well?" Charlotte asked. "He rode out of here a coward, Mollie, on his own steam and his own horse."

"According to you!" Mollie shouted.

Charlotte put her head in her hands.

"I'm sure we'll find someone in this caravan who saw Mews leave," Captain Tayler stated. "And in any event, everyone saw him come back before Biddy Lee and Charlotte returned. He's probably alive and drunk somewhere far off the trail, and he'll wake up tomorrow and wonder where everyone went."

A few people in the crowd laughed, but Charlotte wasn't one of them. Nor were Biddy Lee and Luke laughing, nor the Blisses.

"Those whores tricked my father and brother into meeting them and now half my family is dead!" Mollie moaned.

"It's not true," Charlotte said. "Those men were already out there, waiting for us. If Biddy Lee and I had tricked them, how is it that they were out there first? Is there anyone here who saw them follow us?" Charlotte asked.

She looked from face to face, but she was met with either stony hatred or averted eyes.

Luke stepped forward. "Jake, this is insane," he said, facing Captain Tayler. "It's a shouting match and nothing more."

"I need to hear both sides—all sides of the story," Captain Tayler answered.

"And then what?" Luke demanded. "Decide who most of the people in this crowd believe? I know who I believe."

"That whore services you every day, so what do you care?" Mollie cried out. "Probably both of them do!"

Captain Tayler caught Luke just as he was moving toward Mollie.

"Don't do it," warned Captain Tayler.

"Then stop this insanity!" Luke said. "What the devil has gotten into you, letting a questioning turn into a free-for-all? I'm splitting off from the caravan with anyone who wants to come with me, Jake, and we'll be gone before the day is done. If this is what the caravan has turned into, I want no part of it."

"He's going to take those two murderers away!" Mollie shrieked. "Captain Tayler, you have to stop them!"

Lavinia Smithers was sobbing and wailing, and Amelia Wetherwax was holding her shoulders and crying with her.

"They should be hanged!" Amelia Wetherwax cried out. Her eyes were bright with hatred, her gaunt face red beneath her bonnet. "No marriage in this caravan is safe until those two whores are dead and buried!"

Charlotte felt her blood run cold. Biddy Lee looked frozen with fear, and Charlotte could just imagine why: Many people in the crowd felt she was less than a human being to begin with.

"Jake, get this crowd under control—now!" Luke yelled. "Or I'll do it for you!"

Captain Tayler looked as if he were being torn apart. Charlotte couldn't understand why this man who normally held such command over the group now seemed hardly to know what was going on.

He shook his head, whispered something in Luke's ear, and then raised his right hand in a command for silence. "I know Luke Ashcroft well enough to know that if he's determined to form his own caravan, then so be it. This matter will end here and now; I'm certain we'll never know the truth of what happened—"

"You can't let them get away with this!" Brent Wetherwax cried.

Captain Tayler raised a hand again. "What I know is that we need all our strength for the upcoming journey. A group filled with suspicions and hatred will never make it to the Territories." He sighed. "My wife took sick this morning. I'm laying over right here in this very spot until she's better. Anyone who wants to stay with me is welcome. Anyone who wants to move on with Luke had better go with him."

"You're letting two murderers go free!" Mollie shouted. "How are Mother and Carlene and I supposed to travel without Daddy and Skete, without our slaves? We didn't bury Daddy and Skete, we didn't pray for them—"

"Then pray for them now!" Jake Tayler thundered. "And pray for your own souls, for harboring so much hatred in them!"

Charlotte felt a strong hand on her arm, and she turned. Luke had grabbed her by one arm, grabbed Biddy Lee by the other arm and was heading for the tents. "Pack up," he growled. "We're leaving."

People were already starting to run after Luke— Alma Bliss, the Vestrows, Zeke hobbling on his weak ankle. "We're coming with you, Luke!" he shouted.

"Be sure you don't leave without us!" Nora Vestrow called out.

Word spread quickly through camp. As Charlotte packed, she saw people run everywhere rather than walk, and it seemed as if the majority of people were hurrying to pull up stakes.

"Did you realize you had so many followers?" Charlotte asked as Luke knelt on the ground to check the axles of the wagon.

At first, Luke said nothing. Yet she could see in the clench of his jaw, even in the way he was moving, that something was very, very wrong.

She was about to ask him again when finally he spoke. "Most of the people leaving will follow whoever is heading out first, Charlotte." There was something in the way he had said her name that made her uneasy. "No one wants to be second on the next decent grazing ground when they could be first. Look—even the Clusens are packing up."

"I see," she said quietly, feeling certain he was talking around something rather than about it. And she knew what that something was. He couldn't understand why she hadn't told him about Skete and Jock Smithers. "Luke—" she began.

"Emma Gray needs my help putting her wagon to rights," he said quietly. "Can I leave you and Biddy Lee to check the rest of the wagon and tack?"

"Of course," Charlotte said, her voice so quiet it was almost a whisper.

Emma Gray.

Emma Gray, who had fallen in love with George, only to lose him far too quickly. Emma Gray, who had lost George on the heels of losing her father.

Emma Gray, who was intelligent and courageous and beautiful and harbored no particular plans about going out west other than marrying and then doing whatever her husband wanted her to do.

Charlotte watched as Luke walked away. He hadn't waited for a reply from her; indeed, he hadn't even looked into her eyes as he had spoken.

He's broken up the entire caravan because of you, an inner voice argued.

But Charlotte shook her head as she realized the truth of the matter: Luke had as keen a sense of justice as anyone she had ever met. For all she knew, he had broken up the train to protect Biddy Lee from the Smithers family's supporters.

The man who had just walked away had spoken out on her behalf, and acted on her behalf, and was working to protect her and her friend. But she had finally shown him—unwittingly—that she would always act alone, without sharing her deepest concerns. And his feelings for her—whatever feelings he had ever had—had diminished, dried up to a piece of dust and drifted off on a breeze.

He was moving on.

Twenty-six

"I can't believe we're seeing a real building," Biddy Lee said, catching up to Charlotte. "Can you, Charlotte? And that we're finally going to stop?"

Luke had kept up a brutal pace; they had passed Courthouse Rock, Chimney Rock and

Scott's Bluff, beautiful and amazing formations in the middle of the huge, flat prairie, without a moment's rest at any of the famous landmarks. And now they were finally reaching Fort Laramie.

They had traveled ceaselessly. Charlotte was pretty sure they'd kept up that frantic pace in order to escape all the travelers who had hung back with Captain Tayler. But she didn't know for sure if this was the reason because she and Luke had hardly spoken.

"Look at Luke and Emma Gray," Biddy Lee said, nodding at the two figures ahead of them as they stopped at the high walls that surrounded Fort Laramie.

Charlotte didn't say anything, her voice gone as she followed Biddy Lee's gaze: There was an intimacy in the way Luke and Emma moved and spoke that made Charlotte want to cry.

Luke had been polite, driving the teams when Charlotte needed to do something else, complimenting her and Biddy Lee on their cooking. Yet there was no life in his eyes when he talked with her, no humor, certainly none of the affection or enthusiasm or trust that she had tried earlier to roll up in her mind into some sort of love. But she now saw that she had been trying to create something that simply hadn't existed.

Every night, Charlotte had slept in one tent, Biddy Lee in a another, Luke in a third. Despite aching fatigue and mind-numbing exhaustion, Charlotte had lain awake, hurting from the memory of nights of passion with a man she did indeed love, even if the feelings weren't mutual.

And perhaps as much as the passion, she missed the tenderness that had come before and after Luke's extraordinary lovemaking—the feel of his strong arms as he had clasped her from behind, the warmth of his breath at the back of her neck, the feeling of complete security as she had lain asleep in his arms.

And now, she saw the same enthusiasm that used to shine from his eyes shine only when he was helping Emma; it was at these times that he now seemed to come to life.

"Luke, can you help me soak my wagon wheels tonight?" Emma had asked on the first day out past Courthouse Rock. "Luke, could you help me with one of my oxen?" she had asked on the second. Charlotte had felt her heart break as Luke had casually handed her the whip on that second day, without even a glance, and absently asked her to drive the teams while he helped Emma. For all the attention he had paid to her, Charlotte could have been a man.

And yet, she couldn't fault Emma as she had faulted Mollie in the past for her attempts to interest Luke. Emma wasn't feigning the need for help; Charlotte knew that Luke would want to help her, for as long as she needed help, because of George. Emma had tried to maintain the wagon and the oxen on her own, Charlotte had seen, and called Luke only when she genuinely needed him.

Well, it was the price she was going to have to pay: She had fallen in love with a man who hadn't fallen in love with her—though he was a man of honor and courage. But his offer of marriage had come from duty rather than love.

"Luke has a right to do what he wants," she said to Biddy Lee, trying to sound sincere. At least *part* of her meant the words. "What I need to do is concentrate on finding Jacob, somehow."

"This isn't right," Biddy Lee said, shaking her head. "It isn't supposed to end this way, Charlotte."

Charlotte felt a chill and wave of dizziness. What was important was Jacob; what was important was trying to salvage her promise to Lucinda, and to her own heart. What was important was starting a new life for herself and her baby.

"Do you remember once, Biddy Lee, when you told me I had to keep my eyes on the prize?"

Biddy Lee nodded, her brow etched with memories. "Keep your eyes on the prize, and put one foot in front of the other, Charlotte."

Charlotte took a deep breath. "Well, Luke Ashcroft, despite everything I feel for him, isn't the prize because I've never wanted a man. My sister's boy is the prize, and going out west is the prize. Those are what matter."

Biddy Lee was quiet. "What if you don't find him, Charlotte?"

For some reason, in a place deep in her heart, Charlotte felt that she or Luke would find Jacob—somehow, if the boy was destined to survive. How she would get him from Marcus and Penny was a question she would be able to answer only when the time came.

For now, though, she would keep her eye on the prize.

Yet as she watched Luke slinging an arm around Emma Gray's shoulder as she crossed a rough piece of ground, Charlotte felt a piece of her heart break off. And it felt like a wound that would never heal.

She loved him as she never had loved before, as she had never imagined she could.

Keep your eyes on the prize, she told herself— because Luke wasn't it, and never would be.

"Where have you been?" Charlotte asked Biddy Lee as Biddy Lee came back to the tent in the late afternoon, on the outskirts of the tall wall that surrounded the fort. "I've been worried sick, Biddy Lee."

Biddy Lee flushed, her brown skin turning a deep mahogany. "I met a slave family that's been ahead of us," she said. "One of those men, he brings my Ben Lucius to mind." She was quiet, her face long and drawn in thought. "I miss him with all my heart, do you know? I pushed him away and now I wish I hadn't, and Johnny Washington . . ." Her voice trailed off. "Johnny Washington is his name." Tears welled at the corners of her eyes, and she wiped them away with hands that looked ancient. "Does that sound crazy that I could miss Ben and want to be with another man?"

"Not at all," Charlotte answered, meaning her words. "Ben Lucius is gone. You have to live your life." She hesitated, afraid to ask her next words. "Do you know if he's traveling to California or to Oregon?" she asked, her heart sinking. Oregon had a law that forbade slaves from even entering the Territory, and Charlotte had the feeling she knew what was coming.

"California," Biddy Lee said. "His family, they're good people, and they're freeing all their slaves come California. Every one of them."

"Oh, Biddy Lee," Charlotte said softly. "That sounds so wonderful. I hope you find someone you fall in love with. You certainly deserve it." She felt strange all of a sudden then, and she murmured something to Biddy Lee about the oxen and walked away.

Still feeling strange, exhausted and confused, she walked out to where the oxen were grazing on poor, thin grasses and laid her hands along old Sam's back. She closed her eyes and pictured herself back home for a minute, playing in the barn with her calves and chickens and cows, laughing with Lucinda, planning their futures, their mama in the kitchen baking up pies, Pa wherever— working if they were all lucky, so he wouldn't pick on any of them.

Too much had happened, too much had changed, she said to herself. She missed her mama and she missed Lucinda and she missed Jacob with a deep, piercing ache in her heart. Why was it she had always known she would survive the trip and Lucinda wouldn't? She hadn't reached the Territories yet, of course, but she knew, in her heart and her bones, that she would.

She opened her eyes and looked at poor old Sam again. "I wish I could buy you some new teammates," she said quietly. For a moment, it was as if Sam had answered her. She heard him groan, or thought she did, and then he seemed to shimmer in the late-afternoon, long-slanting rays . . . and sway . . . and then he was engulfed by darkness.

She felt a sharp pain against her forehead . . . and then nothing at all.

At first, she didn't know why she was looking at Luke, why she was in his tent, why he looked so concerned.

And then she remembered Sam shimmering in the sunlight.

"What happened?" she asked softly.

"What happened," he said, "is that you fainted."

For a moment, as Luke looked into her eyes, she thought he was going to reach out and stroke her forehead, maybe sweep her up into his arms. For a moment, she thought he was going to say words she could believe forever. For a moment, she thought Luke would love her forever, not because she was carrying his child but because he truly did love her, and would never change.

"You'll want someone looking after you, Charlotte," he said, "whether you like it or not. Needing help doesn't make you a weak person. When some women are with child—"

"But I'm not," she interrupted.

He looked surprised, then saddened, his eyes questioning hers.

God forgive me, she said silently, and then went on. "Everything is back to normal."

"But the fainting—?"

She shrugged, silently begging forgiveness again. "As I said," she began, but could speak no more untruths.

Yes, this was forgivable, she told herself. This was necessary. If Luke pursued her, somehow talked her into marrying him because he was the father of her child, it would be wrong, as dishonest as what she was now doing.

Yet as she looked into Luke's eyes—quickly, just a glance, because a glance was all she could afford if she was going to stick to her resolve—the stronger part of her heart told her she was doing wrong.

I have no choice, she told herself. *I won't spend my life with a man who isn't in love with me for myself.*

She had to move away from him; she had to distance herself from his scent, the sight of him, the nearness of the man she would always love.

"I shall be fine," she said, for a moment feeling the edges of her world blackening again.

Luke watched her, and he knew what she was feeling. He could see that she was about to faint again, see the weakness in her eyes, the way her mouth half-opened at the point she nearly blacked out again.

And he knew she was lying; he could see the evasiveness in her eyes, a dishonesty he would have bet his life he would never, ever see in Charlotte's eyes.

Ashcroft, he said to himself, *you lost out.* If Charlotte felt so determined not to marry him that she would lie in order to avoid it—

Well, hell. He didn't believe in beating dead horses.

For a moment, it was as if George were suddenly there with him—looking angry, and amazed. "I've never seen you give up that quickly in your entire life!" George cried out. "I've never even seen you give up, Luke."

Luke shook his head then, missing his old friend.

"There's a first time for everything, my friend," he said silently. "I'm not going to ask Charlotte again."

Twenty-seven

Charlotte awakened with a jolt of sickness, closing her eyes against a wave of nausea that reached her throat and then slowly, too slowly, abated.

"Mrs. Dalton?" a woman's voice called from outside the tent.

She didn't recognize the voice, and she was eager to be taken away from her self-pitying thoughts. She hurriedly dressed, and was surprised to see Penny Clusen's mother shivering in the cold, her eyes rimmed red from crying.

"Olive's near passing," Mrs. Clusen said, her voice breaking into a sob. "Lord knows she might have passed while I was coming over here—" Her voice broke again, and Charlotte looked past her to where a few women were beginning to stoke up the previous night's fires. "Now don't ask me why because I'm sure I couldn't begin to tell you—" She wiped at flowing tears. "But my Olive said she needs to speak with you. So follow me and let's hope the good Lord none of my friends see me talking with the likes of you and your kind."

Charlotte bit her tongue against the slew of choice words she could have spoken. But if Olive was near death and needed to speak to Charlotte, obviously she had something important to say.

"She's in here," Mrs. Clusen said, pointing to a small, dark tent.

Charlotte said nothing. She opened the flap and was stunned to see a completely transformed girl, one who had once been beautiful and full of youth and life. Olive Clusen now looked closer to Alma Bliss's age—wizened, pale, the life drained right out of her. Her cheekbones were sharp below dark circles around her eyes, and her lips were chapped and brittle. Her eyes looked glassy, almost unseeing, but Charlotte still kept her distance.

"I told a lie," Olive said, her voice surprisingly strong. "Maybe, if you want to see your little nephew, you should go to Sacramento. Penny always said that was her heart's desire. She wanted to live in a place with a Spanish name and lots of new faces to see."

Charlotte didn't know what to say. She knew why Olive was telling her now—it seemed to have become a trail tradition, deathbed declarations and confessions.

"I know you don't have much feeling for my

family," Olive said quietly, "so you can believe me or not. I just know you love that little boy, so . . ." Her eyes, glassy but still expressive, said it all: She was telling the truth.

"Thank you for telling me," Charlotte said. "I hope you recover from the dysentery," she added, though they both knew this wouldn't happen.

Sacramento, she said to herself as she headed back toward the tent. A chance to find Jacob, a place to head for. . . .

As she neared her tent, she saw Biddy Lee come out of hers, a small, neat bag looped over her shoulder. "What are you doing?" Charlotte asked.

"Saying goodbye to you and Luke and the Blisses. Those Washingtons, the slave family I told you about? Their people, the Joneses, they're pulling out. They're heading for Sacramento—"

"But that's wonderful, Biddy Lee, because I think I might head there too—"

"Then you hurry up and do it, girl, because what the Washingtons heard last night would curl your toes. There was a small wagon train pulled in last night, and they say all kinds of people back with those Smithers women are talking about us. They're stalled up back about fifteen miles with a broken axle, and they talk against us to anyone who'll listen. 'You beware of two of them women if you come upon a train run by Luke Ashcroft,' they tell everyone. 'They'll murder you in your sleep as soon as look at you.'" She shivered and looked into Charlotte's eyes. "They're not going to be laid up forever, Charlotte. And I don't want to be here when they get going again."

Charlotte shook her head. "No one can travel as fast as Luke is pushing us," she said. "That's why half these people followed him. If the weather holds—"

"If the weather holds, if Luke doesn't hang back for some reason . . . If, if, if, Charlotte, and then we'll have a wagon train of people coming who are calling us murderers and whores." Biddy Lee looked down, her dark lashes lush and beautiful. "If you truly might be heading for Sacramento, that's the best news I've had in a long time. But wherever you go, Charlotte Dalton, we'll meet up again because it's meant to be." She took Charlotte in her arms and hugged her. "Just one more thing. I need one little promise from you before I go."

"What kind of promise?"

"The man who fought for my freedom, the man who defended us against all those crazy people—"

"What about him?" Charlotte asked, hoping she was wrong about what Biddy Lee was leading up to.

Biddy Lee narrowed her eyes. "Men like that come along once every thousand lifetimes. I want a promise you're going to marry him, Charlotte."

Charlotte remembered the day she had told Luke she wanted to get to know him in another lifetime. And now it was all over—as if indeed it *had* taken place in another lifetime, or in a dream. "Biddy Lee, I'm not going to marry him."

Biddy Lee reached out and touched Charlotte's cheek, her hand as rough from work as Luke's.

"You would be making the mistake of a lifetime," Biddy Lee murmured. "Don't you do it, girl."

"I know what I'm doing," Charlotte said.

Biddy Lee's lips were set thin and narrow. "I expect to see you and Luke together out west; that's all I'm going to say." She hugged Charlotte again, and whispered before she broke away, "Trust me, Charlotte. Please. I always trusted you."

And then she was gone, running toward a man who was holding out long, strong-looking arms for her. He took Biddy Lee in his arms when she reached him, and they walked off together toward the small caravan that was already pulling out.

"Oh, Biddy Lee," Charlotte said out loud. "Find a better life out there for yourself. Somehow."

Unconsciously, she cradled her belly. *We'll be together and we'll be strong together, and that's all that really matters,* she said silently, a tear rolling down her cheek as she watched her friend disappear.

Twenty-eight

The fire for the night's dinner leapt to life before Charlotte's eyes, and Charlotte tried to concentrate on the flames rather than on the conversation she had had with Emma Gray an hour earlier.

But she knew she wouldn't soon forget Emma Gray's words, her soft voice, her beautiful and honest-looking face. "I'm not in the business of stealing men," Emma had said. "And I'm certainly not ready for anyone at all except a friend in my life. But I have a lot of feelings for Luke. And I thought you two . . . well, if you're involved with him—"

"I'm not," Charlotte cut in, not wanting to listen to any more. "Luke and I are friends. If you want to fall in love with him, run off with him, whatever you're thinking of doing, I'd certainly be the last person on earth to try to stop you. I'll never have anything to do with a man again."

Now, as she mixed a crust for the buffalo-meat pie she was making for dinner, she was amazed she had been able to say so many words without crying or screaming. But she had managed, as she supposed she would have to manage for the rest of the journey.

She had invited Alma and Zeke for dinner, hoping her experimental pie, plus potatoes, cooked apples with serviceberries and biscuits, would keep her mind off Luke and Emma.

As she poured the meat and onions into the pie crust that lined her Dutch oven, she told herself it was just as well she hadn't dared to invite Luke. Not twenty feet away, he was kneeling beside Emma Gray, talking with her—then laughing with her, tucking a lock of her hair back from her face.

Charlotte felt her heart sink, remembering how whenever Luke had done the same thing to her, she had always felt it was a sign of affection.

"If you say nothing," Alma said softly, interrupting Charlotte's thoughts, "then you will have made your own bed, Charlotte." Alma sat down on her haunches beside the campfire like a young girl.

"And what would you have me do?" Charlotte asked. "Proclaim my feelings for Luke after I interrupt their kissing?"

"Just talk to him," Alma said. "If you'd like me to talk to him—"

"Talk leads to trouble," Charlotte said, trying not to look over at Luke as he sat shoulder-to-shoulder with Emma. "Talk leads to false hopes, and I don't intend to have any more for the rest of my life. Everything has fallen apart. I've lost everyone I've ever loved. I love you and Zeke, of course, and Mama back home, and the Vestrows, but you know what I mean."

"You don't have to lose this man," Alma said fiercely. "Everyone always knew he loved you."

"But he didn't," Charlotte said. "He absolutely didn't, Alma." Her voice was cut off, all her attention turned toward the adobe walls that surrounded Fort Laramie and an all-too-familiar wagon train that was pulling into camp.

At the head was Captain Tayler, driving a worn-out group of oxen, the man himself looking stooped over and beaten. Charlotte had the awful feeling Mrs. Tayler had passed on—hadn't Captain Tayler said he was laying over because his wife was ill? There wasn't much of a chance that she had recovered so quickly.

Behind the captain followed the Wetherwaxes' wagons, and then one of the Smitherses' wagons, driven by an unfamiliar-looking, strapping young man, and led by teams of horses instead of oxen.

"Who's that driving the Smitherses' wagon?" Charlotte asked. "And how did they get a brand-new team of horses?"

Alma shrugged. "Maybe the teams are his. Or maybe the Smithers girls and that witch of a mother bought them. They have more money than most everyone else put together, Charlotte."

Mollie suddenly appeared at the front of the wagon. She tugged at the man's sleeve, looking in Charlotte's direction and pointing.

"She can't harm you with all these people around," Alma said. "She wouldn't have the nerve or the strength."

Charlotte thought back to those nights that now seemed so long ago, when Luke had sworn to protect her and had guarded her tent even when she hadn't needed him to. Well, she was on her own now, as she had always claimed she wanted to be. And Biddy Lee was on her way with the handsome and strong Johnny Washington.

Suddenly, Mollie Smithers leapt out of the wagon and ran toward Charlotte like a wild animal, her eyes bugging, her beautiful white skin blotched with angry red spots. "Do you know that my sister-in-law is dead? Do you know that my mother and I are alone now? And that it's all your fault?"

"How would it be my fault that Carlene is dead if I haven't seen you in all this time?" Charlotte asked.

"My Carlene—my best friend in the whole world—is dead because *you* made her sick. You and that slut slave girl made her sick because of

what happened to Daddy and Skete. That bloody
flux killed her as quickly as if you had stuck a
knife up into that poor girl's body and twisted it,
what with us having to do the work of those good-
for-nothing slaves twenty-four hours a day. But the
suffering my Carlene went through is nothing
compared to what will happen to Biddy Lee. That
girl is going to be strung up like a pig going to
slaughter. Have you ever seen a slave killed by
someone who knows what they're doing?"

"You're crazy," Charlotte said.

"What's crazy," Mollie screamed, "is that you
don't see fit to honor the law that says my family
owns Biddy Lee Waters, fair and square. I have
witnesses to the murder of my father and brother,
Charlotte, and you'll hang for those murders. But
Biddy Lee—she'll go under the cleaver for what
she did."

Charlotte said nothing for a moment, thanking
God that Biddy Lee was already gone from the
fort. But how fast would their wagon train travel?

"You should realize nobody in Luke's caravan
believes you, Mollie. You may have some believers
in your group—"

"I have witnesses!" Mollie shrieked. "And they
want to see that slave girl's blood drain out of her,
Charlotte Dalton. When the authorities here at
the fort hear my witnesses, it isn't going to be like
Captain Tayler, staring off into space almost crying. They're going to string both of you up—"

"There are no authorities here," Charlotte said.
"What authorities are you talking about? Did you
think this was a military outpost?"

"It's a fort!" Mollie cried out. "It's Fort Laramie!"

"It's a trading post," Charlotte said, her voice nearly trembling with happiness. She couldn't remember the last time she had been so pleased about proving somebody wrong. "It's a fur trappers' fort. Nothing more. There are no authorities. Nobody's going to listen to your story—"

It was as if the blood had literally drained from Mollie's face. She looked ashen. "This isn't the end," she murmured, looking into Charlotte's eyes. "I have witnesses and I'll see you both pay! Biddy Lee will be strung up as sure as we strung up Ben Lucius. As God is my witness, Charlotte."

It was still light out, way too early to begin working on her secret project, Charlotte knew. She wished darkness would fall. People had put together a party to celebrate reaching the one-third mark of the journey, and Charlotte watched from a distance as Luke danced with Emma Gray. She watched as Luke put his hand at the top of Emma's back and then moved it lower.

She knew how that felt.

She watched as Luke looked into Emma's eyes, talking softly with her.

And she knew how that felt.

She saw Luke let go of Emma's hand and put his arm around her shoulder instead, pulling her close.

And her heart ached, because she knew she would never feel any of those things again. She would never feel his strong, comforting hold, she would never feel his powerful body moving with hers, she would never feel the clasp of his hand or his rough beard, or the soft touch of his lips.

"Get over it," she said to herself. She was made of tougher stuff. She didn't need a man.

"You know," Alma Bliss said softly, suddenly at her side, "I've been known to speak out of turn, my dear. Luke knows me well enough to know that if I talk to him about you, it's probably because I'm nosing in where I don't belong. He wouldn't think you had asked me, dear."

Charlotte felt sadness grip her heart, and she squeezed her eyes shut against tears.

But when she opened them, she was determined to be strong. "I'll always love him, Alma. But it wasn't meant to be. I'll never be with a man, because that *is* what is meant to be. And Luke doesn't love me."

"You know that, child?"

"Look at him," Charlotte said softly.

Alma's eyes followed in the direction Charlotte had nodded. And Charlotte could see Alma's whole expression change, as she watched Luke act as tenderly and caring with Emma as he had acted with her.

"I may be hurting, Alma, but it doesn't matter. Because he isn't. Biddy Lee taught me to keep my eyes on the prize, and for me that means always having baby Jacob in my mind, always asking about him and trying to find new people who might have seen him, and helping Biddy Lee out whatever way I can. Anything else is just selfishness," she finished, knowing that what she needed, too, was time to slow the Smithers women down, and time to start learning who she was, with no one to rely on—or blame—but herself.

Charlotte walked through the darkness, stomach-sickness making what little she could see spin before her eyes. And making her miss Luce and their mama and baby Jacob more than ever.

She felt as if every step was like a thunderclap, threatening to wake up Mollie or one of her supporters.

When she found Mollie and her mother's wagon, its painted white and yellow roses visible even in the midnight's darkness, she knelt down, grateful she had brought her sharper-than-sharp knife from her home farm. She hated to destroy such beautiful tack—Alma had found out Mollie and her mother had bought the team and its tack only the day before—but it was her best chance of slowing them down. If she stole the tack, they would notice its absence at first light. Slicing through it would buy her more time . . . if she was lucky.

As she worked, she made a *clink* here and a *clink* there when metal hit metal, and each time she made a sound, her heart skipped a beat.

With six good cuts, she had rendered the tack unusable, but not so damaged that anyone would notice right away. Mollie and her people might even travel a few miles before the tack gave way.

Suddenly a picture came into her mind of baby Jacob, crying in a broken-down wagon. *Don't let my actions bring bad luck to my boy,* she prayed. For she was indeed doing a terrible thing, she knew, one of the lowest acts anyone could do to someone else on this long, difficult journey.

But she truly felt she had no choice. As she thought again and again of Mollie's ugly, dangerous threats about Biddy Lee, she made more and more cuts, wanting to be dead sure Mollie and her mother didn't get far.

And then, just as she crouched on the ground to make one more slice in the tack for good measure, she felt a cold, steel-strong hand on her shoulder.

It was all over.

It was one of the guards, or a friend of Mollie's, maybe that man she was now traveling with, maybe even one of the trappers who lived at Fort Laramie.

She tried to think about what she could possibly say in her defense, but she knew there were no words that could begin to explain what she was doing.

"Get up now," the voice said.

Luke pulled her up from under her arms and then set her roughly down, standing, as if she were a sack of flour. "You should have let me take care of it," he said.

"I told you a long time ago that I don't need your help," she whispered, her heart crying out, silently, to say something else. *Tell him the truth,* the inner voice said. *Tell him how hard it is for you to trust a man.*

But what was the point? He had made his choices; she had made hers.

She was glad she could only barely make out his eyes as they searched hers. "Fine," he finally said after taking in her features for what seemed like hours. "You get your wish, Charlotte, from here on out."

And with those words, he strode off in the darkness toward Emma Gray's tent.

In the morning, Charlotte felt nervous, alone, even disoriented. What if her sabotage was discovered right away? What if someone had seen her working in the dark? Why had she been so harsh to Luke?

As far as she knew, Captain Tayler was planning a layover of at least one more night. But what if he had changed his plans, and Mollie's wagon fell apart immediately?

Alma and Zeke had invited Charlotte to breakfast, and when she joined them, she almost blurted out everything she had done, just to relieve the pressure. But then she told them something just as important as what she had done to Mollie's tack. "I've decided I'm changing my plans," she said as Alma handed her a plate covered with delicious-looking johnnycakes.

Alma's mouth dropped open. "What on earth are you talking about, dear?"

"I'm going to head for California instead of Oregon Territory," Charlotte said, feeling more secure about her decision with every word she spoke. "Olive Clusen told me that Marcus and Penny were headed for Sacramento, so I know that's where I'll have to go if I want to find Jacob. And Biddy Lee is traveling that way as well."

Alma was looking at Zeke. "Funny all these changes," she said softly. "Pete and Nora and their brood are going to split from the group as well. When they told us that, we thought maybe California would be to *our* liking as well."

"What I like is that California sounds warm," Zeke said, chewing a slab of bacon. "To my old bones, that sounds like it might be just the ticket."

Alma was looking carefully at Charlotte. "How will you travel, dear? Without teams or a wagon or provisions?"

Charlotte imagined Biddy Lee setting off on such a trip without giving it a moment's thought. "Put one foot in front of the other," she would say. And indeed, Charlotte had seen a couple traveling with nothing more than a handcart. "Don't we walk every day anyway? And it's not as if our tents have protected us from the rains," she said with a laugh.

But Alma wasn't smiling. She was looking at Zeke, and Zeke was looking at her. "We *could* go where it's a bit warmer, Zeke."

"I didn't mean for *you* two to go," Charlotte said. "I just know what I have to do. I won't rest until I find Jacob. And this is the first time I at least know where they were headed."

Alma looked over at Luke, who was standing with Emma Gray, talking with his lips nearly touching her ear. "You're sure this is what you want to do, dear?" she asked, looking back at Charlotte.

"Even if things were good between me and Luke, Alma, I would still split off. I need to find my boy. I have to make my own life now, and try to make my boy's life better too."

Twenty-nine

"Do you know what happens to liars?" a voice whispered—Mollie's voice, Charlotte realized as she awakened.

But Mollie had already moved on top of her. Charlotte felt hands clamp around her neck, and she tried to push Mollie away, to push at her arms, to throw her off balance with her hips. But Mollie had planted herself firmly, with strength Charlotte never would have guessed she had.

"How long have you known Biddy Lee was gone?" Mollie breathed. "How long have you known that girl escaped the cleaver I had ready and waiting for her whoring flesh?"

Mollie's fingers tightened, and Charlotte could no longer breathe. The pressure in her head made her eyes feel as if they were going to burst out of her head, and she tried to kick at Mollie, to twist, but her strength was gone. She thought of the baby she was sure was inside of her, she thought of Jacob, whom she would have no chance of saving if she died. . . .

Push! she told herself.

"You think you're so smart, sending Biddy Lee

on her way," Mollie whispered. "Do you know when I think of how my poor Carlene died, I realize hanging would have been too good for you? So you'll get the cleaver that was all sharpened up for that slut—"

Charlotte pushed, wrenching her body off to the side and then shoving at Mollie with her feet.

She thought of the baby and wondered if it had been hurt, thought of what she had almost lost—her life, and that of her baby's—and felt sick with rage and fear. "Get out of here before I kill you!" she screamed.

Behind Mollie, her friend suddenly appeared, the man Charlotte had heard was named Tim Denton. He moved quickly, pulling Mollie roughly to her feet.

"I'll keep a watch on her, miss, but you'd best be moving on before we do," he muttered, dragging Mollie outside.

"She should die for what she did, and for hiding that whore!" Mollie screamed as Tim Denton led her away.

In the early dawn, Charlotte saw that a dozen or so people, men and women both, had emerged from their tents to see what the commotion was about.

And she couldn't help expecting to see Luke. Luke, who had always been there for her; Luke, who was a man of honor before anything else.

But now, as she looked out at the campfires, searching for the one face she wanted to see, she knew that she truly was all alone in the world.

* * *

Luke was forcing the group to keep up a brutal pace, rarely even stopping in storms. "It's as if he's trying to fight the trail," Charlotte heard one man say.

"But look how many groups we've passed," a woman said in Luke's defense.

And her words were true. The cattle and horses were being pushed nearly beyond endurance, and many had died; but for those that had lived, the grazing was far better than it would have been if they had traveled more slowly.

Once again, they passed landmarks without stopping to carve their names or even their initials. At Independence Rock, Luke had nearly bitten a man's head off when he had asked if they could paint just one initial on it before leaving.

The one landmark Luke allowed people to see was Ice Slough, a strange place that made Charlotte feel they truly had entered a new land; a huge bed of ice lay underneath the sod all year round, even on the hot day on which the caravan reached it. Luke called out that everyone could chop at the sod and dig up ice "for one hour, and one hour only."

For a second, Charlotte stood there listening, watching the handsome man she would always love, the father of the baby she might be carrying, the man who had showed her how important it was to be listened to and touched and loved.

And then his eyes met hers, and her heart turned over.

And he looked away.

It's over, she said to herself, her throat tightened

against tears. *I need to find my boy, and I need to live my own life.*

The wonderful news was that Biddy Lee was still free. In the Laramie mountains, when Charlotte's group camped for a night along the Sweetwater River, she heard a woman talking about some slaves and found out that Biddy Lee and Johnny Washington had passed through the day before. "Their caravan wasn't gathering any dust on it, that's for certain," the woman had told Charlotte. "Those slaves and their people, they were racing as if their lives depended on it."

And Charlotte was happy about that. But she felt an ache in her heart that grew deeper each time she saw Luke. Sometimes he drove the teams, sometimes she did, but when the changeover was made, all Charlotte could count on was that few or no words would be exchanged.

She didn't know where he slept, and she didn't want to know.

She tried to be philosophical. She would raise her boy or girl by herself, without a man to boss her around or yell at her or hit her, as her father had done to her mother. Never in her life would she be slapped or pushed, belittled or humiliated.

Luke never would have done any of those things to you, an inner voice said.

But that, she reasoned, was what her mother had thought at first about the handsome, kind man named Henry Collyer when she had first met him. She hadn't expected him to turn into a brutal, angry man with a temper as quick as a snake's.

But Luke's not like that, an inner voice insisted.

Well, that really didn't matter, though, did it? she asked herself. The fact remained that Luke didn't love her. He believed in doing what was right and what was honorable. But that didn't mean he loved her.

And so she would be alone with their baby, and baby Jacob if her deepest hopes came true.

They crossed the South Pass, the Continental Divide, though some people weren't even sure this was the point they had heard so much about. On the chilly, somehow foreboding night they reached it, it just looked like a beautiful, gently sloping meadow encouraging them to continue west.

"In four miles we'll reach Pacific Springs," Luke announced gruffly. "That will be the eastern edge of Oregon Territory, folks, and the end of the easy part of the journey."

A few people laughed in the crowd that had gathered at the edge of the circle of wagons, but Luke didn't smile. "It's not a joke, folks," he said, looking west. "When we reach Fort Bridger, everyone who can would do well to trade their teams in to Jim Bridger and head out without looking back."

Charlotte felt a lump in her throat as she thought about saying goodbye to Luke's once-strong, always faithful oxen.

But she knew that Luke was right; the teams would have a better chance of surviving if they were traded in; then they could get some rest and grazing time before being sold, several weeks in the future, to someone else. And for anyone who could afford to make a trade, refreshed oxen were going to be better than the trail-worn ones they all possessed at that moment.

A few days later, when they pulled in to Fort Bridger, a shabby, cobbled-together structure made of poles and mud, Charlotte felt sadness wash over her as Luke, with Emma Gray at his side, led his teams of oxen to Jim Bridger's corral.

Goodbye, my strongest friends, Charlotte said to herself, turning away.

A moment later, she watched and then listened as men and women in the crowd gathered around an enthusiastic, loud-voiced man named Lansford Hastings. "We need people out in California, ladies and gents," he was saying. "If you follow my route west, I guarantee you'll be weeks ahead of the others heading to the Sacramento Valley!"

Charlotte thought about Jacob. She thought about Luke showing her how to use the sling, Luke holding him as if he had known the baby forever, Luke teaching him to drink. She thought about her and Lucinda's vows and plans, their high hopes and confident dreams.

I promise I'll watch over him, she had said.

She thought about Olive Clusen's words and Penny Clusen's plan to go to Sacramento.

And she wondered. Would Mr. Hastings's way be the better route?

While Luke and Emma were talking to Jim Bridger, Alma and Zeke came up to Charlotte. "Is he telling the truth, do you think?" Alma asked.

"If he is, we'd certainly do well to take the shortcut."

"Pete and Nora and their brood are packing to go," Zeke said, picking up his hat and running a hand over his nearly bald head. He glanced at Alma and then looked into Charlotte's eyes. "So what do you think, dear? Wait to take the trail at Soda Springs, or take the new route?"

"You're definitely going to California, then?" Charlotte asked.

In Zeke's old eyes, gray-looking and cloudy, she saw deep affection. "You're like a daughter to us, Charlotte. If you're leaving with Mr. Hastings, then we'll leave, too, and put your things in our wagon."

Charlotte hugged Zeke, taking his frail shoulders in her arms. "I would dearly love to go with you and Alma," she said as she drew back. "And I suppose if Nora and Pete are going with Mr. Hastings . . ."

"Let's get the show rolling, then," Zeke said. "You hitch a ride with us and talk no more nonsense about walking to California by yourself."

Charlotte looked over at Emma and Luke. "Just promise me, you two, that you won't tell Luke I'm leaving with you."

Alma frowned. "Charlotte—"

"You leave her be!" Zeke said. "She's a grown woman, Alma. Now go pack up, young lady, and we won't breathe a word to a soul."

After giving Zeke another hug, and Alma a hug, Charlotte went into her tent and packed up her few possessions: pots and pans she had gotten by trading along the trail; and Barsina Poole's skirts and blouses, which Mr. Poole had given to Charlotte after Barsina had died in childbirth.

The thought made Charlotte shiver. How quickly life changed on the trail, when one minute, a family consisted of a mother, father and children, and in the next, parents died, babies toppled from wagons, children were poisoned by eating plants along the trail or getting run over by wagons.

She thought of baby Jacob, how hungry he probably was, and cold, and scared. Were Penny and Marcus even still alive?

I'll find you, honey, she said silently. *At least now we're heading for the same place.* And she knew, too, that even if she didn't find Jacob, not at first, anyway, she still had to get away from Luke; she had to get away from his growing relationship with Emma Gray, and she had to start a new life, a strong one, for herself and her baby. Alone.

"Get up, Charlie! Tom!" Luke cried out, raising the whip high in the air. The new teams were frisky and surprisingly well-conditioned, Luke saw, and he cracked the whip across their backs, then stopped himself before doing it again.

Charlotte might be watching, a voice said.

He laughed and shook his head, feeling like a fool. He had worked with stock his whole life. He didn't need a woman to tell him how to drive his teams. He didn't need a woman telling him what to do, how to think, what to feel—

Since Fort Laramie, he and Charlotte had kept

their distance with what he had felt was a complicated series of unspoken, unwritten rules, most of which boiled down to one thing: If she was someplace, he was someplace else. If she hitched up the teams in the morning, he helped Emma. If he started up the teams, Charlotte usually walked with Alma.

He had said an emotional goodbye to Alma and Zeke this morning, worried about their following Lansford Hastings but unable to talk them out of it—

He shook his head, trying to shake some sense into it.

No. Charlotte couldn't have.

He closed his eyes, trying to picture Alma and Zeke's leave-taking. They had been traveling with the Andriessens and the Vestrows, and he could picture them as they had waved to him . . .

Luke pulled his teams up and stepped into the back of the wagon. He knew where Charlotte kept her few clothes, in a small box Alma had given her.

It was gone, as were her pots and pans.

Charlotte was gone.

For a moment, Luke felt as if his heart were being torn apart. Charlotte, gone? As if he were drowning, memories flashed before his eyes: Charlotte when he had first seen her, furious about his cow; Charlotte when he had first kissed her, in his bumpy, lurching wagon; Charlotte when she had pressed her lips against his neck, clinging to him with passion.

But then he brought himself back to real life: Charlotte telling him she would never marry him, Charlotte telling him she wasn't carrying his baby, Charlotte doing everything she could to be as far away from him as possible—

"Is everything all right, Luke?" a soft voice asked from behind him. "You seem upset." Emma came to stand beside him.

He shook his head. "Not at all. I just realized Charlotte must have left for California with Alma and Zeke and the Vestrows."

Emma's hand flew to her mouth. "Without telling us?"

Luke laughed. "I don't think she's much on goodbyes, Emma. She probably just wanted to get going without a lot of fuss."

Emma opened her mouth, then closed it, and looked into Luke's eyes. "You know, Luke, I did talk to Charlotte about you. I've never liked women who try to steal other women's men, and I didn't intend to start being someone I didn't like. But she did seem quite clear she wasn't interested. She said she wouldn't ever be with a man again."

For a moment—a moment too long—Luke remembered the feel of Charlotte's lips against his neck as she cried out his name.

But she didn't need a man. If she had said it, he guessed she was going to make it true.

"I guess I'm just the opposite," Emma said, reaching out and touching his beard with her soft, delicate hand. "Every day I need you more, Luke."

Thirty

"What we try to do is bring God and wisdom to the tribes," Father DeHaven said solemnly, stroking a big, bushy beard that reminded Luke of George. "We've ministered to and converted Indians in the Flatheads, Nez Perce, Coeur d'Alene tribes. We feel that now is the time, before problems with white settlers turn them against our God." The priest looked searchingly into Luke's eyes. "There's something troubling *you*, I see," he said quietly, stroking his beard again. "Is there something you would like to discuss?"

Luke shook his head, feeling disgusted that he was so transparent. From now on, was every man or woman concerned with spirit going to ask what was troubling him?

He shook his head, striking his flint for a spark and missing White Fox. At least with him, he could share a good laugh and a good, long smoke. Buffalo meat, baked marrow and potatoes was the dinner Father DeHaven had been invited to, but right about then, Luke felt like walking away and leaving Emma to do the entertaining.

He didn't want to talk about the women he had lost in his life, or the son he had loved, or the baby he hadn't found. And he didn't want to feel sorry for himself. He wasn't going to wallow in self-pity; he was going to get on with his life.

"What I need isn't to talk, Father DeHaven. What I need is to get out to Oregon Territory."

"Because you know someone out there?" Father DeHaven asked in a strange voice.

Luke shook his head sharply. "No," he said with irritation, though he didn't know why he was so annoyed.

"And you will do what out there?" Father De-Haven asked as Luke blew gently on the flames of the campfire.

"Log," Luke answered. "Log and then log some more. And then log some more."

"By yourself?"

Luke nodded. "A friend and I were going to start a business together. Now it will be a one-man operation." He looked into the priest's eyes. "I'm a private man, Father DeHaven—"

"You are a tormented man," the priest cut in. "Do you think you will reach Oregon when your mind and heart carry such a heavy burden?"

"No offense, Father, but I know plenty of people who bear a hell of a lot heavier burdens than I do. Plenty," he said, meaning it.

"Son, I won't argue about that with you," Father DeHaven said. "At the least, we're talking. At our missions, we have babies who can't say one word, who are lost or orphaned or sick or all three. We have Indian women who have been wounded, white women who have been abandoned, children who don't know where or how or even whether to begin looking for their parents—"

"Father DeHaven," Luke suddenly cut in.

"Yes, my son."

"You say at your missions you have babies. If I told you about a baby, would you know if he was in your care?"

Charlotte winced as she cracked the whip across the oxen's backs, and winced again when they bellowed.

They had all taken an enormous chance when they had chosen to follow Lansford Hastings, believed words that had been spun out of gold, perhaps, or imagination, or just plain hope.

But not made of truth.

Never, in all the days they had traveled the trail so far, had they covered such a short distance unless they had been forced to stop because of rain or sickness. Never had each inch felt like a mile, each foot like a hundred miles; but Lansford Hastings had neglected to mention that everything—wagons, ox teams, even the yokes themselves—was wider than the narrow gorge they were trying to pass through.

As Charlotte looked back at the wagon, she was just able to make out Alma's face behind the tattered, dirty cover. The last time Charlotte had looked in, Zeke had been lying on a quilt inside the wagon, and Alma had been rubbing his forehead with a wet cloth. "He's got some sort of fever," she had said in a hollow, frightened voice. "You keep your distance, Charlotte," she had warned sternly.

Now Alma seemed to be talking to Zeke, shaking her head, tears streaming down her face.

"Oh, Mama," Charlotte said quietly. "Did we

make the worst decision of our lives going with
Mr. Hastings?"

Winter snows would be coming soon—too soon
if they didn't make it out of the gorge.

Suddenly Charlotte heard yelling up ahead,
and the little forward movement each wagon had
been making came to a stop.

Pete Vestrow, his face white even in the sun,
came walking back to Charlotte, glancing past her
into the wagon at Alma. "How is old Zeke faring?"
he asked softly.

Charlotte shook her head. "Alma says he's
struck by a fever."

Pete spat on the ground, rubbing his beard and
then looking up at the sky. "What made me and
Nora want to follow this man is beyond me," he
muttered. "Up ahead, it's impassable for anything
but a mule or horse. We're going to set up a wind-
lass and hoist the wagons up over that there
bluff," he finished, pointing at a slope that looked
to Charlotte just as hard to pass over as the gorge
was to pass through.

"But—" she began.

Pete Vestrow shook his head. "Do you know
what I told Nora and the babies?" he asked. "No
sense doubting, because we've come this far and
lived to tell the tale, Charlotte. We might just as
well try to scale that there bluff as squeeze into a
gorge the width of a kid."

But when he looked into Charlotte's eyes, she
could see the same doubt that hung heavy in her
heart. And she knew that for Alma and Zeke, it
would be the last news they would want to hear.

* * *

The hoisting of the wagons took days, and Charlotte had never seen so many possessions thrown out at any one spot—not just heavy items that people had somehow managed to hold on to that far—chairs, bureaus, chests and stoves and musical instruments. This time, people threw out family albums, linens, even kettles and Dutch ovens and silverware.

Zeke hung on, sometimes not knowing where he was, his face spotted with fever, his eyes shiny with tears. When they began traveling again, Charlotte felt that everyone heaved a sigh of collective relief. At least they were moving. And they were moving West. Zeke's eyes watered with happiness as he whispered, "We'll be there before you know it," to Charlotte and Alma.

But then they hit the Great Basin, a waterless desert that stretched hot and dry as far as the eye could see. "Oh my Lord," Charlotte murmured. It was as if they had come upon something out of a dream, or a nightmare—certainly nothing Charlotte had ever seen or even imagined—white salt everywhere, flat and dry, without a leaf or blade of grass or sprig of anything growing out of it.

And without a drop of water.

Charlotte's heart sand as she looked at Tip and Tom, Alma and Zeke's older team. She had hitched them up second, behind the newer team they had gotten from Bridger, but it was going to be a brutal row to hoe, and they were already showing signs of the heat and the strain. How could they possibly walk for two days without drinking?

All around her, families were unhitching their teams. They would walk the rest of the trail, and their children would walk the rest of the trail, and they would carry whatever babies couldn't walk, or strap them on the backs of their animals.

Alma had jumped out of the wagon, her step spry and determined as she walked toward Charlotte. "Would you water Tip and Tom now or later, Charlotte, if you had saved water to give them?" she asked, her voice high and strange. Her eyes looked almost hysterical, not meeting Charlotte's but looking past her at the teams.

"If we had the water, I would give it to them now, Alma. Later would be too late, and they would probably drink too fast."

Alma nodded, walked away, and came back with a pan of water, walking slowly so she didn't spill any.

"Ho!" she called out, her voice strong. "Tip, come here, dear," she said as she walked up to him.

He drank the water down in one gulp, snuffling it and blowing it out his nostrils while the others mooed and bellowed.

"All in time," Alma called out. "You'll each get water. Now have some patience."

"How is Zeke?" Charlotte asked as Alma walked past her, back up into the wagon.

Alma's mouth twitched, but she said nothing, just shaking her head. "Let me water these boys before we drop any farther behind," she said quietly.

Back and forth she went, getting a pan of water for each, until all four oxen had been watered.

Then she walked up to Charlotte and held out

her hand. "May I have the whip, please?" she asked, her voice quavery.

In her sharp blue eyes, Charlotte saw tears start to well up.

"Alma—" Charlotte began, handing over the whip.

"Zeke is dead," Alma cut in. "He passed on half an hour ago." Tears poured out of her eyes now, but she went on speaking. "I shant try to bury him in this Godforsaken salt, and I certainly won't leave him in this horrible place. But I won't lose Tip either," she said, and then she began sobbing, and Charlotte took her in her arms and prayed that they would make it to the end of the trail alive, and that Biddy Lee was well, and that Jacob knew no fear or hunger or thirst. Or loneliness, she suddenly added, her heart aching from having felt too much.

For she was sure she *had* felt too much, that she had let herself love when simple existence would have been the better course.

Thirty-one

Sacramento Valley, California, March 1847

Dearest Mama,
    I hope this letter finds you well and happy. I am still living in the canvas tent-house, quite nice compared to what we experienced on the trail, and

*we are all working hard planning our wooden
houses and enjoying the amazing beauty of this
valley. If you received my last letter, you know that
some of my friends are freed slaves, and they are so
happy to have their own land, and of course we
are all so relieved to be here.*

*Some of the people I wrote you about, the worst
sort of slave owners, well, I hear the last two members of the one family, the worst one of all, perished
in the Sierra Nevada. And God forgive me for saying I wasn't unhappy to hear the news.*

*The very day we heard about the Smitherses, as
a matter of fact, we had quite a grand wedding for
my friend Biddy Lee and her husband, with a fine
meal of stewed bear and apples and cabbage, with
grape-berry pie and cake for dessert. The war with
Mexico, I am told, should end soon, and then I
hope we will be part of America!*

*I never knew so many Americans already lived
here in this thriving little colony. There are lots of
families, men who were fur trappers and became
carpenters, masons, even soapmakers and wine
merchants. Many have married Mexican women,
and I find people here to be quite friendly.*

Charlotte hesitated, not knowing how to write
words she had never expected she would ever
write.

And so she wrote something else.

*It's kind of funny because Luce and I had vowed
to go to Oregon Territory, and I had thought I
might regret my decision to go to California in-*

stead. But it is so beautiful here, the land quite
rich, with fertile soil and lush grapevines, and I
know Luce would have loved it.

Alma is happy in the little canvas house we put
up for her on land next to mine. She misses Zeke
terribly, of course, but she is planning to plant all
kinds of things with me and looking forward to
when we are all settled in our own houses.

Charlotte swallowed against tears as she wrote
her next words.

Mama, I do feel that Jacob is alive, sincerely and
with all my heart. I don't know why or how I feel so
sure, but I do. Otherwise, I never would have been
able to break the sad news to you in the first place.
I wish I could tell you more, but I do have faith,
and every day ask anybody and everybody I can
ask.

She bit her lip, pulling her shawl around her
shoulders, and began to write again.

But Lily started crying, and Charlotte reached
over and scooped her baby into her arms.

"Oh, honey," she said, kissing her on the lips
and brushing her fine, light-brown hair back
from her forehead. "How should I tell your grandmother who you are?"

Lily looked back at her, blinking eyes that were
sky-blue but looked just like Luke's. Charlotte
could never have imagined that a baby girl could
look so much like her daddy, as masculine a man
as she had ever met, and still be beautiful, but Lily

Rose Collyer was as beautiful a baby as Charlotte had ever seen.

And she was two months old today. It was high time, Charlotte knew, that her grandmother found out she existed. And knew that she was a child born not of marriage but of a deep love, if only on Charlotte's part.

Charlotte lifted her blouse and put Lily by her breast. A moment later, Lily began to nurse, and Charlotte closed her eyes, fighting too many feelings.

How had she ever thought that memories of Luke wouldn't occupy her nights and her days, haunt her dreams and plans and hopes and regrets? How had she ever thought it would be easy?

Not that she would have traded Lily away for anything in the world. But suddenly, every relationship meant more, not less. Had she known how she would feel being a mother, she would have done something—though she didn't know what—to have forced a change in Luke. She would have been more courageous and said things that could have invited hurt; she would have been more honest, with herself and with Luke. She would have taken more risks, asking him things she hadn't been able to ask him.

No, you wouldn't have, an inner voice answered.

She looked down at Lily, drinking carefully and hungrily at the same time, her little mouth moving and her eyes already getting heavy again. Drunk with milk.

I would have done anything for you, she said

silently. *But I didn't know how important that would be at the time.*

And the part that probably broke her heart the most was that this was what Lucinda must have felt for Jacob—this amazing, all-encompassing love, this knowledge that you would do anything at all for this little person. Lucinda had felt this for Jacob.

And she had asked Charlotte to take care of him.

And now Charlotte didn't even know where he was. No one, out of all the dozens of people she had asked in the area, had heard of Marcus or Penny or little baby Jacob.

"Knock, knock," came a voice at the doorway to Charlotte's canvas house-tent.

"Come on in," Charlotte called out, stroking the top of Lily's head to calm her after the voice had startled her.

Alma peeked her head in, wrapping her shawl around her shoulders as she bustled in, her sharp blue eyes bright with excitement. "I've found a source for those grapevines I was telling you about, the grapes we ate at Christmas dinner," she said, but then her voice trailed off as she looked down at Lily, already asleep again, her head resting against Charlotte's stomach. "That sweet little babe," she murmured. "Not a day goes by when I don't thank the Lord she was safe inside you during our long trip. She never would have survived the Great Basin or the Sierra Nevada, the poor thing."

Charlotte stroked Lily's head; her fine, chestnut hair was Luke's color exactly. "I think she would have survived anything," Charlotte said softly. "I think she was meant to be, the way Biddy Lee was meant to meet Johnny and settle out here, the way we were meant to come here instead of to Oregon Territory, for some reason—"

Alma was smiling. "Did Biddy Lee tell you her news?" Alma asked, her eyes twinkling.

Charlotte shook her head. "Did she find more people to help her build the school?"

"Not yet. But she and that fine husband of hers will be needing a school themselves pretty soon. They're expecting a little one, Charlotte."

Charlotte smiled, so happy for Biddy Lee. All the dreams she had never thought possible were coming true, and all the cruelty and pain in her life had been left far, far behind. Yes, it was difficult sometimes living from day to day, but Charlotte knew that for Biddy Lee, these months in California had been the easiest of her entire life.

And Charlotte knew that she had to count herself lucky, as well. She had survived—across the endless, dry Humboldt Sink, glimmering in the heat, up and down the stony mountainsides of the Sierra Nevada, finally walking in bare feet when her shoes had been torn to bits and Alma's beloved oxen could travel no more.

And Lily had survived.

The fact that she hadn't found Jacob had made an ache in her heart that matched the ache in her heart for Lucinda. The fact that she missed Luke more than she could say was just a fact, a part of her existence she would have to live with for the rest of her life.

"I found two more people who are interested in your baskets," Alma said. "That rancher with his senorita wife, the pretty one with five children, would like to buy six for the girls of his family. And the woman who makes the wine with her husband out in the valley would like three for herself and her sisters. She's the one who will share her vines with us in exchange for my pumpkin and gourd seeds. And now I'm going to be on my way again, dearie," she said, gathering her shawl around herself more tightly.

"But you just got here," Charlotte said, stroking the top of Lily's head and cradling her more closely against her belly. "As soon as she's sound asleep, Alma, we can go outside and start mapping out the garden areas." Though Alma had staked out her own plot, a piece of beautiful rolling land right next to Charlotte's, she had agreed that her cultivated acreage would border Charlotte's so that Charlotte could help her with the work.

Alma was already leaving the tent. "I must go," she said, straightening the threadbare bonnet on her head. "Do you have the letter to your mother?"

"Not yet," Charlotte said, carefully laying Lily down on the quilt she and Alma had sewn together in the month before Lily had been born. "I should be finished by tomorrow." She hesitated. "I wish you could at least stay for a pot of tea."

Alma shook her head firmly. "I have another—" She stopped. "I must go," she said again, sweeping out of the tent.

Charlotte followed her outside, to the land that was now hers and the sky that felt as vast as the universe itself. She still could hardly believe that she owned this lush, rolling land that would soon be plowed under and planted with grapevines, vegetables and fruit trees. Chickens, cows and pigs were in her and Alma's plans as well, everything to be added when they could afford to. Charlotte was making a bit of money selling her bullrush-and-ribbon baskets and ministering to anyone's animals that needed help, and Alma was sewing for a wealthy Mexican-American family of ranchers. They figured they would save quite a bit of money by planting together, where their lands bordered.

But in the meantime, Alma did seem to be in quite a hurry. She hoisted her thin frame into the wagon she and Charlotte and Biddy Lee shared with Johnny Washington's family, snapped the reins at the two worn-out-looking black geldings, and took off down a path that was already beginning to look like a road, leading to her landholdings, then Biddy Lee and Johnny Washington's, then on toward the vast ranches owned by the area's early settlers, then on to Sacramento.

Jacob was finally well enough, Luke saw.

It had been three days since they had reached the Sacramento valley, three days since Luke had wondered whether he and Jacob had traveled all this way, only to have Jacob pass on before Charlotte had seen him.

But Jacob's little blue lips had turned pink

again, his pale, white-blue cheeks pink too, and his chest had cleared.

He was breathing, crying, screaming now like a regular baby.

"Are you ready?" Luke asked, bundling Jacob in the little buckskin pants and shawl that the Apache squaw had made him during the winter. "You met Grandma Bliss yesterday, but now it's time for you to see your aunt, honey."

"Whhaaa!" Jacob cried, and Luke laughed. He hadn't heard crying like that in days.

Hell, he said to himself as he walked out of his tent and into the morning sunlight. *I think Jacob is ready to see Charlotte, whether he remembers her or not. It's the big guy here who isn't ready.*

He tucked Jacob into the little buckskin carrier he had made, saddled up old Canton and headed south.

It had been a long road he had traveled, a journey made bearable because he had known he had one goal: to find Jacob, to follow Father DeHaven's directions until he found the boy. The mission Father DeHaven had told him about, near Fort Boise, had burned down by the time Luke got there, and Luke had headed northwest then, up toward Fort Walla Walla, along with Emma Gray and the rest of the caravan.

On the way, Emma had fallen in love with another man—almost a boy, really, in Luke's eyes, but someone who would take care of her and had promised Luke up and down he would treat her well until the day he died.

Luke had felt something shift in his heart as he

had urged Emma to marry young Jess Appleton. He hadn't known quite what it was, hadn't wanted to look at what it meant.

Find Jacob, he had told himself.

He had searched on and on, back down along the Snake River, then west onto the California Trail at the Raft River. And he had finally found Jacob at a Catholic mission in Flathead country, tended to by a woman who looked as old as the hills and reminded Luke of Alma.

He had felt something shift in his heart again when he saw Jacob, and again when he took the boy into his arms and held him against his chest.

He had known he couldn't risk crossing the Sierra Nevada so close to winter; there was no way to cross without getting snowed in. And so he and Jacob had become a small family over that winter, living on salmon and antelope and bear in a tent made of bear and antelope skins.

And all of a sudden, one morning when Luke woke up, Jacob bundled on his chest and breathing softly against his neck, Luke realized that all of his bitterness, the frozen, stone-cold parts of his heart, had melted.

The journey to Sacramento, over the Sierra Nevada at first snowmelt, Luke and Jacob riding all the way on Canton, had felt easy to Luke, because he was bringing Jacob back to the woman he—

The woman he loved.

And he hoped she would forgive him for being so blind.

He had probably loved Charlotte, in little ways, since the day she had looked at him with so much fury over his cow on that long-ago day in Independence. He had loved her more when he had first kissed her, loved her more when he had made love to her . . .

And then acted like a heel, thinking he was doing the right thing. Offering to marry her as if he would be doing her a favor. Offering to marry her only because he had thought she was carrying his baby.

And now, she was fine, though Alma hadn't said anything about a baby. Only that Charlotte was fine, full of plans as big as the universe, and it was high time he went and saw her and showed her whom he had found.

But Jacob wasn't his reason for seeing her. He would never make that mistake again, running as fast as he could away from the truth.

He had promised to find Jacob, and he had found him.

But Charlotte was the reason he was galloping along the path that led from Mr. and Mrs. Johnny Washington's land to Mrs. Zeke Bliss's land to Mrs. Charlotte Collyer's land.

He saw a plume of smoke coming from beside a large tent, and he laughed. "Your aunt will have this place looking like home before you know it," he said to Jacob, trying to slow the beating of his heart.

"So you're finally home," he said to the baby as he dismounted Canton and tied him to a hitching post about twenty feet from the tent.

Jacob was hardly even awake, having been lulled to sleep in the carrier.

But Luke felt as jittery as a teenager. In his thoughts, he had always pictured Charlotte outside at his first sighting of her, maybe working the ground or feeding stock. He had thought there would be distractions—the outdoors, things that would make his thoughts feel less huge.

Only now, it was going to be just him and Charlotte, and Jacob if he was awake.

Just go to her.

Canton whinnied and pawed at the ground, and a second later, Jacob let out a wail.

Out of the corner of his eye, Luke saw movement at the tent. When he turned, Charlotte was at the doorway, a shawl around her shoulders, her eyes squinting at him with an expression he couldn't read. Her hair was disheveled, blowing in the soft breeze, and Luke knew she looked different somehow, though he couldn't say in what way.

And then he could see, in her eyes and the way her jaw dropped, the very moment she realized he was carrying Jacob.

She came toward him, first walking and then running, her hand covering her mouth. "I can't believe it," she said softly, tears running down her cheeks. "You found him?"

"At a mission near the Raft River," he said.

"But how? Why? How did you know where to look?"

"I met a priest near Fort Bridger who knew him; he had met Penny when she dropped Jacob off on her way to Oregon. Marcus had died, and the reason the priest remembered her so well was that she had said she wasn't the boy's mother, and she didn't want him anymore because she was heading to Oregon with a boy she had just married."

"Oh my God," Charlotte murmured, looking at Jacob sleeping peacefully against the chest of the man he probably thought was his father.

"When I got to the mission Father DeHaven had told me about," Luke went on, "it had burned to the ground. I went from one to another then until—" He stopped. He didn't want to talk about the search, about the long winter months or his race over the Sierra Nevada. "Charlotte, I was a fool," he said.

She shook her head, looking confused. "About what?"

"About us. You and me. I never told you I loved you."

He couldn't read her expression. He remembered the day she had lashed out at him, telling him she could never marry him, that their relationship was over. And he still didn't know; had she said those words because she had been hurt by him, or had she really not loved him, only crying out those words in the heat of passion?

"A lot has happened," she began.

"I didn't come here because of Jacob," he cut in. "I vowed to find him for you, and I did. But I'm here for you."

She sighed, her eyes troubled, her whole face troubled. "I think I loved you, Luke, long before I ever told you. But I don't know anymore if love is enough—"

"Why not?" Luke asked. He put his arms around her, stroked her cheeks, brushed her hair back from her face. "We've both made it out here, Charlotte, because we're determined people." He had to smile. "Just the way Alma Bliss was so determined to get us together that she left me a 'meddling note,' as she put it, about where you were all heading." He could hardly believe, though, that he had actually found her, that he was finally looking into the eyes of the woman he loved. "You tell me what you need," he said. "Tell me anything and everything."

Her face twisted in sadness, and then he heard a sound. "Just a minute," she said, heading back to the tent.

It had sounded like—

A second later, Charlotte came out of the tent holding a little bundle—a quilt of yellow and pink and blue and white—

—and a baby.

Bawling and screaming.

Luke's heart turned over. He felt his mouth open, and he looked into Charlotte's eyes, and she smiled—

—and nodded—

—and smiled again. "Lily Rose Collyer, this is your daddy," she said softly.

"It can't be this easy," Charlotte said softly, her lips against Luke's neck. Both babies, miraculously, were asleep, and Luke had just made love to her as slowly and perfectly and passionately as she ever could have dreamed possible.

Yet she was scared. It felt too right, too easy, too impossible all at the same time.

Luke hoisted himself up on one elbow. "I love you, Charlotte Collyer-Dalton-Ashcroft, and you will be Charlotte Ashcroft before the day is done, young lady—"

"But—"

"But what?" he asked. "And speak now, Charlotte, because this is probably going to be the only time for the next five years when both babies are asleep at the same time!"

Charlotte laughed, and she felt tears come to her eyes. "Oh, Luke," she said softly. "What about . . . What about your plans to log? To log and log all by yourself? No ties, no commitments?"

He brushed her cheek with his warm, rough hand. "You should know what the answer is, honey. That was a good plan for the man who couldn't look at his own heart. I finally did that, in the mountains while I walked and slept and took care of Jacob; I did that," he said softly. "Now tell me. Look into my eyes and tell me what's in your heart. The truth."

She could remember all the times on the trail he had asked her to do that, and she had had to look at his nose because she had felt too much; she could remember all the times she had tried not to love him, and she had loved him all the more.

And she knew that she would love him always, whether she wanted to or not. She knew that Jacob would love him, and Lily would love him, and he would be strong and courageous and the man he always had been . . . and always would be. He wouldn't change because that was who he was—

not Francis Dalton, not Marcus Dalton, not
Henry Collyer.

"I guess I'll always love you, Luke Ashcroft," she
murmured, and a moment later, Lily woke up
with a cry, and Jacob woke up before Lily's first
wail had ended.

Luke laughed. "I think that was our last moment of peace, Charlotte Ashcroft. But I'm going
to make you so happy, you're never going to look
back." He kissed her then, long and hard. "I'll always love you," he whispered.

And for the first time in her life, Charlotte
could feel, deep in her heart, that Luke's words
were true.

Crosswinds
CINDY HOLBY

Ty – He is honor-bound to defend the land of his fathers, even if battle takes him from the arms of the woman he pledged himself to protect.

Cole – A Texas Ranger, he thinks the conflict will pass him by until he has the chance to capture the fugitive who'd sold so many innocent girls into prostitution.

Jenny – She vows she will no longer run from the demons of the past, and if that means confronting Wade Bishop in a New York prisoner-of-war camp, so be it. No matter how far she must travel from those she holds dear, she will draw courage from the legacy of love her parents had begun so long ago.

CHASE
THE WIND
CINDY HOLBY

From the moment he sets eyes on Faith, Ian Duncan knows she is the only girl for him. But her unbreakable betrothal to his employer's vicious son forces him to steal his love away on the very eve of her marriage. Faith and Ian are married clandestinely, their only possessions a magnificent horse, a family Bible, a wedding-ring quilt and their unshakable belief in each other. While their homestead waits to be carved out of the Iowa wilderness, Faith presents Ian with the most precious gift of all: a son and a daughter, born of the winter snows into the spring of their lives. The golden years are still ahead, their dream is coming true, but this is just the beginning. . . .

Texas Star

Elaine Barbieri

Buck Star is a handsome cad with a love-'em-and-leave-'em attitude that broke more than one heart. But when he walks out on a beautiful New Orleans socialite, he sets into motion a chain of treachery and deceit that threatens to destroy the ranching empire he'd built and even the children he'd once hoped would inherit it. . . .

A mysterious message compells Caldwell Star to return to Lowell, Texas, after a nine-year absence. Back in Lowell, he meets a stubborn young widow who refuses his help, but needs it more than she can know. Her gentle touch and proud spirit give Cal strength to face the demons of the past, to reach out for a love that would heal his wounded soul.
